EMMA'S BABY

Struggling as a single mother, Emma sometimes wishes that her thirteen-month-old son would just disappear. But when, one quiet Sunday evening, Ritchie is abducted by a stranger from the London Underground, Emma is thrown into a situation worse than she could have ever imagined. But why don't the police seem to fully believe her story? Why would they think that she would want to hurt her own baby? If Emma wants Ritchie back it looks like she'll have to find him herself. With the help of a stranger called Rafe, the one person who seems to believe her, she goes in search of her son. And she is determined to get him back . . . no matter what it takes.

Abbie Taylor is a doctor in her thirties. She was born in Ireland and divides her time between Dublin and London. This is her first novel.

ABBIE TAYLOR

EMMA'S BABY

Complete and Unabridged

CHARNWOOD
Leicester

First published in Great Britain in 2009 by
Bantam Books
Transworld Publishers
London

First Charnwood Edition
published 2010
by arrangement with Transworld Publishers
The Randon House Group Limited
London

British Library CIP Data

Taylor, Abbie.
Emma's baby.
1. Kidnapping- -Fiction. 2. Mothers of kidnapped
children- -Fiction. 3. Infants- -Crimes against
- -Fiction. 4. Large type books.
I. Title
823.9'2–dc22

ISBN 978–1–44480–047–0

Published by
F. A. Thorpe (Publishing)
Anstey, Leicestershire
Set by Words & Graphics Ltd.
Anstey, Leicestershire
Printed and bound in Great Britain by
T. J. International Ltd., Padstow, Cornwall

This book is printed on acid-free paper

This novel is dedicated to
Tom and Olive Glynn

Acknowledgements

Sincere thanks to Marianne Gunn O'Connor, Pat Lynch and Vicki Satlow, and to Francesca Liversidge, my editor at Transworld.

To the Bristol Writers Group, with great affection, especially Louise Gethin, Spencer Gillman and Kevin McGimpsey; and to the Richmond Writers' Circle, especially Joanna Stephens-Ward and Richard Rickford, for their invaluable help with the early chapters of this novel.

To Chief Superintendent Michael A. McGarry, Cork North Division, Ireland, and to the London Detective Inspector who wished to remain anonymous; thank you both for researching and answering my many questions about police procedures. I have retained the right to use considerable artistic licence, and all mistakes are mine.

To Peter Whitty, for uprooting himself to come and live in London, and for making my time there so happy.

And finally, last but not least, Tom O'Connor, for Ritchie.

1

Sunday, 17 September
Day One

At the top of the stairs, a group of teenage boys slumped against the walls with their feet out, taking up most of the passageway. They wore black puffa jackets and had the same expressions on their faces: blank, hard, bored. Emma heard their voices from around the corner, echoing off the tiles. As soon as they saw her, their conversation stopped.

'Excuse me,' Emma said politely.

Very slowly, they moved their feet back. There was just enough room for her to pass. She had to walk straight through the middle of the group, feeling their eyes on her. They watched in silence as she struggled down the steps with the buggy and Ritchie and all the bags.

She was glad when she got to the bottom of the steps and around the corner. The tube platform was deserted and starkly lit. Emma checked behind her. The boys had not followed.

'All right, Rich?' Relieved, she crouched down beside the buggy. She was not normally a nervous person, but with Ritchie there she found herself hoping the train would come soon.

Ritchie, a solid, chubby, thirteen-month-old, had begun to grizzle, sticking his tummy out and rubbing his eyes with his fist.

1

'Tired, eh?' Emma jiggled the buggy. 'Soon be home.'

She was tired herself. It had been a long day: a trip all the way across London to the East End. She'd been desperate to get out of the flat and couldn't face yet another walk to Hammersmith Broadway or the North End Road. They'd made a day of it; wandered around the stalls in Spitalfields Market, bought some trousers and vests for Ritchie, and gone to a busy little café for scones and coffee, and a jar of Banana Surprise. Then they'd got a bus to Mile End and gone for a walk by Regent's Canal, watching the swans and the long boats with their painted flowerpots. But when it turned chilly it was time to go home. In the dusk, the canal had a layer of green scum and a rusting shopping trolley poking out of the water. It took quite a while to find a tube station, and the shopping bags seemed to double in weight, knocking against Emma's legs as she walked. She was relieved to finally spot the familiar blue and red London Underground circle ahead of her in the gloom.

'Muh.' Ritchie leaned out of his buggy to thrust his orange lollipop at her. Sticky liquid trickled down his sleeve.

'Oh, for God's sake.' Emma felt a headache starting. 'Why did you ask for it, then?'

Roughly, she took the lolly from him and wiped his face and hands. She looked around for a bin. None anywhere, of course. It was ten past seven on Sunday evening. Everyone seemed to have finished their travelling for the day and gone home. There wasn't a soul about. She could just chuck the lolly on the tracks. In the end, however, she wrapped it in a tissue and stuffed it into her bag. On the wall of the platform opposite, an ad for bottled water showed a picture of the countryside. Trees, and water, and peace.

Ritchie whined again, straining at the straps.

'Come on, then.' What harm could there be in letting him out?

As she knelt to undo the straps, a faint, scratching noise sounded from deep in the tunnel.

There was something sinister, Emma had always thought, about the sound of a train approaching through a tunnel. The way you could hear but not see it; only the rattle of the tracks ahead of whatever monstrous thing was about to loom from the darkness. Quickly, she lifted Ritchie on to the platform. He'd heard the noise as well and turned to stare, a breeze lifting the blond down on his head. Emma held on to his harness, stooping to fold the buggy with her free hand. The noise grew louder. Ritchie pressed himself against her leg, gripping her jeans in his fist. Distracted though she was, she remembered afterwards the way he had looked. Round little face, eyes wide, mouth in an O as he gaped at the tunnel and waited for the monster to come.

'Der,' he said, thrilled, as the headlights lit up the tunnel. He let go of Emma's jeans to point. The grimy red, white and blue carriages roared into the station. Squeals and screeches filled the platform; the train slowed, then stopped. The roar of the engine died abruptly, like a turned-off fan.

Silence.

A second later, the doors *whoomped* open.

'On you go,' Emma said.

Ritchie didn't need to be told twice. Emma steered him to an empty carriage, keeping his harness taut, lifting it a little to help him climb on board. He struggled in on his hands and knees, the top of his nappy sticking out from his cargo pants. Then he stood up again in the doorway, delighted with himself.

'Muh,' he said, turning to wave her aboard with a fat hand.

That was how she saw him, mostly, in the weeks that followed. Standing there in the doorway with his toothy little grin, his crooked fringe, his blue fleece with the smiley elephant on the front. There was nothing different about him, nothing she hadn't seen a thousand times before. No whisper in her head warning her to snatch him back from the carriage and never let him go. He was still waving as she loaded the buggy on beside him and turned to pick up the bags. Reaching down, Emma thought she felt something with her other hand: a slight, sideways jerk on the harness she was gripping. Just a small thing; but looking back there must have been something odd about it, because she remembered frowning to herself. Even before she had a chance to straighten, to look, she knew that something was wrong.

Whoomp.

She spun around. For a second she found it hard to take in what she was seeing. Her thoughts zigzagged. *What is missing from this picture?* She still held Ritchie's harness in her hand, but the door of the carriage was closed.

Closed in her face, and Ritchie was on the other side.

'Jesus!'

Dropping the bags, Emma sprang at the door and tried to get her fingers around the edges. Through the window, she saw the top of Ritchie's head.

'Hang on,' she called. 'I'm coming.'

Oh God, how did you open the door? For a second, everything was a blur. Then she found the 'Open' button and pressed it. Nothing happened. She jabbed again, harder this time. Still nothing. She began to bang on the door with her fists.

'Help.' She looked wildly around the platform. 'My baby's stuck.'

Her voice rose thinly and trickled away. The platform was deserted. Just dark slabs of concrete, metal benches along the walls, the silent tunnels at each end.

'Shit.' Emma's heart was pounding. She felt very quick, alert. She looked around again and this time spotted a red box on the wall with a glass panel on the front. The fire alarm. Instinctively she jerked towards it. Then she stopped. To reach the alarm, she would have to let go of Ritchie's harness. She dithered, unable to make herself relinquish, even for one second, her contact with her son.

'Help,' she yelled again, louder this time. 'Somebody.'

Surely someone must hear. This was a public place, for God's sake. She was right in the middle of London.

Something occurred to her then. The train hadn't moved. The doors seemed to have been closed for an age but the train was still just standing there.

'They know we're here.' She sagged with relief. Of course. The train couldn't go while the harness was caught in the door. The driver could see her in a mirror or camera or something. Someone would be along in a minute to help. She stood there, waiting, not knowing what else to do. 'It's all right,' she told herself. 'It's all right.'

She looked in again to check on Ritchie. Then she jumped. *What was that?* That movement, way down at the end of the carriage?

Someone was in there. Someone was in there with Ritchie.

Emma felt a jolt of unease. Surely the carriage had been empty before? She searched sharply for whoever it was, just blocked from view by the handrail. Then the person moved again, coming closer to the window, and she saw that it was a woman.

The woman was leaning forward in the aisle, bending cautiously to peer through the glass. She looked older than Emma, closer to her mum's age maybe, blonde and well groomed. She looked sensible. She looked concerned.

She looked . . . normal.

Emma breathed again.

'My baby,' she called, trying to smile. She

6

pointed at Ritchie. 'My baby's stuck.'

The woman pressed her hand to her mouth, a horrified expression on her face. The expression said, *What should I do?*

'Open the door.' Emma pointed with her free hand. 'Find the alarm and press it.'

The woman nodded. She took a step back, and began to look up and around the door.

Christ. What a day. Feeling weak, Emma rested her forehead against the window and looked down at Ritchie. He was sitting on the floor, facing away from her, pulling at the zip on his fleece. All she could see was the top of his head. This was such a stupid situation to have ended up in. It was so exhausting, being a mother. You couldn't relax, you couldn't look away, not even for one second. Probably she and the blonde woman would laugh about it when the doors were open and Emma had got on and had Ritchie safely back on her knee.

'Bit of a close one,' the woman would say, maybe thinking how careless Emma was but being nice about it.

'I know. You'd want eyes in the back of your head.' And Emma would smile, then pull Ritchie to her and turn away. Back to it just being the two of them. The way it always was.

She could feel Ritchie on her knee already; his blocky weight, the apple scent of shampoo from his hair. In her head, everything was normal again. So it was a couple of seconds before she realized that the doors of the carriage still hadn't opened.

She frowned, looking up.

7

At the same moment, the train gave a loud hiss.

Emma's self-control vanished.

'Help.' Wildly, she hammered on the glass. 'Please. The train's about to go.'

The woman was back at the window, mouthing something. Her lips moved: 'Ex. Op. Ex. Op.'

'What?'

'*Ex. Op.*'

The woman gestured vigorously, pointing at Emma, then ahead of her, down the tunnel.

'What?' Emma stared in confusion. Violently, she shook her head to let the woman know she didn't understand.

The train gave a second hiss.

And then a lurch.

'No!' Emma gripped Ritchie's harness and screamed, a high scream of terror. 'Please. Stop!'

The train pulled ahead of her. Emma began to follow it. She was trotting before she knew it.

'Stop! Stop! Stop!'

A second later, she was running. It was that fast. One second the train was not moving at all, the next it was hurtling straight for the tunnel. Emma was sprinting flat out to keep up with the harness. Her ears were filled with noise. Ahead of her, the barriers bristled with signs saying: *Danger! Stop!* The signs were rushing towards her but she couldn't stop. She didn't know if her hand was tangled in the harness or if she was just holding tight, but she knew she would not let go. The barriers were in front of her. Oh Jesus. Oh Jesus. Oh Jesus.

Something grabbed at her arm, jerking her to a stop so suddenly that she flew right around in a circle. There was a burning sensation as the harness dragged across her hand, a vicious twist of her finger as the strap caught on it, then was gone. She stumbled, spun further, landed hard on her knees. The noise increased as the train filled the tunnel, a hollow roar surging back at her, an animal howl of pain and anguish and rage.

And then it was gone.

*   *   *

Silence.

Ritchie, Emma thought, through a haze of horror. She was on her hands and knees at the end of the platform, her head almost touching the tangle of signs and barriers. *Ritchie is gone. I don't have him. He's gone.*

She felt sick. She was going to pass out. Numbness prickled around her mouth and in her hands.

What had that woman said?

Ex op.

Next stop.

Emma struggled to her feet, ignoring the pain in her hand and knees. Strangely, there was a man on the ground behind her. Emma didn't stop to wonder about him. She ran down the platform, frantically searching for the board that showed you how long before the next train came.

Next thing, the man was on his feet beside her, jogging backwards to face her.

9

'Hey,' he shouted. 'What did you think you were you playing at? Why didn't you let go?'

Emma ignored him. The board. Oh God, where was the board?

'Didn't you hear me?' The man moved himself in front of her deliberately, forcing her to stop.

'Please — ' Emma tried to duck around him.

'You could have been killed.' The man was leaning into her, taller than she was, blocking her path. His face was a blur. All she registered was that he was dark-haired and wearing something blue. 'If it wasn't for me you'd have gone under the train. All over a fucking . . . what was it? Designer handbag?'

'It wasn't a handbag,' Emma yelled at him. 'It was my baby.'

'What?'

'My baby!' She screamed it into his face. 'Mybaby, mybabymybabymybaby.' Her voice cracked. She put her hands to her mouth.

'Fucking hell.' The man's face went white.

Emma gave a long, keening sob, pushed past him and headed for the sign. Through spots in her vision, she saw the board. Next train: one minute. Her breath wheezed in her ears. One minute. One minute.

'Fucking hell.' It was the man, beside her again. 'I'm going to press the alarm.'

'No!' She spun to face him. 'Don't!'

'What?'

'I have to get to the next station.' Emma struggled to speak clearly, to make him understand. 'There was a woman on the train. She's going to take Ritchie off there.'

10

'A woman? Are you sure?'

Emma felt the tension around her eyes. She pictured the woman's lips, moving around the words: Ex op. *Next stop*. That was what she had meant. Wasn't it?

Rattling on the tracks. A breeze blew her hair across her face. She swung back towards the tunnel.

'Why didn't she pull the alarm?' the man asked.

Emma bit her lip. Oh God, train, come on. Please. Please. Come on.

The man said, 'Look, I really think — '

'No, you look.' Emma turned on him, almost snarling. 'I know you're trying to help, but please, *don't* press any alarms. You'll stop the trains, and I just want to get Ritchie at the next station, so please, just go away, and *leave me alone!*'

The train had arrived by this time. Emma was on it as soon as the doors were open. She kept moving, power-walking down the aisle to the end of the carriage, as if by doing so she could bring herself closer to Ritchie.

A final shout from the man.

'Hey.' He was waving something. 'Is this your — '

And then the doors closed.

In the train, Emma stood swaying by the window, almost touching it with her nose. The tunnel turned the window into a mirror. She saw her own pale face, like a blob, elongated and distorted in the glass. There were other people in the carriage but she never saw who they were.

11

'Come on, come on,' she whispered. The agony of just having to stand there and wait. She had a physical ache to have Ritchie back with her, a panicky feeling as if she wasn't getting enough oxygen until she could breathe him in. She pictured herself at the next station, grabbing him into her arms, pressing her face into the velvety curve of his neck.

That man's voice.

Why didn't she pull the alarm?

Something sucked at Emma's lungs. She tried to breathe, and nothing came in.

Suppose she got to the next station, and Ritchie wasn't there?

No. No. Don't think it. Of course he would be there. The woman had looked nice. What else would she do but take him off? It was the logical thing. She had said, *Next stop*. She had said it. Emma went back to picturing herself with Ritchie, his stubby, warm little body, his smell. Her eyes prickled. She had been such a crap mother to him. Not just today but every day; ever since he'd been born. He deserved better than her. She put her hand over her mouth, quietening her pain, swallowing back the tears, the guilt. She would make it up to him. She would. In another minute, less than a minute. How long could the train take? When would the tunnel end? How long before she stopped seeing her own face in the window and saw the platform and Ritchie instead?

But what if he wasn't there?

The tunnel vanished. Emma's face was replaced by the outdoors: navy blue sky, brick

12

walls, tracks converging on each other. Then they were in the station; lights and platforms and posters. *Clunkety-clunk*. The train slowed; she whipped her head from side to side, searching the platform, her lungs heavy, struggling to fill with the weight. There was a woman on a seat with a baby and . . . It was her baby, it was Ritchie, it was her woman. Oh God, oh God, oh God. She was going to fall. She managed to hold herself up until the train stopped and the doors opened, then she ran out and flew to the bench. Ritchie was sitting, quite unconcerned, on the woman's knee, chewing his sleeve, and the woman was looking at her and smiling. As Emma reached them, the woman rose to her feet, holding Ritchie up before her like a gift. Emma grabbed him and kissed all over his cheeks and forehead and ears, pulling his feathery head tight into her neck. She squeezed him to her until neither of them could breathe, and wept his name over and over again into the side of his silky little face.

2

'Ngg!'

Ritchie wailed, arching his back and pushing Emma away with his fists. She was squashing him. His breath smelled of rusk, and orange lollipop. Emma's arms were too weak to hold him. She needed to sit down. The sides of her vision were going dark.

'Are you all right?' the woman asked. Her voice echoed from a long way away. 'Shall I take him for you?'

Emma felt Ritchie being lifted from her arms; she felt the seat behind her with her knees and sank into it. A tide sound rushed at her ears. She closed her eyes and leaned forward.

After a minute, the rushing noise receded. The platform returned to normal around her.

Emma sat up.

'Thank you,' she said, and burst into tears.

She didn't know how long she cried. Probably no more than a few seconds, but when she looked up, Ritchie, sitting on the woman's knee, was staring at her, open-mouthed. A long thread of drool hung from his lower lip, inches from the woman's expensive-looking sleeve. It was that which made Emma get herself under control.

'I'm sorry.' She pressed the bases of her hands to her eyes. 'There's only the two of us — my little boy and me. It's so hard sometimes . . . I'm sorry. I'm sorry.' She shook her head. 'You don't want to hear this. You must think I'm a terrible mother.'

'Nonsense,' the woman murmured. 'You've had a dreadful shock.'

She was right. Emma longed to cuddle Ritchie, but her hands were trembling and her face was soaked with tears and mucus. There was blood on her lip as well. She must have bitten it. She looked around for something to wipe it with. This station was much busier than the last one. Where were they? She looked at the sign above the seats. Whitechapel. Another train was pulling into the platform. Two girls stood up to meet it.

'Tissue?' The woman balanced Ritchie with one arm and rummaged in her bag. She did look the sort who would have a clean tissue with her at all times. Sensible, organized, like the headmistress of a school. She looked to be in her early forties, with blonde hair cut in layers to just below her ears. Tweedy trousers. A short, fawn-coloured jacket, with fur at the cuffs and collar.

'Here we are,' the woman said.

'Thank you.' Emma took the tissue and wiped her eyes and face. The woman watched her in a sympathetic sort of way. Close up, she had tiny, spidery veins on her cheeks. It was an outdoor face, despite the pearl earrings and coiffed hair. A horse-rider's or gardener's face. Emma had seen plenty of women like her during her childhood in Bath. They were everywhere at Christmas, lunching in cosy teashops with their daughters, surrounded by shopping bags. Emma had waited on them during her school holidays.

15

'Let me take him.' Emma finished drying her eyes and reached for Ritchie. Immediately he shook his head, leaned back into the woman's elbow and stuck his fist in his mouth.

'What's wrong?' Emma was upset. 'Why won't you come to me?'

The woman gave a little laugh. 'I think he must have got a fright when you squeezed him.'

'I probably hurt him,' Emma worried. It wasn't like Ritchie to be so manipulative. Normally he wouldn't go to anyone except her.

'It was the shock. And of course he doesn't know he nearly went missing, do you, little manikin?' The woman jiggled Ritchie and leaned sideways to look at him. He gazed up at her, chewing his fist. 'You had your mummy all worried, didn't you, you naughty little man?' She looked back at Emma. 'He's adorable, isn't he? Such blond hair. And you're so dark. What's his name?'

'Richard. Ritchie.'

'Ritchie. How sweet. Is that after his daddy?'

'No.' Emma looked away.

The woman didn't push it. 'Would you like another tissue?' she asked. She pronounced it *tiss-yoo*. 'No, give that old one back to me. There aren't any bins down here.'

She took the sodden tissue from Emma and tucked it into her bag.

'By the way,' she held out her hand, 'I'm Antonia.'

'Emma. Emma Turner.' Emma shook Antonia's hand.

'Where do you live, Emma? Are you near home?'

16

'No,' Emma said. 'I live in Fulham. Hammersmith, really, I suppose.'

'Well, you are a long way from home. Shall I come some of the way with you on the train? You shouldn't travel alone in this state.'

'I'll be fine. Honestly.' It was almost true. She was still shaky, but she was starting to recover. She just wanted to be alone now, to get her bearings and get herself and Ritchie back to the flat. And then she remembered. 'Oh, my bag. I left it at the other station.'

'My goodness,' Antonia said. 'You have got yourself in a mess.'

'I'll be all right.' Emma stood up. She'd sort something out. What was a lost bag? A few minutes ago, she thought she'd lost her son. 'Ritchie and I will go back there and ask. See if anyone's handed it in.'

'Well,' said Antonia, 'I think the chances of you finding that bag at this stage are really very small. Perhaps I should wait to see if you need some money to get home?'

'Oh, no.' Emma was horrified. She hadn't meant to sound like she was asking for money.

'I insist. I'm going to make sure you get home safely. You've had a very nasty shock.' Antonia put a hand on Emma's arm. 'Won't you come for a cup of coffee? My treat?'

'I couldn't ask you to do that. You've done enough.' Emma felt her barriers going up. She knew she must look awful, streaky with tears, her hair all over the place. The sleeve of her jacket was ripped from where she'd fallen on the platform, and the front of one of her trainers was lifting off its sole. Antonia seemed kind, but Emma just wanted to be left in peace. Just to get back to herself again, have another little cry, even, if she wanted to. She found it hard enough to talk to people these days, never mind someone like Antonia, who was being very tactful but must be wondering how anyone could be so stupid as to leave their baby on a train.

'Just one coffee.' Antonia was watching her. 'Look, I have an idea. I've been visiting a friend of mine, and I was supposed to meet my husband in town, but why don't I call him and ask him to collect me here instead? He has a car. Let us take you home.'

Emma wanted to say no. She really did, but she felt beaten, weary, unexpectedly over-whelmed at the idea of someone being kind to her. Her shoulders were heavy, as though someone had put a blanket over them.

'OK,' she said. Her eyes prickled. 'Thank you.'

While she was blowing her nose again, Antonia stood up with Ritchie in her arms.

'I'll get this young man settled,' she said.

'He won't let — ' Emma began, but Antonia was already loading Ritchie into his pushchair. He didn't protest at all. His head nodded, his eyelids drooped. Antonia fastened him in with the straps. She seemed to know exactly what she was doing.

'There.' She patted Ritchie's head. 'You need a sleep, don't you? Poor little man.'

Emma went to take the buggy, but Antonia had the handles in her grasp. She took off at a brisk pace, steering Ritchie towards the stairs.

18

Emma had nothing to do but follow them, empty-handed. The platform was open at both ends; a chill breeze blew over their heads. Emma's knees stung beneath her jeans. It felt strange to have nothing to carry, no Ritchie, no bag. She felt out of control. Vulnerable. She would have preferred to carry Rich, to take him out of the buggy and hold him, but Antonia had been so kind, it would be rude to wake him up. She settled for watching him as they walked. My God, my God.

She helped Antonia to lift the buggy up the stairs. At the turnstile, Antonia turned to her and said, 'You've lost your ticket, haven't you? You'll need to report your missing bag to the guard. Ask him to let you through.'

Emma hesitated.

'Go on.' Antonia gave her an encouraging smile. 'Don't worry about Ritchie and me. We'll wait for you at the entrance.'

Wanting to hurry, Emma didn't mention anything to the cheerful, orange-jacketed guard about Ritchie getting caught on the train. She just said that she'd lost her bag at the previous station, Stepney Green, and asked if anyone had handed it in. The guard went into a room at the side to use the phone. Emma glanced through the turnstiles, towards the entrance to the station. It was dark now, outside. Raining, it looked like. The pavements were shiny with light. A couple of people stood inside the doors, sheltering from the rain, or queuing for the little newspaper and sweet kiosk at the side. More people pushed through the barriers: a man

19

wearing a woollen hat, a woman in a hijab, holding the hand of a little girl. Then they were gone, and there were just their footsteps on the wet floor. Emma looked again at the entrance. Then she froze. She took a jerky half-step towards the barrier.

Where had Antonia gone?

She saw her then, just beside the kiosk. She was kneeling by Ritchie's buggy, adjusting the zip of his fleece; that must be why she'd missed her at first. Emma let out a shaky breath. It just went to show how jumpy she was. Ritchie was asleep. She watched him hungrily. His head was on his chest, making him look as if he had three chins. His wispy hair was brushed straight down on his forehead. The smiley blue elephant on his front moved up and down as he breathed. Antonia looked up just then and saw Emma watching. She gave a little wave.

The guard came back.

'No bag, I'm afraid,' he said. 'There's a number for Lost Property if you — '

'It's OK.' Emma was anxious to be back with Ritchie. She gestured to the barrier. 'Is it all right if I go on through? My ticket was in my bag.'

The guard was in a good mood. He tipped his hand to his forehead and released the turnstile for her. Once through it, Emma headed straight for Ritchie. She reached for the handles of the pushchair and instead found Antonia pressing a twenty-pound note into her hand.

'You must take it,' Antonia insisted as Emma began to protest. 'There's a café open down that way, look.' She pointed down a side street to

20

where some lettering on an illuminated window read, 'Mr Bap's'.

'We'll go there to wait for my husband,' Antonia said. 'You can buy the coffees. You might want to get something for Ritchie too, and I wouldn't know what to buy.'

'I . . . Oh, OK.' Emma gave in. Antonia had a point. Ritchie would be hungry soon. She'd buy something for him to eat, but as soon as she was at the table she'd wake him up and take him on to her knee and have him back to herself again.

Mr Bap's turned out to be more of a fast-food restaurant than a café. Inside, the damp air of the street gave way to a strong smell of vinegar and chips. Rows of brown plastic tables and benches took up the front half of the restaurant. Most of the tables were in need of a wipe. At the back of the shop was the counter, lined with giant bottles of brown sauce and mustard. The only other customer, an elderly, bearded man with a beige jacket zipped up to his neck, sat at a table by the wall, staring into a cup in his hand.

'Not very nice, is it?' Antonia wrinkled her nose. 'Still, it's warm. And we won't be here for very long.'

She wheeled the buggy to a table by the window. Ritchie was still asleep. Emma went to order the drinks.

'Two coffees, please,' she said quickly to the grey-haired, stubble-faced man behind the counter. 'And one of those chocolate buns. And a carton of milk.'

'Large or small coffees?'

'Either. It doesn't matter.'

21

Emma fidgeted, gazing around her as the man poked through a tall steel fridge. The wall beside the counter was smeared with something red, darkened and crusted into the paint. Ketchup, Emma hoped. She shuddered. What a dreary place to work on a Sunday evening. Over by the window, Antonia had her mobile phone to her ear. She was talking in a low voice, probably so as not to wake Ritchie. Her hand covered her mouth as she spoke.

'Anything else?' the man behind the counter asked.

'Oh.' Emma looked back at the tray. 'No, thank you. Just what's there.'

The man couldn't seem to work the cash register. The drawer kept springing open at the wrong time. Every time it did, the man tutted and slammed it shut again. Emma wished he'd just hand over the change.

Ritchie had moved in his sleep. Now his head was tipped back, his mouth open, his two white top teeth showing. Antonia was still on the phone. She had her back to Emma, but her head was turned to the side and her hand had moved away from her mouth. Emma could see the movements of her lips as she spoke.

'*Bird rack*,' Antonia seemed to be saying. Or at least that was what her lips made it look like.

For no reason at all, a vivid image popped into Emma's head. Her mum, sitting watching the telly in their terraced house in Bath. Emma was at the corner table, doing her homework. The curtains were drawn; the flames of the gas fire flickered. Emma could see her mum, sat as usual in her brown-and-red flowery armchair by the fire. The half-drunk mug of tea beside her on the coffee table. The fixed, rather sad expression on her face as she concentrated on her programme.

Emma frowned. How many times had she seen her mum watching the telly like that when she was young? What had made her suddenly think of it now? She looked again at Ritchie and shook her head.

Finally the man managed to get the drawer to work, and handed Emma her change. She took the coffees and bun over to the window. Antonia was still talking into her mobile phone. Emma slid the tray on to the table.

'Sorry for the delay,' she began.

Antonia jumped and spun around. Then she lifted her finger and smiled.

'I have to go now,' she said into the phone. 'I'll see you soon.'

She helped Emma to unload the tray.

'That was my husband,' she said. 'He's on his way.'

Emma sat down thankfully and pulled Ritchie's buggy towards her.

'That young man's out for the count,' Antonia said.

'He'll wake up soon.' Emma peeled the wrapper off the chocolate bun. 'He's due his dinner.'

'I don't think he looks like he's interested in eating anything, do you?'

'He will soon,' Emma said, more sharply than she'd intended.

Antonia didn't reply. She drew her cup of

23

coffee towards her, picked up the tiny stainless-steel milk jug from the table and began to pour. Immediately, Emma regretted her tone. What on earth was wrong with her? Antonia was only trying to be nice.

In a politer voice, she asked, 'Do you have children?'

The steel jug stopped pouring. Antonia held it in the air for a moment before she answered.

'Yes, we do,' she said. 'We have a little boy.'

She tipped the jug again and went on pouring.

Emma was surprised. For some reason, she'd have thought that if Antonia had children they'd be grown by now. Teenagers at least. Antonia looked much too groomed to be the mother of a young child. Maybe she had a nanny. Before she could ask her where the child was, Antonia put down the jug and nodded at Ritchie's pushchair.

She said, 'I gather from what you mentioned about it just being the two of you that this little chap's father isn't around?'

'No,' Emma said. 'We split up before he was born.'

'But your family helps out?'

'I don't have any family. My parents are dead.'

'I see,' said Antonia. 'Alone in the world.'

Emma stirred her coffee.

'Money must be tight, I imagine,' Antonia said, eyeing Emma's bobbly woollen sweater and faded jeans. 'How on earth do you cope?'

'We manage.'

'But it isn't an ideal environment for a child, is it? No money, no family support. Hardly fair on him, I would have thought.'

24

Emma felt uncomfortable. She really didn't want to discuss this any more. She went to undo the straps of Ritchie's pushchair. He stiffened at once and scrunched up his face. Emma knew she was forcing him out of sleep and he'd be cross, but she wanted to wake him, to have him back to herself.

'Shh,' she soothed him, tugging on the straps. He pushed against them, tightening the buckle.

'Still tired,' Antonia remarked. 'Perhaps you should leave him.'

'Rich, look.' Abruptly, Emma turned to the table. 'Do you want some bun?' She steadied her hands by breaking a piece off the muffin on her plate.

When she turned back, Antonia had Ritchie out of the pushchair and on her knee.

Emma didn't know what to say.

'You shouldn't let him eat sweets,' Antonia said. Ritchie sat on her knee, rubbing his eyes. 'Should she, little man?'

Emma's heart was hammering. She was thinking: I won't take the lift. We'll just go.

'Oh look,' Antonia said. 'Your lip's started bleeding again.'

Emma put her hand up to her mouth. Wetness on her lower lip. She took away her fingers and saw that the tips were red.

'Oh dear.' Antonia's face creased with concern. 'And I'm afraid I don't have any tissues left.'

Emma jumped up to get a paper towel from the counter. But she couldn't see any. The man behind the counter had disappeared, presumably through a doorway beside the fridge hung with coloured plastic strips.

'Hello?' Emma called to the plastic strips. 'Hello?'

Antonia's voice: 'You might find something down there.'

Emma turned. Antonia was pointing at a gap between the counter and the wall. Through the gap, a narrow passage led to a brown door marked 'Toilets'.

Without speaking, Emma marched to the gap and down the passage. She was going to get some tissues, wipe off the blood, take Ritchie and go. Just as she reached the brown door, she looked back. She could see all the way to the front of the shop where Ritchie was sitting on Antonia's knee, still rubbing his eyes. Then he saw Emma and his face lit up. He gave a heartbreaking smile and held up his arms.

'Muh,' he said.

She almost turned back to take him. Her weight went to one foot, then the other. But her face and hands were all bloody, and if the toilets were anything like the rest of the café, she could imagine only too well what condition they'd be in. She didn't want to take Ritchie in there if she could help it. There was something funny about Antonia — something about her superior attitude that Emma didn't like — but she'd done a good job minding Ritchie on her own already, those few minutes when she'd taken him off the train. Ritchie would be OK with her. Just for a few seconds more.

Emma smiled at him.

26

'I won't be a minute,' she said.

Then she opened the door, and went in.

As soon as she smelled the air, she was glad she'd left Ritchie outside. The toilet was just one room, with a tiny sink covered with grey cracks and no window. A ventilation fan in the wall above the sink was clogged on the inside with lumps of blackish material. This really was a horrible place. Emma would be just as glad to get Ritchie out of here as soon as possible, even if it meant him having to wait till much later to get anything to eat. She looked at herself in the mirror over the sink. The glass was rippled and bendy; her face looked wider than normal, but it was enough for her to see the swollen area on her lip, oozing from the cut in the middle. Blood streaked her cheek and chin. She looked a right mess.

On the cistern at the back of the toilet was an industrial-sized roll of loo paper. Emma reached for it, avoiding looking into the actual toilet. She unrolled some of the sheets and tore them off. They were probably filthy but she didn't care. She wet the tissue under the tiny trickle from the tap and scrubbed at her face. There. That was the worst of it sorted. She threw the tissue into a bin under the sink and tore off a second piece. This she held to her lip, pressing it on the cut for a few seconds to stop the bleeding. But when she took the tissue away, it stuck to the cut and pulled the scab off, making the bleeding start all over again. Emma sighed with impatience. It took two more pieces of tissue before the cut finally stayed sealed. A final quick scrub at her chin, and a rinse of her fingers, and she was done. She didn't bother looking for anything to dry her hands.

When she came out of the toilet, she was too busy at first breathing in the fresher air to fully take in what she was seeing. She was looking down the passage towards the front of the restaurant; she had a good view of most of the tables from here. She could see the window with its flaking red lettering: 'Mr Bap's' spelt back to front. But just inside that, where she would have expected to see Ritchie, with his flushed, sleepy face, and Antonia with her flicky blonde hair, there was a gap. Ritchie's pushchair was gone. The table by the window was empty.

Emma didn't start to worry straight away. They were here somewhere. She just wasn't seeing them. She came out into the main part of the café and looked around. The table tops were sticky and yellow in the fluorescent light. The bearded old man sat with his eyes closed. The man behind the counter was still nowhere to be seen.

Uncertain, Emma stood in the middle of the room. What was happening here? What was going on that she didn't understand? Then she got it. They'd gone outside! Antonia's husband had arrived. They'd got Ritchie ready and put him back in his buggy. They were all out there, waiting for her in the street.

She went to the door and yanked it open. She looked up the street and then down. Cars and buses on the main road. Some shops still open, their lights glistening on the pavement. Music

28

thumping from one of them, an unfamiliar Eastern beat. Groups of bearded men, some wearing round, coloured hats. No sign of a woman in a furry jacket, pushing a buggy.

A few feet along, the street turned on to another side road. Emma went to it and looked down. Railings along the pavement, three buses in a row. Blocks of flats, a pub.

No woman with a buggy.

Trying hard not to panic, Emma hurried back to the café. This was ridiculous. They *must* be here! Antonia must have taken Ritchie to some other table, some section of the restaurant Emma hadn't noticed before. She should have told her first, though. This was definitely the last straw. When she found Ritchie now, she really was just going to take him and go.

But even as she quickly examined every wall of the restaurant, and all around the counter, she knew what she'd known when she'd first walked into the place: that it was just one square room, with the window and door to the street at the front. There was no stairs and no corners, no tables she hadn't seen. No other section to the café at all.

Emma hurtled down the passage to the toilet. She flung open the door, just in case there was a second toilet in there and she'd missed it. But there was just the one stinking room.

Hands shaking, she ran to the front of the counter.

'Excuse me,' she called, her voice high-pitched. 'Excuse me.'

The coloured plastic strips moved. The man

with the stubbly beard poked his head through.

'Did you see them?' Emma asked.

'Who?'

'My son.' Emma looked past him, through the coloured strips. 'Are they in there? Did they go into your kitchen?'

The man began to lift his hands in incomprehension. Emma opened the flap on the counter. She ran to the doorway and shoved her way through the strips. Behind them was a steel kitchen, cluttered with pots and piles of plates and smelling of bins. No Ritchie. No Antonia.

'What are you doing?' The man was behind her.

Emma turned on him.

'There was a woman.' She struggled to stay calm. 'By the window, with my son. Did she take him? Where did they go?'

'I didn't — '

'Did she leave him on his own?' Emma was shouting now. 'Did she take him, or did someone else? You must have seen something, are you blind?'

The man backed away, looking alarmed.

'I didn't see nobody,' he said. 'I don't know where they go.'

Emma pushed past him, back to the shop. The old man by the wall was peering up at her. His eyes had a bluish film on the front.

'Did *you* see them?' Emma begged.

The man just gripped his cup. He was more elderly than she'd thought, shaky and vague. She couldn't tell if he even understood what she was saying.

'Call the police,' she shouted to the man at the counter. 'Someone's taken my child.'

The two men stared at her.

'Call the police,' Emma screamed at them, and ran out into the street.

There was still no sign. She couldn't even run, she didn't know which way to go. The street blurred; she was dizzy and sick.

'Ritchie,' she called. 'Ritchie.'

Her throat was clicky with fright. She looked up and down again, standing on tiptoe. People everywhere, in coats and scarves and hats, but no one with a baby. Ritchie seemed to have completely vanished. Emma wanted to vomit. She tried to cross the road to the island in the middle, to get a better view of the street on both sides of the café, but there were railings everywhere, blocking her way.

'Ritchie,' she yelled. And then: 'Oh God. Please. Somebody help me. My baby's been kidnapped.'

A man in a baseball cap and jacket was striding towards her on the path.

'Please.' Emma tried to stop him. 'Please. I need help.'

The man veered past her and kept going.

'Someone. Please.' Emma was breathless with terror. She had to force herself to stay standing. Her legs were like water. She couldn't think straight. What should she do? Someone had to help her, she couldn't, she couldn't think about anything.

A large, middle-aged lady, laden with plastic shopping bags, slowed down to have a look.

'What's going on here?' the lady asked.

Emma almost threw herself at her.

'Please. Oh please. Someone's taken my baby.'

'Who's taken your baby?'

'The woman, she . . . Did you see them? A woman and a little boy? Did you pass them on your way up here?'

'I don't . . . ' The woman hesitated. Around her, more people were stopping. People were talking, mostly in foreign languages, she couldn't understand what they were saying. One or two English phrases came through:

'Who's taken a baby?'

'That thin girl with the torn coat.'

'Is that blood on her face?'

'My child has been *kidnapped*.' Emma couldn't believe it. Why were they all just standing there? She grabbed the middle-aged woman by the front of her jumper.

'Call the police,' she yelled at her. 'What the hell is wrong with you?'

The woman recoiled, her mouth a rectangle: *What have I got myself into?* Someone else said in a sharp voice to Emma, 'Hey, hey, no need for that.'

Emma let go of the woman. She sprinted down the street in the opposite direction from which the woman had come, trusting her that if she'd seen Ritchie on her way up she'd have said. Her breath sounded thin and whistly. Only a tiny amount of air was coming in each time. Oh God, don't black out. Oh please, let her not black out now, there wasn't time, she had to find him before he got too far away. She was trying to

32

look everywhere at once, at the lighted windows, the darker corners and side roads, straining to see Ritchie's tufty little head and blue fleece in all the colours and the gloom. Had Antonia's husband come; had the two of them bundled Ritchie off together? Did Antonia even *have* a husband? Or a child? Or was she just some nutter who . . . ? Oh Jesus.

Ice.

Maybe Ritchie wasn't with Antonia at all. Maybe Antonia had got bored, and walked out of the café and left him, and someone else, some person Emma couldn't even begin to imagine, had seen him there on his own and come in and taken him.

The street disappeared. The road came and went in flashes, like the strobes at a nightclub. Then she was pushing past people, shoving them violently out of her way. She was flying down the street, spinning down side roads at random, then sprinting back up them again. She didn't know which way she was going, whether she was searching the same places over again or different ones, they all looked the same, the same people and roads and buildings. Had she missed him, gone right past him? Was she flying around in circles, not making any progress at all, while all the time he was getting further and further away?

The flashes were coming faster. She screamed his name all around her, again and again and again.

'Ritchie. Ritchie. Ritchie.'

Then she knelt in the road and shrieked, no words coming out, just sounds. Car horns

blared. Through the flashing lights came voices:
'Look at her. She's not well.'
'Is it drugs?'
Emma's head was full of noise. There was too much colour and movement. She couldn't cope; everything was coming too fast. She couldn't think. Too many things to think about. Too urgent. Too much. She fell forward on to her hands. The road rushed at her face.
'Are you all right?' a woman asked.
'Someone call an ambulance.'
They swirled, blurred, and were gone.

3

The light was blue and dim. Gentle on her eyes. Outside the patterned curtain, a muffled symphony of voices and footsteps; inside, a little square of hush where she was. She was in a bed and her knees were sore and stiff. She'd had a terrible dream that Ritchie had died. No, she'd left him on a train. She couldn't remember. It was all right now anyway. She was awake. It was over.

At the end of the bed, a girl in a blue tunic was busy writing something into a folder. Emma watched her drowsily. She felt sleepy, comfortable and secure; a sensation of well-being such as she hadn't had for a long, long time. The girl turned a page, checked something, turned back and wrote again. She had a delicate way of moving her fingers. Soothing. Hypnotic. As a child, sleeping at her gran's house, Emma had woken one night to see her mum sitting at the dresser under the window, going through some old letters. The lamp was tilted low, the only light a yellow pool over the paper. Emma had lain there for a long time, cosy and safe, listening to the rustlings and watching her mother's fingers turn the pages.

After a while she murmured to the girl in blue, 'Where am I?'

The girl glanced up quickly. 'Oh. You're awake.'

She put the folder down and hurried over to Emma.

'You're in hospital, Emma. The Royal London

Accident and Emergency department. Do you remember the ambulance bringing you in?'

Ambulance? Emma frowned. Something struck her then, and she pulled herself up in the bed. She stared around the quiet, blue cubicle.

'Where's Ritchie?' she asked. 'Where's my little boy?'

'Excuse me.' The nurse dipped under one side of the curtain and beckoned to someone outside. The curtains shadowed, bulked, pulled aside. A shaven-headed man came in. He wore a short-sleeved white shirt and bulky black vest. A radio jutted from his left shoulder.

Emma's heart sank.

'Ritchie.' She sat up further. 'What's happened to Ritchie?'

The policeman didn't say anything. Emma began to sob wildly. 'Ritchie,' she cried. 'Ritchie, where are you?' It wasn't a dream, then. Ritchie was gone. But what was wrong with her? She felt so sluggish and strange. Why couldn't she remember what had happened?

'Find him,' she begged the policeman. 'Please. You have to find him.'

'We're trying to,' the policeman assured her. 'The problem is, there's been some confusion as to exactly what happened. You've been uncon- scious for the last two hours. I believe you've had some kind of . . . ' he glanced at the nurse, ' . . . sedative?'

The nurse said defensively, 'She was screaming when the ambulance brought her in, trying to run back into the street. A danger to herself. We didn't know.'

36

It was as if they were talking about someone else. Emma had a vague memory of shouting things at a crowd of people, but it didn't seem real. She felt so dim and underwater now, it was hard to believe she'd been how the nurse said. She struggled to wake herself, to free her brain from the rolls of cotton wool wrapped around it.

The policeman took out a notebook.

'Would it help,' he said, licking his finger, 'if I repeated back to you what you told the paramedics at the scene? Clarify what we've managed to gather so far?'

'Please,' Emma begged him. 'Please do.'

The policeman flipped through the notebook until he came to the right page.

'Your name,' he said, 'is Emma Turner, and you are aged twenty-five?'

'Yes.'

'And Richard — Ritchie — your child, is one?'

'Yes. Last month.'

'Good. So. You met this woman . . . Antonia?'

'Yes.'

'And you were talking to her in the café, and then you went to the bathroom and when you came out, she and the child were gone?'

'Yes. Yes.' The cotton wool lifted. She was there, in the café, and Ritchie was holding his arms out to her, smiling and saying, 'Muh.' It was so real she almost cried out, lifting her hand to touch him.

'Now, if I could just clarify.' The policeman tapped his notebook. 'Because this is where things become a little confusing.'

He cleared his throat and looked at Emma.

'Whose child was it that the woman took?'

Emma gaped at him in astonishment. 'Mine.'

'You're quite sure about that? You're sure the child didn't belong to the other woman?'

'Of course I'm sure.' Bewildered, Emma looked at the nurse for help. Why was he saying this? 'There were witnesses. Ask them.'

'We already have, Ms Turner. This is where their version differs from yours. The general impression from the witnesses we spoke to in Mr . . . er . . . Bap's, seems to have been that this lady and the child came into the café together, and that *you* approached *them*.'

'No.' Emma struggled to sit up in the bed. 'That's wrong. We'd met each other already. In the tube station.'

'Yes, that is correct. You had previously approached this lady and her child at Whitechapel station. A staff member witnessed that, a guard at the barrier — '

'What?'

'You went to the guard and reported to him that you had lost your bag. When you spoke to him, you were on your own, no child, no buggy — '

'No!'

'You then left him and approached a woman at the entrance to the station who was with her child. You seemed to be asking her for money, and she gave you . . . Please, Ms Turner, I'm just summing up what's been said. She gave you some money, then she left you and went into the café. Some minutes later, you were seen to approach her again. At this point, there was

38

some kind of argument. You went to the bathroom, and the lady left with her child.'

He looked up.

'Is that what happened?'

'No!' Emma cried. 'It is *not* what happened. Ritchie is *my* child.'

'All right, Ms Turner. Try to stay calm. I'm here to hear your side of the story.'

Emma's breathing was harsh and rapid. She couldn't control it; it was like she was having an asthma attack. Her mouth was filled with saliva. She couldn't swallow. The spit was dripping out of her, on to the pillow. The nurse put a bowl in front of her.

'Breathe slowly,' she advised, rubbing Emma's shoulder.

Emma spat into the bowl, smelling bile and plastic. She forced herself to breathe properly. Everything was coming back to her now, the cotton wool veil over her mind split by great, jagged tears.

'*Listen*,' she said, desperate to tell them before it all disappeared again. '*This* is what happened.'

The story tumbled out. She started with Ritchie scrambling on to the train before the doors closed, his wide little face aglow with triumph. By the time she got to where she was sprawled in the road, with all the faces, and the horns blaring at her, she was crying. The policeman nodded, writing everything down. He was quiet when she'd finished, tapping his notebook with the top of his pen.

'He *is* my child.' Emma's voice shook. 'He *is*.'

'Yet according to your story,' the policeman

said, 'you went to the bathroom, and left him with a woman you'd never met before.'

The nurse squeezed Emma's hand.

The policeman said, 'You said that the child got trapped on a train when the doors closed. Did anyone else see this happening?'

'No.' Then Emma remembered. 'Yes. A man. He pulled me back from the tunnel.'

'Did this man give you his name?'

'No.'

The policeman didn't say anything.

'Why would I lie about something like this?'

'I'm not saying you're lying, Ms Turner. But why didn't you report this to anyone? Press the alarm to call for help? Mention it to the guard you spoke to? He says you only reported a lost handbag.'

'I have a child,' Emma shouted. 'Why would I be here telling you he's been kidnapped instead of looking after him?'

She was kneeling up on the bed by this time, thrusting her face towards the policeman. He didn't react. He calmly held his notebook and focused on a point between Emma's eyes.

'Is there any way,' he said, 'that you can verify that you have a child?'

'What do you mean?'

'Who do you live with? Who else knows Ritchie?'

'I don't live with anyone.'

'There must be someone who knows you both. Family members? Friends?'

Emma thought wildly.

'Even a health visitor or GP?'

40

'My GP. Dr Stanford. In Hammersmith. She knows Ritchie.'

'We'll contact her immediately. Do you have an address?'

'It's Walker Square. The health centre. But what about Ritchie? What are you doing about him?'

'As soon as we've spoken to Dr Stanford, we'll be able to proceed from there. We'll go as quickly as we can.'

'But — '

'I'll be back as soon as I can, Ms Turner.' The policeman was halfway through the curtains. 'As soon as I've confirmed these details you've given.'

He pushed his way out and left.

'Look for him,' Emma shouted after him. 'Find my child. You have to believe me.' She slammed against the pillows, weeping with frustration. The cotton wool was back. She forced it away. She had to stay awake. She had to make them look for Ritchie. Oh God, how long had he been gone? Every minute he was moving further away from her. She sat up again, her heart racing with terror. Where was he? What did that woman want with him? What if Emma never saw him again? The thought made her want to throw up. This was a nightmare. It wasn't real. Any minute now, she would wake up and find herself back in her flat, with Ritchie in the cot by her bed. Only, a too-large part of her knew that she wouldn't. She had an enormous sense of failure. She had failed Ritchie. She'd always known it was going to happen and now, at long last, it had.

A man in a pink shirt was beside her bed,

41

saying something. His mouth opened and closed. Emma stared at him in confusion. His voice swam at her brain.

'Are you listening, Emma?' he was saying.

'I've told you,' she said in despair. 'I've told you everything I know. Why aren't you out looking for him?'

'Bear with me, Emma. Just a few more questions. Is Ritchie your only child?'

'Yes. Yes, he is.'

'How is it that you are so isolated? A young woman like you. No family, no one to call. Where's Ritchie's father?'

'We're not in touch.'

'What about your family? Your parents?'

'They're dead.'

'I'm sorry.' He was writing this down. 'Were you close to them?'

'No . . . yes . . . my mum.' Tears in her eyes. Viciously, she rubbed them away.

'Have you any history of psychiatric illness?'

'Sorry?'

'Depression, for example. Are you attending a doctor for treatment?'

'Why are you asking me this?' She stared at him. 'Are you a psychiatrist?'

'I'm Dr Canning, from the psych — '

'Do you think I have a mental illness? Is that it? You think I'm imagining all this?'

'Of course not.'

'Right.' Christ, she'd had enough of this. She pushed at the sheets to untwist them from her legs and began to climb off the trolley. 'I'm leaving.'

'Emma, please.' The pink-shirted man sat back, his hands in the air. 'You're very upset. Let's think about this. How are you going to get home?'

'Where are my shoes?'

'If you leave against medical advice, you'll have to sign — '

'Fine. Whatever you want. My child's been kidnapped and no one's doing a fucking thing about it. I'll have to go and find him myself.'

She muttered to herself as she stooped to find her trainers. Fucking doctors. Fucking police. Fucking everyone. She felt weird. Dizzy. She couldn't feel her feet. The one thing she knew was that she had to get out of there and find Ritchie. In this city, the only person you could depend on was yourself.

The curtains swished back again. It was the shaven-headed policeman.

'We've spoken to Dr Stanford,' he announced.

Emma stared up at him, gripping the bars of the trolley. Harsh white light surrounded him from behind. She couldn't see his face.

The policeman said, 'Dr Stanford confirms that you do have a son whom she knows very well and has seen many times. On the basis of that, we'll be starting a full investigation into the disappearance of your child.'

4

Emma's first memory of Ritchie. Yeah, you didn't forget that kind of thing. He was purple, wrapped in a crocheted blanket, lying like a mollusc across her bed. She felt it was someone else's baby the midwife had just put there for a minute.

'Aren't you breastfeeding?' the brisk, navy-uniformed midwife asked, busy rolling up a blood-pressure cuff beside the bed.

'No.'

'Oh? You do know it's best for his immune system?'

'My mother didn't breastfeed me.' Emma lifted her chin. 'And I did all right.'

The vicious pain of the labour was behind her, but her body felt ripped and bruised, from her belly button right down to her knees. She felt weak, heavy, flattened into the pillows. Blood dripped from a transfusion bag above her wrist. The baby miaowed, then bawled, gumming his knuckles. He lay on her bed, dirty, hungry and helpless, and the responsibility overwhelmed her.

The midwife pursed her lips.

'In that case, you'd best give him his bottle. We don't want his glucose levels to drop.'

'Will the social worker come before I leave?' Emma asked, more timidly now she had won her small battle. 'The maternity grant — '

'Oh, she'll be here.' The midwife clattered her

44

equipment back into its basket. 'Don't you worry.'

She left the room, rattling the blood pressure stand ahead of her.

Unfriendly cow, Emma thought.

Left to herself, she propped the yowling baby in her arms, holding him a little away from her in case she hurt him. She took the bottle from the nightstand and looked from it to the child. What now? Did she just put the bottle to his lips? How would he know what to do?

While she was wondering, the teat happened to touch the baby's mouth. Instantly, he lifted his face and hoovered it in. He sucked so hard that Emma grabbed the bottle in alarm, afraid the thing would disappear down his throat. After a few seconds, however, she relaxed. The bottle wasn't going anywhere; the baby seemed to know what he was doing. She just had to balance the bottle with her hand and let him get on with it.

She watched him cautiously as he drank, surprised by how alert he was. She'd thought they couldn't see anything for the first few days, but here he was, pear-drop eyes wide open, gazing steadily up at her. He had a strange little face, wide and squashy, like a toy football. His wrinkly neck stuck out of the top of his Babygro. The room was quiet, the only sounds the steady *suck-suck* on the bottle and a murmured conversation from a radio turned low. The baby's expression was one of grave understanding.

'I do apologize,' he seemed to say. 'I need to drink this, but I'll do it as fast as I can and let

45

you get back to yourself.' A slow blink: 'I'm on your side, you know.'

Very slightly, the anxiety clawing at Emma's insides began to ease.

On the radio, the DJ announced, 'And now we have a classic from Keane.'

The opening bars of 'Somewhere Only We Know' filled the room. Emma's throat hardened. She let her head drop back against the pillow. She was in Hampshire with Oliver, and the song had played in the car on the way down. They were walking along the river. 'Wait till you see this place,' he had said. 'It's like an enchanted forest. Not many people know about it.'

They passed under old stone bridges, one after another, into green, misty light. Heavy branches dappled the water. They walked for a couple of miles and saw no one but the midges. Oliver pushed his dirty blond hair back from his forehead. In the silence, his mouth came down on hers.

Emma's arms were tired. She relaxed them, and the baby settled in against her body. She lowered her head, still feeling the ache in her throat, and the baby's wispy hair brushed against her lips.

She couldn't call him Oliver. Not after what had happened. But she could call him . . . what were the names of the band members in Keane? Was one of them called Richard? She had always liked that name.

'Would you like to be called Richard?' she asked the child.

He didn't answer. His eyelids had begun to

46

droop; his mouth was slack around the teat of the bottle.

'All right then. That's what we'll do.'

One less thing to worry about. The sun slanted from the window across the bed. Emma felt tired, peaceful, as if she might sleep too.

Monday, 18 September
Day Two

'The first twenty-four hours are crucial,' Lindsay, the Family Liaison Officer, said. 'We need to gather information as quickly as possible. Some of the questions we ask might seem intrusive or personal, but it's all part of the procedure, so please try not to take offence.'

It was five hours since Ritchie had been taken. Lindsay was so tall and shiny and efficient. Beside her, Emma felt very small and cold and thin. Mostly she was numb, but every so often a sheet of panic would open in her head, whiting out her mind. Where was Ritchie? What was happening to him? She got bouts of shivering every hour or so, where all her muscles, especially those in her neck, were so shuddery and tense that they were painful.

'Do you think he's alive?' she whispered.

'I'm sure he is,' Lindsay said. She put her arm around Emma's shoulders. 'A lovely little boy like him? No one would want to hurt him. I'm sure he's being treated well.'

Lindsay must have been a couple of years older than Emma, but looked younger. Her skin was plump and smooth. Her hair, as long and dark as Emma's, was thick and shiny. She had a cheerful, worry-free face; a face that wore a half-smile in repose. You would call her a girl, not a woman.

She had come to meet Emma in the hospital after the police had finally agreed to start looking for Ritchie.

'I'm going to be your Family Liaison Officer while we're looking for Ritchie,' Lindsay explained. 'Think of me as the link between the police and you. Any time you need to speak to someone, you can phone me, and I'll call and visit you regularly until Ritchie is found, so you always know what's happening.'

It was Lindsay, along with a couple of other policemen, who accompanied Emma from the hospital back to her flat in Hammersmith. Emma's keys and security swipe card were still in her bag somewhere in the East End, but the police had managed to get her an emergency replacement set from the housing association. Dazed, Emma stood under the lit shelter at the tower-block entrance and swiped the new card through the security slot by the doors. Most of the windows in the block were dark. The new card worked. The heavy metal doors opened with their deep double click.

In her flat on the fifth floor, the smell of cold toast and baby cereal hit her as soon as she opened the door. The breakfast things were still piled in the sink in the kitchen. There was Ritchie's plastic bowl with the picture of Bob the Builder on the bottom, partly obscured by lumps

48

of dried porridge. His toys were lying about the flat where he'd left them. The red truck he'd just learned to push himself around on, recklessly aiming it straight at the furniture. His train that shrieked 'All aboard' when you pressed the funnel. A rusk lying in a shower of crumbs under the table, the edges scalloped with tiny teeth marks. His cuddly frog named Gribbit. Each item made Emma's chest grow heavier and heavier, until the pain was almost unbearable.

The police, after asking Emma's permission to take a look around, began to search the flat. They searched everywhere: the narrow, yellow-painted bedroom, with Ritchie's cot and Emma's single bed; the bathroom with its olive-green bath and rubber shower hose on the taps, and Ritchie's yellow plastic bathtub under the sink. His spill-proof beaker lay upended behind the tub. She'd been looking for that for a week.

The policemen rummaged through the cupboards and peered into the laundry basket. They got down on their hands and knees to examine the floors: the speckled lino in the kitchen, the green scratchy carpets in the bedroom and sitting-room.

'What are they looking for?' Emma kept asking. 'Ritchie wasn't kidnapped from here. Why aren't they doing this at the café?'

'It's routine,' Lindsay soothed.

The policemen picked strands of Ritchie's hair from his cot, and they took away his toothbrush. They took his blanket and some of his clothes.

'For scent,' Lindsay explained, 'and DNA. To help us with the search.'

49

'Have you any clothes similar to what he was wearing at the time?' one of the policemen asked.

Emma was able to give them an exact replica of Ritchie's trousers; they had come in a two-for-one pack at Primark. The man labelled the trousers and took them away. Emma described the fleece Ritchie had been wearing.

'Any photos of him in it?'

When she went to look, she was shocked at how few photographs she had of either of them. It had never occurred to her that she should have taken more. The last one she had of Ritchie struck her as a lonely little picture. Ritchie on his own, astride his truck against the empty yellow background of the wall, smiling shyly into the camera. Oliver's languid, drowsy-eyed smile. It had been taken on his birthday. August. He wore denim shorts and a blue T-shirt with 'Surfer Dude' printed across the front.

The man had to pull it before he got it from her hand.

'Have you got a copy of this?' he asked.

'No.'

'Sorry.' His voice was kind. He looked like a father himself; shaggy and rumpled, as if people had been climbing on him. 'We do need to take it. Put your name and address on it. We'll do our best to get it back to you.'

'What should *I* do?' Emma asked Lindsay. 'I feel like I should be doing something. Looking for him. Not just sitting here.'

'You need to stay by the phone,' Lindsay said. 'If anyone tries to ring. You know, for a ransom or something.'

'A ransom?' She had to be joking.

'You never know,' Lindsay said.

'But they don't know where I live. They don't have my number.'

Lindsay repeated: 'You just never know.'

She made some hot, sweet tea and tried to persuade Emma to drink it.

'I can't.' Emma held the tea in her mouth for a moment, then spat it into the sink. 'It won't go down.'

'You should have something, Emma. Something with sugar in it. You're as white as a sheet. You'll be no good to Ritchie if you fall sick.'

But she was shivering too much, and her throat just wouldn't swallow.

'Isn't there anyone we can phone?' Lindsay asked. 'A friend, or a neighbour, even? Someone who'd come and stay with you tonight?'

'I don't need anyone with me.' Emma shook her head. 'The only thing I need now is for you to find Ritchie.'

A large man with dark hair and a moustache loomed in front of the couch.

'Detective Inspector Ian Hill,' he said, holding out his hand. 'Senior Investigating Officer, in charge of the case.'

Detective Inspector Hill looked exactly as Emma had always imagined a proper police detective should look: tall, with huge, bulky shoulders and a belted, tan-coloured coat. She grabbed his hand between both of hers, holding it in a tight grip, as if to stop him from getting away.

'Promise me,' she implored him. 'Promise me

51

you'll find him. Promise me you'll get him back.'

Detective Hill scratched at his moustache and said, 'We'll do our best, Ms Turner.' He tugged, very slightly, at the hand Emma held.

'In the meantime,' he said, 'if I could just ask you a few questions.'

It was all so mundane. So ordinary. They might have been discussing the theft of a bicycle. The calmness of it disorientated Emma, so that she sat there at first and answered all of Detective Hill's questions in a quiet and rational way. Then Detective Hill said, 'Now, can you tell us about the moment you noticed your son was missing?' That was when the reality of it hit her all over again. She thought, This is *me*, this is happening to *me*. *My son is missing!*

Her throat closed. Her lungs swelled; her chest wasn't big enough to hold them. This was not happening. She could not be here. She fought not to get up and thrash her way out of the room. They had to stop the interview while Lindsay sat her back in her chair and made her put her head between her knees.

★   ★   ★

Detective Inspector Hill wanted to know everything about Ritchie. He asked for Emma's permission to view Ritchie's medical records from the GP.

'Are you sure you'd never seen the woman at the tube station before?' he asked. 'Did anyone strange call to your flat recently? Approach you or Ritchie in the street? Follow you when you were out and about?'

Emma had recovered enough to answer all of these quite definitely. No one had followed her. No one had called to the flat. She had never seen Antonia before.

'Does Ritchie's father have any contact with him?' Detective Hill asked.

'No.'

'Is that by his choice or yours?'

'His.'

'Would he have tried to take him, do you think?'

'No.' Emma shook her head. If only she could think it *was* Oliver. At least then she'd know Ritchie was all right. 'I know he wouldn't. He's not the type.'

Detective Hill gave her a cold look, a look that said, 'I'll be the judge, thank you, of who is the type.' For some reason, it was as if he'd decided he didn't like Emma very much. He wrote something into his notebook and said, 'We'll need to talk to him anyway.'

Once, Emma would have been ashamed at the thought of Oliver knowing she'd been incompetent enough to lose her child. Their child. She didn't care now. In less than twenty-four hours, all thoughts of Oliver had been wiped from her mind as completely as if he'd never existed. She gave Detective Hill his sister's phone number in Birmingham. Oliver wasn't close to his family, but presumably Sasha would at least know where he was.

The questions continued.

'Do you have a boyfriend? Someone you've been seeing?'

'I haven't been with anyone since Oliver.'

'Who else do you know in London?'

Emma thought.

'My ex-flatmate, Joanne. But we're not that friendly now.'

'What about your neighbours here?'

'I don't really know any of them.'

Behind Lindsay, two of the policemen exchanged glances. Emma caught them and said angrily, 'Why do you keep on and on asking me about people I know? I told you, the woman who took Ritchie was a stranger. I'd never met her before.'

'I'm sorry, Emma.' Lindsay touched her arm. 'I know the questions are upsetting. But at the moment, we can't rule anything out.'

'What are you doing to find Ritchie?' Emma jerked her arm away. 'Apart from asking me questions, I mean. What are you actually doing to find him?'

Lindsay said patiently, 'We're doing quite a lot, Emma. We've spoken to some of the witnesses at the scene earlier — the tube station, and the street outside Mr Bap's — and we'll do our best to find and talk to as many more as we can. Your table in the café wasn't cleared after you left, so we've taken the coffee cups you and Antonia used. Antonia might have left some of her DNA on hers. Also, we're checking to see if any CCTV cameras are in operation on the street outside the café. If so, we might get some pictures of who took Ritchie and which way they went. The tube stations, at least, will have cameras, so we've put in an urgent request to look through those. And we've passed Ritchie's details to all the newspapers. You saw the late-evening edition.'

She had. A short paragraph on page five: 'The alleged snatching of a toddler from . . . ' But why hadn't they put him on the front page? Put him on *TV*? It all seemed so passive. So . . . so . . . Surely in films they did more to hunt for lost children? Emma floundered, lost for what else to ask.

'What about dogs?' she said. 'Helicopters?'

Lindsay said: 'Anything that's appropriate, we're doing it right now.'

Emma wanted to argue, but her breathing was coming too fast again, the way it had in the hospital. She put her hands to her mouth, trying to get it under control. More exchanging of glances between the policemen.

'My son does exist,' she said, and her voice came out as a sob.

'I know he does,' Lindsay said gently. 'I know.'

★   ★   ★

She had to get away. All these people in her flat, asking about Ritchie, and none of them knew him at all. He was just another job to them. She felt like a goldfish, frantically swimming around and around in a bowl, trapped and banging off the sides, while these calm, trained people looked at her from the outside and took notes.

The only private place was her room. She took Gribbit the frog from Ritchie's cot and crawled into bed, holding him in her arms. She wrapped them both in her duvet and lay there, exhausted, yet unable to slow down her thoughts.

What are they doing to my child? That was one of the worst things, nasty, ugly, lodged like a roll of barbed wire in her stomach. Lindsay had said she was sure he was being treated well, but then she had to say that, didn't she? The truth was, none of them knew who'd taken him or what was happening to him. She pictured Ritchie drugged, breathing in a loud, obstructed way, his eyes rolled back, waiting in a van or shed somewhere for . . . what? Or shivering in a corner, eating things off the ground and crying because no one had changed him and he was dirty and sore. She pictured him with tears rolling down his cheeks, emitting little high-pitched hiccups of distress, wondering what he'd done for her to leave him like this. To ease the horror of it, she concentrated on trying to send a hug to him. She focused on him; the bed swam away and there was just Ritchie, sitting by himself in a cot in a darkened room. He looked up, puzzled, the tears still on his cheeks. Emma felt a fierce tenderness and joy. Her arms went around his fat little body and he gave a glad cry and snuggled into her. She soothed him, weak with thankfulness; felt the way he trembled as he clung to her, wanting her to bring him home. The sensation was powerful enough to wake her, jerking her back to the bed. It wasn't Ritchie she held, it was Gribbit, his wide, stitched-open eyes blank with misery. Emma wept with the pain of it. She wasn't with Ritchie, she was here and he was God knew where, all alone. Crying for her.

What were they doing to him? What was some sick, twisted pervert standing over him doing to him?

Emma writhed in agony. She couldn't take much more of this. Why? Why had she taken her child for coffee with Antonia? A complete stranger! She'd been so naive, so desperate for someone to talk to. Why *had* she gone to the bathroom and left her small child — her baby — with a woman she'd never seen before? What sort of mother was she? Why had she let Ritchie get trapped on the train? Why hadn't she been watching him properly? Again and again she saw him there, standing in the doors. Over and over she replayed it in her mind: that strange tug on the harness, the sense that something was not quite right. But her bag was an inch out of reach, so that she spent that extra fraction of a second groping for it before she turned around.

She could never have that moment back. It had come and gone, and when it mattered most, she had chosen a bag of vests and trousers over her son.

★   ★   ★

If she slept at all, she didn't remember it. The hours dragged as she lay in the bleak silence, that barbed-wire coil in her stomach. At six in the morning, she abandoned the farce of trying to sleep and got up again. The phone hadn't rung once. She picked it up to check there was a dial tone. There was. Lindsay had left a note written in thick, black marker on a Post-it, stuck to the receiver: *Here's my number again, just to make sure. I'll be back tomorrow. Or sooner if there's any news.*

Emma was still wearing her jeans and jumper from the night before. She left her bedroom, trying not to look at the cot under the window. She made herself a cup of tea and sat without drinking it at the round table in the sitting-room. The curtains to the balcony were open. Through the glass doors, she saw the black tower block opposite, a grey halo in the sky just softening its edges. The heating in their building hadn't come on yet. The coldness exaggerated the loneliness and emptiness of the flat.

A whole night. He'd been gone a whole night. She'd thought she'd known what misery was, but now she knew she hadn't at all. She'd known nothing, nothing compared to this. Gribbit sat on her knee, his long fuzzy legs brushing off her calves, just at the place where a toddler's feet might reach. Emma stroked him, over and over, feeling her fingers bump over the dents on his tummy where his stuffing was wearing out.

How long she sat there for, she had no idea. The buzz of the intercom, belching harshly through the silence of the flat, brought her to. Emma started. Lindsay had said she'd call round today, but surely she hadn't meant this early? Why would she be here now, unless it was to say they had some news? Oh Jesus! She jumped up, flinging Gribbit off her lap, and hurried to the intercom.

But it was only Dr Stanford, her GP. What was she doing here? She didn't normally make

58

house-calls. Emma pressed the button to open the main door below. Dr Stanford arrived up in the lift a few minutes later. She had a second person with her: a youngish, frizzy-haired woman in a green top.

'Emma, how are you?' Dr Stanford floated into the tiny hall of the flat. She was tall, greyhound-thin, with ash-coloured hair smoothed back in a bun. She wore her usual uniform of immaculate grey skirt suit and silk blouse with a bow at the collar.

'This is really awful,' she said. 'You must be at your wits' end. You've met Alison Regis, haven't you?' She indicated the woman in green. 'Our health visitor?'

'No,' Emma said listlessly. She'd met several health visitors after Ritchie was born, but it seemed to be a different one each time.

'I've been on maternity leave,' Alison Regis explained. 'Today is my first day back.'

'I've been away myself,' Dr Stanford said. 'All last week. At a conference in San Diego.'

'San Diego?' Alison brightened. 'Lovely. That's where I went for my honeymoon.'

There was a pause. Dr Stanford cleared her throat.

She said to Emma, 'The police were at the surgery. They asked to see Ritchie's medical records. I hope you don't mind? I saw the form you signed, giving permission.'

'That's fine.'

'They asked if I'd check on you,' Dr Stanford went on. 'I would have anyway, of course. After your last visit to me, if you remember, I had left

59

an urgent message for Alison here to come and see you. Unfortunately, I didn't realize at the time that she was still on her maternity leave.'

For some reason, Dr Stanford seemed nervous. Her bony fingers shook as she fixed a loose strand of hair. Usually she was very calm, efficient, remote. She'd seen Emma and Ritchie for various ailments; had given Ritchie all his vaccinations, and twice some antibiotics for an ear infection. Emma had worried the infection wasn't clearing up properly, but Dr Stanford was always briskly reassuring. The ten-minute slot didn't leave much time for chat. The last time Emma had been to the surgery was just over a week ago, and Dr Stanford had been just the same.

'You look exhausted, Emma,' Dr Stanford said now. 'Have you managed to get any sleep?'

Emma's eyes stung from fatigue, and from the salt of a constant seepage of tears. Her jaw ached; no matter which way she held it, she couldn't seem to get it into a comfortable position. They'd given her some Valium at the hospital; she'd taken one and it hadn't worked at all. She wanted nothing more than to sleep, to get away from the panicky, relentless *thinking* about Ritchie, the horror of what might be happening to him, the helplessness and acid panic of not knowing what to do. But Lindsay had said to stay near the phone. Emma couldn't imagine how Antonia would have got her number, but if there was any chance at all that she would ring, she didn't want to be too drugged to take the call.

'You really should try to sleep,' Dr Stanford advised her.

'I will,' Emma said. 'But for now, I need to be awake.'

★ ★ ★

And then, just after five o'clock that evening, the phone rang.

Lindsay and Detective Inspector Hill were in the flat. Lindsay had been there most of the day, making endless cups of tea, and nipping round to Sainsbury's to buy soup that Emma wasn't able to eat. Detective Hill had arrived an hour ago — to take Emma's official statement, he said. Lindsay explained to Emma how this was done.

'Just tell us everything you've told us already, as it occurs to you,' she said. 'Plus anything else you may have remembered in the meantime. Don't worry if you get confused or if things aren't in the right order. We'll be recording everything you say, so we can put the full statement together later from the tape. At some point we'll ask you to read it through, and if you're happy we'll ask you to sign it.'

Emma spoke into the tape recorder and repeated most of what she'd told the police the night before. She didn't remember anything new. When the statement was finished, Lindsay got up and went into the kitchen to boil the kettle. Emma went to the bathroom. She was just unbuckling her jeans when the low *brrr-brrr* started up from the sitting-room. She froze. In the mirror over the sink, a white-faced scarecrow, harshly lit from above, gaped with black, sunken eyes. Emma listened, hardly breathing, very still.

The ringing was cut off. Lindsay's voice spoke, paused, spoke again.

And then — Oh sweet Jesus! — there came running footsteps and a hammering on the bathroom door.

'Emma.' Lindsay's tone was urgent. 'Quick, quick.'

Emma let go of her belt and stumbled to the door.

'It's a man,' Lindsay hissed. 'Wouldn't give a name. Are you expecting a call?'

Emma shook her head. She couldn't think . . . Unless it was Oliver, ringing to say he'd heard? She took the phone. There was no feeling in her fingers; she had to use her other hand to stop it slipping.

'Hello?'

A man's voice said, 'Is that Emma Turner?'

It wasn't Oliver.

Emma went rigid. Beside her, Lindsay's eyes were so wide Emma could see the white bits around her pupils.

'Yes?' Emma said.

'Oh, hello. My name is Rafe Townsend.'

She had never heard the name.

'Yes?'

'We met yesterday. In the tube station, remember?'

Emma's legs buckled. Lindsay gripped her arm. Emma clutched a table for support.

'Hello?' the voice was saying. 'Hello? Are you still there?'

'Yes,' Emma said coldly. 'Yes, I'm here.'

'You left all your bags behind when you got on the train,' the man said. 'Your number was in your wallet. I hope you don't mind me ringing, but I wanted to check you got your baby back all right.'

5

Emma couldn't speak. It was a while before she could even understand what the man was talking about. Feelings rushed at her. Relief that this man on the phone wasn't the kidnapper. *Disappointment* that he wasn't. It was too much. Too much. She backed away, dropping the phone on the floor.

Lindsay and Detective Hill were with her at once. Who was this person? they wanted to know. Where had she met him? How much had he seen of what had happened?

'He tried to help me in the station.' Emma was shaking. 'He pulled me back from going under the train.'

Detective Hill picked the phone up off the carpet.

'Hello,' he said into it in his deep voice.

The man on the other end was obviously still there, because Detective Hill, after listening for a moment, spoke again. Emma was still too flustered to hear much of the conversation, apart from the occasional 'Mmm' and 'I see'.

When Detective Hill had hung up, he said to Lindsay, 'Mr Townsend was planning to drop the bags here this evening. Apparently he'll be cycling past on his way home from work. I've told him we'd prefer it if he dropped them at the station.'

Lindsay was nodding. But Emma's brain was

64

starting to work again. How much had this Rafe person seen? Had he seen Antonia? Had he noticed something about her that might identify her?

'No,' she interrupted. 'Can't he bring the bags here? I want to talk to him. I want to meet him properly.'

'It might be better to let us take care of it,' Lindsay advised. 'We can take his statement at the police station.'

'I want to hear what he says,' Emma insisted. 'He was there. He saw Ritchie. You ask him. He saw what happened, he'll tell you.'

Lindsay hesitated. She looked at Detective Inspector Hill, who was busy cleaning something out from under his thumbnail. He shrugged.

'All the same to me,' he said. 'We can do the statement here.'

'You're sure about this?' Lindsay asked Emma. 'You're sure you're in a fit state to have this man come here?'

'I am. I want to see him. I want to hear what he says.'

Lindsay phoned Mr Townsend back. They agreed between them that he should call at the flat in twenty minutes.

While waiting for Rafe Townsend to arrive, Emma pushed back the sliding glass door to the balcony and went out for some air. She walked up and down, pacing and re-pacing the three steps it took to go from one end of the balcony to the other. The balconies of the tower block opposite bulged with jumble: drying clothes, pushchairs, strings fluttering with flags. Windows, hundreds of them, studded the block, some blacked out with tinfoil or paper, like missing teeth in a row of mouths.

Imagine, Emma kept thinking. Imagine if this Rafe Townsend had seen Antonia. Recognized her, even.

'Oh, yes,' he might say to the police. 'We're regular travellers, that woman and me. I see her most days. She gets off every evening at Tower Hill.'

And there was another thing she kept thinking: *Now they'll have to believe me.* For some reason, she just couldn't shake the feeling that the police were suspicious of her. As though they didn't believe her version of what had happened. They were trying to get CCTV footage, they said, that would show Ritchie getting trapped on the train. But so far they'd had problems finding the film. 'Did anyone else see what happened?' Detective Hill had kept asking her. 'Did anyone at all see you with Ritchie?' It was driving her mad. Well, now she had a witness. They'd have to stop all the endless, pointless questions and get on with looking for Ritchie properly.

The intercom buzzer sounded. Emma stopped her pacing and rushed to the sliding door. Voices swelled from inside the flat.

' . . . good of you to come . . . '

' . . . awful. I can't believe . . . '

Quickly, Emma stepped through the door. Detective Hill was standing in the middle of the sitting-room, talking to a dark-haired man in a red T-shirt. Rafe Townsend, Emma presumed.

66

She stared hard at him, trying to figure out what kind of a witness he might make. Whether he looked the type to be observant. Her first thought was how young he looked. She'd had an impression in the tube station of a much older man. This person was about her own age, lean and tanned. He wasn't as tall as Detective Hill, but that didn't mean he still wasn't fairly tall. He was carrying a canvas rucksack with holes frayed in the corners and his jeans and T-shirt were faded. Damp circles spread under the arms of the T-shirt.

'You look familiar,' Lindsay was saying curiously. 'Weren't you in the police?'

'Only for a while,' Rafe Townsend said. 'I finished Hendon, but left my training after a year of probation.'

'Oh?' Detective Hill raised an eyebrow. 'Why was that?'

'Personal reasons,' Rafe said politely. He had a London accent, not a posh one.

There was a chilly pause.

Detective Hill said, 'And what do you do now?'

'I work for a landscaping company. Digging. Knocking walls. That kind of thing.'

Hurry *up*, Emma thought. Ask him what he saw.

Detective Hill stood there, stroking his moustache, moving his thumb from left to right and back again over the hairs. He was staring at Rafe as hard as Emma had done.

'You've been told what's happened,' he said after a moment.

'Yes.' For the first time, Rafe glanced towards Emma. 'I'm sorry.'

'You don't mind if we ask some questions about what you saw?'

'No. I'd be glad to be of any help.'

Lindsay looked at Emma. Before Rafe had arrived, she had asked Emma if she would mind waiting in a separate room while he gave his statement.

'Witnesses usually give their accounts in private,' Lindsay said. 'But you'll have a chance to talk to him afterwards if you want.'

Emma went back out to the balcony. She slid the glass door shut and heard the voices in the sitting-room drop to an incomprehensible murmur. She leaned on her arms on the railing for a while, letting the breeze numb her face. The car park below was a twilit blur. She didn't notice that the murmuring in the flat had stopped until she heard the balcony door open behind her.

'Mr Townsend would like to see you,' Lindsay said.

Emma turned. The door slid open further. Then there was a scuffling sound, and Rafe Townsend and his rucksack were beside her on the balcony.

'I brought your stuff back,' Rafe said.

Emma swung all the way round to face him. Close up, he wasn't so much tanned as sallow, as if he had Spanish or Italian blood. His eyes were very alert.

'What did you tell them?' Emma asked. 'What did you say?'

Rafe said, 'Well, the first thing they wanted to know was what I'd been doing at Stepney Green tube station. I said I'd been on a gardening job near Epping Forest, and my boss gave me a lift to the station on his way home. When I got on to the platform, I saw you running after the train and thought you were about to get yourself killed, so I ran down the tunnel to pull you back.'

'Did you see her? Did you see Antonia?'

'The woman on the train? No. I'm sorry.'

Emma slumped. But what had she expected? Even if he *had* seen Antonia, he wouldn't have been able to tell them much more about her than she herself had.

To comfort herself more than him, she said, 'Well, at least you saw Ritchie. The way the police have been talking, some of them seem to think I've been making him up.'

Rafe shuffled a bit on the cement floor of the balcony.

'You know,' he said, 'I didn't actually see your kid.'

Emma stared at him. 'But you must have. You were there.'

'Yeah. Well, it's like I said to the police, I saw you holding on to a strap of some kind outside the door of the train. But I only knew when you told me afterwards that it was your baby.'

'But you — '

All over a fucking designer handbag. Of course. Emma remembered now. He had thought Ritchie was a handbag. This person was blind. He couldn't help her at all. She turned away. Her throat felt like there was something in

69

it, like she might choke. She didn't want to hear any more.

'I'm sorry.' Rafe sounded subdued. 'Really, I am.'

Emma couldn't answer.

'How are you doing?'

How did he bloody well think?

'I feel like the world's biggest loser.' Rafe hit his fist off his rucksack. 'I shouldn't have left you. I should have pressed the alarm.'

Emma said dully, 'Why would you have? I told you not to.'

'But I shouldn't have listened. You were in no state to know what you were doing.'

Emma picked at a piece of rust on the railing. Beside her, Rafe shifted unhappily from foot to foot. One of those restless types who always had to be doing something. She didn't attempt to make it easy for him.

'Well,' he said at last, 'I'll go, then. Give you some peace.'

He disappeared from the edge of her vision. More scuffling, as he tried to fit his rucksack back through the door. On an impulse, Emma swung around.

'Wait.'

'Yes?' Rafe turned. In the light from the sky, his eyes were a peculiar colour; so light brown they were almost golden.

He'd tried to help her, she couldn't deny that. It may not have worked, but at least he'd tried. It was far more than any of those other people, the ones who'd been outside the café, had done.

'You were in the police,' she said. 'Would you

know if there's something they're not telling me? Some reason they're not looking for him properly?'

'Why would you think that?'

'Something's wrong.' Now she was saying it, it made her even more certain. 'I don't know why, but they don't seem to believe me. The newspapers aren't interested either. Ritchie wasn't in the headlines this morning, and he's a little boy who's been kidnapped, he *should* be in the headlines. He *should* be. It's like they think I've made the whole thing up. Why on earth would I do that? If Ritchie hasn't been kidnapped, then where on earth do they think — '

Her voice had been rising, and now it turned into a croak. She couldn't finish the sentence.

Rafe said, 'I'm sure for something like this, a missing child, they'd be doing everything they could.'

'Then why haven't they found him?' Emma cried. 'Why are they just *here* all the time, sitting in the flat instead of going out looking for him?'

Rafe looked distressed.

'Sometimes you just need a lead. I'm assuming you've been over it all a hundred times? You haven't missed anything, even something really small, that could help identify the person who took him?'

'Don't you think I'd have said if I did? I keep thinking about it. On and on and on. It's all I think about.'

'I know,' he said. 'I know.'

Emma turned away. It was hopeless. Hopeless.

71

He was no good to her at all.

'Maybe I should get a private detective,' she said, more to herself than to him.

'I wouldn't like to say.' Rafe sounded uncomfortable. Then he said, 'What is it? What's wrong?'

Emma was gripping the railing, staring over the balcony. At the grid of streets, the cars, the rows of wheelie bins five floors down.

'Are you all right?' Rafe asked.

'Something . . . ' she said.

What had it been? She thought back, trying to recap the last few seconds. They'd been talking about the police and then . . . what? What had put Antonia into her head, flashing by, so suddenly like that? She strained to pull the image back but it fled, tapering to a dot, like a rat showing the tip of its tail.

'No.' Frustrated again, she shook her head. 'No. It's gone.'

'It'll come back,' Rafe assured her. 'When you're ready, if it's important, it'll come back.'

⋆   ⋆   ⋆

The two of them didn't have much to say to each other after that. After Rafe had left, the pain in Emma's jaw worsened, spreading upwards to her entire head. Lindsay commented on her pale face and slitted eyes, and persuaded her to take two painkillers. Emma went to bed and lay, fully dressed, under the duvet.

She held Gribbit, puzzling again over what had made her think of Antonia like that.

72

Something had sparked that flash of recall, but what? And there was that image of her mum again, watching television in the house in Bath. Why did she keep seeing that? The scent of sour milk rose from Gribbit's fur. Think, Emma. Think! There was the sense that her mind had recognized something important, and jumped with shock so that the memory had been knocked out of place. But no matter how hard she drew at it, it refused to come back.

A tap on her door.

'Emma?' Lindsay's dark head peeped around. 'Are you feeling any better? DI Hill would like a word before he leaves.'

Something in Lindsay's voice made Emma sit up.

'What's wrong? Something's happened, hasn't it?'

'No, no.' Lindsay wouldn't look at her. 'Nothing's happened. It's just a few more questions. If you could come to the sitting-room for a moment.'

Emma fumbled, trying to get her legs out from under the duvet. Now what? She managed to escape from the bed and followed Lindsay out into the hall.

'Please.' Lindsay held the door open to the sitting-room. 'Come and sit down.'

Lindsay accompanied Emma to the couch and gently pressed her shoulder until she sat, before taking a seat beside her. Detective Inspector Hill squashed himself between the arms of the chair opposite. He looked so enormous, sitting there. Ritchie, who was fascinated by men, would have gazed at him in awe. At this giant, who could have fitted little Ritchie twice over into one of his pockets without anyone even noticing he was there.

Lindsay touched Emma's hand.

'Try not to take this personally,' she said. 'Sooner or later, we ask this to almost every family in your situation.'

'Ask them *what*?'

Detective Hill cleared his throat. He said, 'I was intending to discuss this with you earlier, before we were interrupted by Mr Townsend. I had a long talk with your GP this morning. When we were looking through Ritchie's medical records.'

'My GP?' Emma was confused. What did Dr Stanford have to do with this?

Detective Hill leaned forward. He clasped his huge hands in front of him.

'Ms Turner,' he said, 'I'm sorry, but I have to ask you. Is there any chance at all that you may have done something to your son?'

Emma stared at him.

'I don't understand,' she said. Her cheeks grew hot. 'Ritchie's been kidnapped. You know he has. Why are you asking me this?'

'Dr Stanford has told us a few things,' Detective Hill said. 'She was reluctant to do so, but given that you had allowed us to view the records, she felt she had no choice. She thinks you may not be telling us the truth about all of this.' He paused. 'In fact, based on a visit you paid to her recently, she's worried that you may have harmed Ritchie.'

74

Ha-ha-harmed. The Ha sucked in her chest. *You may have Harmed Ritchie.*

'Emma?' Detective Hill's eyes were very cold. They bulged at her, laser-blue. 'Do you remember your last visit to Dr Stanford, eleven days ago?'

'My last — '

A fizz rose in Emma's belly. In a second, she was back there in the surgery. The lurid coughs from the waiting-room. The gravel-rattle of rain on the window. The stench of socks and antiseptic.

The expression on Dr Stanford's face. Sitting there, so shocked and upright behind her desk.

Emma hunched forward until her elbows were on her knees. She put her hands to her face.

'Do you remember?' Detective Hill was saying. 'Do you remember what you told Dr Stanford that day?'

In a low voice, Emma said, 'Yes. Yes, I remember.'

So, at least, now she knew. The reason they weren't taking her seriously. From the balcony came a seagull-like cry.

Oh Ritchie. Ritchie. What have I done?

Lindsay was pulling at her, trying to take her hand. Her face was a blur of smoothness, all professional concern. But her thoughts sprang at Emma as clearly as if she'd spoken them aloud:

And here we were feeling sorry for you! What kind of mother are you?

Emma kept her face covered. She couldn't look at Lindsay. She turned away.

6

From the first, Ritchie had Oliver's smile, and every time she saw it Emma's heart skipped a beat. Ritchie was a solemn child; the smile usually had to be coaxed out of him, often appearing around a fist or a toy or a rusk in his mouth, but it was there. Some day, some woman was going to be floored by that smile, and Emma didn't know whether to pity her or envy her.

Because, of course, it was that smile that had stopped her in her tracks one evening, halfway across the Blue Grape in Clapham with three drinks in her hands. The owner of the smile wasn't even looking in her direction at the time, but it knocked the breath out of her for a second.

'Who's that bloke Barry's talking to?' Emma hissed, back at the table, sliding Joanne and Claire over their glasses of vodka and cranberry juice.

Joanne twisted around on her high stool to see.

'Oh, him,' she said. 'Oliver Metcalfe. Works in Barry's company.'

'He's got a girlfriend, if that's why you're asking,' Claire Burns said. Claire had been to uni with Emma and Joanne, and was one of those people who always seems to know everything about everyone. 'I've seen him with an Asian girl with hair down to her bum.'

'Oh.' Emma was disappointed. The best ones were always taken.

Still, though, she couldn't help checking out Oliver Metcalfe as the evening progressed. What *was* it about him? She hadn't felt this attracted to a bloke in ages. She watched him over Claire and Joanne's shoulders as he laughed and chatted with his mates. He was tall, half a head higher than most of the people around him, standing under the window with the streetlight in his hair. The hair was dark blond, long enough so that his fringe brushed his eyes. He was part of the work-suited crowd, but where the others had shirts and ties under their jackets he wore a yellow T-shirt with a picture of Homer Simpson on the front. He had a pair of extremely tatty trainers on his feet. The outfit would look ridiculous on a normal man — Barry, Joanne's boyfriend, for example, whose pink belly strained at the buttons of his shirt — but Oliver got away with it. Emma guessed he was a person who knew absolutely what he was doing with clothes. They just hung right on him.

Two Sea Breezes later, Emma had made her mind up. She slammed her glass on the table and grinned at Claire and Joanne.

'Well,' she said, 'I don't see any Asian girls over there tonight. How about I go and say hello?'

'Cheeky bint,' Joanne called as she left the table. 'Hasn't that Brian bloke from your work been begging to take you to dinner for weeks? You never chase men.'

'So maybe it's time I started,' Emma muttered. She checked her reflection in the mirror behind the bar. Her new green Topshop dress was holding up well. The neckline was perfect; not too low, not too high. Her hair was freshly washed and shiny. Her mascara was still in place, not yet at the stage where it had begun to slide down her face. OK, so no one was about to mistake her for Kate Moss's younger sister, but she wasn't an absolute toad either. She looked all right.

Barry looked astonished to find Emma greeting him as enthusiastically as if they were the best of friends. Normally they didn't have that much to say to each other. He grunted at her, and she turned to Oliver.

'Hi.' She smiled. 'I'm Emma.'

'Oliver,' he said politely, shaking her hand.

She was slightly thrown to find that up close he was even better looking than she'd thought. In fact, there was no way around it, he was very, very good-looking. He waited, eyebrows courteously raised, clearly wondering what she wanted. Emma's confidence wavered but she stood her ground.

'We know people in common,' she explained. 'I live with Joanne, Barry's girlfriend.'

'Oh, really?' Oliver had a lovely voice. Deep, very well-spoken. 'How do you know each other?'

'We were on the same course in Bristol. Business Studies and Marketing. And we went to Sydney for a year together after uni.'

'Sounds interesting,' he said. 'Bristol's a good place.'

'Yeah, it is.'

A pause.

'What are you reading?' Emma asked, spotting a book sticking out of the pocket of his jacket. There was a picture of some sort of cockroach on the front.

'Kafka,' Oliver said. '*Metamorphosis.*'

'I've heard of that. What's it about?'

'A man wakes up one morning and finds he's changed into a giant insect.'

'Oh.' Typical male. 'Sci-fi.'

Oliver laughed then, as if she'd said something funny.

'I have to go,' he said, putting his glass on the counter. 'I've arranged to see someone in town. But it was nice meeting you. I'm sure we'll bump into each other again.'

'Great,' Emma said politely. 'I'm sure we will.'

'No vibe,' she said, deflated, to Joanne and Claire a couple of minutes later.

'He only goes out with really attractive girls,' Claire said. 'Not that I don't think you're attractive,' she added quickly as Emma looked at her, 'but you know what I mean.'

Emma did. Claire had been green with envy in case Emma hit it off with Oliver and ended up going out with him. She'd always been like that, all through uni. Putting people in their place, in case they got ideas above their station. Emma often wondered why they still hung out with her. But that was London for you. It was so huge, and so hard to get to know new people, that even though you'd moved there to do precisely that, you ended up hanging out with all the old ones, just for security.

'Oh well.' She shrugged, refusing to let

Claire's snide remarks get to her. 'I gave him a chance, but I have my pride.'

Back at Joanne and Emma's flat, two streets away, there was a message for Emma on the answering machine.

'Hi, Emma. Mum here. I haven't heard from you for a few days, so just checking that you're well and hope to hear from you soon.'

Emma jabbed the Erase button.

'That's the third time this week,' she complained. 'It's only recently she's started doing this. Phoning me at all hours.'

'Why d'you never ring her back, then?' Joanne called, clattering around in the kitchen.

'Sunday is the day I ring. She knows that. Why's she calling the flat on a Friday night? Does she think I have no life, phoning on a Friday?' Emma's voice rose. How tantrummy and hysterical she sounded. There her mother went again. Turning her straight back into a nine-year-old.

'My mum's a nag too,' Joanne said. 'It's being on their own does it.'

Emma fiddled with the switch on the answering machine. She hadn't meant to imply that her mother was a nag. And then she was frustrated. What was there to feel guilty about? She owed her mother nothing. Nothing at all.

'Your mum does care about you, love,' her gran had assured the five-year-old Emma whenever her mother snapped at her. And the eight-year-old, when her mum forgot to collect her from school. And the eleven-year-old, when Emma was spending most evenings and

80

weekends at her gran's because her mother was too tired to look after her. 'She's just worn out because of her work. It's so there'll be money in the bank for you for university.' But really, her gran didn't see what the big deal was about Emma going to university. Emma didn't either, at the time. But she loved her gran, and the arrangement of spending so much time with her suited them both. Who needed her cold, distant mother?

She marched through to the kitchen to explain it properly to Joanne.

'I would ring her more,' she said, 'but once, when I was four years old, I tried to climb on her knee and she pushed me off so hard I fell and smashed my face on the fireplace. Look.' She pulled her hair to one side and tilted her head, jutting her chin at Joanne. 'You can still see the scar. What kind of mother does that to a child?'

'Keep your hair on. I was only saying.' Joanne had seen the scar before. She had lost interest and was reading a fashion magazine, winding her long, blonde hair around the top of her head.

★   ★   ★

Emma saw Oliver a few times after that, usually in a Friday-night group with Barry and the City boys. The Grape was the magnet for most of the twenty-somethings in their area. It had high ceilings, a dark wood floor, plenty of tables. The pub grub was cheap and tasty: steak and ale pie, chicken curry, sausages and mash. No snooker tables, which pleased the women. The blokes liked it because there was a large selection of real ales. Emma didn't try to approach Oliver again, but secretly she was still fascinated by him. The way he rarely spoke to anyone; just stood there sipping his pint of Spitfire, sometimes staring off into space. What was all that about? What did he think about when he half closed his drowsy eyes while those around him shouted over each other to be heard? And yet, despite his aloofness, he always managed to be right in the middle of the coolest group. How did he do that? He didn't seem to make any particular effort to attract people; they just gathered around him. On the nights she spotted him, she felt a little snip of excitement in her belly. She held herself straighter, became more animated, made sure she was always laughing and having a good time. Easy enough to do, because the Grape, with Oliver in it, suddenly seemed like the very centre of London. The place everyone wanted to be.

'You know he's an orphan,' Joanne told her one evening. 'His parents were killed in a car crash when he was seven.'

'No!' Emma was shocked. 'That's horrible.'

'He was sent to live with an aunt somewhere in the country but I don't think they got on too well. She chucked him out when he was about fifteen.'

'Poor Oliver,' Emma sighed. 'No wonder he's so reserved.'

'Yeah,' Joanne said. 'Comes across quite deep, doesn't he? Likes it that way.'

'I thought he was a friend of yours?'

'Oliver's all right, you know. Barry says he

works at that laid-back image of his. A mate of ours lived with him and he said Oliver spent all his time checking himself in the mirror, turning his head from side to side when he thought no one was looking. He makes sure he reads all the right books, knows all the right on things to say. I don't know how much depth there actually is to him, to be honest.'

'Hmm,' Emma said.

The trouble with Joanne was she didn't like any men now that she'd met Barry. Emma could take or leave Barry. He was a bit middle-aged, considering he was only twenty-six. He'd been born and spent his whole life in Wandsworth, had a beer belly already, and held views on things like immigration and single mothers. But he was doing well in his career, slowly clambering to the top of the IT world. He had bought his own flat. Joanne had always wanted to marry young.

It was raining one evening in September when Emma sloshed down the steps to put her key in the lock of their basement flat. The end of yet another glorious day at the call centre, being shouted at by clients who couldn't get through to technical support. The calls were recorded so she couldn't tell the clients to piss off, or even agree with them that yes, actually, PlanetLink was the worst broadband provider in the UK and the best thing they could do would be to take their custom elsewhere. What made things even more unbearable was that she had no one to bitch to during her breaks. Most of her colleagues were either several years younger than her, only there for a few weeks to fund their gap year, or else many years older, worn down and embittered by life, trying to scrape together the cash to save the house their ex had remortgaged without telling them. The only person in the place remotely her age was Brian Cobbold, Emma's would-be admirer, who'd been working at the call centre for six years now, and wearing the same V-necked jumper for most of them.

Six years! Emma felt faint. She'd been there for ten months, and already she could feel mould growing on her. She really needed to get out of there. Fast.

Her humour didn't improve when she got in the door of the flat and found a letter from a renowned hotel chain waiting for her.

Dear Ms Turner,
Thank you for applying for the position of Assistant Marketing Director at the Globe Rendezvous Group. We regret to inform you that you have not been shortlisted for this post.

'London is so *competitive*,' Emma moaned to Joanne. 'Any of the really good jobs I've applied for, all the other people have got Masters and first-class degrees. It's hopeless trying to get anywhere.'

'You're aiming too high,' Joanne advised. 'You should just take something. Get on the ladder. You've been at that call thingy for a year now.'

'I don't want to be tied into a job I'm not happy with,' Emma said. 'The thing about the call centre is, you can leave at short notice if anything turns up.'

She crumpled up the letter, chucked it into the bin and went to the sink to fill the kettle. Even though it wasn't half past six yet, she had to switch on the light. Emma and Joanne's two-bedroom flat was in the basement of a terraced four-storey house divided into flats. The flats on the upper floors had high ceilings and big windows with views towards Clapham Common. Emma and Joanne's ceiling was so low they could practically touch it sitting down, and the only view from their iron-barred windows was of peoples' feet as they passed. This evening was darker than usual, due to the rain. Water ran down the kitchen window. Through the bars, looking upwards, Emma saw the grey street, littered with flapping To Let signs.

'I might travel again,' she said in a dreamy way.

'Where?' Joanne asked.

'I don't know. China? I've always wanted to go there.'

The phone rang.

'Hello . . . Emma?' It was her mum. 'I must have missed your call yesterday evening.'

The Sunday-evening phone call! Blimmin' hell! Emma closed her eyes.

'I was out,' she lied. 'At . . . er . . . to dinner. I got in too late to ring.'

'Not to worry,' her mother said cheerfully. 'Where did you go? Somewhere nice?'

'It was all right,' Emma mumbled.

Time for a change of subject.

'I'm thinking of moving to China,' she announced.

'To China?' Her mum sounded puzzled. 'Why would you do that?'

'To work there for a while. Experience a different culture.'

'But what sort of job would you get? You don't speak Chinese.'

'I could learn, couldn't I?'

There was a pause.

'Do you think this is a good idea?' Emma's mother asked.

'Why wouldn't it be?'

'Well, you've only got back from that waitressing job in Sydney — '

'It wasn't just waitressing.' Emma gritted her teeth. 'I was in charge of all their PR work as well.'

'I know that, love. I know. All I'm saying is, shouldn't you try to get some proper experience or further qualification here before you head off again? Build some networks? You'll find you have nothing to come back to.'

'And you know so much about the business world?' Emma said coolly.

'Oh, Emma.' Her mother sighed. 'I can't say anything to you, give you any kind of advice.'

You should have done all that a long time ago, Emma thought.

'When are you coming to visit in Bath?' her mother asked.

'Soon. Work's kind of busy at the moment.'

'You haven't been home for a while.'

'I will be soon,' Emma promised. 'Look, I've got to go now. I'm going out. I'm meeting someone at eight and I still have to get ready.'

'All right, love,' her mother said. 'Have a good evening. Stay in touch.'

They said their goodbyes and hung up. But it was a while before Emma took her hand from the phone.

I wish I could have the last few minutes back, she thought, as she often did after speaking to her mum.

One day this would be sorted out, once and for all. Emma had it all in her head, all planned out. One day when she had a proper job, a job her mother would be proud of, she would visit Bath and she and her mother would sit down and talk. Really talk, and they would both say everything they wanted to say. Emma would tell her mother how hurt she'd been as a child, never having been hugged or held, never brought anywhere by her mum, always left at her gran's. Her mother would explain why she'd been so cold. There must have been some reason. She would ask Emma's forgiveness, and because Emma was now so happy and successful, she would graciously agree to let bygones be bygones. She and her mother would hug each other, and Emma's bitterness would melt away and she would let herself be as close to her mum as she sometimes longed to be.

Because then she wouldn't be so angry any more.

Three days later, at work, she received a phone call.

'Is that you, Emma?' an elderly female voice asked.

87

'Yes?' Emma was confused. The voice, vaguely familiar, sounded out of place in the high-volume, frantic surroundings of the call centre.

'This is Mrs Cornes. Your next-door neighbour in Bath.'

'Oh.'

And then Emma felt a slow, cold finger at her throat. Why would Mrs Cornes be phoning her at work on a Thursday afternoon?

'Emma, love.' Mrs Cornes' voice trembled. 'I'm sorry to have to tell you this. It's your mum.'

⋆ ⋆ ⋆

Sub-Arachnoid Haemorrhage, the post-mortem said. Mrs Cornes had been worried when she hadn't seen Emma's mother for a few days. She'd taken the spare key and called around to the house. In the hall, at the bottom of the stairs, lay Mrs Turner, her dark hair spread around her head. She'd been dead for more than forty-eight hours. On the train to Bath, light headed and frozen, Emma traced the tiny mark on her chin.

There were more people at the funeral than she had expected. Mrs Cornes must have mobilized the citizens of Bath. Neighbours, none of whom Emma really knew, all had kind things to say about her mother. Afterwards, she spent a few days going through her mum's things to see what she wanted to keep or throw away. Mrs Cornes helped her. They didn't have much time; already there were new tenants waiting to move in to the house. There were mainly clothes, old letters, a few bits of jewellery. That was about it really. Her mum had left so little to show for her life.

In a frame on the mantelpiece, Emma found a photograph: herself, her mum and her gran, taken when Emma was about thirteen. Emma remembered the day. It had been her gran's birthday and a neighbour had taken the photo. Her mum and gran sat on the couch, side by side. Emma stood behind them, resting a hand on each of their shoulders. All of them were smiling, even her mum. Her gran showed no sign of the tumour that was already beginning to vanquish her right lung. Emma's mum looked young and fresh, wearing a rose-pink dress, so different from the grey tunic she wore to her job as a healthcare assistant at the nursing home. Her hair was loose, the same dark brown as Emma's. She had the same blue eyes.

That had been a good evening. They'd taken Gran to dinner at a restaurant. The three of them had drunk a bottle of wine. Emma took the photograph down and stared at it. *What was it all about, Mum? Did you want me? Did you love me?* She'd never know now. She wrapped the photo in a sheet of newspaper and put it into her bag.

Mrs Cornes saw her to the station to catch the train back to London.

'Who do you have up there, Emma?' Mrs Cornes was distressed. She had on the navy Sunday coat she'd worn for the funeral, buttoned up to the neck, with a patterned silk scarf underneath. In the harsh morning light, her lipstick, crookedly applied, was too pink for

89

her face. She peered up at Emma.

'Your mum worried about you,' she said. 'All that travelling you'd been doing recently. Not putting down any roots. I hate to think of you not having someone you can depend on.'

'Joanne, the girl I live with, is a good friend,' Emma assured the kindly woman. 'She won't let me down.'

She went to shake Mrs Cornes' hand and somehow found that she was hugging her instead. Mrs Cornes smelled of rosewater and scones. They held each other tightly for a moment. The guard blew his whistle. Emma let go of Mrs Cornes. She stepped away and walked through the barrier.

★ ★ ★

Emma was in the Grape one evening with Joanne, when Oliver came in. She hadn't seen or thought about him for a while. He was with friends, but left them to come over and speak to her.

'I heard about your mum,' he said. He stood in front of her, looking down. 'It's a tough thing to happen. If you need to talk to someone about it, I'm here.'

Whatever he saw in her that night made him decide to stay with her instead of going back to his friends. He sat beside her for the rest of the evening. They drank a bottle of wine and talked about death, wondering what the point of everything was if it all came to nothing in the end.

'What's the point of beauty, even?' Emma asked in a low voice. 'My mum loved the sea.

90

Especially in the evenings. She loved the sunsets in Cornwall.'

'Beauty is a myth,' Oliver said. 'The sea and the sun aren't beautiful. We're just programmed to think they are because they represent water and heat — the fuel we need to survive.'

The morbidness of the conversation suited Emma's mood. She didn't notice that Joanne had disappeared. Tears filled her eyes at the waste of it all; the futility of her mum's short life.

Oliver held her hand.

'Come out with me,' he said. 'This weekend. A friend of mine is in a band. They're doing a gig in Brixton.'

★   ★   ★

The gig was upstairs in a pub, somewhere in the maze of side streets between Clapham and Brixton. Emma didn't make a massive effort to dress up for the evening. She wore her jeans and the reliable black top she'd got in the LK Bennett sale, with the shiny bits around the neckline. At the last minute, Joanne insisted she put on a pair of dangly jet earrings. But she wasn't really in a party mood. Her mum had just died. This was no date she was going out on. Oliver was being a friend.

A very handsome friend. He met her outside Brixton tube station, looking very tall, wearing a blue shirt and dark wine velvet trousers, and Emma knew she was lost. The pub was on a corner, a spacious brick building with outsized windows and a large green canopy. Under the

91

patio heaters, the wooden benches on the pavement were packed with people chatting and laughing. Inside, the pub was even more crowded. Emma followed Oliver up a narrow set of stairs. At the top, a very pretty blonde girl with a clipboard and a fluorescent wrist-stamper flung her arms around Oliver and showed him and Emma to a table with a good view of the stage. The stools were low and very close together. Every time Oliver leaned over to say something to Emma, the tips of his knees brushed against hers.

The music was a mixture of blues and jazz, some upbeat and lively, some slow and sad. The singer, a tall black girl with long, braided, blonde-dyed hair, was good enough that, at times, everyone fell silent to listen.

Oliver talked about his girlfriend.

'Sharmila and I have split up,' he told Emma over seafood chowder and Guinness. 'She had to move to Edinburgh for work.'

'I'm sorry,' Emma said. 'You must miss her.'

'I do, a bit,' Oliver said. 'But she was always going to put her career first. I don't blame her. If there'd been anything real between us, I might have gone to Edinburgh or she might have stayed here. But neither of us wanted to make the sacrifice.'

By the time the gig was over, it was after one and the tubes had all stopped for the night. Oliver walked Emma home to her flat in Clapham. One minute they were walking through streets lined with littered doorways and steel-shuttered shops, the next, as was often the way in London, they found themselves turning down much posher roads, with tall, sprawling

92

houses surrounded by trees. Clapham Common, lit partly by streetlights, partly by the glow from the houses around the edges, looked black and leafy and romantic. Emma probably wouldn't have cut through the park at this hour on her own, but with Oliver she felt safe. Her corner of London had never looked particularly beautiful to her before, but it did that night.

Especially when Oliver stopped her under a vast, old horse chestnut tree to kiss her.

This was it, then, this was the one. There was something so special about him. Emma had fallen under a spell. She'd read that in books, but thought it was just something people wrote. Now she knew what it meant. Everything about Oliver was magical, not quite human. His skin was so smooth and clean. He didn't smell of sweat, even after a long day, like normal people, just of warmed cotton, as if he wasn't really there.

Emma heard all about Oliver's childhood: about the car crash, the aunt who'd made it plain she'd never wanted a child. Oliver had an older sister living in Birmingham whom he rarely saw. This shocked Emma. How could a sister and brother lose touch like that? Her concern for Oliver made her forget her own unhappiness. She'd had her gran, at least, when she was young and her mum was . . . not herself. Oliver seemed to have had no one. She imagined him as the seven-year-old child he'd been, alone and frightened, and the thought of it almost broke her heart.

Oliver was always full of ideas for outings and exhibitions and music festivals. Over the next few weeks there were surfing trips to Cornwall, a weekend on Skye, the green river in Hampshire. He took her to a party in an underground tunnel in the Docklands where an unexploded bomb from the Second World War was embedded right there in the wall. Emma was thrilled. Although it did occur to her to wonder why, if it was common knowledge that a live bomb was sitting directly under London, the authorities hadn't got around to doing something about it.

Oliver could be moody at times, but Emma didn't let that put her off. He worked hard, often spending weekends and nights at work, supervising the transfer of money to and from accounts all over the world. Emma stayed in with him when he was tired and wanted to slump in front of the TV. This lowness was a part of him that other people didn't see.

'You're such a caring, genuine person,' he said to Emma during one of these down times. 'Sharmila was colder, less giving. I'm a bit like that myself, I think.'

'No, you're not,' Emma reassured him. Then she hesitated. Was this a good time to bring up something she'd been thinking for a while? 'You know, you should try to see more of your sister.'

'Sasha? What for? We saw each other last Christmas.'

'Well, you could see her at other times too,' Emma said. 'You should phone her. Spend some time together.'

Emma often fantasized about meeting Oliver's sister. She would look a bit like Oliver, she thought, maybe with a sparkier personality. She and Emma would hit it off straight away. It was coming up to Christmas now. Emma and Sasha would go shopping together for Oliver's present, and Sasha would have them all to her house for dinner on Christmas Day.

Oliver was looking baffled. 'Well, she doesn't phone me. How often do you see *your* sister?'

'I haven't got one,' Emma said.

'Oh.' Oliver stared at the television. 'I'm sorry. You did say.'

'I wish I *did* have a sister,' Emma said. 'At the end of the day, your family are the people you can rely on the most.'

Oliver yawned.

'Well,' he said, 'Sasha's ten years older than me. Married with three children. She's nice enough, but a bit, you know. Bourgeois. Never done anything with her life. I wouldn't know what to say to her.'

'Maybe I could call her?' Emma suggested. 'It might be easier that way. You know, woman to woman. We could organize dinner.'

'It's all right, Emma.' Oliver was polite. 'The thing is, you don't really know my family.'

When he phoned Emma the next time, he had some news for her. He hoped she hadn't got the wrong idea but he didn't want things to go too far between them. Sharmila was moving back to London, and they were going to give things another go.

Emma would have been shocked except that she was already too shocked to get any worse. She had just realized that her period was nearly three weeks late.

95

7

Friday, 22 September
Day Six

What . . . ?

Emma woke, clawing at something under her face. A cushion, rough and scratchy, dug hard into her cheek. She was lying on her side on the couch, her body jerking in time with her heart. She'd been dreaming. She had a vague awareness of a picture, a scene of some kind, dissolving into dots and flitting from her brain.

What was it that had awoken her so suddenly like that?

She held herself still and listened, but the flat was quiet. The only sound was the buzzing of the fridge from the kitchen. Emma raised herself on her elbow and gazed blearily around. Her mouth was dry. How long had she been asleep? The room had been bright when she'd decided to lie down for a while. Now there was just a grey gleam, high on the walls. The carpet was dotted with ground-in crumbs. A mug lay on its side under a chair.

The flat was cold and empty. Nobody here but her. The police had packed up and left some time ago. They weren't looking for Ritchie any more.

★   ★   ★

They hadn't said that straight out, of course.

'What Dr Stanford said won't affect the investigation in the slightest,' Lindsay had tried to claim. 'There's no evidence you've done anything wrong.'

But it was five days now since he'd disappeared. Five days, and nothing! Not one single lead. The police might be going through the motions, but if their hearts weren't in it, Ritchie would not be found. Lindsay was being patronizing, with her fake concern, and her insolent, cheerful face that said she put Emma and Ritchie out of her head the second she went home every evening to her boyfriend. Emma could see right through the act. Next thing they'd be arresting her for having done something to Ritchie. She didn't trust Lindsay any more. She didn't trust anyone.

'I'd like some privacy,' Emma had said coldly to Lindsay. 'If you've all finished searching my flat, I'd like you to leave.'

'Emma, I don't think — '

'I *said* I want you to leave. You can't stay if I don't want you to. I have a right to spend some time in peace in my own home.'

But after Lindsay had gone, the silence swelled, humming and crushing inwards at Emma's ears. She curled up on the couch and put a cushion over her head. She lay there, shivering, trying to think. She had to get her head together. She couldn't just stay here; she had to do something. If the police wouldn't help her, she'd have to find someone else who would. But who? Who in the world was there, who cared

97

about Ritchie as much as she did?

Nobody, was the answer to that question. Nobody at all.

★ ★ ★

She'd had phone calls, of course, once people had heard. The newspapers had finally got around to publishing the picture of Ritchie on his red truck, although never on the front page. Whenever the journalists mentioned the kidnapping, they always used the word 'alleged'. As in: 'The alleged abduction,' or: 'The mother of the child alleges that . . . '

And there was worse. Lindsay had warned Emma not to take anything she read too much to heart, but still, it was a shock to open the pages and see the horrible things that people she and Ritchie had never even met had written about them.

'The single mother is reported to have had difficulties coping . . . '

'After a fling with the child's father, whom she has not seen since . . . '

'Miss Turner claims to have left her small child in the care of a complete stranger in a chip shop while she . . . '

Emma couldn't read any more.

Emma's old supervisor from the call centre phoned, as did a couple of her ex co-workers. So did Claire Burns, who was now living in Brighton. They all said how sorry they were, and how they hoped that Ritchie would be found soon. But none of them knew Ritchie. None of them had even met him.

Mrs Cornes, shocked and quavery, rang from Bath, sounding twenty years older and frailer than the last time Emma had spoken to her. She kept saying, 'Poor Robbie. Poor little Robbie.' She offered to come to London, but Emma knew she'd be better staying where she was. She managed to put her off by saying that Joanne was staying in the flat with her.

But Joanne wasn't. Joanne had made one phone call: 'Sorry to hear about Ritchie. Call me if you need anything.' She hadn't phoned a second time, though. Hadn't called around. Clearly, ridiculous as it was, she hadn't forgiven Emma for the comments she'd made about Barry the last time they'd spoken.

Karen, Emma's oldest friend from Bath called, and that meant a lot. Karen had travelled to Australia with Emma and Joanne after they'd all finished their finals. The three of them had shared a tatty, sunny house off the seafront at Bondi Beach. Emma missed Karen very much. She'd been a good friend — in the light of things, a much better friend than Joanne had ever been. In uni, it had been Karen and Emma against the world, best mates since they'd been eleven years old in school. Joanne, new from Middlesbrough and not knowing a soul, had been put in the room next to Karen's in their halls of residence. Emma and Karen had found her there one evening, crying her eyes out, saying she was lonely and hated Bristol and was going to drop out of her course and go home. Soft-hearted Karen had insisted she join them for a pizza to rethink her decision. Once Joanne had recovered, she'd turned out to be a good laugh, always up for a night out, and they'd all ended up staying friends.

But while three of them, had gone together to Sydney for a year of sun and fun, only two of them had come home again. Karen had stayed behind to move with Conor, her new Australian boyfriend, to Melbourne. She was settled there for ever now. She and Conor had just got engaged. Karen accidentally let this information slip during her phone call to Emma, and then became tearful and couldn't stop apologizing. In the end, Emma couldn't wait to get off the phone.

The worst phone call of all was the one from Oliver. The police had tracked him down in Malaysia. It seemed he was living there now. It was the first time he and Emma had spoken since before Ritchie had been born, apart from the single email Oliver had sent from Thailand when Ritchie was about six months old. In the email, Oliver had said he felt guilty about the way things had turned out and hoped they were doing OK. At the end of it, he'd written: 'You gave me no say or choice in this.' He had never met his son.

'How awful for you,' he said now on the phone, sounding genuinely distressed. 'Really awful. You must be going through hell.'

'It might be nothing compared to what Ritchie's going through,' Emma reminded him.

'Don't say that. He's my son too.'

Emma cried quietly into her sleeve. How

100

much hearing something like that from Oliver would have meant to her at any time during the past thirteen months.

'The police interviewed me,' Oliver said. 'They were able to do it over the phone. They said it's unlikely for now that I'll need to come to England.'

Emma said nothing.

'That's not to say I won't come if you want me to,' Oliver said. He paused. 'I saw all those things they wrote in the papers. About whether you were looking after him properly. But of course, that doesn't mean anything. I know more than to believe half of what these people say. If you want me to come, then I will. I'd have to arrange things, obviously, but under the circum-stances . . . '

Emma wiped her nose with her sleeve.

She said, 'You don't need to come.'

'Are you sure? Because if there's anything — '

'You don't need to come.'

She put the phone down. Strange — all those feelings she'd once had for him. There'd been a time when she'd have done absolutely anything for him. Anything at all. She felt nothing for him now. He was wasting her time, taking up the line, when someone more important might be trying to get through with news of Ritchie.

★   ★   ★

All of those people who'd called. And not one of them had really known Ritchie, or cared about him, or could be of any use to him now. How

101

had this happened? How had she let him down so badly? How had she got them both into this friendless, loveless position?

Emma shifted, twisting her face into the seat.

So easy, so very easy, to let go of the people you'd once thought were so important. And so very, very hard to replace them.

She continued to lie there. It was still too early in the evening for the central heating to come back on. She was wearing a T-shirt and tracksuit bottoms. Her arms were starting to go numb. Her fleece was draped over her legs; she didn't have the energy to pull it up. The sun went in behind a cloud. The room, never bright anyway, dimmed further as the sky darkened. A shadow closed over the couch.

Emma knew before she heard the voice that she'd been expecting it.

'You've failed,' the voice said.

A deep, dry voice; neither male nor female. Each word was clearly pronounced. It came from the corner, from somewhere in behind the television.

Emma had heard that voice before.

'You lost him,' the voice said. 'You've failed.'

'I know,' Emma wept. 'I know.'

It hurt, it hurt so much; and she had to do something, but she was so exhausted, so heavy, like something was pressing on her, stopping her from getting up. A chill in her hands and feet, spreading up her limbs. Ice in her heart. She closed her eyes. Please, she thought. Please.

And then, for several merciful hours, she didn't think anything else.

★ ★ ★

And now.

What was it that had woken her? It was important, she had a definite feeling it was. Something about the flat? No. Something she'd been dreaming? That triggered a faint niggle. What had it been? Something to do with . . .

Antonia.

Jesus!

Emma shoved the cushion away and sat up.

Antonia! She remembered now. The thing that had flashed into her mind on the balcony the day that man — Rafe? — had brought over her bag. Something then had made her think of Antonia, and now, finally, it had clicked in her head and she knew what it was.

Clear as day, she saw Antonia again in the café with Ritchie. Saw her lips move as she murmured into her mobile phone.

'*Bird rack,*' she'd thought Antonia was saying. But she hadn't been saying 'Bird Rack' at all. She'd been saying, 'Bergerac.'

Emma's heart hammered. Now she knew why she'd thought of Antonia that day. 'Bergerac' was the name of a detective programme her mum used to watch on TV when Emma was a child. On the balcony, Emma had been saying something to that man — Rafe somebody — about hiring a private detective. And that was the exact moment Antonia had come slithering into her mind.

Bergerac! The way Antonia had pronounced the 'g' — the way a French person would say it.

103

Even though Emma hadn't been able to hear most of what she was saying, she'd caught that 'g'. Recognized the accent without even knowing it at the time. Her subconscious, at least, had picked it up. And had responded by showing her that picture of her mum, watching telly all those years ago in front of the fire.

Emma got up off the couch. She wrapped her fleece around her and began to walk up and down the room. OK. OK. Think about this. Suppose 'Bergerac' *was* what Antonia had said. What could she have meant by it? She'd hardly been sitting there discussing 1980s cop dramas on the phone, in a grimy chip shop in Whitechapel, with a strange toddler by her side. Emma concentrated, trying to recall the expression on Antonia's face. What she'd been saying was important. The more Emma thought about it now, the more she was certain. Antonia had jumped a mile when Emma had come up behind her with the tray. She hadn't wanted Emma to hear what she was saying. If she'd been plotting something, did that mean it definitely *was* her who had taken Ritchie? Or was Emma remembering things now that had never happened at all?

BZZZT. BZZZT.

The intercom! Emma almost tripped over the leg of a chair. At the same time, a wave of dizziness rolled over her. She must have got up off the couch too quickly. She ignored it, hurrying to press the button. Whoever it was might be something to do with Ritchie. Even as she thought it, she braced herself for disappointment. It was probably just another journalist.

104

She'd stopped letting them up to the flat, ever since a sneery-faced woman in a red skirt suit had asked her if she could prove that Oliver was Ritchie's father, while behind her, her colleague used Gribbit's foot to clean his camera lens.

The other person it could be was Mrs Alcarez, the Filipino nurse who lived next door. Emma hardly knew the woman but she was constantly accosting the police in the lifts, asking them if they'd found Ritchie yet.

But the voice on the intercom was none of these.

'Emma Turner?' a man's voice said.

'Yes?'

'I'm sorry to bother you. This is Rafe Townsend.'

Rafe Townsend. Rafe Townsend! The man who'd been on her balcony. Emma was too astonished to respond. She'd been thinking about him only a couple of minutes ago.

'I brought your bags back to your flat,' Rafe was explaining. 'Last Monday.'

Emma said, 'I know who you are.'

Before she knew what she was doing, she'd pressed the switch on the intercom to let him in. Then she clicked her tongue against her teeth. What had she done that for? What the hell was this Rafe person doing, calling over here again?

When, a minute or two later, she heard his knock on the door of the flat, she was tempted to ignore it. She was still dizzy from getting up off the couch. Then she sighed and went to open the door. In the hallway stood the tallish dark-haired man she recognized from the last time. He had the same beaten-up rucksack slung over his shoulder. His face was flushed, from exercise or the cold, and his hair stuck up in little spikes of drying sweat.

'I hope I'm not intruding,' Rafe said, peering at her in a worried way.

'Can I help you?' Emma asked. His face was beginning to blur. The dizziness was getting worse.

'I was cycling past,' Rafe said, 'and I just . . . ' His eyes moved down. His voice faltered. ' . . . wanted to see how you were.'

Emma glanced down at herself too and caught a whiff of sweat. She hadn't got around to showering recently. Her scalp itched and her hair hung over her face in greasy, separated handfuls.

'Cops not here?' Rafe asked.

'They're not coming any more.'

'What?'

Emma clung to the door. The light shifted, moving in strange shapes across the carpet.

Rafe said, 'Do you need to sit down?'

Cautiously, still watching her, he pushed the door open further. When she didn't object, he came right in and closed it behind him. He took Emma's arm and led her to the couch.

'Sit,' he said.

Muzzily, she did. The black dots that had been creeping towards the centre of her vision began to recede.

'Are you all right?' Rafe asked. He was hunched on the floor, looking up at her. His face, furrowed with worry, was close to hers, then far away. Close; far away.

106

In a faint voice, Emma said, 'I've remembered.'

'What?' Rafe looked puzzled.

'The thing.' She tried to explain. 'You were there. The thing I was trying to remember. I know now what it was.'

She knew she wasn't making her point very well. She didn't really expect him to know what she was talking about. But to her surprise, he seemed to get it straight away.

'On the balcony,' he said. He got to his feet and sat down beside her on the couch. 'I remember. What was it? What did the police say?'

'I haven't told them.'

'Oh.'

She felt him looking at her.

'Why don't you tell me, then?' he said. 'I'll listen. I might be able to help.'

The way he said it. As if he really was interested. As if he really thought it might be important. Emma found herself describing to him exactly what Antonia had said; how the way she'd pronounced the word 'Bergerac' had reminded her of her mum watching the TV. How Antonia had muttered and put her hand over her mouth as if to hide what she was saying. How flustered she'd seemed when she'd realized that Emma was right behind her.

'It might be nothing,' Emma said at the end, aware of how woolly it all sounded, even to her. 'Except — '

Except, now she was going over it again, she couldn't help being convinced it was important. Why else would Antonia not have wanted her to hear?

107

'Bergerac.' Rafe wrinkled his brow. 'Someone's name, do you think? Her husband's?'

'I don't know,' Emma said helplessly. The doubts were creeping back again. 'It mightn't mean anything at all. Maybe I'm wrong, and she didn't say it at all.'

'If it's a name,' Rafe was still frowning to himself, scratching his chin, 'then maybe she was talking *about* someone. Maybe the police could look up all — '

He stopped.

'Hang on a minute. Isn't there a place in France called Bergerac?'

'Is there?'

'Yeah. You're always seeing it in the travel supplements. Loads of Antonia types go there on holidays. And you said her French accent was good.' Rafe got up off the couch and began to pace around the room. 'You know something, it could fit. If they kidnapped a child, it would make sense to get him out of the country as soon as possible. If they had connections in France . . . Shit.' He stopped pacing. 'It's worth looking into.'

'But how?'

'I don't know. Look up passenger lists? See if anyone flew to Bergerac with a child. Course, they could have gone by train. Or ferry.' He chewed his thumb. 'Or road. But Bergerac's got an airport. It's worth a try.'

Just for a second, Emma felt a wild, panicky sense of hope. Were they really on to something here? Then she said, 'But Ritchie doesn't have a passport.'

108

'They could have got him a fake one. Or used some other kid's passport. Kids all look the same at that age, don't they?' Rafe froze. 'Sorry. That was a stupid thing to say.' He looked around the room. 'Where's your phone? You have to tell the police about this.'

'They won't — '

'Yes, they will.'

Rafe had spotted the phone on the table beside the window. He went to grab it. Lindsay's number was still on the Post-it stuck to the receiver.

'Ring her,' Rafe ordered.

His enthusiasm was infectious. Emma's fingers felt thick and squashy, like sausages. She managed to press the buttons to dial Lindsay's number. She got through to Lindsay straight away.

'Bergerac?' Lindsay repeated. 'Can you spell that? And you think she might have meant the place in France. We'll do what we can, Emma. We'll look into it immediately.'

Emma hung up. Rafe was leaning against the table with his arms folded, watching her.

'They're going to look into it,' she told him.

'Of course they are.'

'For what it's worth,' Emma said, suddenly tired. The excitement was fading again. This was ridiculous. 'Bergerac' could mean anything. Anything at all. The name of Antonia's dog. A type of perfume. What were the odds that hearing one random word could make a difference? You might as well drop a coin from a cliff and expect to pick it up again on the shore. The wooziness was back, weaving the edges of the walls and furniture. She hoped Rafe would leave soon.

But he wasn't showing any signs of going anywhere.

'Have you had anything to eat today?' he asked.

Without waiting for an answer, he pushed himself off the table and headed for the kitchen.

'Excuse me.' Emma followed him. 'Excuse me, what do you think you're doing?'

Rafe opened the fridge. A funny smell floated out. Yoghurts and jars of baby food were clustered on the lower shelves. Two blackened bananas lay on the middle shelf, beside a loaf of bread splodged with green. On the top shelf was a plastic milk container. The contents were yellow and lumpy.

'Not much here, is there?' Rafe said.

He closed the fridge.

'Tell you what,' he said. 'I'm going to cycle to the shops and stock you up on some food. When I come back, I'm going to cook you something to eat.'

'You don't need to.' Emma shook her head. 'I'm not hungry.'

'I don't mind,' Rafe insisted. 'I like cooking. Where are your keys?'

Emma didn't answer. She folded her arms, pulling her fleece closer around herself, and faced Rafe.

'Can I ask you a question first?' she said. 'What do you want, exactly?'

'To make sure you eat something.' Rafe sounded surprised. 'You look as if you haven't

110

had a decent meal in days.'

'And why does that bother you?' Emma asked. 'It's not as if you know me. A few days ago, we'd never even met. Why do you keep coming here?' She narrowed her eyes. 'Are you hoping I'll have sex with you? A free shag? Is that it?'

'Excuse — '

'Let me tell you something,' Emma interrupted, 'about what kind of person I am. And then we'll see whether you still want to . . . *cook me dinner.*'

The last three words came out with a sneer. She could guess what sort of dinner it was he wanted. Rafe had a shocked expression on his face. Well, good. He might as well know what she was really like. It would get rid of him. He'd be out of here as quickly as everyone else.

'A couple of weeks ago,' she said, 'before Ritchie was kidnapped, I went to my GP and I told her that I hated him.'

'You what?'

'You heard me. I told my GP that I hated Ritchie.'

Rafe said nothing.

'I told her I wished he'd never been born,' Emma said angrily. Wasn't he going to make any kind of response to that? 'I told her I hoped that Ritchie would *die.*'

But the word 'die' came scraping out of her throat like sandpaper. Despite her defiance, she flinched. Once again, she was back in Dr Stanford's surgery. The hiss of gas from the heater. The smell of feet. Ritchie, beside her in his buggy in his elephant fleece, crying and crying and crying.

111

Emma pressed her hand to her chest. She couldn't catch her breath. A big bulge was in there, trying to tear its way out. *Enough*, she thought, cringing inside. *Enough. Don't tell him any more.*

'My own son,' she said instead in a hard, cold voice, when she could speak. 'So that's the kind of pathetic psycho bitch I am. And you've clearly decided I'm so messed up, you can call around here and cook dinner and I'll collapse into your arms and have sex with you and no one will ever know. That's what you're here for, isn't it? Why else would you want to do all this for someone you don't even know?'

Success at last. Rafe was angry now. His chest was puffed out, his shoulders up around his ears. He raised his eyebrows, looking up and to the right, and sucked in a breath. His lips formed an O shape, the prelude to 'Wh'. It was so obvious he was going to snap, 'Why indeed, you pathetic psycho bitch?' and stamp out.

But he didn't say that. He let his breath out again, and paused before he spoke.

'The reason I'm here,' he said quietly, 'is because I care about what happens to Ritchie. That, and no other reason. I don't know Ritchie, I've never met him, but I was there the day he was taken. I could have done something. I *should* have done something. I was a policeman, for Christ's sake. I should never have left you in the state you were in. I've thought about nothing else over the last few days and I can't forgive myself for letting it happen.'

His voice was shaking. His face was red and

112

his arms were tightly folded.

'And about what you said to your GP,' he added. 'I don't know why you said it, but I'm sure you were under a lot of pressure at the time. People say things all the time that they don't mean.'

Emma couldn't speak.

'So if I'm too much, if you want me to leave you in peace, then you just tell me and I won't come here any more.'

The dizziness was back with a vengeance. Emma stepped back and felt her hip knock against something. There was a clatter as the table hit the wall. The phone slid to the floor, landing with a thump. Emma sank on to her knees.

'I keep thinking of him,' she said. She gripped her head between her hands. 'I can't get him out of my mind. I feel like I'm going mad. Every time, *every time*, I do anything, lie down, or drink a glass of water or have a cup of coffee, I think, How can I do this? How can I be comfortable when Ritchie might be suffering right at this very minute?'

'You can't think like that. You don't know — '

'He's being punished because of me,' Emma cried. 'I didn't take proper care of him. It wasn't just an accident. It wouldn't have happened to someone else. You heard the way I talked to Dr Stanford about him, what I said . . . you heard . . . '

She shoved her fists to her eyes, blocking it out.

There was movement beside her. Rafe,

113

hunching down so that his face was next to hers.

'Listen to me,' he said. 'You're going to find him. You're going to get him back.'

'Stop saying that,' Emma wept. 'It means nothing. None of you know where he is or what's happening to him. You don't know. You don't know.'

'You told the police that Antonia seemed to know about children,' Rafe said. 'You said she knew how to hold him, how to put him in his . . . pram, or whatever. It sounds to me like she took Ritchie because she wanted him for herself. Not to hurt him, but to raise him as her own.'

'You can't say that. You don't even know it was her who took him.'

'You *have* to say it. You have to think it. Ritchie is going to be OK.'

His strange, yellowish eyes met hers. Very straight, very calm. If he was lying, he was bloody good at it.

Rafe stood up. He took Emma's arm and helped her to her feet. He pointed her in the direction of the bathroom.

'I'll be back soon,' he said.

The keys were in the lock in the door. He took them and left.

Emma went into the bathroom. She undressed and stepped into the olive-green bath. She turned on the taps, and held the shower nozzle over her hair. Warm liquid streamed down her face, and she didn't know whether it was water or tears. The police *had* to say nice things about Ritchie. It was part of their job. They didn't want her getting hysterical, making things more

114

difficult for everyone. But Rafe didn't have to say anything, did he? Why would he bother, unless it was what he really thought? She desperately wanted to believe him. In all of this, he was the first person she'd met who hadn't treated her like some kind of a criminal or liar. After what she'd told him about Dr Stanford, she'd expected him to back off, to behave, at least, with more coldness or caution, but his eyes just now when he'd looked at her had held nothing but understanding and compassion. Emma's mouth crumpled. More tears! She put the shower nozzle to her face and waited for them to pass. Crying wasn't going to get her anywhere. The only thing that was going to help her now was to know for certain that Ritchie was all right.

When the tears had settled, she turned off the shower. She got out, and dried herself, and put on a clean pair of jeans and a top. And when she'd done all that, she found, to her surprise, that she did feel a tiny bit better.

Even hungry.

Rafe was back when she came out of the bathroom. Clattering noises filled the flat. She found him in the kitchen, slicing a stick of bread. Plastic Sainsbury's bags littered the worktops.

'A few days' supplies,' Rafe said awkwardly, following her gaze. 'I hope you like pasta?'

'Yes, I do.'

'Good stuff.'

Rafe put down the knife and used a tea towel to lift a steaming pot from the hob. A waft of basil and tomato curled into Emma's nose. To her amazement, her stomach gurgled in response.

115

Pass some of that down here.

They ate at the round table beside the door to the balcony. The block of flats opposite glowed in the last of the sun. The tinfoil windows gleamed, turning the missing teeth into bright gold fillings. Emma ate cautiously, taking small mouthfuls. Her stomach felt shrunken and tight. She didn't know how it would cope with the food.

'Is that Ritchie's?' Rafe asked with his mouth full, gesturing at the red plastic truck. It was pushed in behind the couch. Emma hadn't wanted to be able to see it.

'Yes,' she said shortly.

'It's a good one.' He nodded. 'I had one like that as a kid. Wait and see, he'll remember it when he's older. You don't forget your first truck.'

Emma put down her fork. The way Rafe had spoken about Ritchie. As if he really was certain he'd be back with her soon. As if Ritchie was just away on a holiday somewhere.

'He looks so funny when he drives it,' she said shakily. 'Concentrating, all busy, as if he's on some vital mission. He gives me this worried look, as if to say he'll be with me in a minute but he has this job to finish first.'

She bent her head again to the pasta, trying to swallow away the lump in her throat. Rafe didn't ask any more questions. He let her eat in peace. The food was simple and appetizing, easy to swallow. Before Emma knew it, she'd managed to finish more than half of what was on her plate. She began to feel much less dizzy, more clear headed.

116

She'd been meaning to ask Rafe something. 'You mentioned you'd left the police,' she said. 'Why was that?'

Rafe pursed up his lips and shook his head.

'It's not an interesting story,' he said. 'I've got a big mouth. It's got me into trouble before.'

'But I am interested,' Emma said. It wasn't any of her business, what he'd done. Whether he'd got kicked out. It was just, if she was telling him stuff about Ritchie, then maybe she should know.

Rafe shrugged.

'OK. It's not a secret. Man!' He shook his head again. 'Those guys. I'm not trying to turn you against them or anything, but the attitudes you come across, I'll tell you. The reason I left was, they crushed this animal rights protest outside a chicken farm in the Midlands. Poor little guys.' He picked up his fork and stabbed at a strand of spaghetti. 'Those morons were cramming them into crates, ten at a time, legs, wings getting broken, still forcing them in. The protesters wanted the place shut down. They got up a big crowd, made plenty of noise to attract attention. Out went the PCs, a load of self-important types. Made themselves so obnoxious they provoked a protester into punching one of them in the face. And then, of course, every cop in the country turned up to arrest everyone they could get their hands on.'

His voice had got louder. He seemed to hear it and put his fork back down.

'Anyway,' he said. 'I heard all the comments in the station afterwards. They were calling the

117

protesters criminals, and scum, and loonies. For trying to help a few little chickens. Well, I had a problem with that, but they told me I was Mr Nobody and I could either shut up or leave.'

'So you left,' Emma said.

'No,' he said facetiously. 'I stayed and got promoted to head of Chicken Torture.'

Emma said, smiling faintly: 'And now you're a gardener.'

'Yeah, well, I like gardening, you know, but it's just a temporary thing. I'm trying to put some cash together. I'm finishing up my current job soon, and then I'm travelling to South America for a few months.' He cleared his throat. 'Actually, my flight's already booked. I'm leaving the week after next.'

'Oh.' Emma was taken aback. 'Well. Good luck. I hope you enjoy it.'

'Yeah.' Rafe looked at the remains of his pasta and tomato. 'Yeah. I'm looking forward to it.'

He stood up after a minute, and began to clear the plates. 'Shall I make some coffee?'

★ ★ ★

The gold fillings faded from the tower block opposite. The balconies darkened, then flared, one by one, into a patchwork of lights, all shades of cream and yellow and orange. Emma sat on at the table, calmed by watching the ritual of coffee-making. It was soothing just to have another person there, pottering about, rattling spoons, pouring milk. Rafe was easy to be with. Mainly because he didn't seem to expect Emma to say anything. He just talked on, though not in a pushy way, and not about himself. Just about things in general. The ridiculousness of the queues in Sainsbury's. The habit London cycling lanes had of apparently leading a person into the middle of a three-lane motorway and then vanishing. He was a funny mix. One minute thoughtful and serious, leaning back in the shadows. The next, excited by something or other, hunching forward and coming over all street, using his hands and chin for emphasis, stabbing at the table and saying things like 'Man' and 'It kills me', as if he'd spent his childhood hanging out with street gangs. His face was dark and expressive, his movements graceful. She could see him in a band, playing drums. Or being a rapper.

At ten o'clock, he stood up and said, 'I'd better get going. I live in Stockwell and I'm on my bike.'

'That's a long way from here.' Emma was dismayed. 'I'm sorry. I didn't mean to keep you so late.'

'I'm used to it,' Rafe assured her. 'I do gardening jobs all over London. Cycle twenty miles a day sometimes. Quicker than the bus in rush hour.'

Emma could believe the distance was nothing to him. He had a fit, healthy look to him, like an athlete. He pulled on his sweatshirt and hauled his rucksack up from the floor. Then he patted his pockets until he heard the jingle of keys.

'Well.' He gestured towards the hall. 'I'll be off.'

119

But he stayed where he was, bumping the rucksack off his knees.

'If you don't mind,' he said, 'I'll stay in touch? I'd like to hear what happens about that Bergerac thing.'

'I don't mind,' Emma told him.

She held the front door open for him. As he was passing through, she said suddenly, 'I'm glad you came.'

'I'm glad too,' Rafe said.

'No, I mean . . . '

What did she mean? Rafe had spent the evening here with her, not because he was paid to do it, or because he wanted something in return, but because he wanted to help. Because he cared about what happened to Ritchie. The only person in the world apart from her who did. Emma blinked in the glare from the hall.

'I mean,' she said, 'I'm really glad.'

'I am too,' Rafe repeated. He smiled at her. 'Take care of yourself, Emma. Hang in there. Don't go under.'

She cried again a little when he had gone, standing in the hallway with her face in her hands. Then she went to the bathroom to blow her nose. She felt weary, very tired. Properly tired this time, as if she might actually sleep, not the futile, acidic fatigue of the past few days. She went to the kitchen to wash the dinner things, trying to put off going to bed for a little while longer.

She was in the middle of drying a saucepan when the phone rang.

It was Lindsay.

'Hello, Emma.' She sounded excited. 'Can you talk for a minute?'

The tea towel fluttered to the floor. The Bergerac thing! Dear God, they'd actually found something.

'I can talk,' Emma managed.

Lindsay said, 'There's been something. It might not lead anywhere, but I'm just telling you. On Monday afternoon, the day after Ritchie was kidnapped, a couple flew from London to Bergerac with a sixteen-month-old boy.'

Emma's heart turned upside down in her chest. She groped for the couch and lowered herself on to it.

'Ritchie?' she whispered.

'We don't know yet,' Lindsay said. 'But there is one slightly odd thing. As it happens, shortly before you phoned us this evening, we received a call from a woman who works at the check-in desk at Stansted airport. She saw the story about Ritchie in the papers and remembered checking this family in on Monday. One thing about them struck her as unusual. The parents had booked seats for themselves in advance, but at the last minute they arrived with this child with no booking who they wanted to bring as well. The child had a passport, so he was able to fly.'

'What was the woman's name?' Emma interrupted. 'Was it Antonia?'

'No,' Lindsay said. 'No, it wasn't.'

Emma twisted the cord of the phone.

Lindsay said, 'I don't want to get your hopes up too much, Emma. The child's passport was in the same name as the couple's. Chances are high

121

they're just a normal family. But we're going to check anyway.'

She hesitated.

'I wanted to tell you. So you'd know we were following everything up. Doing everything we can. As soon as I hear anything, I'll let you know.'

★ ★ ★

Emma lay in bed, very still. She held hope in her head like an eggshell. It would be hours again before she slept.

She spent the time coming up with a new way of sending a message to Ritchie. Holding him was no good, because neither of them could cope with that. Instead, after a while, she dreamed she was standing by a gate. It was a wooden gate, with slim gaps between the bars. Beyond the gate was a little hill. On top of the hill was a thin, brown tree. And under the tree sat Ritchie, by himself, playing with something in the grass.

Emma watched him through the gate.

'I'm here,' she whispered to him. 'I'm here.'

Ritchie didn't look up. But his smile told Emma that he knew she was there. That whole night, she stayed by the gate, and she guarded him for as long as she could.

8

For the first few months, Emma hardly knew she was pregnant. She had no morning sickness. All her clothes still fitted her perfectly. She began to tell herself that she must have been mistaken. After all, she hadn't seen a doctor yet, or even done a pregnancy test. Since when had she got her obstetrics degree?

One evening she happened to be watching a documentary on TV about the conflict in Darfur. The camera panned over ragged tents in rows, crying women, bloodstained streets. Then it zoomed in on a tiny child on his own, stick-thin and starving. The sight of the child's gaunt, haunted face pierced Emma with a sudden sharp grief that shocked and unsettled her. That night, lying in bed, her body felt strange, as if she was falling, or rising, and couldn't find anything to hold on to. A couple of mornings later, she suddenly went off the Boots guava shampoo and conditioner she'd been using for months, and she knew for certain that her body, whether the change was visible or not, was not the same any more. She couldn't pretend to herself any longer.

Joanne didn't seem to have noticed anything, and Emma didn't tell her. She couldn't talk to anyone about the pregnancy because she hadn't decided yet what she was going to do about it. The only thing on her mind was Oliver, and she couldn't make any decisions until she had discussed them with him. And she couldn't discuss anything with him until she knew whether he was going to come back to her.

'I owe it to Sharmila to give things a chance between us,' Oliver had explained on the phone.

'But you owe it to me, too,' Emma said, fighting to keep the tears from her voice. Now wasn't the time to become hysterical. 'Can't we still see each other at least?'

'It's not that I don't want to, Emma, honestly. But I've known Sharmila for three years. She needs it to be just the two of us, just for a while.'

When he stopped taking her calls, she wrote him a letter telling him how much she loved him and hand-delivered it through his letterbox. Part of her was shocked at herself. She'd never behaved this creepily with a bloke before. But she couldn't help it. What did Oliver whisper to Sharmila when he was with her? What was the expression on his face when he looked at her? Tender? Protective? Or was it *she* who loved *him* more? Emma didn't know which was worse. Oliver being so wanted by someone else made him seem even more precious and further from her reach. She ached to touch him, to push back his hair. To see him staring at her mouth with that intent expression that made her insides disappear. She spent so much time picturing him, longing to be with him, that days went by without her thinking about the pregnancy at all.

And then, quite suddenly, Emma came to her senses and realized what she had to do. One thing was certain: Sharmila and Oliver would not last. Hadn't Oliver said how caring and giving Emma was? How cold and self-centred Sharmila was, how obsessed with her career? In Emma's experience, once a man went off a woman, that was it. The candle rarely re-ignited. Even if Sharmila had managed to get Oliver back temporarily, it wouldn't be long before he realized how much more special things had been between him and Emma. In the meantime, Emma had to back off; give him some space. Oliver was not a person to be pressurized. Now was certainly not the time to tell him about any baby.

So she stopped phoning, stopped trying to contact him. When he was ready, he would come back.

It was hard though. These days she seemed to be spending a lot of time on her own. Joanne was always with Barry. When they weren't out partying, they were snuggled up together on the couch in front of the TV, Barry massaging Joanne's feet through her tights as he watched the football. Every so often he muttered something in Joanne's ear that made her shriek and giggle and roll her eyes at Emma as if to say: 'Men, eh? What can you do?'

Sometimes, out of sheer boredom and desperation, Emma went out and caught the number 56 bus, which took the route along Oliver's street. She sat on the upper deck and felt her heart speed up as they approached his flat. She averted her head as they passed, just sliding her eyes sideways to look out, in case Oliver was at home and saw her. Just to see where he lived

125

gave her a high, like a smoker drawing on a cigarette. She tried to guess from whether the lights were on or off what he might be doing. Sometimes he went to the gym after work. At least if he was out, she comforted herself, he wasn't alone with Sharmila. Lights on was worse. Lights on meant they were having a quiet evening at home.

'They're not *officially* back together,' Joanne reported one morning after a night out with Barry. 'Oliver's not sure whether now is a good time for him to be in a relationship. I get the impression our Sharms is kind of hard to brush off. I think Oliver feels under pressure. He was asking for you, Ems. I reckon he still likes you. Just play it cool.'

So Emma waited, but as the weeks went by and she didn't hear from him, she rode the number 56 bus more and more.

One evening in April, she was passing Oliver's flat and noticed that the windows were dark, the curtains all open. It was after nine o'clock.

Emma thought about this. It was Thursday, not Oliver's usual gym night. He sometimes went out with his work friends on the Strand for drinks on a Thursday evening. If he wasn't home by now, that's where he must have gone. It would be hours before he came back. On an impulse, she pressed the red Stop button beside her seat. Around the next corner, the bus drew into the kerb.

'Goodnight, madam,' the driver called as she stepped off.

'Goodnight,' Emma said, surprised. A friendly

126

bus driver! It was as if she'd been accepted by Oliver's community. His bus driver liked her. It was a good omen.

Feeling happier, she walked back to Charmian Avenue. There was little risk of bumping into Oliver if he was miles away in town, but even so, she'd have to be careful. It would be one thing to meet him on Lavender Hill or the main road; she could just say she was visiting someone or going for a walk. She didn't live so far away that it was strange for her to be in the area. But to be actually caught on his street! Emma held her breath as she reached the turn, peering cautiously around the corner. No one. The street was empty. Just trees, and cars parked, nose to bumper, on either side.

She walked along the footpath. Charmian Avenue was a nice road. Like everything associated with Oliver. Special. Different. More affluent than the streets around it. There were more trees, with more and thicker leaves. The houses were better kept and posher-looking. The street started as a terrace, but halfway down, near Oliver's part, the houses became larger and semi-detached. Emma was across the street now from Oliver's flat. The house was grey brick, painted white around the windows and door. A huge tree almost hid a large, three-sided sash bay window with its own roof. That was Oliver's window. His flat was on the ground floor.

So there it was. Emma walked up and down the street, repeatedly passing the flat, as if to absorb some of its specialness. The road was damp from earlier rain, and very quiet. Just the

127

sound of Emma's footsteps, scraping occasionally on a pebble. Some of the windows in the other houses were lit. In one room, a woman stood with a baby, surrounded by people. Seeing her, Emma all at once felt sad. What was she doing here, walking up and down a strange street, looking in strangers' windows? This wasn't like her. This wasn't the way a normal person behaved. She had a lonely, odd sensation, of being on the outside, of peering into other people's lives like a stalker. That was what she was doing, she realized with a shock. She was stalking Oliver. What if someone spotted her here, loitering? They'd think she was up to no good. Might call the police even. That stopped her. She'd had enough of this. She'd go back down now and get the bus. She wouldn't come here again.

And that would have been it, if one final thought hadn't struck her. What if she took one quick peek through the window at the back of Oliver's house, just to see what the living-room looked like now? Whether he'd done anything with it in the four months since she'd seen him. Whether *Sharmila* had done anything with it. She'd come this far; she might not get this chance again. She had to know.

The flat above Oliver's was dark. The couple who lived there were plainly out. Nobody would see Emma in the back garden. Just one quick look, then she'd be out of there. Checking to make sure no one was around, Emma slipped down the side path to the rear of the house. The back garden was small, paved-over, with big,

128

stone pots filled with plants. Emma and Oliver had drunk Pimm's there one evening, listening to Rufus Wainwright float from the speakers in the living-room.

Emma went to the window and cupped her hands around her face. She stared in. From what she could see of it, the room still looked the same. Giant bloke-TV in the corner; woven rug on the dark wood floor; white-painted shelves, stuffed untidily with books and the twisty metal sculptures Oliver liked.

She was peering at one of the shelves, trying to make out the faces in a photograph, when, to her utter horror, the room was suddenly flooded with light. Appalled, Emma jerked her head back. She caught a glimpse of a figure — man? woman? — approaching the window before she threw herself to the side, out of view.

Bloody hell! Emma stood, shaking, at the corner of the house. Why hadn't she been paying attention? She'd never heard the front door open. Thank God it was dark outside. Whoever was in the room wouldn't have been able to see her. She hoped. She held her breath and listened for footsteps, voices, shouts from the front. Nothing. They hadn't seen her. She'd give it a couple of minutes, then she'd sneak back out to the street and leave. God. She blew her hair off her forehead. She would never do anything like this again. *Ever!*

She counted under her breath: *one* thousand, *two* thousand, *three* thousand. At twenty-five, she reckoned she was safe. She began to creep through the side lane, watching where she put

129

her feet. The last thing she needed was to stand on a cat or knock over a bin. And then, just as she was almost through, the light from the street was blocked by a tall, dark shape.

'Hey!' a voice shouted. 'You! What are you doing looking in my window?'

Oliver! Emma nearly died of fright. Should she turn back, run for it, try to climb over the back wall? She went to spin around, but footsteps crunched over the gravel and someone grabbed at her arm.

'What the hell . . . ?' Oliver began. Then he sucked in a breath, dropping Emma's arm as if she had leprosy. He leaped backwards and said in a stunned-sounding voice, 'Emma?'

God, he looked just the same. His hair a bit shorter, maybe. He had on a white shirt, open at the neck. A dark jacket slung over his arm. He was staring at her in amazement. Emma stared back, literally struck dumb. She could not think of one single thing to say.

A slim silhouette appeared at the entrance to the lane.

'Ol?' A silvery, feminine voice. 'Are you OK?'

Oliver jerked his head.

'Yeah. Thanks, Sharm. Just give me a minute.'

He looked at Emma again.

'What are you *doing* here?' he asked.

Emma opened her mouth.

'I need to speak to you,' she said.

Oliver looked bewildered.

'Sure,' he said. 'Here?' Then, before she could answer, he shook his head. 'No. Chilly out here. Let's go inside.'

He gestured with his arm, the one with the jacket over it, for Emma to walk ahead of him. Sharmila led the trio to the front of the house, her high heels clicking on the path. She was wearing something black, glittery and short. Her heavy hair was twisted high on her head.

Oliver's hall smelled exactly the same. Aftershave, or washing powder, or whatever floor polish it was he used. The familiar scent squeezed at Emma's chest. Oliver closed the front door. Streetlight filtered through the stained glass, casting a ghostly red and green glow over the hall. Before anyone could say anything, Sharmila murmured, 'I'll give you some privacy.' Barely glancing at Emma, she gave Oliver's arm a little squeeze, then slipped past them both into the living-room and closed the white-painted door.

Emma was left feeling even worse than before. OK, so she hadn't wanted Sharmila hanging around. But she'd hoped it would be Oliver who'd tell her to leave. The other girl's impeccable manners — or else utter lack of curiosity — made Emma feel clumsy, crude, unbelievably intrusive.

'Let's go into the kitchen,' Oliver said.

He switched on the light. Feminine things glittered everywhere. A gold cardigan was draped over the back of a chair. A shiny handbag perched on the table. New photos littered the front of the fridge — mostly of a dark-haired girl with sparkly teeth and big sparkly earrings, laughing into the camera. New plants lined the window sill, dark leaves tumbling over the edge.

131

Oliver had never owned house plants. He'd said he wouldn't remember to water them.

'Can I get you something?' Oliver asked. 'A drink?'

'No, thanks,' Emma said. Seeing him there in the light . . . it brought it back to her, ten, twenty times over, how much she loved him and always would. Everything about him hurt her. His sultry, sleepy eyes. His sunny hair. His smell.

'I'm pregnant,' she blurted.

And held her breath.

Naturally — she wasn't stupid — she didn't expect Oliver to start prancing around the kitchen with delight at her news. He'd be shocked, who wouldn't be? Angry even. How could she blame him? In all her own reunion fantasies, it was just the two of them, she and Oliver, slim-bodied and free, lying together on Oliver's white-sheeted bed. Not a baby or a swollen stomach in sight.

So she was prepared for the gasp, the backward step, the slackened jaw. So far, so expected. But then there was a quick glance towards the living-room, where Sharmila was. Emma hadn't expected *that*, and her heart sank. And then the third thing, so quick and subtle that if she hadn't been watching him so carefully she might have missed it.

A tiny, faint curl of the lip.

Distaste.

It took him less than a second to recover.

'I won't ask the obvious question as to how it happened,' he tried to joke.

Emma was still reeling. She was floppy, gasping, like a fish slammed against a wall. If he'd hit her, it couldn't have been worse. She saw herself in the window, dressed in her tracksuit and trainers, lank-haired and lumpy around the middle. This was the woman who had just been caught stalking someone in their garden at night. Spying on the man who had dumped her for someone else. Emma compared herself to the cool, slim girl who had slipped so discreetly into the other room, and wanted to crawl through a crack in the floor. You knew it, she told herself. You knew he'd be like this. Just get away. Get away now. Don't stay here any longer.

'You needn't worry,' she said. 'You don't need to be involved. I just wanted you to know.'

'I feel very bad about this, Emma.' Oliver pushed his hair back from his face with both hands. 'Whew. Should I ask if you need some money?'

'I don't need anything,' Emma said.

'Can I give you a lift somewhere?'

'No. Thank you.'

Emma kept moving towards the front door. Low music wafted from the living-room. The door was tightly closed. Oh, how truly perfect Sharmila was. So very clearly *not* eavesdropping.

Oliver followed her, accompanying her to the outside gate.

'What do you think you'll do?' he almost whispered. The cold air made everything louder. 'About the pregnancy?'

'I haven't decided yet.' The thought of it

133

brought Emma to a stop. She stood there on the path, cupping the backs of her arms with her hands.

Then, very deliberately, she looked at Oliver and said, 'Probably the best thing will be to get rid of it.'

That would shake him. It would force him to contact her. He might not be happy about a baby, but no one could make a decision about an abortion just like that. No matter what Oliver thought, he'd have to say, 'Wait. Let me think about this. Don't make any hasty decisions. I'll call you and we'll talk.'

An abortion — well. It would be so final. There would be no reason for Oliver ever, ever to contact her again.

'You're right,' he muttered, not looking at her. 'That's probably best.'

Emma didn't feel anything. Just numbness. So that was it. That was really, really it. She turned away.

'I'm really sorry about this, Emma.' Oliver sounded upset. 'It's just that Sharmila and I ... It seems a bad way to end things. We had a good time together.'

'Yes,' Emma said. 'We did.'

She pulled open the gate. The bottom of it screeched as it caught against a tile.

Oliver said, 'And you'll be all right with, you know . . . er . . . ?'

'Absolutely fine,' she assured him. 'Well,' she said, 'goodbye.'

And she left him standing there, pallid in the street-light, and walked off down the road.

134

★   ★   ★

How she got herself home, she never knew. There must have been a bus, and she must have sat on it. But she never knew.

In bed, she lay and waited for the pain to hit. 'Gone,' she kept saying to herself. 'Over.'

Funny, after the first shock, she was surprised the pain wasn't worse. She prodded her mind for damage, like an athlete carefully checking each limb after a fall. But everything stayed numb. The pain would come later; the race still had to be run. She had a decision to make. She was four and a half months pregnant.

'What now?' she whispered into the cool side of the pillow. 'What do I do?' But no one answered.

The obvious thing was to do as she'd said to Oliver and get rid of it. How on earth could she have a baby? She had no idea how to look after one. Never even seen one, hardly. She had no money, no one to help her. The very thought was ridiculous. But the days went by, and every time she picked up the phone to book a doctor's appointment, she ended up putting it down again.

This wasn't just any baby. This was Oliver's. All she had left of him. And the difficulty was, she still loved Oliver. You didn't get over people just like that, just because they wanted you to.

There was another thing. This baby was her mother's grandchild. The only part of her she had left, too.

Emma became very short-tempered. She

135

couldn't even talk to Joanne because Barry was always around, stuck to her like a snail. One evening Emma came in from work, her back killing her after a crowded tube journey, and found Barry on his own in the sitting-room, sprawled on the couch with his fly open. A pizza box and two beer cans lay on the floor. The telly was turned to the football, loud enough to rattle the windows.

'Where's Joanne?' Emma asked.

'Working late.' Barry's eyes were glued to the box. According to the scoreboard at the bottom of the screen, Arsenal were playing Wigan.

'How did you get in?'

'Wuh?' Barry's eyebrows scrunched as he concentrated on the screen. Then he shot into the air and waved his fist at the TV.

'Come on,' he roared. 'Get past him. You could fit a bloody bus through there.'

'I *said*,' Emma raised her voice, 'how did you get in?'

The sharpness of her tone forced Barry out of his football trance. He looked at her as if only just now realizing that another person was in the room.

'I've got a key,' he said.

A key! He had a key! Who the hell did he think he was?

'Can't you watch the football in your own place for a change?' Emma snapped. 'You're in here blimmin' every evening. Is it too much to ask that I can come home to my own flat after work and have some peace?'

Barry looked very shocked at her outburst.

136

Without another word, he stood up and walked past her, out of the room. Emma heard the floorboards rattle as he went on down the hall to Joanne's bedroom. The door slammed.

Later, when Joanne came home, she bypassed the sitting-room and went straight to her room. Voices floated through the wall. Emma thought she heard her name being mentioned. Neither of them came back out for the evening.

And then, before Emma knew where she was, she was five months pregnant. The button on her jeans wouldn't fasten. She seemed to be going to the loo all the time. One day, standing waiting for the kettle to boil, she felt a sharp stab just below her ribcage. She stepped back in surprise and alarm. Then she felt it again. A brisk, thumping sensation.

Like a foot.

A foot kicking her.

Emma put down her mug. She crept her hand to the spot where she'd felt the kick. There it was again. A determined bumping against her fingers.

Could she even have an abortion now? Wasn't there a law about how late you could have one?

Over the course of the evening, Emma became very calm. All right, then. All right. So she was going to have a baby. In a strange way, the decision cleared her mind. Four months to go. There was suddenly very little time to get things sorted. Money. Her job. She didn't have a clue. How did you find out these things? But they were practical issues, issues you could actually do something about, and Emma was nothing if not a practical person.

Her first step, the next day, was to book an appointment with a GP in Clapham. Maybe she could begin by asking some of the questions there.

She was as taut as a wire going to the surgery. The last time she'd been to see a doctor was years ago, in Bath. Doctors and hospitals made her nervous. She hoped the GP wouldn't have a go at her for not having come in sooner. In a magazine in the waiting-room she found an article: 'My 45-Hour Labour Hell'. According to the article, the woman who'd given birth was twenty-nine. In the accompanying photo, with her blood-spattered NHS nightgown and stare-eyed smile, she looked at least fifty. Emma gawped at the photo. *She'd* have to go through labour. Was she off her head, having a baby? Maybe it still wasn't too late to change her mind. She turned to another page: 'How to Hold on to Your Man'. An elderly woman looked at Emma's stomach and beamed. Emma managed a thin-lipped smile in return.

'Emma Turner,' the receptionist called.

A nurse showed her in to the surgery. Dr Rigby was tiny and red-haired and looked as if she should still be at school. She was busy writing something at her desk and waved at Emma to sit down. The surgery smelled of lemon. A row of Teletubbies sat along a shelf over the weighing scales.

Dr Rigby finished writing and turned to Emma. It didn't take long for them to establish why she was there.

'Pregnant!' Dr Rigby said.

She gave a warm smile.

'Congratulations,' she said.

She made no comment that Emma should have come in sooner. She asked her to lie on a table covered by a paper sheet, and came around the desk to examine her. Her small, silver earrings dangled as she felt Emma's stomach with gentle hands. She listened near Emma's belly button with a black thing shaped like a horn.

'I can hear the baby's heartbeat,' she said.

Emma's eyes filled with tears.

Back at her desk, Dr Rigby asked, 'What about the father?'

'Won't be involved,' Emma said shortly.

'Oh.' Dr Rigby looked sympathetic. 'What kind of arrangements have you made for after the birth?'

'Well, I'll have to give up work for a while, obviously,' Emma said. 'I have some savings but . . . I was going to ask you . . . '

'You should be entitled to maternity leave, to start with,' Dr Rigby said. 'And child benefit. That will give you some breathing space.' She made a note. 'I'll put you in touch with a social worker. There may be other help you're entitled to. Will you have somewhere to live?'

Emma still hadn't told Joanne about the baby. A pregnant flatmate. And a screaming infant. Emma bit her lip. It was a lot to ask. But she didn't have any choice. Where else could she go? She'd have to stay on in the flat, at least until after the baby was born.

Joanne would help her, though, she knew she would. They'd been through a lot together. Boyfriends, exams, holidays . . . all the usual stuff, but maybe, in their particular case, these things had meant a little bit more. Joanne, like Emma, had never seemed very close to her family at home. She was secretive about the details, but there'd been something about her dad having a problem with alcohol. Her friendship with Emma and Karen, Emma knew, was what had kept her going through uni. In Australia, when Karen had announced she wasn't coming home, Joanne had become very emotional after a couple of Bacardi Breezers and clutched Emma's hand and made her promise that no matter what happened, the two of them, at least, would always look out for each other.

'Yes,' Emma told Dr Rigby. 'I'm sharing a flat with my friend.'

'That's something, anyway,' Dr Rigby said, smiling.

Coming down the surgery steps into the yellow morning, Emma felt happier than at any time since she'd found she was pregnant. She put her hands over her stomach. Dr Rigby was really nice. Emma was glad she was going to be her baby's GP. The knowledge that she would have money coming in and wouldn't starve relieved the worst of her anxiety. She felt the waistband of her trousers digging into her bump. She'd been using a safety pin for the past week to keep them closed. This weekend she'd go shopping and she'd buy some proper clothes.

And tonight, Barry or no Barry, she would

break the news to Joanne.

When she got home from work that evening, Barry and Joanne were sitting side by side on the couch, surrounded by takeaway cartons from the Star of the East.

'Hi, Ems,' Joanne greeted her. 'Haven't chatted to you for a while.'

'That's right.' Emma made herself sound cheerful. 'I've hardly seen you.'

Barry bent his head and concentrated on his biryani.

'What've you been up to?' Joanne asked. 'I've been meaning to catch up. We must have a girls' night out soon.'

She seemed in a great mood.

'Wine?' she asked, waving a bottle.

'No, thanks.'

'Not like you not to have a drink,' Joanne said.

'Yes, well,' Emma began. 'I've been meaning to have a talk with you — '

'Listen, Ems,' Joanne interrupted. 'There's just something. You know our lease is coming up soon?'

'Yes?'

'Well, have you thought about what you're going to do? Because Barry's flatmate's moving out, and he's going to need someone to help him with the mortgage.'

Emma's knees began to wobble. Joanne slid along the couch and took Barry's hand.

'Well,' she beamed, 'we might as well tell you. Barry and I are moving in together.'

Emma sank on to the arm of the couch.

'I hadn't thought what I'd do,' she said. The

141

palms of her hands were slippy. 'I assumed we'd renew. There's only a month to go on the lease, Joanne.'

'Yeah, sorry about that,' Joanne said. 'But you can get another person in here, can't you?'

Not likely. Emma tried to ignore the fluttering sensation under her ribs.

'How many bedrooms does Barry's flat have?' she asked.

Barry's head shot up from his biryani. Joanne gave him a quick look. *I'll deal with this.*

'Well,' she said, 'I *think* three, but the flat's quite small — and the thing is, we don't know yet what we'll do with the rooms, do we, Bar? We'll need a study anyway, and storage. I'd make other plans if I were you, Emma, honestly.'

Barry, clearly sensing that things were about to get sticky, removed his hand from Joanne's and muttered something about needing the bog. This was Emma's big chance. As soon as Barry had left the room, she said to Joanne, 'I'm pregnant.'

The effect on Joanne was electric. A lump of bhuna fell off her fork. Her mouth opened; her head jerked from side to side, as if she was a puppet.

'Oliver's,' Emma added, to save her asking.

'Well.' Joanne looked as if a piece of prawn had gone down the wrong way. 'That's . . . that's . . . that's *great*.'

'Yeah.'

'When is it due?' Joanne managed to ask.

'August. I'm five months gone.'

'Oh.'

'So the thing is,' Emma said, 'now isn't a good

142

time for me to find a new flatmate. I only need somewhere until the baby is born. I'll be able to look for somewhere proper then. I'll be in a condition to pack and move and lift boxes. I'll be gone before you so much as see a nappy.'

She could hear the pleading in her voice. Joanne heard it too and shifted on the couch. She pushed away her carton of bhuna.

'Look, Emma,' she said, 'I'm sorry if it makes things difficult for you. But Barry and I have discussed this, and we can't just change our plans.'

Emma looked at her stomach. She couldn't see her feet from here.

'OK,' she said. 'OK.'

'You should have said something before. Five months, Emma.'

'I know.'

'Things are just getting really serious between Barry and me,' Joanne wailed. 'And you and him have never got on, have you? You completely lost it with him the other night, he said, over something really trivial, he didn't even know what he'd done. You like your space, Emma, you know you do. I really couldn't see it working if you moved in with us. And if I don't move in with him now, he'll get another flatmate, and it could be years before we discuss it again. This is my one chance, Emma. You've no idea how much I like him. I've been waiting for this for so long.'

'It's OK,' Emma repeated. 'Honestly, I understand.'

There was a silence. Then Joanne got up off

the couch. She came over to give Emma a hug.

'You're a great mate, Ems,' she sniffled. 'And it's great about the baby, really it is. It's going to be really cute. And me moving out, you know. It's not going to affect anything between us. If you need any kind of help with the baby, babysitting and that, just feel free to ask.'

Emma smiled. But there was a cold space inside her. She allowed herself to be hugged, but her mind had moved to somewhere else entirely. She stared over Joanne's shoulder at the wall.

What on earth was she going to do now?

9

Saturday, 23 September
Day Seven

In the dusk, on the steps of the Fulham Palace Road police station, Lindsay waited in her neat, dark coat.

Emma walked faster. She was out of breath by the time she arrived at the station.

'Am I late?' she asked anxiously.

'Not at all,' Lindsay said. 'I've only just got here myself.'

Lindsay was carrying a slim, dark green handbag over one shoulder. Her hand was on the door, but she paused for a second to tilt her head and give Emma a concerned little smile.

'Sure you're ready for this?' she asked.

Emma nodded. But the blood was drumming in her ears.

The policeman at reception buzzed them through. Emma followed Lindsay into a dark, narrow corridor. Their shoes clumped on the hollow-sounding floor. The corridor turned into another, then another, until Emma had lost all track of where they were. Then they turned right again, through a doorway and into a room with a large, round table in the middle.

'Afternoon, Ms Turner.' Detective Inspector Hill straightened up from the table. He was wearing his tan overcoat and carrying a rolled-up *Metro* newspaper.

'Good afternoon,' Emma said warily. When-ever Detective Hill looked at her, which he seemed to avoid doing, it was as if he despised her. As if she was wasting his time. Once she'd caught him raising his eyebrows at another policeman, clamping his mouth in a tight line as if to say, 'Can you believe this woman?'

'I'm sure all of this has been explained to you,' Detective Hill said. He pointed his *Metro* at a woman who was doing something at a computer in the corner. 'Our computer expert, PC Gorman there, has got some CCTV footage, taken at Stansted airport the day after Ritchie was kid-napped. We've got a view of the couple and child who checked in for the Bergerac flight. In a minute we'll show you the film, and you can tell us if the child in it is your son. Understand?'

'Yes.'

Detective Hill held out a grey plastic chair for her in front of the computer. Emma sat down. Behind, she heard scraping and shuffling as several more people came into the room. She didn't look round to see who they were. The only thing on her mind was what might be about to appear on the screen.

'All right, lovey?' the woman at the computer asked. She had short, greying hair and a kind face. 'Now, when I start the film, the first thing you'll see will be a set of doors. After a couple of seconds, you'll see three people come through. A man first, then a woman carrying a child. For the time being, we're going to block out the faces of the man and woman. We just want you to concentrate on the child. Let me know when you're ready to start.'

'I'm ready,' Emma said. Her left leg was jiggling up and down. She pressed her hands on her knee to make it stop.

'Lights off, please,' the woman called.

The fluorescent glare disappeared. Now there was just the glow from the computer, casting a blue halo around the heads in front of it: Lindsay's smooth, dark bun; Detective Hill's moustache.

Emma's chest fizzed.

What if this was Ritchie?

No. Don't even think it. Don't get your hopes up and end up even more of a wreck than you already are.

But if it *was*?

Emma gritted her teeth. She'd been at this all night, her mind swinging first one way, then the other, until she didn't know which way was up. Footsteps clumped along the corridor outside the room. 'Oi,' a man's voice shouted. 'You going to Tesco?'

The footsteps faded. On the screen, an image lit up. A white hall, with double doors at one end. White metal and glass.

'Watch now,' the woman at the computer said.

Behind the glass doors, a shape loomed. Then the doors slid open and a man came striding through. He was tall, wearing jeans and a navy, short-sleeved shirt. An oval-shaped blur covered his face, breaking it up into tiny pink and yellow squares. The man was pulling a wheelie case and walking very quickly. In no time at all, he was

147

past the camera and gone from the screen.

'Wait . . . '

Emma sat up. The film was moving way too fast. If the rest of it was like this, she wasn't going to be able to see it properly. But beside her, Lindsay was still focusing on the screen. Detective Hill, PC Gorman . . . everyone was busy watching the film. No one but her seemed to be having trouble following it.

'Here come the woman and child,' PC Gorman said.

Panicking, Emma jerked her eyes back. Her vision blurred. Now she couldn't see anything at all. Roughly, she scrubbed at her eyes. When she looked again, a woman, her face also obscured, was coming through the doors, holding something bulky in her arms.

A child.

Emma strained, using every muscle in her face to try to see the child. But it was impossible to get a proper view of him. The woman's body was turned away from the camera. All you could see of the child was a tuft of hair — darker, surely, than Ritchie's? — and a small foot, sticking out.

'Look up,' Emma wanted to shout. 'Ritchie, if that's you, look up.'

But it was the woman who glanced up instead. Although her face was covered with little squares, she appeared to be looking straight at the camera.

The film froze.

'Are you all right?' Lindsay asked.

Emma was staring at the screen. Even taking the blurring of her features into account, this

woman had nothing familiar about her whatso-
ever. Her hair was dark, tied back instead of
down by her ears. She wore baggy trousers and
some sort of hooded top. Very casual. Very
different from the posh, horsey woman at the
tube station.

'I don't think that's her.' Emma chewed at her
thumbnail. 'I don't think that's the woman who
was in Mr Bap's.'

'Take your time,' Lindsay advised. 'We haven't
seen the child yet.'

But Emma had lost her nerve. Face it. It
wasn't them. It wasn't Ritchie. She should have
known. The police could be looking for Ritchie
some other way, instead of all of them just sitting
here. Emma wanted to scream with frustration.
She wanted to get up and run out of the room.
This was a complete waste of everyone's time.

She had her mouth open, about to say as
much to Lindsay, when the film started again.
The woman's face moved in jerky little squares.
A second later, she turned her body towards the
camera, and all Emma's thoughts flew away.
There was the child in the woman's arms, in
plain view for the first time. A solid little lump, a
sheen of hair. Emma's head shot up, she felt
herself lifted off the seat. Her body knew before
she did. She was on her feet, pointing at the
screen.

'That's him,' she said. 'That's Ritchie.'

Someone drew in a breath.

'What . . . ?'

'Did she say . . . ?'

The exclamations faded. Emma was rising,

floating in the room like a ghost. Oh, Ritchie, Ritchie, my precious baby, you're alive. You're alive! She wanted to touch the screen, to hold it, to take his head in her hands. It was real. It wasn't real. A cold drink in the desert which you couldn't feel in your throat. Her own breath filled her ears. Everything else, the people, the room, all had been subtracted. There was just her, breathing like Darth Vadar, gazing down a quiet tunnel at her son. Here they came, the dark-haired woman in her hooded top, Ritchie in her arms. Ritchie had dark hair too now. How funny it looked on him. He was wearing a green top that Emma had never seen, and brown trousers. Brown boots, which made his feet look huge. His arms dangled at his sides. The only thing she couldn't see was his face, which was turned into the woman's shoulder. He was slumped against her, clearly asleep.

'Emma.' Detective Hill's voice echoed down the tunnel. 'Emma.'

Emma's ears popped. Dazed, she looked at Detective Hill.

'Are you sure it's him?' Detective Hill asked. 'You can only see the top of his head. And this child has brown hair, not bl — '

'His fringe,' Emma babbled.

She'd cut Ritchie's fringe herself, the day before he was kidnapped. He wouldn't stay still, and the right side ended up an inch shorter than the left. There it was now, on top of his head. Right side shorter than the left. Exactly the same.

'They've dyed his hair,' she said. 'But I know

it's him. I know what the rest of him looks like. He's in France, isn't he? They've taken him to France. What happens now? How do we get him back?'

Detective Hill scratched the back of his head. He said to PC Gorman, 'Haven't we got any proper views of his face?'

'No,' PC Gorman said. 'It's the same in all the pictures. He's got his head in her shoulder the whole time.'

'She's trying to hide him,' Emma said, caught between joy and exasperation. It was so obvious. 'A child that age wouldn't stay asleep that long in a noisy place like an airport. Ritchie definitely wouldn't. He'd wonder what was going on. He'd be trying to get down, get into everything.'

'Then maybe it isn't Ritchie?' Detective Hill suggested.

'She's drugged him,' Emma said grimly. 'It *is* him.'

Detective Hill opened his mouth, but PC Gorman got there first.

'She's got a point,' she said. 'My granddaughter's the same. You'd have to drug her to keep her quiet in an airport.'

A ripple of chuckles from behind.

Detective Hill said, 'All right, then. We'll check them out. We'll get on to it straight away.'

'What will you — ' Emma began again, but Detective Hill had already left the room.

The fluorescent lights came on. Emma blinked. She couldn't see the screen so clearly now. Five days ago, that video had been taken. Today was Saturday. Five days ago, while she

151

had been weeping in their flat and answering a million questions about Oliver, Ritchie had been in an airport, wearing a strange green top and sleeping on this woman's shoulder. While Emma had lain in bed, clinging to Gribbit, Ritchie had boarded a plane and flown almost directly over her head.

Around her, people in navy jumpers with badges on the shoulders were stretching in their grey plastic seats. Some of them were still chuckling over the comment the woman had made about her granddaughter.

'Hurry up,' Emma wanted to shout at them. 'Time is passing. Get back to your jobs and find him.'

Five days. Ritchie could be anywhere by now. Her happiness at seeing him was replaced again by fear. She couldn't feel her legs. She had to sit down.

★ ★ ★

Outside the station, she was still having trouble believing it. Had that really been Ritchie in there? It was hard to keep still. She pulled at the zip of her fleece, tugging it up against the cold, then down again, shifting from foot to foot on the steps. The urge to do something, anything, was overwhelming. It was after eight, but the traffic was still flowing. Saturday shoppers on their way home. The headlights picked out the trees in the park and cemetery across the road.

'You did so well,' Lindsay kept saying. 'What an amazing breakthrough.'

'You do believe me, don't you?' Emma asked anxiously. 'That it was him? You are going to follow it up?'

'Of course we are. This is wonderful.'

'It doesn't mean he's OK now, though.' Emma was still agitated.

'But it's much more likely,' Lindsay said. 'That footage was taken nearly twenty-four hours after he disappeared. And he looked OK, didn't he? Things are looking more hopeful for him now, really they are.'

'No thanks to you.' Suddenly, Emma was very angry. 'What were you all waiting for? Why has it taken this long for us to get anywhere? I'm his mother. You should have believed me from the start.'

'We never *didn't* believe you, Emma.' Lindsay sounded troubled. Her smooth, beautician's face gleamed in the lights from the cars. 'It's just that . . . with Dr Stanford . . . We had to think of every . . . I admit it would have been helpful if we'd had more CCTV evidence. But the cameras at Stepney Green tube station had been vandalized. They'd been having trouble there recently with gangs of schoolkids messing about. Two of the lenses were painted over. Someone was supposed to come and sort them out. And the street outside Mr Bap's had no CCTV at all.'

Emma said bitterly, 'That's funny, because I heard that in London the average person gets caught on camera three hundred times a day.'

'Well, they're not all police cameras,' Lindsay said. 'But you're right. I've heard that too. Just, unfortunately, not in the one place where we

153

needed a camera to be.'

She turned to face Emma. She tucked her green bag under her arm and put her hands on Emma's shoulders.

'Look,' she said, 'after all this, we're definitely on the same page now, aren't we? What's happened this evening is wonderful. Really it is.'

Emma chewed again at her nails.

'What will the police do now?' she asked.

It was at least the third time she'd asked that, but Lindsay didn't seem to mind.

'We'll give the passport details of those people to Interpol,' she said. 'Copies of their photos as well, from the passport office. The French police will start looking for them over there.'

'But if they used false passports?'

'We'll still find them. There'll be cameras in the airport at the other end. We'll be able to see who met them, how they left the airport. From there, we'll know where they went. We know who we're looking for now,' Lindsay said. 'That's the difficult part. Once we're on the trail, it's hard to get us off.'

'What time will they look until?' Emma asked. 'Who?'

'The police. What time do they work until?'

'All night if we have to, Emma.' Lindsay was patient. 'You know that.'

Emma did. But she still needed to hear it said.

'We'll find him,' Lindsay repeated. 'Hey.' She gave Emma's shoulders a little shake. 'We will.'

Emma knew that Lindsay was trying to get her to look at her but she couldn't make herself do it. It wasn't that she didn't want to, but her eyes

154

seemed to be moving around by themselves, very fast, taking in the street, the steps, the people walking past with their bags and coats. She didn't seem able to focus on just one thing. Lindsay pulled her in for a hug. Emma let her. Lindsay patted her on the back while Emma stood there, awkward in the unfamiliar embrace.

'Will you go and look with them?' she asked Lindsay. 'I'd feel better if there was someone there I knew.'

'Why don't I come home with you for a while?' Lindsay suggested. 'It'll be hard, waiting on your own.'

'I'll be all right. I don't want to go back to the flat just yet. I'd like to go for a walk. Buy some things for Ritchie. Food and stuff.'

'It may be a while before you can see him,' Lindsay warned.

Emma stiffened.

'If he's in France, I mean,' Lindsay reminded her. 'Plus, he might need to be seen by a doctor. You know, to be checked over.' Then she added, 'But I'll tell you what would be helpful. If you got some stuff together in a bag for him? Some of his favourite toys, and a change of clothes. When we find him, we may need to take whatever he's wearing.'

Emma nodded. 'Phone me the minute you hear anything,' she begged.

'I'll do that,' Lindsay promised.

They said their goodbyes. Emma went on down the steps of the police station. *Checked over.* What did Lindsay mean by that? She'd said it was less likely now that Ritchie would be hurt.

She walked on, keeping her hand in her pocket, curled around her mobile phone. She had to keep moving, keep doing something, even if all she could do was cling to the phone and wait for it to ring. She walked quickly, hardly noticing where she went. She turned left on to the Fulham Road and kept going. The further she walked, the buzzier the street became. The pavements were packed with people her age, all heading out for the night. Lights and noise and smells radiated from the bars and restaurants. Some of the restaurants had their windows open to the street. Rows of bottoms faced outwards in the dusk. People jostled around her. She crossed to the other, quieter side of the road so that she could walk undisturbed.

Scenes chased through her head. One minute she was imagining the reunion. Ritchie calling in his clear little voice, 'Muh. Muh,' with his arms out, and she grabbing him, pulling him to her. Then she remembered that they hadn't found him at all yet. How would they get him back? Would they have to break down the door of the house where he was? Would there be guns? Would the kidnappers try to kill him?

Her mobile rang, buzzing against her hand. Emma jumped, fumbling in terror to pull it out.

'Hello? Hello?'

'Emma?' The voice was familiar. 'It's Rafe Townsend here.'

'Rafe.' Emma stopped. She never would have thought it, but he was exactly the person she needed to hear from right now.

'Rafe,' she blurted. 'The Bergerac thing. I saw

156

the tape from the airport. It's him. It's Ritchie.'

'What?' The phone crackled.

A crowd of people, men in jackets and polo shirts, girls in tight, pastel coats had all arrived together outside an Italian restaurant. Emma put her finger in her ear. She shouted into the phone, 'That was Ritchie at the airport. They're going to track him down in France.'

'Jesus.' Rafe sounded stunned. 'That's fantastic.'

'Yeah.' All of a sudden she was smiling. 'Yeah. It is.'

The maître d' of the restaurant had opened the doors. The men and girls were crowding into the warmth. Emma could smell garlic. She saw red and yellow lights along the inside walls.

'How did he look?' Rafe asked. 'Did he look OK?'

'He looked as if he'd been drugged.' Emma tried not to think about it. 'And she'd dyed his hair. And put different clothes on him.'

For some reason, even with Ritchie being given drugs and having chemicals put in his hair, the thing that really bothered her was the new clothes. She kept coming back to them. She'd been picturing Ritchie all this time as still in his elephant fleece.

'But the clothes looked warm,' she had to admit. 'Clean. He looked . . . comfortable.'

'I can't believe it,' Rafe kept saying. 'I can't believe it.'

'I thought he might be dead,' Emma said in a low voice. 'I really did. Part of me thought that. I never thought it would really be him.'

157

Rafe said, 'But it was.'

The customers had all gone in now. The street had quietened. The restaurant doors were closed.

'You couldn't see his face properly,' Emma said. 'On the film. Detective Hill kept saying, are you sure it's him, you can't see his face.'

'But you *were* sure,' Rafe said.

'Yeah.' Happiness filled her. 'Yeah. I can't wait to see him.'

Again, she pictured Ritchie, trying to run to her with his funny little waddle. His delighted beam when he saw her. Or would he cry? Would he be so traumatized he wouldn't be able to smile at all? Would he have to go to hospital? Once more, her gut clenched. God. Was this ever going to end?

'It's going to be fine.' Rafe seemed to be thinking the same things she was. 'Stay positive, Emma. You'll have him back with you soon.'

She held the phone, letting the words slow her heart. It was so good, hearing them. Knowing he was interested in what was happening. Having him there.

'I'd better go,' she said at last. 'They might be trying to reach me.'

'Ring me any time you want to,' Rafe said. 'Any time you want to talk. You know where I am.'

★ ★ ★

Even though Lindsay had said it would be a while before she saw him, Emma stopped in at Sainsbury's to buy things for Ritchie. Rusks.

Milk. Strawberry yoghurt. The sticks of mild Cheddar cheese he liked to carry about with him. Choosing the familiar items calmed her. The child's bright colours on the pots in the fridge; the comforting shuffle in the queue with the other mothers. The whole routine of it made Ritchie's coming home seem more real.

Lindsay had said there might be a delay, but as it turned out, things moved very swiftly over the evening. Lindsay phoned several times, each time sounding more and more excited. Now they had an address in France. Interpol was involved. A team was going to the address straight away. Lindsay would phone as soon as the British police heard back.

Emma hung up, her heart racing. This was really it. She was really going to see him. She spent the next hour and a half cleaning the flat from top to bottom. She turned on all the lights and kept her head down, scrubbing the kitchen, hoovering the carpets, scouring the bath and sink. She made up Ritchie's cot for him, covering the mattress with clean, lavender-smelling sheets and smoothing out his fleece blanket with the green and purple Barney on it. She sat Gribbit right at the top, and arranged Ritchie's five soothers in a circle around him.

And then, suddenly exhausted, she sank down on to the edge of her bed, still with her hand on Gribbit's soft, green, semi-chewed head. She let her head droop, resting her forehead against the bars of the cot.

'Did you hear, Grib?' she whispered. 'Did you hear? He's coming back to us.'

★ ★ ★

It was after midnight when the intercom finally sounded. Emma flew to answer it. Moments later, Lindsay arrived at the flat, dressed much less formally than usual in a pink shirt and jeans. She was out of breath, her cheeks shiny and red. Her hair stood up in straggly wisps around her face. Clearly she had some news.

'Did you find them?' Emma managed to ask. 'Were they there?'

'Yes. They were there.'

Oh, thank God. Emma's whole body relaxed. Thank God. Her muscles had gone loose, as if someone had taken a wrench and opened all the bolts. At last. At last it was all over.

'So where is he?' she asked. 'When can I see him?'

Lindsay came into the flat. She closed the door behind her.

'Why don't you answer?' Emma was surprised. Then something struck her, and a needle of ice slid into her throat.

'Is he hurt?'

'It's not that,' Lindsay said quickly.

'Well, what then?' Emma was confused.

Lindsay said, 'Why don't we sit down?'

'Sit down? Sit down? Sure.'

Emma almost ran over to the couch. She plopped down on to it. Lindsay sat beside her, looking grave.

'Emma, it's not him.'

'It's not . . . ?' Emma stared, uncomprehending. 'Sorry. I'm not with you.'

160

'The little boy you saw at the airport. It's not Ritchie.'

'But — '

'Interpol have made some enquiries. They're an English family who've lived in France for several years. They'd spent some time abroad and were passing through London on their way home to France. I know the child looked like Ritchie, but it wasn't a good view.'

Emma couldn't believe it. She felt stunned. Sick.

'I . . . ' she kept saying in a little gaspy voice that didn't sound like her own. 'I . . . '

'I'm so, so sorry, Emma,' Lindsay was saying. She'd been so sure. The fringe. It was him.

'It is him,' she said. 'It is Ritchie. I know it is.'

'Emma, I hoped it was too, I really did. But the fact is, the passports all check out and not only that, the family is well known in their neighbourhood in France. They had the baby there in the local hospital. Everybody knows him. The husband's parents live in the same village. The neighbours. The local English-speaking family doctor. It all checks out.'

'No. No. You don't understand. I don't care what checks you've done. It is him. It is Ritchie.'

'We can't take it any further, Emma. But listen to me . . . no, listen. We've still got plenty of other options. Several people have called in after reading the news stories about him. We've had a possible sighting in Manchester, we're following all — '

'Please. Please. That was him in the airport. You have to believe me.'

161

'When you want something so much you can convince yourself.' Lindsay looked distressed. 'I'm sorry, but we can't take this any further.'

'Where is he? I want to see him. I want to see him for myself.'

'We can't tell you that.'

'Well then, get out.'

'Emma — '

'*Get out!*'

Emma sobbed, rocking herself back and forward, cradling the empty space in her arms.

10

Lindsay refused to leave the flat. She spent the next twenty minutes trying to persuade Emma to let her call someone.

'You shouldn't be here on your own,' she insisted. 'You need someone with you.'

And Emma kept repeating in a blank, dead voice, 'I'll be all right. Just go.'

Lindsay tutted, then sighed. She went out to the hall to use her phone. She closed the door behind her, but Emma could still hear what she was saying.

'She wants me to . . . I know. I know. I feel bad for her, but I'm meant to be . . . Well, am I going to get overtime for this?'

After a few minutes, she came back in.

'I can't leave you,' she said flatly. 'You really shouldn't be on your own. Can't I call a social worker? Someone from Victim Support? They're a charity that helps people in your situation. They could send someone to be with you while all of this is going on.'

'I don't want anyone.'

'Emma.' Lindsay was beginning to sound desperate. 'Listen to me. You're not making any sense.'

Emma put the tips of her fingers to her eyes, circling them around and around. When she pressed them inwards, she thought she was going to faint.

'I'll call Rafe,' she said at last.

'Rafe?'

'The man who found my bags.'

'But, Emma.' Lindsay looked perplexed. 'You hardly know him. It's one o'clock in the morning.'

'Well, that's the person I want.'

She wouldn't have called him, of course; she was only saying it to make Lindsay leave. But Lindsay, raising her eyebrows at Emma between digits, as if to say, 'Are you sure about this?' went ahead and dialled Rafe's number herself. And in what seemed like a very short space of time, the intercom buzzed again and it was him.

Lindsay went to let him in. Once again, urgent whispers emanated from the hall. Then Rafe spoke in his normal tone.

'It's all right,' he said, his voice sounding very loud after all the whispering. 'I'll stay with her.'

'You don't mind?' Lindsay's relief couldn't have been more plain.

Emma stayed where she was, hunched in a chair by the window. She heard the front door close behind Lindsay. As soon as Rafe came into the room, she said, 'I'm sorry she called you. You don't need to stay. You can turn around again and go home.'

'But I don't want to,' he said. He was wearing a bright blue rain-jacket, zipped up over his jeans. His eyes were small. His hair was pushed-back and messy, as if he'd just got out of bed. 'I'm glad I'm here. I'm glad she called me.'

Emma didn't have the energy to argue. She sank her head on to her arms.

'I can't bear this,' she said into the table. 'I can't. I can't take this any more.'

'I'm sure you can't.' Rafe was grim.

'What can I do?' Emma asked. 'What can I do?'

'Don't blame yourself,' Rafe advised. 'I've seen those kind of tapes. It can be hard to see faces properly.'

Emma interrupted him with her hands, lifting them up and spreading her fingers in the air around her head.

'There was no problem with the tape. I know it was Ritchie.'

'But — '

'*Listen* to me.' She turned on him. 'I've been thinking about this. I've worked it out. That couple are lying. They're family members, those people in France, of course they'd back them up.'

'But the police spoke to the neighbours as well. And their doctor — '

'I'm not *interested* in the neighbours. Or their bloody doctor. There must be a way to prove this. We don't have long. Those people must know now that the police have been asking about them. They'll move on and we'll lose them.'

'You could be right, but — '

'I know I'm right,' Emma hissed. 'Jesus, you think I don't know my own child?'

Rafe was silent.

'What kind of a country is this anyway?' Emma slammed her hands on the table. 'I'm looking at a film of someone kidnapping my child — I'm *watching them taking my child in*

165

front of my nose — and you're all telling me it's in my head. Telling me it's someone else's child. You were in the police. You must know some way. You said you felt guilty about Ritchie; well, now's your chance to do something. Oh!' She turned away, rigid with frustration. 'Forget it. You don't believe me.'

Through the haze of anger and self-pity and pain, she heard Rafe's voice.

'I do believe you.'

It took a second for that to get through.

'You do?'

He shrugged. 'Sure. You said it yourself. You know your own child. If you say it's him, then it must be.'

How weird. How weird, after all this time, to have a conversation like this with a person who actually seemed to believe what she was saying. A person who didn't think she was delusional. Emma had been beginning to seriously wonder if she was going mad, and she was the only one who couldn't see it.

But what was the point? It wasn't as if Rafe believing her was going to get her anywhere. Bitterly, Emma slumped back on to her arms. She said, 'What can you do about it anyway?'

She didn't expect an answer. But when, a few seconds later, Rafe still hadn't responded, something made her look up. Rafe was squinting slightly, looking off to the left, as if in thought.

'What?' Emma said. 'What?'

Rafe said, 'A mate of mine's a cop.'

'So?'

'So, maybe it's time to bring in your private

166

detective. If I talked to my mate, and he could get us the address where Ritchie is — '

'*Excuse me?*' Emma thought she'd heard him wrong. 'What did you say? Get Ritchie's address?'

'Well, yeah. It'll have to be somewhere; on a computer; somewhere. It's just a matter of — '

'Hang on a minute.' Emma still couldn't believe her ears. 'You're saying *you* could tell me where Ritchie is? You're telling me I could *see* him?'

'Look.' Rafe sounded alarmed. 'I didn't say that. I can't promise anything. My mate might not agree to help. And if we did get the address, you'd have to be careful. You'd have to go about this the right way.'

'What? What do you mean?'

'If you're thinking of trying to snatch him, you could get yourself arrested.'

'Do you think I'd care?' Emma's voice had risen to a squeak. She was on her feet now, clutching the back of her chair.

'Listen to me, Emma.' Rafe stood up straight. He spoke very firmly. 'For a start, just getting the address would be against the law. My mate owes me a couple of favours, but I can't guarantee he'd do something like this. And just say you found Ritchie — and I'm not saying you will, but just if. And if you went to see him, and they saw you. They'd take Ritchie and run. You might never find him again.'

Emma hadn't thought of that. For a moment, she was still. Then she said in a quieter voice, 'I wouldn't try to snatch him.'

'What would you do, then?'

'I . . . I . . . '

What would she do? Never mind that now. She had to convince Rafe to get her the address. The rest she'd worry about later.

'I just want to see him,' she said. 'Just to prove it's him. They'd have to believe me if I saw his face. I wouldn't touch him. I swear.'

Rafe seemed to still be hesitating.

'Please.' Emma's voice crumpled. 'Please. I have to do this. You don't know how much I need to see him.'

Her distress was beginning to get to him now, she saw. He was taking deep breaths. Scratching the side of his head. Emma kept her eyes fixed on his. It seemed like a long time since she'd done that. Stared someone in the face and not backed down.

In the end, it was Rafe who looked away first.

'I'll need your crime reference number,' he said.

'My . . . ?'

'The police would have given you one. So they can look up your details on the computer when you phone them.'

It sounded vaguely familiar. Emma went to scrabble amongst the pieces of paper by her phone. Near the top was the Post-it Lindsay had left with her contact details. Emma hadn't noticed it before, but there was the crime reference number, neatly printed underneath.

'I'll need to take this home,' Rafe said, copying the number on to a separate piece of paper. 'Make a few calls. I'll phone you as soon as I know anything.'

* * *

He rang her as the sun came up. Emma hadn't moved from her place at the table. The sky was pink. The streets below were quiet. The drunken teenagers had smashed their last beer bottles and gone home; the early traffic had yet to clog the roads.

She only realized how cold she was when she went to pick up the phone and felt the little shocks in her fingers.

'Hello?'

He'd hardly have heard anything. It was too soon. The only question was whether his mate had agreed to help. If he'd even managed to reach him yet.

So she was stunned when Rafe announced, 'I have an address.'

An address!

Emma felt for her chair, and sat down.

'Where?' she asked.

She heard a papery, rustling sound.

'According to this,' Rafe said, 'the people in the airport are a married couple. David and Philippa Hunt. The child's name is . . . um . . . X . . . Exa . . . ' He spelled it out.

'Xavier,' Emma said. She twisted at the shirt button near her throat.

'Zah-vee-ay.' Rafe repeated. 'OK. Zah-vee-ay Hunt. Aged fifteen months.'

Xavier Hunt. Xavier Hunt. Emma pictured Ritchie's fringe; his new top and trousers. The way he slept so tightly curled into the woman in the airport.

169

'Should I go on?' Rafe asked.

'Please.'

'They're in a place called St-Bourdain,' Rafe said. 'I've a map up on the screen here, and it's about forty kilometres outside Bergerac. It's a tiny village. Outsiders will stick out, so we'll need to be careful.'

'We?'

'I'll be honest here, Emma. My friend was very reluctant to give out the info. If there's any trouble, his job could be on the line. He was only happy to pass on the address if I promised I'd go with you. In case you were a loony or something.'

'Oh.'

'I know you're not,' Rafe added. 'But I told him I would.'

'I want to go straight away,' Emma said flatly.

'Haven't you got work?'

'I was finishing at the end of the week anyway. I can take the last few days off. It's not a problem.'

He still thought she was going to make a grab for Ritchie. Well, she'd worry about that later. She could shake Rafe if she had to.

'How do we get there?' she asked.

'We can fly to Bergerac, or to one of the other airports near there. Bordeaux, I think. Whichever is quickest. Do you want me to book the flights?'

'I'll do it.' Emma had the phone book open already and was fumbling through it. She didn't know where she was looking. She opened it at the beginning, and started at A, for Airlines.

Sunday, 24 September
Day Eight

Passport. Check. There in her bag. The flight numbers were written on a piece of paper, safely tucked into her back pocket. The only clothes she was bringing were the ones she was wearing: jeans, plain T-shirt, navy fleece. She'd flung her toothbrush, deodorant and a change of underwear in her backpack. And in a separate compartment, carefully zipped, was Gribbit, his long legs folded neatly over his shoulders.

That was it then. She had everything.

Just as Emma closed the door of the flat, the phone in the sitting-room started to ring.

Shit! Emma scrabbled to get the key back out of her bag. Don't say it was Rafe, phoning to say he'd be late. It was after twelve already. They were supposed to be meeting at Liverpool Street station at one.

She let herself back in and flew to the phone.

'Hello?'

'Emma.' It was Lindsay. 'You weren't asleep, were you?'

'No. I was up.'

'That's good,' Lindsay said. 'I was just calling to say I'll be over later this afternoon, if that's all right with you? I've got some things we need to discuss.'

'I'm going out,' Emma said.

'Where?' Lindsay sounded surprised.

'I'll have my mobile with me.' Emma was desperate to get off the phone. She couldn't hang up

171

too quickly though, or Lindsay might get suspicious.

'I see,' Lindsay said. 'Well, it was really to discuss how you might feel about appearing on TV. To give a press conference. It sounds intimidating, I know, but you'd have a chance to appeal directly to the people who took Ritchie. Also to anyone who might know them or live near them who might — '

'It sounds like a great idea,' Emma interrupted. 'Let me know when it's happening.'

She ended the call and grabbed her backpack off the table. She glanced at her watch. Twelve fifteen. She left the flat and ran all the way down the stairs, not bothering to wait for the lift.

Hammersmith was its usual grey, chilly self as Emma hurried past Charing Cross Hospital and down the ramp to the underground walkway into Hammersmith Broadway. Then out again the other side, to the old station on the corner, looking, with its old-fashioned blue sign and Victorian clock on the top, utterly quaint and out of place in the midst of all the double-decker buses and flyovers. Emma waited for the lights to change, drumming her fingers on the traffic-light pole. By the time she reached the station, she was sweating. A train pulled in just as she arrived on the platform.

Liverpool Street station was white and high-ceilinged and jammed. People in suits strode around with briefcases. Every route seemed blocked by gangs of teenage tourists with puffa jackets and very hairy eyebrows, loaded down with giant rucksacks and chattering

172

incomprehensibly. Emma, pausing by a bench to look for Rafe, felt a sharp blow to her ankle. She turned to see a jowly man wheel his case past her, clicking his tongue with annoyance.

She spotted Rafe beside a large board with an 'i' on the top, wearing his blue rain-jacket and reading the announcements on the board. As she watched, he tipped his head back and took a long gulp of water from a bottle. His black rucksack, bulgier than before, hung by its strap from his hand. He finished his drink and started to wipe his mouth with his hand. Midway through, he caught Emma's eye. He raised the bottle towards her and smiled. Emma tightened her lips in return. She wasn't quite sure what to say. It was odd, them meeting like this, away from the flat.

'The train for the airport's leaving in five minutes,' Rafe said as she reached him.

'I have my ticket.'

'Then let's go.'

They ducked and zigzagged through the crowds, Emma following the blue flash of Rafe's jacket. Announcements dinged over the loud-speaker: 'The. Next. Train. From. Platform. Three. Will be the — '

The whistle blew just as they stepped on to the train.

'Perfect timing.' Rafe grinned, dumping his rucksack on the floor between his feet.

'A good omen, maybe?' Emma tried to return the smile.

The train was full; they had to stand. A woman who looked to be in her thirties appeared

173

at the door and lifted a small boy into the carriage. The woman held the child's hand and remained on the platform to continue a conversation with someone on the other side of the turnstile. The boy was about two years old, with thin curly hair and bright red cheeks. He seemed very excited to be on the train. His eyes almost popped out of his head as he swivelled from side to side, anchored by the woman's hand, trying to see everything at once. Then he froze, clearly spotting something of interest further down the crowded carriage; Emma couldn't see what it was. The woman on the platform was still chatting. The boy gritted his tiny teeth and hauled himself from her grip. A second later, he was free. He took off down the carriage, disappearing into a forest of legs. Emma looked quickly at the woman. She didn't seem to have noticed.

'*Definitely*,' she was saying in a loud voice to her friend. 'Well, as soon as I hear from Barbara, we'll arrange — '

Beep-beep-beep. The carriage doors sounded their warning. Emma's heart pounded. She stepped forward. At the last second, just before the doors whipped shut, the woman turned, hoisted her straw shopping bag higher on to her shoulder, and stepped on to the train.

'James,' she called. 'James.'

The little boy reappeared, poking his chubby face around a metallic wheelie-case.

'*There* you are, darling,' the woman said. 'What did Mummy tell you about keeping close?'

Emma shrank back against the rail. The woman and child headed off together down the carriage.

The train started with a lurch, causing those passengers who were standing to stumble and step on each other's toes. The crowds were a good thing; they meant that Emma wouldn't have to talk to Rafe during the journey. She needed time to think. As the platform slid past, she realized she was holding her breath. What if Lindsay had become suspicious and decided to have her followed to see where she was going? What if the police had bugged her phone? What if the train stopped again, and Detective Hill came on board, telling her for some reason that she wasn't allowed to leave the country?

But the train didn't stop. It kept on moving, click-clacking its way through the North London suburbs. Some shift in the crowd just then pushed Rafe towards her. His knuckles whitened as he gripped the rail beside her head. The veins on the back of his hand stood out as he steadied himself, keeping the crowd from her.

★   ★   ★

All the way through the airport, Emma couldn't stop thinking, *Ritchie's been here.* She'd never been to this airport before, but he had. Her tiny son had been somewhere before her, had seen a place that she had never seen. She looked around at everything, trying to view it all through his eyes. Was this the door they'd walked through on the CCTV? Was this the desk they'd checked in

175

at? Those three check-in girls in their dark blue uniforms — was it one of them who had seen Ritchie that day, and remembered him enough to speak to the police? Had he woken at all during the journey? What had he thought of the plane, the noise of the engines? Had he been cross? Excited? Afraid?

She was relieved when the plane finally took off without any sign of its being stormed by the police. She'd been allocated a seat beside the window. The woman next to her had busied herself during the safety demonstration by arranging an inflatable rubber tube around her neck and wrapping a woollen pashmina around herself, right up to her chin. Now her eyes were closed and her head rested sideways on the tube, bouncing with the turbulence. She seemed to be already asleep. Rafe was sitting several rows behind.

For some reason, Emma found herself remembering a holiday she'd gone on to Greece, five years ago. Four of them had gone together. Her, Karen, Joanne and Claire Burns. They'd stayed in a gorgeous apartment, with pink flowers in baskets outside their window. Emma had had a holiday romance with a rather intense engineering student from Vancouver called Vernon. They'd all gone snorkelling one afternoon, and two Greek fishermen had given them a lift home on their boat. They'd had a good laugh. Emma pressed her forehead to the window, watching the sun gleam on the clouds.

We're so small. So small, and no one cares.

What was she going to do when she found

Ritchie? She couldn't think beyond just seeing him again, confirming it really was him. Would he still be at this St-Bourdain place? What if the kidnappers had moved on? They must have got a fright when the police came around asking questions. What if they'd sold Ritchie, or . . .

No! No. She wasn't going to think like that. Rafe had said that Antonia wanted Ritchie for herself. She'd taken a liking to him, and wanted to raise him as her own.

And Ritchie had liked her back.

Liked her very much, in fact.

He hadn't wanted Emma to take him.

You shouldn't give him sweets.

Emma squeezed her eyes shut. How dare she! How *dare* that woman tell Emma what to do with her child! But didn't that sound as if Antonia did mean to look after him? Not to hurt him? But, Christ, it was weird, if so. How did she think she was going to get away with something like that? Just taking someone else's baby and pretending he was hers?

★ ★ ★

Bergerac was sunnier than England. The airport, a pale, prefab-like building looked like nothing so much as a large garden shed. Emma came down the steps of the plane, smelling warm, unfamiliar air. The trees and sky and ground had a different colour to England. It was as if she was seeing everything through yellow-green lenses. Inside the shed, the passengers gathered in a crush along the luggage belt. Everyone seemed

177

to be wearing the same thing: sandals and shorts or combat trousers, and fleeces tied around their waists. Voices, mostly English, rose around them.

'Jeremy, did you pack George's tennis shoes?'

'Mummy, tell Emily to stop putting things in my bag!'

Emma and Rafe hadn't checked in any luggage, so they were able to bypass the crowd. They proceeded to passport control, where a man in a round hat waved them languidly through.

'Do you think there's a bus to St-Bourdain?' Emma asked, looking around the tiny hall.

'I doubt it,' Rafe said. 'We'd be better off hiring a car.'

'Driving licence, *madame*?' said the man at the car-hire desk. He had a moustache like Detective Hill's.

Emma was flustered. 'I never thought — '

'It's all right.' Rafe held up a plastic wallet. 'I brought mine.'

Emma fumbled in her wallet for euros. Were they the same as pounds, or less? She hoped she'd brought enough for a car. She'd never thought about how she was actually going to get to the place where Ritchie was.

'I'll get the car,' Rafe said. 'You paid for the flights, remember?'

'I can't let you — '

'Keep your money. Please. You don't know how much you might need.'

When the paperwork was done, the man told them, 'The hire parking is at your left as you go out of the exit.'

The car park was dusty and quiet. The sky was white, the sun gleaming off rows of chrome. Space B5 was occupied by a silver Peugeot hatchback. In the car, the smell of hot polish and rubber hit Emma's nostrils like a wall. Rafe opened the map of the region that the man at the car-hire desk had given them. It was very basic. Bergerac was the smallest town marked on it. They had no way of knowing which direction a tiny village like St-Bourdain was in.

'I should have brought a proper map.' Emma cursed herself. Hadn't she thought of anything?

'We'll buy one, don't worry,' Rafe said. He peered through the window. 'Town centre, look, that way. Five kilometres.'

At the car-park exit, the Peugeot squealed and leaped forward, throwing Emma against her seatbelt.

'Sorry.' Rafe scowled, yanking the gearstick. 'Bloody thing keeps sticking.'

The town of Bergerac had a functional appearance. Rows of pale, square shuttered buildings, some in need of a coat of paint. It was hard to say whether the few shops they saw were open or closed because there didn't seem to be any customers in them. On one side of a square, a canopy jutted from the front of a café, shading a collection of red plastic chairs and tables on the pavement. The tables were all empty. Paris this certainly wasn't.

They parked the car close to the square and found a bookshop across the road. A bell tinkled as they pushed open the door. The elderly man at the counter looked up from his newspaper.

'*Avez-vous un . . .* ' Emma scanned the shelves of books and magazines.

'Map?' she tried, but the man behind the counter looked blank. She craned again, peering up at the top shelves. Cartoon books, mostly, for children. Asterix. The Smurfs. A whole row of books with pictures of a bald boy and a small white dog. Then a memory rose in Emma's mind. French lessons, Year Nine, in the blue prefab in her school in Brislington. The wooden desks, the smell of cheese and onion. Kevin Brimley, the boy beside her, standing up to read aloud his essay about his *vacances* in Le Havre.

'*Plan,*' Emma said with triumph. '*Avez-vous un plan?*'

'*Oui. Plan,*' Rafe said. '*De France,*' he added proudly.

'*La-bas, monsieur.*' The man pointed to a rack below the counter.

Back in the car, between sips from plastic bottles of water, they studied the folded-out map.

'There it is.' Rafe pointed at a tiny circle, marked in green. 'St-Bourdain. We keep going south and we basically hit it.'

They found the route easily enough, a medium-sized road with little traffic. The few cars they saw were plain and useful-looking. A gleaming London Mercedes or Jaguar would look vulgar and out of place here.

'You're on the wrong side of the road,' Emma warned, clutching the dashboard as they came off a roundabout. Then, spotting another car in front of them, she realized her mistake. 'No, I'm

180

sorry. You're right. I don't know how you remember.'

'Keep the bitch in the ditch.' Rafe grinned sideways at her. 'Works every time.'

They drove on in silence in the early-evening sun. Gradually, the scenery changed. Billboards, and garages with rows of parked cars gave way to fields dotted with yellow and white flowers. Across the fields, thick, cloudy masses of trees darkened to blue in the distance.

'You know,' Rafe squinted at the rear-view mirror, 'we're going to need to come up with some sort of plan.'

Emma pretended not to hear. She was hunched towards the window, closely watching everything they passed. Signs, painted with pictures of grapes, pointed down narrow side roads with grass in the middle. 'Chateau Mireille,' the signs read. 'Chateau de Montagne.'

'Have you thought about what you're going to do?' Rafe asked. 'Are you going to just sit outside the house all night?'

'I don't know.'

More fields. Rows of plants tied with wooden posts and wire.

'All right, then.' Rafe relented. He pushed on the gearstick. 'We'll think of something when we get there.'

Drive, Emma thought. Just drive.

With each village, her pulse was rising. The deeper into the countryside they drove, the closer they came to St-Bourdain and the more beautiful the villages became. The houses were built with yellow-coloured stone, like in the

Cotswolds. Behind them spread rows of dark, leafy crops, higher than a man; you could run into them and not be seen. She saw farmhouses with hens in the gardens, creeper-covered walls, rows of vegetables. Was Ritchie in a house like this? In a garden like that?

I'm coming, Rich. She sent the promise to him, over the fields. *I'm almost there.*

And in return she felt his presence, as strongly as if he was in the car beside her. She knew she was right. Somewhere amongst these yellow houses, these cloudy trees, her little boy was waiting for her to find him and bring him home.

Ritchie was here. She knew that for certain. He was here.

11

Bringing Ritchie home from the hospital had been an anticlimax.

He'd looked so adorable in the taxi, dressed in his tiny new blue-and-white striped Babygro and a woolly beanie hat that made his head look like an egg. He kept staring at the window in astonishment, as if he'd spotted something amazing out there, but unfortunately his head kept wobbling to one side. Emma jiggled him, gently helping him to bump it back up again so he could see.

'Bit of a bruiser, in'ee?' the taxi driver said admiringly.

Emma smiled with pride.

But when they'd arrived at the flat, and the taxi driver had helped her bring all her stuff to the lift, and they'd reached the fifth floor and closed the door of the flat behind them — when all that was done, it was just the two of them, sitting there looking at each other. After the buzz of the hospital ward, the flat seemed very bleak and silent. No other babies wailing, no mothers in their dressing gowns smiling and saying hello as they passed. No nurses popping by to coo at Ritchie and say what a good sleeper he was. There was no one to greet them, no one to hold Ritchie up to and say, 'Look at him. Isn't he the most beautiful baby on earth?'

At least they *had* a flat by then.

'How am I going to be able to afford somewhere on my own?' Emma had uneasily asked the social worker, two weeks before the lease on the Clapham flat ran out. She'd been doing some calculations and realized, with a shock, that once she stopped work she wouldn't be able to afford even the rent she'd been paying with Joanne.

'You'll be entitled to some benefits,' the social worker assured her. 'Though if your mum has left you some savings, you'll have to contribute towards rent and council tax.'

Emma had expected that. Still, it worried her, having to dip into her nest egg so soon. She'd hoped to be able to keep it for a rainy day. Which, of course, this was.

'How long do you think it'll take to find somewhere?' she asked.

'We would hope to have you placed by the time the baby is born.' The social worker frowned at her clipboard. 'I have to say, though, that accommodation is fairly tight at the moment. I can't guarantee anything.'

'But what will I do in the meantime?' Emma asked. You couldn't just move into a flat for a few weeks; you had to sign a lease. Pay a deposit. Why hadn't she looked into this long ago?

'If you're stuck, we can find you a B&B,' the social worker said. 'It shouldn't be for too long. We've placed you on our emergency waiting list, as you're a vulnerable homeless person.'

A vulnerable homeless person. In the grimy B&B room beside a laundrette in Balham, Emma stood with her bags at her feet and felt the first pricklings of real fear. Vulnerable homeless people featured on *Panorama*. They lay under bridges and shouted at empty seats on the tube. A brown patch in the middle of the mattress disgusted her, filling her with nausea. She put her hands on her stomach. No way could she have a baby here.

To her utter relief, ten days before Ritchie was born, Emma was offered a flat in a housing association complex between Hammersmith and Fulham. It was miles away from Joanne and Barry, and from her new GP, Dr Rigby. She'd have to change doctors. But she was in no position to argue.

By that stage, she could just about still walk. It was more of a waddle really, the weight of her stomach pulling her this way and that. The social worker, a chatty woman with a grey bob, came with her to view the flat. It was in a tall, brown tower block, facing an identical block across a concrete car park. Swirly red and orange graffiti daubed the walls as high as an arm could reach. A sign above a row of wheelie bins read, *To all tenants. Please place rubbish IN the bins, NOT beside.*

The social worker dug a card out of her bag and ran it through the strip beside the steel and reinforced-glass doors. Inside, the hall was tiled and dim, with a browning yucca plant in a plastic pot beside the lift.

One lift, Emma couldn't help noticing. For a block with eleven floors.

'Don't worry.' The social worker eyed her swollen belly. 'The management here is quite

185

good. If anything breaks down, they usually fix it within a couple of days.'

The tour of the flat didn't take long. The yellow-painted hall was so tiny that with Emma's belly the way it was, she and the social worker had to take turns standing in it. Three doors led off the hall. The first led into the bathroom, which had no window, just a fan; but it did have a bath.

'A bonus when you have a baby.' The social worker smiled.

The bedroom had a single bed with a clean, stripy mattress, a built-in wardrobe with white doors, and a desk with two drawers in it under the window. The desk would have to come out if they were to fit a cot in there for the baby. The sitting-room was very dark, despite the fact that it was three in the afternoon and the curtains to the glass balcony doors were open. It was furnished with a maroon-coloured corduroy couch, and a round, glass-topped table with two metallic chairs. A doorway with no door led through to a windowless kitchen. No room for a table in here; just an oven, fridge and stainless-steel sink, and three mustard-coloured cupboards at eye-level. The white and grey speckled lino was held down in places by sticky tape.

The balcony, though, was nice. It was a plain, cement rectangle, barely the length of a person lying down. But she could put plants out there, make it nice in the summer. The carpets in the flat were threadbare but clean. No brown stains anywhere. That was really what made Emma breathe a sigh of relief. Not the Ritz, then, for sure, but miles better than the B&B. She didn't know what she'd have done if the flat had been as bad as, or worse than, that awful place.

'I'll take it,' she told the social worker.

'Not much choice, have you, love?' the social worker said cheerfully.

Emma moved in the next day. Even with all her possessions, it only took one trip in a taxi. Clean though the flat seemed to be, Emma went to the Sainsbury's down the road and bought a cupboard full of supplies to scrub it all over again. Over the next couple of days, she used some of her mum's money to buy things for the new baby. A pram which converted to a pushchair, a cot, blankets, bottles, a sterilizer. Mugs, plates, cutlery, nappies. A green stuffed frog with friendly eyes from a stall in Hammersmith Broadway.

That weekend, she lay in bed and listened to the *thump-thump-thump* of music from somewhere above her head. Someone was having a party. Well, let them; it was Saturday night. Shouts came from below, followed by the sprinkly crunch of breaking glass. Emma's hands moved to her stomach. But she was safe in here. She was on the fifth floor; it wasn't like anyone was going to climb up. She'd been given an electronic coded card for the heavy doors at the bottom, and a separate, normal key for the lock on her own door.

They'd be OK here. Her and the baby. They'd manage.

For a while anyway.

* * *

And then, eight days later, Ritchie arrived, and for the next few weeks everything was a blur. All of Emma's time and energy was taken up just with concentrating on him. There was so much to do. She had to feed him — more or less continuously, it seemed. With pauses, where she had to sit him up and pat his back until he burped, the way the health visitor had shown her. She had to change his nappies. Sterilize his bottles. Wash his clothes. Every other minute there was something.

She was surprised, though, at how quickly she got the hang of it. She'd been worried she wouldn't know how to look after him, never having known anyone with a baby. But the sleepless nights weren't as bad as she'd expected. It was tiring, definitely, all that getting out of bed to give him his bottle, but after a few weeks he was sleeping right through and they'd got a routine going for the day. Up at six thirty. Bottle. Both of them back to sleep until nine. Two further naps during the afternoon. Bed for the night at eight to eight thirty.

Ritchie was a placid baby; he only cried when he was hungry or wet and she was usually able to work out the reason. He wasn't the worst baby, Emma knew that from what she'd read. There were some infants who just screamed and screamed, night and day; you couldn't do anything to get them to stop. But Ritchie didn't do that. She was lucky. And she'd read that you were supposed to sleep whenever the baby did during the day, so that was what she did. She got enough sleep; the housework got done. There really was nothing very difficult about it.

Only that you had to keep on doing it.

Over and over and over again.

It wasn't until the worst of the nights were behind her that Emma realized properly for the first time how alone she was. How hard it was to get out of the flat with a small baby, and how few people she ever saw.

She was delighted when Joanne called over one evening on her way home from work. Ritchie was about six weeks old by then.

'Ems,' Joanne cried, flinging her arms around Emma as soon as the door was open. She looked amazing. She was wearing high, spindly heels and a pale blue trouser suit. Her hair was cut to her shoulders, with a new, long fringe swept to the side. 'Sorry it's been so long. We've been redecorating the new place; Barry and me've been living out of boxes. And I've been promoted at work. I'm regional sales manager now. It's been mad.'

She kept flicking her fringe back as she looked all around her, at the corduroy couch, the boxes of nappies and wipes in the corner, the towels and Babygros drying on the backs of Emma's two chairs.

'Your flat's *gorgeous*,' she said in a very bright voice.

'Sit down.' Emma was thrilled to see her. 'I'll make us some coffee.'

Joanne gave the couch a quick check before she lowered herself on to the edge.

'Isn't he sweet,' she cooed at Ritchie, asleep in his pram.

But she drew the line at picking him up.

'Babies don't like me,' she giggled, tucking her knees in the opposite direction. 'I'd be afraid I'd drop him.'

'Oh, go on,' Emma said. 'He's lovely to hold, honestly. He's tougher than he looks. He won't break.'

She was lifting Ritchie out of the pram as she spoke, trailing blankets all over the floor. She placed him in Joanne's lap, dying for Joanne to get to know him. Ritchie stirred, screwing up his face. And then, just as Joanne lowered her hands to take him, he turned purple and launched into a high-pitched, waspy wail. Joanne put her hands back in the air at once.

'I told you babies don't like me,' she said, trying to poke Ritchie back towards Emma with her knee.

'Just give him a minute,' Emma urged. 'He gets colic. It goes away once he's settled.'

She realized how much she wanted to see someone else apart from her holding Ritchie. Giving him a cuddle. Loving him. It was funny. In the past few weeks, this tiny, pink scrap had managed to sneak his way under her skin in a way she'd never expected. If Joanne would only take him for a minute, then she'd see. But then Ritchie opened his mouth and spewed a long white fountain all over Joanne's pale blue trousers.

'I'm sorry. I'm really sorry.' Emma couldn't stop apologizing.

'It doesn't matter.' Hastily, Joanne lifted the ruined material to hold it away from her leg. 'But maybe you'd better take him back now.'

Emma soothed Ritchie, rocking him on her knee while Joanne sponged the sick off her trousers with a J-cloth and told Emma all about her new job. She and Barry were putting in a new bathroom and knocking though the wall between the kitchen and living-room. She didn't know if she was on her head or her heels these days. Ritchie kept up an uncharacteristic, monotonous wail throughout, which meant that Joanne kept having to raise her voice to be heard. Emma missed most of what she was saying because she had to keep putting Ritchie in different positions to try to settle his tummy.

Once, when he seemed to have gone quiet, she asked, 'Have you . . . do you see Oliver at all?'

'Oliver?' Joanne frowned. 'Now you mention it, Barry hasn't met up with him in a while. I don't think they're working together any more. Oliver must have left the company.'

'Oh.'

Ritchie bawled again, and Emma was forced to turn her attention to him.

'He's not usually like this,' she said with relief when Ritchie had finally stopped howling and fallen asleep, face down across her lap. His nose and mouth rested partly in her hand, filling her palm with warm, wet snuffles and hiccups. 'I shouldn't have woken him. Next time you come over, he'll be all smiles, wait and see.'

'Why don't we meet for a drink some evening instead?' Joanne suggested. 'Somewhere halfway between us both. We can have a proper chat, and it'll be good for you to get a break.'

Emma was startled. 'But what would I do about Ritchie?'

'Oh. Um. Babysitter?'

'He's a bit small,' Emma said doubtfully. 'I don't know if anyone would take him. And babysitters cost such a lot.'

Joanne shrugged. 'Oh, well. When he's big enough, let me know. We can arrange something then.'

★   ★   ★

Emma was surprised that Joanne hadn't commented on the way her hands had trembled when she'd mentioned Oliver's name. Half an hour after Joanne had left, she still hadn't recovered. She managed to drop two spoons and the sugar bowl when she was clearing up the coffee things. From the casual way Joanne had answered Emma's question, she obviously thought that Emma was long over Oliver; but, distracted as she'd been these past few months, no day had passed that she hadn't thought about him.

Because Ritchie looked so like Oliver! Same heavy eyes, same wide mouth built for smiling: everything. Ritchie being born had stirred up all sorts of feelings, all over again. Did Oliver even know that Ritchie was here? The last time she'd spoken to him, she'd told him she wasn't going to go through with the pregnancy. Clearly Joanne, at least, had not informed him otherwise.

Emma yearned to have someone to share

192

Ritchie with. Someone she could turn to and say, 'Oh, look, did you see what he just did?' She had tried so hard to get over the break-up and move on, but with Ritchie there it was impossible; she was looking right at Oliver every day. In the end, the need to talk to him grew too strong to ignore.

It took a while for her to work up the nerve to call him. The first few times she tried, she got as far as dialling the first few digits of his number before hanging up again. The fifth time she did this, she banged the receiver down and ordered herself to get a grip.

'This is your son's father,' she said sternly to herself.

To settle her nerves, she got up and walked around the flat a few times. She pulled the curtains closed across the balcony doors, checked on Ritchie in his pram, wiped a smear off the glass table with a cloth. She even went to the bathroom to brush her hair. Her hair was well past her shoulders now; it was quite a while since she'd been to a hairdresser's. It was a bit thin to have this long. Straggly, she thought. Most days, she tied it back.

When she felt ready, she sat back down at the table and dialled again. The entire number this time. Heart thudding, she put the phone to her ear. Then she heard a woman's voice: 'The customer you are calling is out of range.'

Over the next few days, Emma tried Oliver's number many more times, but each time she got the same out-of-range message. Now she'd made up her mind to call him, the delay in reaching him was frustrating. Had he changed his number? Was he on holiday somewhere?

In the end, she decided to call his sister instead. She'd never spoken to Sasha before, but she had her phone number. Early on in their relationship, she'd copied it from the notice-board in Oliver's kitchen, assuming a time would come one day when they'd all be friends and call each other all the time.

Making the call to Sasha meant having to work up her nerve all over again. It wasn't easy, contacting a complete stranger out of the blue. Although, as Emma reminded herself, Sasha was Ritchie's aunt! Still, though, a stranger.

To ensure some peace and quiet for the conversation, she chose an evening when Ritchie was in good form. She fed him before his bedtime, adding an extra couple of ounces to the bottle to make sure he wouldn't want more again in an hour. He was going through a hungry phase. Ritchie was delighted with the bonus; he sucked on the bottle until his eyes crossed with pleasure and his tummy grew tight and round. Emma patted it with satisfaction. No way would that go down for a while. She got him settled in his cot and pulled the bedroom door so it was just an inch or two open. Then she turned the TV right down, took her diary and the phone to the couch, and dialled Sasha's number.

Brrr-brrr. Somewhere in Birmingham, on a table in a hall, maybe, or in a kitchen, a phone was ringing. Emma cleared her throat. She wondered what Sasha would sound like.

The phone clicked. A woman said, 'Hello?'

194

Emma asked, 'Is this Sasha?'

'Yes, it is.' A brisk, no-nonsense tone. The 't' in 'it' was sharply pronounced.

Emma swallowed. She said, 'My name is Emma Turner.'

She waited, but there was no sign of recognition.

She said, 'Oliver, your brother, may have mentioned me?'

'I'm sorry,' Sasha said, 'but what did you say your name was?'

'Emma. Emma Turner. I used to . . . I used go out with Oliver. A little while ago.'

'Oh. I see.'

Sasha didn't sound all that interested, or friendly. Emma's heart sank but she ploughed on.

'I've been trying to reach him,' she said, 'but his phone doesn't seem to be working.'

'I see,' Sasha said again. 'Well, he's not in the country at the moment. He's gone to Indonesia with his girlfriend.'

So. Oliver was still with Sharmila, and they were travelling together. Emma kept her voice light.

'Do you know when they'll be back?'

'I've no idea,' Sasha said. 'You know Oliver. He doesn't really tell people his plans. But I believe he's taken some time out from work, so they could be gone for a while.'

After a pause, she said, 'Did you want to leave him a message?'

Emma had been trying to decide whether to tell Sasha why she was phoning. She took a breath.

'Yes,' she said. 'I did. I mean, I do. The last time I spoke to Oliver . . . the last time I met him . . . I was pregnant.'

Sasha said nothing.

'I don't know if he told you,' Emma said. 'But anyway, what I was phoning to tell him was that I . . . ' She had to stop to swallow again, but continued, 'I was phoning to tell him . . . I had it.'

Still Sasha didn't respond.

'I had the baby, and it's a boy.' Emma sat up straight. From the bedroom, the faint sound of snuffly breathing.

Still nothing from the phone, though.

'Hello?' Emma took the receiver away from her ear. 'Hello?'

'I can hear you,' Sasha said from a distance. Emma put the phone back to her ear.

'I heard you,' Sasha repeated. 'I'm still here.'

'It must be a shock, I know.'

'No, well, of course. I was just going to say. How wonderful for you.' Sasha added politely, 'If it's what you wanted.'

'Oliver didn't tell you.' Emma fiddled with the cover of her diary.

'No,' Sasha said. 'I'm sorry.'

The diary cover tore. A piece of it came off in Emma's hand.

'All right,' she said. 'All right. Well, now you can see why I need to talk to him.'

'Of course I can,' Sasha said. 'And if I do hear from him, I'll tell him you called.'

Despite her politeness, she seemed to be signalling the end of the conversation. Emma

196

searched hard for some way to continue, to get a rapport going between them, but she couldn't think of anything, and Sasha didn't seem the slightest bit inclined to help her. After her initial surprise, that seemed to be the sum total of her interest in her new nephew. She didn't ask Emma one single thing about the baby. What he looked like, whether he was healthy. Nothing. How reserved she sounded, Emma thought, somewhat shaken, finally putting the phone down after a much shorter conversation than she'd expected. Much more like Oliver than the sparky girl Emma had imagined.

She waited and waited to hear from Oliver, but there was nothing. Maybe Sasha hadn't told him yet. Surely if he knew he had a son he would contact Emma, even if only out of curiosity? It was true that he hadn't wanted Ritchie. She couldn't forget that look of revulsion on his face when she'd stood there in his kitchen and told him she was pregnant. But Ritchie was here now. Emma imagined Oliver getting straight on to a ship or plane when he heard, the news making him realize at last what had been missing from his life. How could all these feelings, still there after so long, be coming only from her side? She missed him so desperately, especially at night; missed having his hand or foot to touch in the dark hours and feel the reassuring connection of another living being.

It was strange, though. When she pictured them together, it was always just the two of them, walking in the sun by the river. Oliver had never been to this drab, cardboard flat, with a baby who cried to be fed. He had never stomped about searching for a clean shirt in the mornings, trying to get ready for work after another bawling, sleepless night. He didn't change nappies that smelled like rotting seaweed. Oliver had not watched Emma retch and vomit during childbirth. He had not seen her ruined stomach and stretched, crinkled skin. Emma couldn't imagine him doing any of those things, and she didn't want him to. She wanted to keep him as he was, and for him to remember her as she'd been. The girl who'd had so much potential; the freedom to be anyone and do anything. When the world was still hers, and she had made no decisions yet which could not be unmade.

After thinking it over for a while, she didn't put Oliver's name on the birth certificate. Let the CSA come after her, or him, for the money. But she wouldn't be the one to force him to be a father if he didn't want to be.

'Looks like it's going to be just you and me, buddy,' she told Ritchie with a heavy heart.

Ritchie studied her gravely from his orange bouncy chair, his bald head making him look like an elderly professor thinking of writing her up for a conference. Young babies were like that, Emma had often thought. Wise. They couldn't move around by themselves so they had to sit where they were put and had nothing to do but observe. What did Ritchie think of her? she wondered. What sort of opinions went through his head when he gazed at her like that? She wanted him to think well of her, but was afraid he could see her for what she really was.

Impoverished single mother. Alone in the world. Loser.

★ ★ ★

Money was tight. Ritchie seemed to grow out of his clothes every week, not to mention the mountain of bottles and nappies he got through every day. By the time Emma had finished buying things for him, there was very little left over for anything else. Even a latte in Starbucks, an old favourite treat, was almost the price of a new Babygro.

To get them out of the flat, she took instead to bringing them both on long walks. It was hard work sometimes, pushing the heavy buggy over kerbs and across busy roads, but the exercise made her feel better afterwards. She set out most days, determined to explore her new neighbourhood, which she hadn't really got to know yet. Fulham was similar in many ways to Clapham. The people on the streets were a mixture of students, families and young professionals, dressed in the coloured shirts and dark, trendy suits that Oliver's City workmates wore.

On the North End Road, Emma discovered a whole street full of market stalls selling cheap household goods, fruit and vegetables; even clothes. The stalls smelled of fresh fish and apples. The stall-owners all seemed to know each other. They gathered in twos and threes to chat, keeping an eye on their own produce, dressed for the outdoors in thick jackets and woollen hats

199

and gloves. Some of the women wore saris. At one stall, Emma found a bright red all-in-one snowsuit for Ritchie for only £2.99. That would do him nicely for the winter.

Though scruffy in parts, the area seemed a friendly enough community. Groups of mothers strolled together and chatted. Children ran ahead, shouting. Some of the families lived in blocks of flats, like Emma's. Others lived on the roads she came to think of as being characteristic of Fulham, with their rows of terraced houses, mainly grey or pale brown brick, with bay windows and pretty, pointed roofs. The nicest streets were the ones off Fulham Palace Road, near the river, or those around Fulham Broadway tube station.

But the really gorgeous houses, the jaw-droppingly beautiful ones, were the ones she saw when she walked along the Fulham Road towards Chelsea. Here, hidden away down quiet side streets, were some of the most magnificent houses Emma had ever seen, more impressive than even the poshest ones she'd seen in Bath. Glowing, red-brick buildings, four or five storeys high, with huge windows; or spotless white mansions, with gleaming black railings, and steps up to pillars and polished doors. Emma stared up at them, wondering what sort of people lived there. She rarely saw anyone. The streets here were so hushed and quiet compared to the cheerful hubbub of Fulham. Once or twice she saw a child walking along with its nanny — or at least, she guessed it was a nanny when the child spoke with a London accent and the woman a foreign one. The school uniforms were bizarre. Some of the children wore quaint 1940s-style outfits: rust-coloured shorts, and brown, sleeveless, V-neck jumpers, like posh versions of the Famous Five. Others flitted about in swingy coats and woollen hats with long bits pointing down the back: woodland elves or pixies in an Enid Blyton story. All very different from the navy skirts and sensible, shapeless, machine-washable anoraks Emma herself had worn to school.

'Well, what did you think?' she asked Ritchie as she turned him around to head for home. 'Would you like a pair of those shorts?'

Ritchie looked bored. He sat scooched down as far as the straps would allow, both feet planted on the step of the buggy. He looked like the bad boy at the back of the class.

'What am I saying?' Emma sighed. 'You'd bully those kids, I suppose.'

★　★　★

Ritchie's teeth came through, turning his cheeks hot and red. When he was cranky, the movement of the buggy soothed him better than anything else. On those days, Emma packed a bottle and a spare nappy for Ritchie, and some water for herself in the netting under the pushchair, and set off for an extra-long walk along the river. She liked Chiswick Mall, with its brooding grey mansions overlooking the water, and cobbled streets and old lamp-posts, like something from a Charles Dickens novel. But the nicest walk was south of the river, heading west towards Barnes. Emma had been amazed when she'd discovered it. It was like having the countryside right in the middle of London. There were fields and fences, and people actually on horses, riding ahead of them through the trees. The track was muddy sometimes, and difficult to steer the buggy through, but it was worth it. The walk tired her out, took away some of the constant, gnawing worry inside. Ritchie leaned back, chewing his teething ring, watching everything in a hypnotized way with his eyes half closed. Now and then he made a lunge to grab at something: a horse clopping past, or a seagull perched on a wall.

Coming home again, there was Hammersmith Bridge, Emma's favourite of all the Thames bridges. When she'd first moved to the city, she'd thought that Hammersmith Bridge was in some way connected to Harrods, because green and gold were the same colours as the Harrods bags. It was worth navigating the gloomy underpass and life-threatening traffic around Hammersmith Broadway just to come down and glimpse the magnificent pointy turrets and lamp-posts against the yellow sky. In the evenings, from this angle, the sun set almost directly behind the bridge. Across the river, Castelnau village, with its old-fashioned shops and restaurants and swans gliding past on the Thames, was another homely slice of the countryside right in the middle of London.

And the walk back north again, across the bridge in the dusk; the lights just coming on in the old houses and pubs along the river making her homesick for some seaside fishing village she'd never known.

⋆ ⋆ ⋆

Sometimes the endless days really got to her. There was only so much walking you could do on your own. She rang Joanne a few times to meet up, but there always seemed to be some excuse. Joanne was in the middle of a vital marketing campaign, or she had to buy new shoes for a sales awards dinner, or Barry had been working himself half to death and needed her by his side.

'I'll come to *you*,' Emma suggested. 'I'll bring Ritchie on the bus. You can show us what you've done with your new flat.'

'That would be great,' Joanne said. 'But the thing is, Barry's here. He's working from home at the moment.'

'So? We won't disturb him.'

'But Ritchie seems to cry a lot. And if he kicks off and Barry gets distracted . . . '

'Joanne.' Emma couldn't be listening to this. 'Barry's a bloody computer technician. Not a heart surgeon. The world won't collapse if he leaves out a decimal point.'

As soon as she'd said that, she realized how dismissive it sounded. But she was hurt by how little interest Joanne seemed to have in her these days, and how rarely she'd bothered to contact Emma since Ritchie had arrived.

'I'm sorry,' she said. 'You know I didn't mean — '

'You never did think much of Barry, did you?' Joanne spoke in a cold voice. 'As I say, Emma, today really doesn't suit us. I'll be in touch.'

★ ★ ★

Emma was sorry she'd made the dig about Barry. She hadn't thought it was that bad, but Joanne was clearly offended and had taken the chance to toss Emma yet another rejection. It hurt, the way she just seemed to have thrown their friendship aside. You did hear about friendships breaking up when one of the women had a baby, but Emma had always assumed that was the new mother's fault, losing all interest in everything apart from her child. She was more than prepared to continue to make the effort with Joanne, but Joanne had a new glamorous life now, with her expensive suits and her promotion, and she didn't seem to want to know. Maybe it was down to Barry's influence. It was true that Barry and Emma had never seen eye to eye. And Barry probably thought even less of Emma now she was a single parent, dumped by Oliver. But that didn't mean Joanne had to completely take his side.

But then, that was Joanne all over. She'd done it before: dropping all her friends the minute a man came along. Emma and Karen hadn't seen her for months one time in Bristol when she'd started seeing a medical student called Andrew. Then Andrew had ended the relationship, and Joanne was back again as if nothing had happened, insisting Emma and Karen come out with her on Friday nights to Corn Street or to a rave in the Carling Academy.

Emma had been really looking forward to catching up with Joanne. To seeing her flat and having a good old natter, maybe even a glass or two of wine. Joanne had said the flat was amazing since they'd got the interior designer in. Barry's building was right on the river, with floor-to-ceiling glass walls. People said how prestigious those flats were, though to be honest, Emma had never seen the attraction. True, the people in the apartments could see right out over the river, but then so could all the people outside see in. She'd passed there one evening a few months ago on her way towards Wandsworth Bridge, and seen a man on the second floor with the lights on, stark naked, examining something in his armpit. But it would have been great to hear all of Joanne's gossip: what people were up to these days, where everyone went for drinks, who was going out with who. Whether anyone had heard from Oliver, or knew where he was. Emma was lonely. It seemed a long time since she'd had a proper chat with someone her own age.

The other thing she really wanted was for Ritchie to have someone to play with. He was getting big and curious now, his face and bald head like a moon or beach-ball, always poking his nose into everything and staring at people, especially other babies and children. Everywhere they went, they passed women with pushchairs. Babies all over the place. Emma had never noticed until she'd had Ritchie how many babies there were in London. It struck her how happy the other mothers all seemed. They beamed as they trundled along, burbling instructions to their offspring: 'Look at the *tree*, darling!' Emma wondered if she should be talking to Ritchie like that. But she couldn't make her voice sound as sunny and natural as theirs. 'Look at the tree' — it just sounded stupid and flat when she said it.

One afternoon, she tried taking Ritchie to Ravenscourt Park. They fed biscuits to a grey squirrel who inched right up to them and snatched the pieces from in front of their feet. He sat there holding a biscuit between his paws, nibbling at it with his squirrel front teeth. Ritchie, panting with enthusiasm, nearly turned himself upside down in Emma's arms to grab at him until finally the squirrel dropped the biscuit, whipped around and streaked off to the trees. Emma put Ritchie back in his pushchair and wheeled him over to the playground, where the other mothers and children were. But Ritchie was too small yet for the brightly coloured swings and bars. He wriggled and cried, looking around for the squirrel. Emma knew he was tired. He was rubbing at his eyes. She left him in the buggy and sat in the chill March air, pushing the buggy backwards and forwards to settle him. The other children ran and climbed and screamed. Finally Ritchie, snug in his red snowsuit, fell asleep as she rocked him.

On the way home, it started to rain. Great, freezing sheets, blowing straight at them from the side. Emma ducked into a café for shelter.

The café was warm, with red, wobbly tables, and salads displayed in tubs behind the glass counter. Ritchie, awake again and in better form, took some juice from his bottle, and sat on happily in his pushchair, chewing at a spoon. Emma drank dark brown tea from a polystyrene cup and flicked through a copy of the *London Lite* that another customer had left behind.

A small boy marched up to Ritchie and poked him in the chest with his finger.

'Hello, baby,' he shouted.

Ritchie opened his mouth. The spoon he'd been chewing fell into his lap. Fascinated, he stared up at the boy. The boy poked him again.

'Hello,' he shouted. 'Hello.'

A woman in a cream and gold headscarf came rushing from a nearby table.

'Jamal,' she scolded, 'don't do that. You might hurt the baby.'

'He's all right,' Emma said, taking in Ritchie's round, thrilled face. 'He didn't mean any harm.'

Ritchie kicked his feet with excitement.

The woman put her arm around the little boy.

'Say hello to the baby in a nice way,' she said.

Jamal looked at Emma and put his finger in his mouth. He pressed his face into his mother's knee.

'Oh, so now you are shy?' The woman patted the child's head. She smiled at Emma. Her eyes were large and dark, beautifully made-up, with mascara and brown smoky liner. Emma tried to smile back, but it was weird: her smile felt stretched and strange. As if her mouth was out of practice.

'They are so full of energy, these boys,' the woman said. 'You will see with your little one when he begins to walk. He will drive his daddy demented. Just like Jamal here.'

The woman was so confident and friendly. Emma wanted to seem interesting back, but all she could think about was what she must look like in her parka jacket and man's woolly jumper, which had seemed like such a good idea for the park in this weather. The other woman was so chic and feminine, in her fitted jeans and short pink jacket.

The woman said to Jamal, 'Shall we have another try at saying hello to the baby?'

Ritchie kicked again and made an excited screeching noise: 'Ah-ha-ha-ha-ha.' Jamal shook his head into his mother's legs. The woman looked at Emma and laughed. She seemed to be waiting for Emma to respond in some way. Emma tried as hard as she could, but she just couldn't think of anything to say. She stared into her cup of tea.

After a few minutes, the woman looked towards the glass door of the café. She said to her little boy, 'Well, Jamal, the rain seems to have stopped now. It looks as if we can go.'

They went back to their table to gather their things.

'Goodbye,' the woman said as they passed Emma's table on the way out.

'Goodbye,' Emma said.

The café door closed. Ritchie stared at it. He had stopped screeching and kicking his legs. His moon face was round with disappointment. For a second Emma had an urge to run out and call Jamal and his mother back. The table where they'd been a moment ago seemed very empty.

★ ★ ★

'If you don't know many people in the area,' the health visitor suggested, 'why don't you see if there's a mother and baby group you can join? You'll find the details in your local library.'

The idea of a mother and baby group didn't appeal all that much to Emma. She was unnerved by the way she'd reacted to the woman in the café, and didn't fancy repeating the experience in front of a load of strangers. She must be going a bit odd. She'd never had any problem meeting people before. But Ritchie had been so thrilled when he'd thought that boy Jamal was going to play with him. He would adore being in a room full of children. For his sake, she would give it a try.

Waiting with Ritchie in his pushchair for the lift, she heard an exclamation behind her: 'Oh, what a beautiful baby.'

Emma turned. A woman with dark eyes and rosy cheeks was staring at Ritchie, her hands clasped. She was wearing jeans and a pink flowery T-shirt. Emma had seen the woman a couple of times, coming in and out of the flat next door.

'What age?' the woman asked, still gazing at Ritchie.

'Eight months,' Emma told her.

The woman opened her eyes wide.

'Only! But so big. I thought he was older. He is the same size as my daughter, but she is one year.'

'I don't think I've seen your daughter,' Emma said politely.

'Oh, no.' The woman shook her head. 'You wouldn't see her. She is back home with my family in the Philippines.'

'Oh . . . um . . . ' Emma didn't know what to say.

'I am working in London,' the woman explained. 'I am a nurse in the hospital. Chelsea and Westminster. But it's better for my daughter to be at home. She can be with my mother while my husband and I are working.' She sounded wistful. 'I have not seen her for four months. Only photographs.'

'That must be difficult.' Emma was shocked. She'd thought *she* was badly off. How desperate must this woman be, to come here and leave her daughter thousands of miles away to be brought up by someone else?

'It is hard,' the woman agreed. 'But this is the best way for our family. My mother loves having her, and with the money, my daughter will have a good life in the future.'

Shyly, she addressed Ritchie: 'What is your name?'

'Ritchie,' Emma answered for him.

'Well, Ritchie, I am Rosina Alcarez. I live right next door to you. Maybe you could call to visit me sometime? You can remind me of my daughter.'

Rosina Alcarez smiled at them both as she left

the lift. Emma smiled back. Rosina seemed nice, and about her age. And how sad for her not to have her daughter with her. Maybe she *would* take Ritchie over to see her.

All the same, for some reason, she felt very flat as she wheeled the buggy away.

On her way to the library, she found herself waiting at a crossing with two other women, one a girl in her twenties, with her long hair in a plait, the other an older lady in a pleated skirt and puffy jacket. Between the women, in a pram, snoozed a tiny, wrinkly baby, wrapped like a birthday present in a blanket with little pink hearts on it.

'Let me take Lucy for a while,' the older woman urged the younger. 'Give you a chance to get some of your shopping done in peace.'

'Do you mind, Mum?' The girl's face lit up.

'Of course not.' The older woman stroked the baby's cheek in a longing way. 'The two of us will go for a little potter. We'll have a lovely time.'

Emma couldn't take her eyes off the three of them. Would her own mother have been like that if she had lived? Then the girl lifted a hand to push back her hair and Emma saw something flash on her finger. A wedding ring. So the girl had a husband as well. Someone who would be thinking about her during the day and who'd rush home in the evening to see her and their baby. He'd bounce the child on his knee while the girl told him about their day. Her mother would wag her finger at him and say, 'You look after my two darlings now, do you hear?' And he would say, 'Oh, I will, don't worry, because I love them as much as you do.'

In the library, Emma stood for a while reading the noticeboard, checking to see if there was anything for her and Ritchie. Sheets of paper, anchored by thumb-tacks, fluttered in the breeze from the door. Book clubs. Art tours to Florence. A geology trip to Scotland. Finally, near the bottom of the board, Emma spotted what she was looking for. A mother and toddler music morning. Right here in the library. That sounded good. Then she read further. Oh. The child had to be over one year to join.

Emma sighed. It was probably for the best. She hadn't been at all sure about the notion of sitting in a draughty hall, listening to a load of women blither on about their families and how they'd all gone to Kew Gardens together at the weekend. Maybe having met Rosina Alcarez was enough for one day. She'd leave it at that for now, and get something to read and go home.

She pushed the buggy past the noticeboard and went to the shelves. She picked out a couple of novels, easy ones she'd read before, and a squashy waterproof book for Ritchie who liked turning the pages in the bath. She was bringing the books over to the counter when she spotted a woman talking to a group of people under the window. She stopped.

The library was dark. It was getting to that time of day just before the lights came on. The sky outside the windows was pale grey, silhouetting the woman's shoulder-length hair and slim figure. She had her back to Emma, but Emma had the strangest sense of how like her mother this woman was. She stood there, staring in the aisle, between the high shelves filled with encyclopaediae. The way the woman stood. The way she moved her hands when she spoke. The feeling became very strong: that if this woman turned around it would be Emma's mother, and when she saw Emma and Ritchie she would smile with pleasure.

'What are you *doing* here?' she would say. 'It's so wonderful to see you.'

She would leave the people she was with, and come to take Emma's hand.

'This is my daughter and grandson,' she would say, her voice filled with pride. 'What are you doing now, Emma? Why don't we go somewhere, just the three of us, and have lunch together?'

Emma squeezed the handles of the buggy. The grey from the windows was getting very bright. And then the woman turned, and it was a different face, and the grey light went dark.

Emma's mum would never have been chatting and smiling in a group like that anyway. Emma's mum was always alone.

★   ★   ★

Ritchie got temperatures; he spat up his food; his poo went a funny colour. Emma worried constantly that she was doing something wrong, missing something, and there was no one to tell her.

'All new mothers worry,' her new GP, Dr Stanford, reassured her. 'He's growing very nicely. Putting on plenty of weight.'

Yes, he was. He was putting on weight. He could see. He could hear. He was starting to crawl now. But there were all the things that Emma could not ask.

Is he happy? Does he smile enough? Are we alone too much? Should he see more people?

Do I love him enough?

Because sometimes, just lately, the thought had been coming into her mind.

What if Ritchie just . . . wasn't there?

Sunday, 24 September
Day Eight

The blue and white sign leaning into the hedge read: *Bienvenue à St-Bourdain*.

Rafe pulled the car over to the side of the road. Stones crackled under the tyres. He turned the key and the engine went dead.

'There it is,' he said. 'The directions said to look for the first set of gates after the sign. I'm pretty sure that's the place.'

Emma pulled herself forward in her seat to stare.

Long shadows lay over the fields. Across the road and up a little way stood a pair of yellow stone pillars with high iron gates. Through the gates, a driveway curved up a hill. At the top of the hill, the reddish roof of a house was just visible through heavy branches. The grass on the sloping front lawn was uneven and ankle-high; some weeds, not many but a few, poked through the centre of the driveway.

'Garden's a mess,' Rafe observed. 'Looks like they've been away for a while.'

The garden might have been a mess, but it was still beautiful. The grounds were rich with trees, swaying in the faint breeze. Piles of chopped logs glowed against a wall. Just inside the gates, a cat lay on its side in the sun. Geese ran and ducked under the trees. Emma made her breath come slow and steady. She had to be calm now.

She opened her door and climbed out of the car. Summery, croaky sounds came from the fields. Rafe got out as well, and made a sign for Emma to close her door as quietly as possible. He came around the front of the car to stand beside her.

'What do you want to do?' he asked in a low voice.

'I don't know.'

'Let's just take our time,' he said. 'Let's just think about this for a minute. We don't know what they might — '

Then he took a quick, backwards step.

'People,' he hissed, ducking and putting out his hand. Emma ducked too, automatically, before looking up again towards the house to see.

On the driveway, several people had appeared, walking down to the gate.

'Careful,' Rafe warned, as Emma took a step forward. 'Come back a bit.'

'We're too far away. They won't look this way.'

Now she could make the people out. First came an older couple, tanned and grey-haired. Then a younger man, and a woman in a

215

cream-coloured top and trousers. Halfway down the drive, they all stopped. They gathered in a circle around the cream-coloured woman.

The woman was Antonia all right. No doubt about it. Her hair was darker than Emma remembered from Mr Bap's, but of course she'd dyed it for the airport. The rest of her was the same. The beige clothes; the brisk, straight-backed walk.

And in her arms, the little boy, his ears sticking out, his hair a light halo in the sun. The roundness of his head made Emma still with longing. Briefly, Antonia tilted her head to let the older woman kiss the child, then she pulled him back to her, closer than before. The love and tenderness were hard to witness. The child, dressed in a white T-shirt and red shorts, held his finger in his mouth and gazed at the geese under the trees.

'Is it him?' Rafe asked.

'Yes.'

She cried softly, putting her fingers to her nose, trying to sniff as quietly as she could.

She wasn't aware she'd moved forward again until she felt Rafe touch her arm.

'Don't,' he warned. 'Don't let them see you.'

'What, then?' she said through her teeth. 'What do I do?'

'Hang on.' Rafe had his mobile in his hand. He squinted at the screen, tapping a number with his thumb.

'Hello?' he said into the phone. 'Hello?'

The older couple were walking again, down the driveway to the gates. Antonia, however, was

216

turning back towards the top of the hill. In another minute, Ritchie would be out of sight. The swaying trees would surround him and he'd be gone.

'Ritchie,' Emma cried.

Rafe's hand tightened on her arm.

'Let me go.' She pulled against him. And then, in sudden panic, not caring who heard, she began to scream, 'Ritchie. Ritchie.'

Rafe's hand was slipping but still he tried to pull her back. Up till then he'd been calm, but Emma's anguish was clearly unnerving him. His phone clattered to the road. Swearing, he bent to retrieve it, and Emma freed herself from his grip.

'Emma,' Rafe called, as she started across the road.

She heard his footsteps as he started after her; but then someone must have answered his phone because he stopped again to speak into it.

'Police,' he said desperately. 'Please. Help us.'

12

Dusk had turned everything from green and gold to blue by the time the car turned into a stony courtyard set back from the road. The buildings in the courtyard looked older and darker than the other buildings in the town. Long windows gleamed in the headlights.

'What's this?' Agitated, Emma sat up in the back of the car. 'Why are we stopping?'

'This must be the Consulate.' Rafe peered up at the grey walls. 'This is where that British bloke said he'd meet us.'

'But,' Emma was confused, 'I thought we were going back to the house. I thought we were going back to get Ritchie.'

Rafe said gently, 'We can't, Emma. Not right now. Those people called the police at the same time we did. Remember? They wouldn't let us stay there.'

Emma did remember. Bits of it anyway. Ritchie in his shorts, with his finger in his mouth. That part was very clear. Much of the rest of it was a blur. She remembered pulling away from Rafe, running across the road and through the gates, pounding up the driveway towards Ritchie. The people ahead of her were running as well. In a second, they were around the trees and out of sight. Emma followed them grimly. She rounded the trees, and came to a large house. The people from the driveway were

218

all piling in the front door. Emma reached it just as the last person was about to enter. He was the man who had been with Antonia on the drive, a tallish person, mid-forties, with curly brown hair. It struck Emma that he seemed to be moving slower than the others on purpose, glancing behind him, as if waiting for her. She flung herself at the door, trying to push her way through, but the man held it and wouldn't let her past.

'Get out of my way,' Emma yelled at him.

She looked into his face, and saw that he was looking back at her. Emma held his gaze.

'Please,' she said. 'Please. You have my little boy.'

The man hesitated.

'I'm sorry,' he said, and closed the door.

Emma kicked at the door, and banged it with her fists. She didn't need to remember that part now to know it had happened. The sides of her hands were swollen and sore. Her throat was sore as well, and rough; she must have been shouting. You would shout, if you were banging on a door. At some point, she remembered, she had spotted a rock in a flower bed, and stopped banging to go and pick it up. She flung the rock at a window. It smashed straight through one of the top panes; she hadn't thought a window would be so easy to break. The broken pane was too high to reach, but she'd got the idea now. She started looking around for more rocks. Then there came the sound of car engines, and skidding tyres. Doors slammed. Men in round hats surrounded her, all shouting in French.

At first, Emma thought the men were on her

side. These were the police, surely, and Rafe had called them; they'd come here to help. But the men did not look or sound in any way friendly. They shouted again, pointing at the house, then at their dark cars under the trees. If they spoke English, they made no attempt to make themselves understood. Then Emma saw the guns, huge, heavy pistols in holsters at their belts, and her insides shrank.

Rafe and one of the men were arguing. They looked exactly alike, fierce and lean, standing over each other, gesticulating and stabbing at the air. They were speaking in different languages, but Rafe must have managed to get his point across because after a minute the other man put his hands up. He stood back, watching, as Rafe came and spoke to Emma.

'They want us to come to the station,' he said. 'They won't arrest us if we leave now.'

'Arrest us?' Emma was incredulous. 'Why would they want to arrest us?'

'The Hunts could have us charged with trespass,' Rafe said. 'Or even breaking and entering, since you tried to force your way into their house.'

'But don't they know?' Emma cried. 'Don't they know why I'm trying to get in there? My son is there. I'm not leaving without him.'

She tried to run back to the house, but the fierce-eyed policeman blocked her way. Rafe took her hand.

'You don't have a choice here,' he said urgently. 'If you don't leave voluntarily, they'll drag you off.'

Emma looked at the guns again. Black and

oily in their belts. She'd never seen a real one, and here they were, all around her. Guns! With Ritchie only a few feet away. These policemen made her afraid. They didn't look anything like the British street bobbies you saw in London, polite men and women in checked hats and bright yellow jackets. These men looked like soldiers, tough and angry, as if they were used to living in the mountains, hunting animals for food, with knives between their teeth.

'These aren't people to mess with,' Rafe agreed. 'The quicker we go with them, the quicker we can find someone who speaks English. Get the British Consulate involved. They'll help us sort this out.'

The next thing Emma remembered was being in a car, twisting and turning on the darkening roads. In a cream-coloured building, a man in a checked shirt approached them and said in English to come with him in another car — Emma thought, back to the Hunts' house.

But instead, here they were at this Consulate place.

She climbed out of the car. The grey buildings surrounded them in a threatening U. Rafe was on the cobbles, talking to the check-shirted driver. Emma had a strong sense of unease.

What was she doing here? Why had she let these men take her away from the place where Ritchie was?

She followed Rafe and the driver up some steps and through an arched door. In a high hall, their heels echoed on the tiles: *plunk-plink-plunk*, like drops falling into a well.

'Wait, please,' the check-shirted man said, and disappeared.

The hall was cold. A bare, too-bright bulb hung from the ceiling, driving stark, black shadows into the corners. Heavy pictures hung on the walls, of elderly men with beards and sneering eyes. And what was that thing, over there in the alcove? Emma stared up at it. A life-sized statue, a robed, marble woman with hollow eyes, crouching over a baby in her lap. The marble-woman's face was shadowed, the bones sharp above sunken cheeks. The jutting brow emphasized the expression of malice. The baby stared up at her in fear. The woman's hand was lifted as if to strike it.

'Hello!'

Emma spun around.

'Brian Hodgkiss,' the breathless, red-cheeked young man said, coming forward from the back of the hall. He had a hand raised in salute. 'Duty Officer. I cover the Consulate out of hours, for emergencies. I believe you're in a bit of a situation.'

'Yes.' Emma stepped to meet him. 'Yes, I am. I want my son back, and I want him tonight.'

'I understand,' Mr Hodgkiss said. He looked worried. 'I'm aware of your story, and I sympathize. The trouble is, the family say that this isn't your child.'

'Yes, he is.' Emma made her voice sound as hard as possible.

Mr Hodgkiss gave a cough.

'I've just been talking to a Detective Inspector Hill, in London,' he said. 'I believe the identification of the child — '

'The identification is not in question,' Emma snapped. 'I saw him myself less than an hour ago.'

'I'm not disputing that.' Mr Hodgkiss lifted his hands, then lowered them through the air, as though smoothing a duvet. 'Not disputing it at all. However, according to the police, you shouldn't have been there in the first place. The family would be within their rights to charge you with trespass.'

'What else was I supposed to do?' Emma whimpered.

Beside her, Rafe touched her arm.

'Isn't there some way we can sort this out?' he asked. 'You can see this problem isn't going to just go away.'

Mr Hodgkiss turned to him, plainly happy to have someone rational to talk to.

'You have to understand,' he said. 'We're seeing both sides of the story here. The child's family has also contacted us for assistance. Incidentally,' he glanced again at Emma, 'they are very sympathetic to your plight. Mrs Hunt, especially, would like it passed on to you how much she feels for you, missing your child, but — '

'She's lying,' Emma shouted. How could any woman be so brazen? 'She knows perfectly well why my child is missing. She took him, the lying cow.'

'Excuse me,' Rafe said. 'What about a DNA test?'

There was a silence.

Rafe said, 'It seems to me that that would sort the problem out once and for all.'

Emma was too wound-up to speak. A DNA test! Why hadn't she thought of that herself? It was by far and away the most obvious way to sort out this whole mess. She looked at Brian. He wiped his forehead with the back of his hand.

'Well, yes,' he said. 'Yes, I suppose it would.'

'So how do we organize one then?' Emma demanded.

'I'm not a lawyer,' Brian Hodgkiss said, 'so I can't say for definite. But I'd imagine it would depend on whether or not the Hunts agreed.'

'And if they don't?'

'In that case, I'm not sure you could make them.'

'What do you mean, we couldn't make them?' Emma said angrily. 'Why *wouldn't* anyone make them? Why would you believe them and not us?'

'It really isn't up to me,' Brian said. 'My advice to you would be to come back to the Consulate first thing in the morning and we'll put you in touch with an English-speaking lawyer. In the meantime,' he felt in his pocket and pulled out a card, 'if you need a bed for the night, here are a couple of numbers you can — '

'A bed for the night?' Emma exploded. 'Are you mad? Do you think I'm going to go to bed while Ritchie is still in that house with those people? You must be absolutely off your head.'

Brian Hodgkiss heard her out in polite silence. When she had finished, he said, 'That's up to you, Ms Turner.' When she still didn't take the card he was offering, he added, 'I would say to

224

you, though, that if you go back to the Hunts' house, you could find yourself charged with trespass or harassment. In that case, there would be nothing the Consulate could do to help you.'

His coldness bewildered Emma.

'They've told you, haven't they?' she said.

'Who?'

'The police in England. They told you what Dr Stanford said. That's why you won't help me.'

'Ms Turner, I really have no idea what you're talking about.'

She stared at him, unsure whether to believe what he was saying.

'Now,' Brian said, 'although I'd prefer not to have to get the police back here tonight, I really —'

Rafe had stepped forward. 'I'll take the card,' he said, holding his hand out.

Brian, looking relieved, gave the card to him.

'Speak to the lawyer, all right?' he said in a confidential, man-to-man way. 'Come back here in the morning. About nine should do it.'

'We will,' Rafe said shortly.

'Well, then. Goodnight.'

Brian held the door open. Emma was so stunned that she found herself walking back outside and down the steps into the courtyard. She couldn't believe it. They'd come here for help, and been thrown out, like a pair of drunks from a pub. This had to be a joke. Surely Brian Hodgkiss couldn't be their only contact with the British Embassy in France? There had to be someone else there they could call, someone who'd have a better grasp of what to do.

'What now?' she asked Rafe. 'What do we do?'

'I don't know.' He stood on the steps, holding Brian Hodgkiss's card, looking more uncertain than she'd seen him. 'Maybe we should wait and speak to that lawyer in the morning?'

'In the *morning*?' What was the matter with him? 'The Hunts will be gone in the morning. They'll take Ritchie and escape. They're probably leaving right now.' Emma began to panic again. 'Why did we leave him there? I was right beside him. He was right there. *Right there*, and I *left* him. Jesus! We need to go back there. Right now.'

Rafe tried to say something but she swung away from him. She'd take the car and . . . but no, she couldn't, where was it? The hire car was still at the Hunts' house! Oh God, what was she going to do? Not a single car had passed on the road. The entire town was shut down, hardly a light to be seen. She didn't even know any French numbers to call on her mobile. Taxis. Directory enquiries. Nothing.

Somewhere nearby, a door closed. A soft click, but it echoed off the walls. Brian Hodgkiss appeared, zipping up the top of a brown leather bag. His shoes scraped on the cobbles. He walked past without seeing them. Emma watched him as he headed for the road, his jacket swinging on his arm, the brown bag bumping up and down on his shoulder.

Then she began to run.

'Wait.'

She couldn't let him go. Useless as he was, he was all they had.

'Wait,' she called again.

Brian turned, his posture wary. His elbows pointed stiffly outwards, as if for protection. The moonlight gleamed on his cheeks, his nose, his forehead, and on the stones. Emma reached him, wrenching her backpack from her shoulder.

'Look,' she said, pulling at the flap with trembling hands, 'I've got pictures of Ritchie.' She rummaged in the backpack for the envelope she'd brought. 'See?' She tore one of the photographs out of the envelope and shoved it towards Brian's face.

'You tell the French police to compare that child with these photos. You'll see if you look at them, it's my son. They have to do that DNA test. They *have* to. You have to make them.'

Brian tried to slide his eyes from the picture of Ritchie in his pyjamas, his hair brushed to one side in the comical comb-over that made him look like a tiny mogul, but Emma kept after him, following his head with it until he was forced to look.

'I've told you,' he said. 'I can't influence what the police do. I have no legal powers here.'

'Is that all you can say?' Enraged, Emma shook the photo at him. 'Everything we say to you, your answer is: 'I'm not a lawyer. I'm not a lawyer.' Is that the only thing you're able to — '

Behind her, Rafe cleared his throat.

'Mr Hodgkiss,' he said, 'do you have children?'

'I'm sorry?'

'Do you have children?'

Mr Hodgkiss raised an eyebrow. 'As it happens, I do, but — '

'What ages are they?'

227

Mr Hodgkiss hesitated.

'Two and four.'

'And would you recognize them?' Rafe asked. 'If someone took them, and said they were theirs? Would you still recognize them as your own children?'

Brian Hodgkiss licked his lips. His T-zone shone with perspiration. His hair was thin and far back on his forehead. Despite the baldness he looked very young — more like a schoolboy himself than a father of two. He didn't look as pompous as he had in the stately Consulate hall. Here in the night, with just the three of them, he seemed like a good person. Earnest. As if he wanted to do the right thing.

'Look,' he said. 'The thing is, one of our staff here at the Consulate is actually a good friend of the family's GP. A Dr Ridgeway, I believe.'

'And that puts the Hunts above suspicion?' Rafe said impatiently.

'No, of course not. Of course it doesn't. But Dr Ridgeway has lived here for over twenty years, and is extremely well known and respected in the area. He's a Brit himself, so of course takes a keen interest in all of our ex-pats. And there were certain issues with this particular family . . . ' He paused.

Then he said, 'Perhaps I shouldn't tell you this. But I don't see the harm. Everyone in the area knows about it. Apparently, the Hunts' child was very ill as a baby. A genetic condition, I believe. The lining on his nerves, or some such. He was seen by all kinds of specialists — the parents stopped at nothing, you can imagine

— and Dr Ridgeway looked after him whenever he was here in France. So you can see how he ended up getting to know the family, and their child, extremely well.'

'So you're telling us their kid is sick?' Rafe said. 'Because I have to say, I'm no doctor myself, but he looked pretty healthy to me.'

'Well,' Mr Hodgkiss said, 'it's interesting because, what happened was, the Hunts got to hear about a new treatment in India. Some spiritual cure or other; I don't know all the details. Anyway, Dr Ridgeway thought it wouldn't help, and he wasn't keen for them to go there, but they'd tried everything else, so in the end they took him over there for a few months, and . . . well.' He spread his hands. 'It worked. The child was cured.'

Emma said in despair, 'But that's a different child we're talking about. The child I saw today — the one they have with them in the house right now — is *my* child.'

'Ms Turner — '

Emma cried to Rafe: 'Let's go back. We're wasting our time here. I should have taken him while I had the chance.'

She turned to the road.

'They'll take him away,' she whimpered. What was she doing here? What in God's name had possessed her to allow Ritchie out of her sight for one second once she had found him?

The sound of a mobile phone ringing. Brian's voice: 'Hello?'

Emma kept going. Blimmin' ignorance of him, taking a phone call at a time like this. Then Brian said in a loud voice, 'What?'

What now? Emma half-turned. Brian put his hand up to her, a sharp *wait-there* gesture.

'That's incredible,' he said into the phone. 'Yes. I think they will. In fact, we've just been discussing . . . yes, yes. I'll get back to you.'

He snapped shut his phone.

'*Well!*' he said. His cheeks glowed. His expression was transformed. He was a smiley, jovial Santa Claus now, with a lovely surprise for them both.

Rafe and Emma stared at him.

'That was Philippa Hunt,' Brian explained. 'As I've already mentioned, the Hunts are very sympathetic to your plight. They want to help, if only by ruling themselves out of this situation and allowing you to concentrate on other avenues.'

Rafe asked: 'What does that mean, exactly?'

Brian swelled out his chest. He said: 'Mrs Hunt has volunteered to do a DNA test.'

★ ★ ★

The guesthouse Brian Hodgkiss directed them to for the night was just around the corner, part of a terrace on a side street. The windows were dark, but Rafe and Emma were plainly expected. As they reached the house, the door creaked open to reveal a very wide, elderly woman in a flowery buttoned-up coat.

'Ssh.' The woman put her finger to her lips. Then she beckoned the two of them into a dim, biscuit-smelling hall and closed and bolted the door behind them. Still flapping her hand at them to be quiet, she led them up a flight of stairs with a brown patterned runner carpet. At the top, she opened a door to the right and pressed a switch on the wall.

They all blinked at the gigantic, four-foot-high bed taking up most of the room, covered with a glistening pink counterpane, like a giant tongue.

'*Voilà*,' the woman said complacently.

Emma was too dazed to say anything.

'This room,' Rafe said in an awkward way. 'It is for . . . ' He pointed at himself and Emma. 'For both of us?'

The woman looked shocked. She tutted and shook her head.

'*Deux chambres*,' she said, raising two fingers. She crossed the room and pushed open a second door. Emma caught the gleam of tiling, a white bath and sink. Beyond the bath, yet another doorway led to a room on the opposite side.

'Ah,' Rafe said. '*Merci*.'

The woman nodded, pointed to some folded towels on a chair, and left.

Still dazed, Emma sank on to the edge of the bed.

'How accurate is the DNA test?' she asked.

Rafe said, 'As far as I know, pretty accurate.'

'It can't give a false result and show he's someone else's child if he's not?'

'No.'

She absorbed this.

'How will they do it? Will they have to stick something into Ritchie?'

'I don't think so. No. They'll just use a swab to

231

take some saliva from his mouth.'

'Who will?'

'A doctor. Or a nurse. It'll be the same for the Hunts. They'll take all the samples at the same time, and send them off to the lab together to see if they match.'

'As simple as that,' Emma said. She had a shaky sense of having pulled back, just in time, from a steep fall to a drop miles below. It was hard to grasp. How nearly all of this — finding Ritchie again, getting this test organized — might never have happened. How close she had come to never getting him back.

'Thank God,' she said. 'Thank God we came here. They'd never have done this otherwise.'

Rafe didn't reply.

'What?' Emma asked. 'What's wrong?'

Rafe said slowly, 'Why do you think they've agreed to do the test?'

Emma frowned. On the wall across from her was a framed painting of a horse and foal, noses touching, standing together in a stable yard.

'I don't know,' she said. 'Maybe they feel remorse?' She remembered how the man had said 'sorry' to her before he closed the door in her face.

'Or maybe they don't know how conclusive the test is,' she said. 'I don't know. All I do know is, if they do it and it really is as accurate as you say, then it will show he isn't theirs.'

Rafe nodded.

'Won't it?' Suddenly she was less sure. 'What do *you* think? You think while we're all sitting around waiting for the test to happen, they'll run off without any of us suspecting?'

She jumped up off the bed.

'Oh, God. We should go back. We should go back and watch the house.'

Rafe said, 'Brian Hodgkiss called the house again, and the police were still there. He doesn't think the Hunts are going anywhere tonight.'

'And you believe him?'

'Why would he lie?'

'Because he's not on our side. He doesn't believe Ritchie is mine.'

'Emma.' Rafe tried to calm her. 'He doesn't know who to believe. He's just doing his job.' He scratched his head, looking annoyed with himself. 'I wish I hadn't said anything now. I don't know why I had to go mouthing off like that. All I can tell you is, if we go back there and the Hunts see us, they might change their minds about doing that test.'

Change their minds! Emma went still.

'You look exhausted.' Rafe touched her hand. 'Try to get some sleep. Look.' He pointed at the window. 'Nearly dawn. They'll be doing the test in a couple of hours. There's nothing else we can do for now.'

When he had gone, Emma eyed the lurid pink bed. Try to get some sleep! She might as well try to swim the Atlantic. Instead, she unpacked Gribbit from the side pocket in her bag. He was all crumpled, his legs twisted in different directions. Emma smoothed him out. Then she stood there, holding him to her face. The pain of it; she was struck with it all over again. She'd never felt Ritchie's loss getting any easier, but somewhere along the line she must have got used to it because now it suddenly seemed a thousand times worse. Her need for him was so acute, after being so close to him she could have touched him. His little yellow head; she missed him so much. Should she be doing this? Just waiting here in this room, while Ritchie was still down the road with those people? It seemed strange. To have him so near and not go to him; it seemed wrong. If only she knew the right way to act. If only an arrow of some kind would appear, pointing and saying to her: this is what you do. No matter how hard it was, she wouldn't hesitate for a second. Should she go back to the house by herself? Sit outside and make sure they didn't try to take Ritchie anywhere? Smash down a door or a window and take him, and refuse to let him go?

Restless, she took Gribbit to the window. No cars outside. No lights anywhere, apart from her own. Just low buildings, huddled under the moon. The scene could have been from any time, a hundred, two hundred years ago. Several times, she stooped to put her shoes back on, then changed her mind and took them off again. If she went there, and they cancelled the DNA test . . . In the end, exhausted, she gave up. She took her shoes off for the final time, turned off the light and crawled in beneath the slippery bedcover, not bothering to pull back the woollen blanket underneath. She lay there with Gribbit, little needles poking at her head. Then she sat up again, bunching the pillows up into a heap behind her back. She curled her arms around her knees. Her eyes were too stretched, too wide and dry for sleep. The heavy curtains were not completely closed. A faint light shone between them.

Ritchie had looked so well. So small and sweet and beautiful. No wonder Antonia had held him so closely, protecting him even from the members of her own family. He'd looked well fed, well cared for. Even from a distance, she'd seen that the clothes he was wearing were new and expensive. You could see that he wasn't being tortured. He wasn't suffering. Seeing it was like the loosening of a weight or a claw inside of her, the first real relief she'd had since all of this had started.

From the hall, the slow, heartbeat tick of a clock.

Did he miss her? Did he think about her at all?

You loved small children so much, more than you could ever think possible. But it was different for them. They lived from day to day. They forgot things the way adults never did. And of course Ritchie would be busy. So many people, all wanting to hold him and love him.

And such a beautiful house. It really was, such a beautiful place. A place that caught at your throat. The geese under the trees. The cat in the sun. The fields with their dark corn crops, as high as giants.

Imagine being a little boy and growing up there.

The moon had faded. Pale light filtered between the curtains. Emma put the pillows down and rolled on to her side. The roll of barbed wire in her middle had gone. In its place, a raw, scraped hollow.

13

Monday, 25 September
Day Nine

First thing in the morning, Emma was on the phone to Brian Hodgkiss.

'They're still there, aren't they?' she asked as soon as he answered. 'They haven't taken Ritchie anywhere?'

'They're still there,' Brian placated. 'I spoke to Mrs Hunt not five minutes ago.'

Emma's grip loosened on the receiver. She had no idea why the Hunts were being so cooperative, but as long as they were, that was fine by her.

'When is the test being done?' she asked.

Brian said, 'This morning. Mrs Hunt is bringing Ritchie to their GP's surgery at ten. Mr Hunt is refusing to be tested. He doesn't see that it's necessary. But that shouldn't affect us because even though, strictly speaking, the test should be done with both parents, for our purposes all we need is the maternal — '

Emma interrupted him: 'How long before we get the result?'

'Twenty-four hours, at a minimum. If we can get the lab to prioritize it.'

'And you're absolutely sure they're not going to take him and run off in the meantime?'

In a very patient voice, Brian said, 'It's extremely unlikely. One of our staff here is going to check in regularly with them until the DNA result comes back. The Hunts don't have a problem with it. I'm sure that should set your mind at rest.'

Emma couldn't think of anything else to say.

Brian asked, 'Could I speak to Mr Townsend, please?'

While Rafe was on the phone, Brian's voice came tinnily through the receiver. Emma could hear everything he was saying.

'You know, she can't go near them,' he warned Rafe. 'Certainly not in that state. She'll be arrested if she harasses them again. The Hunts are frightened for the child. It was they who asked if we could keep an eye on them until the test is done, and to be honest, I can't blame them.'

'I see.'

'So, for her sake as well as theirs, keep her away from them until the DNA result is back.'

Rafe said, 'I will.'

★ ★ ★

Someone had brought their hire car back to Bergerac from St-Bourdain and left it parked in front of the B&B. Rafe suggested they go for a drive. He turned off the main road and took the smaller side routes, driving at random, anywhere to keep moving. The morning was lemon fresh; the roads, though narrowing in places to barely a single lane, were clear of cars. Castles on the hillside poked their turrets through the treetops, like towers in a fairytale.

'What do you think's happening now?' Emma asked for the fifteenth time.

Rafe glanced at the clock on the dash.

'Just gone ten,' he said. 'They're probably taking the swabs now.'

Emma wondered what Ritchie would think of it all. He didn't like doctors one bit. The day she had taken him in to have Dr Stanford look at his ears, he'd flattened himself into her like an octopus, highly suspicious, knowing full well there was something funny going on. Just the torch shining near his face was enough to make him howl. She could picture him now, recoiling from having his mouth swabbed, trying to reach out and grab the thing they did it with.

'He loves sour things,' she said, out of nowhere. 'Slices of lemon. Things like that. Even though they make him scrunch up his face, he insists on eating them.'

'Bloody men.' Rafe grinned at her. 'Do we ever learn?'

'He *is*,' Emma insisted. 'He's a real little man. You'll see when you meet him. Once he caught his finger in the door, and even though the nail went blue he didn't cry at all. He just crawled over, and made a face and held it up to show me. And he's been learning how to kick a ball. He's nearly got it. You just have to hold his other leg down.'

She couldn't stop talking. What were they all doing now? Had the test been done? Had the doctor been nice to Ritchie?

After a while, her voice ran out, and she and Rafe drove in silence. They passed more

238

vineyards, then along a road lined on either side by a row of tall trees whose tops met in the middle. The car was filled with light, then shade, then light again. Light, shade, light . . . The next thing Emma knew, her mouth had a dry, bitter taste, and she was slumped to the right, her forehead bumping against the window.

Startled, she sat up. Her neck was stiff. The view from the windscreen had changed. They were on a much bigger road, a motorway, crawling with cars and long, rumbling trucks. Rafe, concentrating on the busy lanes, was squinting in the hard, bright light from the sky.

'Was I asleep?' Emma asked.

Rafe grinned, keeping his eyes on the huge, padlocked lorry in front.

'Just a quick nap,' he said.

Emma was astonished. She hadn't even known that she was tired. The clock on the dashboard read eleven thirty. She rubbed the side of her neck.

'Where are we?' she asked.

'Just approaching Bordeaux.' Rafe nodded at a green road sign. He glanced at Emma. 'What should we do? Take a break, or keep going?'

'Keep going, if you can.' Emma wasn't in the mood to visit a large city.

Rafe nodded. At the next roundabout, he took an exit away from the signs for Bordeaux. Gradually, the traffic began to ease. The number of trucks decreased, though they were still surrounded by plenty of cars. Tall trees crowded the edges of the road, a change of scene from all the fields and vineyards. The sun was very strong now. The temperature in the car was beginning to rise.

Emma, fully awake again, was thinking hard. Maybe whatever she'd been dreaming about had set her off, but something was bothering her. In Mr Bap's café, Antonia had said she'd had a child. A little boy. Later, Emma had assumed she must have been lying about that. But now, from what Brian Hodgkiss had said, it seemed as if Antonia did have a child after all. But where was he? According to the CCTV tape from the airport, the only child the Hunts had brought with them from London was Ritchie. And yesterday as well, on their driveway, Ritchie had been the only child in sight. If the Hunts did have a child of their own, then what on earth had they done with him?

At a T-junction, Rafe had to stop the car. Ahead of them, a tractor pulling a trailer with some kind of machinery on it was trying to make a right turn around a high stone wall. The young male passenger had got out on to the road to help the driver. The sun beat down. With no movement to keep things cool, the temperature in the car rose further. The air coming through the windows was dry and dusty. Below the high wall, a sharp, black line on the road marked the division between light and shade.

Emma frowned. Why *were* the Hunts doing this DNA test? It was weird, weird, weird. Rafe had commented last night on how odd it was, and he was right. It made no sense, to steal a baby and then keep on hanging around, even after the police had twice been to the house.

240

Antonia must have brought Ritchie for the test this morning, or the Consulate would surely have been in touch. But that didn't mean she had any intention of sticking around for the result.

Emma turned to Rafe.

'Let's go back. Let's go back to the house.'

'Emma — '

'It's a public road. No one can stop us going there, or parking in a public place.'

'As it happens,' Rafe said, 'I agree with you. But that's not how the police would see it.'

'They're going to take him,' Emma insisted. 'They're just waiting till we think we're safe, and then they're going to go.'

'Emma, think about it.' Rafe's T-shirt was damp. He looked flushed and hot. 'How is sitting outside their house going to help? If the Hunts want to leave, there are plenty of other exits they could use. They live on a farm, they're surrounded by fields and lanes and back roads. If they want to sneak away, there isn't anything we can do to stop them.'

'For God's sake.' Emma had listened to more than enough of this crap. 'You make this sound like some sort of *training* exercise, with rules that we have to follow. This is my *son* we're talking about. I don't care if I'm too stupid to understand how these things are normally done. I don't *want* to play any of these bloody games. I just want to go there and get him back.'

'I know how you feel.' Rafe sounded frustrated. 'And I wish I could help you, but I know how these people work. This whole thing is

241

a fucking game to them. You have to follow the rules or they won't lift a finger to help you.'

'Follow the rules?' Emma's voice rose. 'Follow the rules? That's rich, coming from you. I doubt you've ever followed a rule in your life. You couldn't even work for the police for more than a few months without packing the whole thing in in a temper, so what makes you such an expert on rules?'

'Well, maybe if I'd bothered to follow them, I wouldn't have made such a mess of my life, would I?' Rafe snapped.

Emma fell back in her seat. She put her hand to her eyes. All the time, *all the time*, every step she took, she was pushing through some giant, clinging web, and with every step, the web grew and recoiled on her, pushing her right back again to where she'd started.

After a minute, Rafe said, 'I'm sorry. I really am. I don't know how to advise you. I don't want to make things worse for you. I could tell you to just walk away from them and do your own thing, like I did. But you can't, can you? *You* don't have a choice.'

She didn't answer. Neither of them spoke again for a while. They sat there, limp and miserable, velcroed to the sweaty seats. Out on the road, the tractor droned on. Through the window, Emma breathed petrol and hot tar. Another quicksand day. Well, she'd come this far. She could do this. She pressed her eyes with her finger and thumb. A game, was it? Fine. Ridiculous as it was, she would play it. She would get through this. She would keep on going, and sitting here, and breathing in and out, and no doubt, at some point, the DNA result would come back and all of this would come to an end.

At least she knew that Ritchie was all right. She'd seen that for herself. Right now, that was if the Hunts hadn't taken him off somewhere, he was probably asleep in bed. He should have gone for his nap an hour ago. Or was he keeping to the same timetable here as at home? Would Antonia notice he was tired? Would she insist on him staying up, or would she let him have enough rest?

And he had no Gribbit here. He never went to sleep without Gribbit. Did he miss him? Or did he have another one now? A newer, plusher, shinier Gribbit; a Gribbit that didn't smell or have stains.

Emma forced the thoughts away. This waiting and hanging around was doing her head in. But she had to trust Rafe that waiting was the best thing to do. If it wasn't for him, she wouldn't have seen Ritchie at all.

Thank God, they were moving again. The tractor had finally made it around the wall. The youth waved at Rafe before hopping back up into his seat. Rafe didn't follow the tractor, but turned left to where the road was clear. They were coming into a town now. They seemed to have reached the coast. A fresh, welcome breeze lifted Emma's hair from her eyes. Between pale-coloured buildings, she glimpsed the sea. Boats bobbed in the distance; the blue-grey water was dotted with bright, white triangles.

Further into the town, people in shorts and flip-flops thronged the paths. Children skipped ahead, trailing towels and fishing nets.

'This is Arcachon,' Rafe said. 'I think we should stop here. Stretch our legs a bit. There's a famous sand dune somewhere nearby. The Dune of Pyla. I read about it when I was looking up the area. Biggest sand dune in Europe, supposedly. We can climb it, if you like? Get some exercise?'

On cue, through some trees ahead, rose what looked like a massive yellow wall.

'That's a sand dune?' Doubtfully, Emma peered up at it. Little black specks dotted the side. People, she realized.

'Impressive, isn't it?' Rafe said. 'Come on.' He indicated to pull in. 'Let's give it a go. It'll take our minds off the wait.'

It was a relief to get out of the car. Being in there was like sitting in an oven. They walked through some trees, stepping over heavy growth and fallen branches to reach the dune. Emma tilted her head back to see the top of it. It really was steep.

'I don't think — ' she began.

Rafe was already climbing.

'Come on,' he called. 'There'll be a great view once we're up.'

Emma made a half-hearted attempt to follow him. Within a minute, she was out of breath. Her feet sank in the sand, sliding backwards with every step. Her bag swung down in front of her, getting in the way. She didn't seem to be getting anywhere at all.

'How are you doing?' Rafe called. He had

stopped to wait for her.

Emma straightened, pushing her hair off her face. Her T-shirt stuck to her chest. This was crazy. Here she was, climbing a pile of sand while her child was being held prisoner in some madwoman's house. What did she think she was doing?

'I'm not going any further,' she said. 'You go on if you want to. I'll wait here.'

Rafe slid back down the dune.

'Take off your shoes,' he advised. 'Look at the way those people are doing it.' He pointed. A couple of hundred yards away, a group of teenagers were climbing the dune on all fours.

'I'm not doing that,' Emma said scornfully.

'Why not?'

'Because I don't want to. This is stupid.'

'Just give me your bag and shoes,' Rafe tried to persuade her. 'Free up your hands.'

He really was irritating her now.

'I don't need your help,' Emma snapped. 'I'm perfectly able — '

'I *know* you're able.' All of a sudden, Rafe sounded annoyed as well. 'But you're carrying more of a load than me. All I'm doing is trying to help you.'

The two of them glared at each other. Then, to Emma's own surprise, she bent down and took off her shoes. One by one, she slapped them into Rafe's hands.

'Happy now?' she asked.

She dumped her bag on top of the shoes. Then she turned back to the dune. She planted one foot on the sand, placed her hands to either side of it, and began to climb.

This time, without the bag and shoes, she moved faster. Now she could see herself climbing, making progress. Drops of sweat rolled from under her arms, soaking her T-shirt, and her tongue stuck to the roof of her mouth, but she kept going. The higher she climbed, the steeper the slope became; but by now it didn't matter because she was concentrating, chest burning, everything forgotten except her determination to get there.

Then she was over the top, and the grey sea, the whole of the Atlantic spread out before her.

'Oh.'

She was surrounded by whiteness. Wind swept her face and hair. A lid had been lifted off the world, and all of its contents had flown away. All that was left was the sheer pleasure of being up there and of not having to climb any more. Her legs felt like jelly. It would be OK. Everything would be OK.

'Well done,' Rafe called. He had reached the top ahead of her and was sitting a little way away, cross-legged on the sand.

Emma was too out of breath to reply. She let her knees fold, sinking her to the ground, and lay on her back, arms out, staring up at the sky. The wind cooled her forehead and neck and lifted the hem of her T-shirt. She closed her eyes, listening to the waves and the faraway cries of seagulls, like babies. Her breath slowed. The jelly feeling faded from her legs.

A little while later, she sat up again. Rafe had been busy. A knee-high sandcastle stood in front of him, dampened into place with Evian water. The lower, squarer part of the castle was decorated with stones. In the centre was a tower, with finger-marks down the sides. On top of the tower, the wooden stick from an ice lolly pointed into the sky.

'The fortress of Helm's Deep,' Rafe explained when he saw Emma looking. 'Impenetrable to all forces of darkness.'

A breeze came up. Helm's Deep trembled, very slightly, and collapsed into the sand. Rafe muttered something to himself.

'So,' he said to Emma, 'how are you feeling now?'

'Better,' she admitted. She began to brush sand off her T-shirt.

'Can I ask you something?'

'Sure.'

'Where is your family?'

Emma stopped brushing. Of course. He didn't know. She took a moment to push her hair behind her ears.

Briefly, briskly, she told him about her mother's death.

'I'm sorry.' Rafe looked at her. 'So soon before Ritchie.'

'And my dad,' Emma added, 'left when I was three. Went to Swindon to live with a woman called Jackie. So now you know the story of my family.'

'Do you still see your dad?'

Emma shook her head. 'He died when I was nine. I never really knew him anyway. He didn't stay in touch much after he left.'

'Must have been hard on your mum,' Rafe said.

'Well, yeah, it wasn't exactly a barrel of laughs. She was left in a lot of debt. She had to work two jobs to keep us. But she just got on with it. It's what you do, isn't it?'

Rafe paused. Emma could almost hear the inevitable next question: *And what about Ritchie's father?*

She didn't feel like going into all that, not now, so she said, 'So, what about your family? Are you from London?'

'I grew up in Lewisham,' Rafe said. 'My mum still lives there, with my stepdad. My real father moved out when I was a kid.' He made a face. 'Snap. Like yours.'

Ritchie's too, Emma thought with a pang. Was there something wrong with them all, that none of them had fathers who wanted to see them grow up?

'Do you keep in touch with him?' she asked politely.

'Now and then. He moved to Spain a few years ago. Fifty-seven, and still trying to find himself. He plays guitar with a band in Malaga, can you believe that? Got himself a twenty-three-year-old girlfriend.'

Rafe's grin faded. He picked up the wooden lollipop stick and stirred the fallen heap of sand.

'Since I left the police,' he said, 'I can see myself turning into him. Drifting about. Trying to find myself.'

'I'd say you were a good policeman,' Emma said. She meant it.

'Yeah, well. I grew up in a pretty tough estate, gave my mum a hard time after my dad left. A few of us got into nicking cars and the cops used to come and chase us up and down the estates. Lucky we never killed anyone. Or ourselves, come to think of it — not that that would have been any kind of loss. Most of the time, no matter how fast we went, the police caught us. After a bit, I was impressed by that. I thought about how pointless I was being, just pissing about and stealing things, when I could actually try to do something useful with my life.'

'Didn't you have a problem getting into the police?' Emma was curious. 'After you'd stolen the cars?'

'Nah. Well, I walked into our local station when I was about fourteen — they all knew me by then — and told them I wanted to join, and the bloke behind the desk thought it was the most hilarious thing he'd ever heard. But when they'd all finished having a laugh, one of them was actually quite helpful. He told me to keep out of trouble, go back to school and stay there, and who knew what might happen.' Rafe smiled, remembering. 'My mum was thrilled.'

'You liked it, didn't you?' Emma said. 'Being in the police?'

'Yeah.' For a minute, his face lit up. 'Yeah, I did.'

His eyes were narrowed against the light. The narrowing gave them a keen, watchful look, made him seem the type of person he was: active, energetic, used to the outdoors. Emma had no trouble picturing him zipping easily over fences and walls, leaping off a bridge to bring down the baddie with the gun. But to balance that, what so many of the police didn't seem to have, or had lost: the kindness and compassion he had shown the day he'd called to her flat to see if she was OK.

'I couldn't believe they were paying me to work for them,' Rafe was saying. 'I'd have done it for nothing. For a while anyway. But then . . .' He lifted a shoulder. 'You know the rest. I had this clichéd notion I could make a difference. But it's such a machine. They were all so full of shit. I didn't want to be a part of it.'

'All the more reason to stay,' Emma said. 'People who care are needed everywhere. If the good people are on the outside, nothing will change.'

She was watching a child roll, squealing, down the dune. A woman slid after him, laughing and calling. The child had blond, wispy hair. She thought she saw Rafe looking at her, but when she turned to him he was gazing at something over the other side of the dune.

'Let's cheer that couple on,' he said, jumping up. 'They look like they could do with some help.'

A man and woman who looked to be in their seventies were climbing the dune. The man, breathing hard and purple in the face, gallantly tried to push his well-padded partner from behind. She had given up and was lying face down in the sand, only a few feet from the top.

'Keep going,' Rafe called. 'You're almost here.'

'I keep telling her that,' the man gasped. He had an American accent.

'Listen to you,' the woman said. She lifted her head to shoot him a look. 'Don't you pretend you're not glad of an excuse to stop.'

But she got to her knees and started to climb again. By now, several other people were peering over the edge of the dune. A group of teenage girls who had been sitting in a circle, eating crisps and chattering in French, jumped up and arranged themselves in a line along the top.

'Come on,' they shouted, their hands around their mouths. 'You can do eet.'

When the couple finally reached the top, the girls, all long legs and skinny, cut-off jeans, squealed and clapped, jumping up and down. Emma surprised herself by clapping too.

'Oh, my.' The woman knelt in the sand, blowing her cheeks out and fanning herself with her hand. 'How nice of you. I really thought I wasn't going to make it.'

'Of course you were,' Rafe said.

Emma noticed several of the French girls looking over at him. He'd caught the sun today. Already he was dark enough to be French himself. He looked like an overgrown kid, loping and messing about there on the dune with the American couple; but there was something adult about him as well, a toughness, like he could take care of himself if he had to. What did they call it? Streetwise. He glanced towards her then, and she smiled. For a second, Rafe looked surprised. Then he smiled back, straight at her. Emma's mind had moved on. She was thinking again about the little boy, rolling down the hill and shrieking. She hugged her arms to herself.

251

She would bring Ritchie here. They'd never really, properly, had fun together. It would be like this.

⋆   ⋆   ⋆

On the way back to Bergerac, they stopped in one of the yellow stone villages for something to eat. Inside, the restaurant had walls of rough brick, and candles in wine bottles on the tables. Waiters in waistcoats and white aprons bustled about with buckets of ice and menus.

The walls of the building were inches thick. Emma had to step outside again to get a signal on her mobile. Further downriver, a bridge with arches caused the water to divide and ripple. Where the water was disturbed, the moon cast blue tips. Emma phoned Brian Hodgkiss again, and waited in the shadow of walls that must have seen a hundred generations of mothers like her come and go.

'All well,' Brian Hodgkiss said when he heard her voice. 'The test has been done. I spoke to the Hunts a little while ago. They're still in the area.'

Oh, the relief of it. She still had no idea what the Hunts were playing at, but whatever it was, at least Ritchie was safe.

She said, 'I was wondering if there was any way I could see him tonight?'

'I don't think that would be possible.' Brian sounded apologetic.

'Even a quick meeting,' Emma pleaded, 'even with other people there? Even with *her* there, I don't care . . . '

252

'It wouldn't be possible,' Brian repeated. 'Not unless they agreed to it, and I really don't think they would. I'm sorry.' He did sound as if he meant it.

He added, in a kinder tone, 'Not too much longer now. The results should be back by tomorrow.'

He sounded a lot more friendly than before, as if he was finally coming around to her side.

Emma reported the conversation back to Rafe. 'I could have him soon,' she said, her voice wobbling.

Rafe was quiet. His earlier high spirits on the dune seemed to have passed. A waiter appeared at their table, a row of plates along his arm. Pyramids of ham, cheese and tomatoes; chunks of warm French bread. Emma sampled them all, hungrier than she'd been for days, but Rafe ate very little. Tired, no doubt, after all that climbing. Plus, he'd done all the driving again that day. She was in no doubt as to how much she owed him.

The B&B was shut up and silent by the time they got back. They let themselves in the front door, careful not to jingle the keys or trip over the rug in the hall. Emma followed Rafe up the stairs, tiptoeing on the steps, peering to see her way in the sepia light from the window.

Rafe's room had its own entrance, a little way down the hall from Emma's. He stopped outside Emma's door to say goodnight.

'Thank you for today,' Emma said, keeping her voice low so as not to wake their hostess. 'It helped a lot. Kept me from thinking too much.'

It was true. She felt easier inside now, less knotted and hopeless than before. Things were going to work out. She just had a feeling.

'I enjoyed it too,' Rafe said. 'I'm glad it helped.'

'We owe you a lot,' Emma said. 'Ritchie and I. You found the address for us. None of this would have happened without you.'

Rafe's hands were at his sides, just hanging there between them. Emma reached down and took them in hers.

'Why did you do this for us?' she asked. 'You hardly know us.'

Rafe had taken a breath, as if to say something. But then he didn't.

'Well, whatever it was,' Emma smiled at him, 'I'm glad we met you.'

She went to kiss him goodnight. But then a peck on the cheek didn't seem enough. On impulse, she released his hands and put her arms around him.

'Thank you,' she said.

Rafe's arms came around her too, holding her as tightly as she held him. His cheek, solid and a bit scratchy, pressed against hers. He smelled of sweat and the sea, and some faint, appley scent.

'I was happy to do it,' he said.

They held each other for a moment. Rafe was the first to let go. He took his arms away from her and stood back.

'We should get some sleep,' he said. 'Tomorrow could be a busy day.'

'I hope so.' Emma was fervent.

But once in her room, Emma knew she was

still a long way from sleep. When she pulled her jeans off, sand drizzled out over the carpet. Her socks were stuck to her feet. A bath might be the thing to settle her; tire her out.

She went into the bathroom. Quietly, so as not to disturb Rafe, she pulled off her T-shirt and draped it over the towel rail. She reached behind her to unhook her bra. In the mirror over the sink, she saw the lines on her stomach, the folds of extra skin. There were blue veins on her legs that hadn't been there before. Ritchie had put those veins there. She'd freaked a bit when she'd first noticed them, but she was used to them now.

She was leaning over the bath, about to turn the taps on, when the door to Rafe's room opened and in he walked, holding a toothbrush. He looked up and saw her, and jerked back, sucking a breath between his teeth.

'Shit.' Emma flailed. Towel, quick, where? She grabbed her T-shirt off the rail and held it up in front of her.

'Sorry. Sorry.' Rafe was backing out of the room. 'The door wasn't locked. I'll leave you to it.'

Emma saw herself in the mirror again and cringed. How embarrassing. Caught here in all her wobbly glory by some bloke she still hardly knew. What was it she'd said to him the day he'd called to the flat and tried to cook her dinner? What had she accused him of trying to do? It just seemed funny now. If she'd known then the standard of girls he was used to attracting: French, teenaged, slender as willow trees. He

255

must have thought, In your dreams, dearie; but been nice enough not to say it.

'It's all right,' she called. No point making things awkward between them. 'Come back and brush your teeth. I'll wait next door.'

But he was gone. A china soap dish wobbled for a moment, teetering on the edge of the bath. Then it crashed to the floor, shattering to pieces on the tiles. He must have managed to knock it as he went.

★ ★ ★

Ritchie was sitting on Emma's knee. The warm weight of him pressed on her legs, and his eyelashes lay along the curve of his cheek. Her arms were around him and she was cutting up a muffin for him.

'He loves muffins,' she explained to Antonia, who was sitting opposite. 'Chocolate especially.'

'I never knew that,' Antonia said.

Ritchie beamed and held out his hands. He grabbed the muffin and stuffed it into his mouth.

'See.' Emma kissed him. 'I told you. I told you he was mine.'

Antonia's face darkened. She picked up a heavy mug. She began to bang it on the table.

Thunk. Thunk. Thunk.

'Stop.' Horrified, Emma put her hands over Ritchie's ears. 'What do you think you're doing? You'll frighten him.'

Thunk. Thunk.

'Emma.'

Thunk.

'Emma! Wake up!'

She was lying on something slippy and pink. The curtains were framed with light.

Someone was banging on the door.

'Emma!' It was Rafe. 'We got a call. They want us at the Consulate.'

Emma was out of bed in a second. Why hadn't they phoned her? She must have missed the ring of her mobile. She got dressed, struggling to haul up her jeans. She shoved her feet into her trainers, not bothering with socks, and flew out of the room.

They didn't speak. She ran all the way, sprinting ahead of Rafe. The Consulate was just around the corner.

They were greeted at a side entrance and shown through to an office. The office was modern and ordinary, with a swivel chair, a wooden desk and a computer; completely different from the ornate hall of the other night. Brian Hodgkiss was waiting for them in front of the desk.

'Good morning,' he said.

'Good morning,' Emma said, breathless, darting her eyes around, taking everything in.

Standing beside Brian was another man who could have been his twin. Same beige trousers, same retreating hairline, same stripy tie under a round-necked jumper. This new man was holding a torn brown envelope and a folded sheet of paper. Emma's eyes went straight to the paper. She knew at once what it was.

'The DNA result is back,' Brian explained unnecessarily.

Emma stepped forward; she actually went to take the paper out of the man's hand. He moved back, lifted it away from her.

'I can see you're in a hurry,' he said. 'I won't delay things any longer.'

He unfolded the page. Looked at it for a moment. Cleared his throat.

'The report is quite detailed,' he said. 'So I'll just try to cover the main . . . ' His eyes skimmed down the page. His voice trickled off. 'Testing conducted in accordance with . . . hmm . . . child named . . . yes . . . the alleged mother . . . probability of . . . Ah. Here it is.' He cleared his throat again. 'So. To summarize. The result of this test indicates, with a probability of parentage of 99.999 per cent, that the mother of the child in question is . . . '

He looked up again. Thinned his lips in apology.

'Mrs Philippa Hunt.'

14

Tuesday, 26 September
Day Ten

A cold hand pulled at Emma's insides, toppling her until she thought she might fall. The floor shifted. The room glittered and spun.

'I don't understand,' she said. Her lips felt like the stiff, plastic lips on a mask. She turned to Rafe. 'You said the test was accurate.'

'I thought it was.' Rafe's face was pale.

'It is,' Brian's twin put in.

'He's not hers,' Emma pleaded. 'The test is wrong. There must be something we can do.'

Brian Hodgkiss was shaking his head, his mouth all pursed up.

'I'm a British citizen,' Emma cried. 'You have to help me.'

'I'm sorry.' Brian Hodgkiss was colder and stiffer now. As if getting involved in all of this had got him into trouble in some way. 'I'm sorry, there's nothing we can do. Go home. Forget about here. Maybe you'll have news of your child in England.'

'Couldn't I do the test with *my* DNA? Maybe it's a coincidence. Maybe there's more than one match.'

'I don't think it works like that.'

'I'm not leaving this country without him.'

'I must warn you,' Brian Hodgkiss said. 'If you harass this family again, you *will* get yourself arrested.'

'Arrest me then,' Emma shouted. 'I'm not leaving. I'll kidnap him if I have to.'

Brian exchanged a glance with his colleague. He said, 'I wouldn't advise that, Ms Turner. As it happens, the family have gone to stay with friends at the moment, for their safety. They plan to leave the area soon. Their house is up for sale.'

'They're moving house?' Emma was shocked. 'To where?'

Brian didn't answer.

'To *where?*' Emma brought her fists down on the desk. Pens and paperclips hopped. Out of the corner of her eye, she saw Brian's colleague swiftly leave the office. Most of the desk was taken up with a large computer with a bulky screen. Emma put her arms around the screen. She began to drag it towards the edge of the desk.

'I'll smash this on the floor,' she warned. 'I mean it. I'll break every window in here. I'm not leaving until you tell me.'

'Ms Turner.' Brian rushed to push the computer back into place. 'We'll get the police in here. I'm warning you. I'll have you arrested.'

Emma hauled at the screen again and he shouted, '*Ms Turner.*'

Rafe's calm voice in the background: 'Emma. Emma, listen.'

'Get off me.'

'There's no point here, Emma. Come with me. We'll talk about this, we'll work something out.'

'Leave me alone.' Emma began to sob. 'I should have taken him at the house but you

260

made me come away. If it wasn't for you, I'd have him.'

Rafe tried to take her hand. She let go of the screen and swung around, shoving him with all her strength.

'Get *away* from me!' she screamed. 'Get away, get away, get away!'

She pushed him off her and stumbled, collapsing against the desk, just managing in time to stop herself from falling to the floor.

Brian said, 'Mr Townsend, I'm going to have to — '

'Give us a minute,' Rafe snapped. 'Please.'

And then, quite suddenly, all of Emma's energy drained away. Squeezed out of her, like the final drops of water wrung from a sponge. *Over*, she thought, surprised at the sense of release. It was as if the sponge was relaxing again, dry and light. *Over now*. Inside, a tightness unravelled, the tightness that said they thought she was lying or mad, or else they just didn't care, because in this world some people mattered and some did not. Some people had power and some didn't; that was how it was; and how you got that power she didn't know, it was a secret she'd never know now, it would never be for the likes of her. She was no one. She was no good for Ritchie. She knew that now. She sank to the desk, propping herself up with arms that felt like bags of sand.

'It's all right,' she whispered. 'It's all right.'

Rafe said, 'You'll come away from here?'

'Yes.'

The door of the office burst open. Three or

261

four large men pounded in, all heading straight for Emma. Rafe put his hand up.

'She's just leaving,' he said coldly. 'Back off, will you?'

Brian must have made some signal. The men stood back.

'All right, Emma?' Rafe held his hand out to her. She had to lean on it to walk.

'I believe it's your fault she's here at all,' Brian Hodgkiss said to Rafe as they passed. 'I've no doubt there'll be questions back in London about this.' He raised his voice after them. 'There are reasons for the Official Secrets Act, you know. This sort of thing happens otherwise.'

Rafe muttered, 'Yeah, yeah.'

Their car was parked outside the B&B. Rafe opened the passenger door and helped Emma in.

'Wait there,' he said, putting his hands in the air, palms facing her. Then he closed the door and ran into the B&B. Emma leaned forward until her forehead touched the dashboard. Grey, bumpy plastic blurred before her eyes. Minutes later Rafe was back with their bags. She felt him peering anxiously into the car, as if afraid she might have disappeared, but here she still was, hunched in her seat, as limp as a strand of seaweed.

They drove away from the town.

'What do you want to do?' Rafe pleaded. 'If you want to stay, I'll stay with you. But I don't know what else we can do here.'

Sunflowers; fields of them. Nodding their yellow heads.

'Maybe we should go to the airport,' Rafe said.

'Get a flight home. Take it up with the Foreign Office in England.'

Emma said, 'I told Dr Stanford I wished he was dead.'

'I know,' Rafe said. 'You told me.'

'That wasn't all, though. It was worse than that. I didn't tell you all of it.'

'People say things — '

'I told her I was thinking of hurting Ritchie.'

'But you didn't mean it.'

'But I *did*.' Her voice shook. 'I did mean it.'

'You went to your doctor to ask for help,' Rafe said loudly, banging his fist on the steering wheel. 'That's what people do.'

'I wasn't *asking* for help,' Emma said.

She started to weep, twisted in her seat.

'I was planning to kill him.'

★   ★   ★

'Muh,' Ritchie said, the day he first walked.

He waddled across the sitting-room, sticking his hands in the air to keep his balance. He staggered to Emma and put his arms around her neck.

'You clever boy!' Emma grabbed him and planted kisses all over his pudgy little face. 'You're the cleverest boy in the whole wide world.' She kissed each temple, then his eyes, then his ears, and then finally the most precious part of him, the part where the curve of his cheek met his throat, just below his ear. Neither of them could stop smiling.

For emergencies, however, he went back to

crawling; it was still faster. He went to the kitchen and put the yellow plastic mixing bowl over his head.

'Aloo?' he shouted. 'Aloo?'

He loved tidying up. He put all his bricks back in their box, panting and grunting with the effort of opening and closing the lid between each brick.

'You can leave the lid open,' Emma told him. Sometimes he made her laugh.

But there were all the other times that he wore her out. He was hard work. He was always there, looking for her, bursting into tears if she left the room even for a second. If she went to the loo, he would stand outside and shout, 'Muh, Muh,' until she came out. The constant whining got on her nerves. She began to snap at him more, shouted at him even, until finally he stopped wailing and looked at her in bewilderment.

$$\star \quad \star \quad \star$$

With Ritchie's teething came a row of ear infections, one after another. He often woke in the night, crying, and Emma had to get up and take him into the bed with her where he spent the next hour or so fussing and snuffling and trying to lie right on top of her. She took him back to Dr Stanford who said it was just a virus and he didn't need any more antibiotics. Emma didn't agree. She was sure there must be something more serious going on. Why else would he be so cross and clingy? Dr Stanford became impatient with her.

'In again, Emma?' she took to saying whenever Emma appeared in the chair across from her desk. 'What is it this time?'

These days, for some reason, Emma found she was much more tired than she'd been at the beginning. She stopped taking Ritchie for long walks; she just didn't have the energy. She often slept during the day, lying on the couch, while Ritchie crawled around the sitting-room on his own, laughing to himself with his dirty little chuckle: 'Huh huh huh.' This new tiredness worried her. Sometimes while doing something, eating her dinner or pushing Ritchie's buggy, she would just . . . stop. Unable to move. Literally as if some weight was pressing on her shoulders. She wondered if it might be a problem with her muscles. Ritchie's birth had taken its toll on her in a way she hadn't expected. He'd been a big baby, and she was small. Over the past few months, she'd developed all kinds of problems she'd never had before: bladder infections, anaemia, backache. She'd never been the type to worry about her health, because she'd never needed to. But Jesus, if she became ill now! What in God's name would she do about Ritchie?

Emma became obsessed with eating properly. She and Ritchie got free milk, and she stocked up on tins of beans, which she'd heard were good for you. Potatoes as well; you could just put them in the microwave. You could buy a loaf of bread for forty-six pence and it lasted all week. She got free vitamins from the healthcare centre and made sure to take one every morning. Despite that, she managed to pick up a throat infection that got gradually worse over a few days until she could barely get out of bed. It finally went away, but not before she'd become very stressed. If she had to go into hospital, what on earth would happen to Ritchie?

The thinking didn't stop there.

What if — she went cold! — what if she fell one day, in the bathroom, say, and broke her leg and couldn't get up? Who would miss her and come looking for them? Ritchie could starve to death in the flat, and no one would know.

★   ★   ★

Twenty-eighth August. Ritchie's first birthday. The sun poured in through the balcony doors. Emma dressed Ritchie in his shorts and blue Surfer Dude T-shirt. He waddled around the flat for a while, bimbling about with his various toys, before Emma sat him into his pushchair for his lunchtime nap while she cleaned up in the kitchen.

After a while, she glanced around the doorway to check on him. He was asleep by the balcony, the sun lighting the lower half of his face. Emma stood there, holding the J-cloth and watching him. One year old today! Who would have thought? His head was flung back. Little snores and whiffles came from his nose. Even like that, he was so beautiful. She went to the pushchair and stroked his cheek, using just the tip of her finger, so he wouldn't wake up.

'Happy birthday,' she said softly, 'my gorgeous little darling.'

Today of all days, she would make an effort for him.

'We're going to get your present today,' she told him. 'Something really nice.'

After lunch, they got the bus to the King's Road, a place Emma normally never went to shop as it was way too expensive. But Ritchie was always dressed in cheap clothes from stalls or low-price department stores. Today, for once, she was going to buy him something really good.

They got off the bus at Sloane Square and headed west back along the King's Road. It was a long time since Emma had been here. She kept on looking around her in amazement. How gorgeous and colourful and clean everything looked. The people were so beautifully dressed. Teenage girls wearing chiffon tops and waist-length strings of beads tossed their long, straight hair as they passed. Elderly women, some of them a bit mad-looking, wandered around with giant sunglasses and collagen lips, carrying tiny dogs in their handbags. An elderly man in a uniform lined with medals trundled along the path in a motorized wheelchair. People sat near the fountains in the Duke of York Square, drinking coffee, reading, chatting. And the shops! God, she'd forgotten about the shops. Everywhere you looked: gorgeous vintage and high street clothes; shoes; jewellery; handbags. Once she would have drooled at the handbags. She and Joanne used to read in awe about people fighting to get on waiting lists for bags that cost thousands of pounds. It just seemed weird now. To spend that much money on a bag. Obscene, even, if you thought about it.

The children's clothes shops, though. Look at the stuff they had! Beautiful. In one window, a row of tiny white cashmere Babygros hung on padded hangers. Emma was astonished at the size of them. Had Ritchie really ever been able to fit into one of those? His big toe wouldn't go near them now. She looked at the prices and was shocked all over again. Who on earth would spend that much on a Babygro? On something the baby would only wear for a month? And then in one window, folded on top of a giant wooden alphabet block, she spotted an utterly adorable blue fleece top. Emma stopped. How sweet would Ritchie look in that fleece? Beside the zip was a felt, stitched-on elephant with big, shy eyes. The elephant was standing beside a pond, smiling and pouring water over himself with his trunk. Ritchie would love him! But a fleece would be too hot for this weather. Then Emma thought about it. At these kinds of prices, a fleece would be a much better buy than summer clothes. Look how often Ritchie had worn his red snowsuit last year. He'd practically lived in it. If she got the fleece a little bit too big — for aged eighteen months, say, instead of twelve — it would last him all this winter. He'd get wear out of it most days. It would be worth the extra expense.

In the shop, she took Ritchie out of his buggy to try on the fleece. He grinned up at her from inside the hood, which fell over one of his eyes.

'So cu-ute,' the tall, wafty shop-girl cooed. They always said that, to get you to buy their things. But in this case the girl was right. Ritchie did look adorable.

'It's too big for him now,' the shop-girl said, 'but when the weather is cold, it will fit.' She smiled at Emma. She wore a long, silky top over linen trousers, and her white-blonde hair reached her waist. Her name badge said 'Ilona.' Emma looked away. She knew she should smile back, but it was like she had a hand on each cheek, dragging her face down. It jarred her now when people spoke to her; she had to come from such a long way away to answer them. And when she did, her voice sounded deeper. She could see the way people looked at her. It was easier not to engage with them, or talk to any of them.

While the girl wrapped the fleece in frothy blue tissue paper, Emma waited by the counter and watched Ritchie totter around, examining the toys. He was still new to walking, a bit wobbly and inclined to fall over. He stopped in front of a red plastic truck with black wheels and a dip in the middle for a seat. He grasped the bar sticking up at the back and gave the truck a push. It moved.

'Muh!' Delighted, he turned to check she'd seen what he'd made it do.

'It's lovely,' Emma told him. The shop-girl was tying a blue bow at the top of the bag. 'But we have to go now.'

Ritchie ignored her. He gave the truck another push.

'You like it, don't you?' the shop-girl called to him. 'You like our truck.'

'Come on, Rich.' Emma took his arm.

Ritchie wailed, trying to pull away from her. Dramatically, he stretched his other hand out to the truck and wailed again.

'Poor thing,' Ilona said from the counter. 'He just wants to play.'

Emma said nothing. She gave Ritchie's arm another yank and hefted him into the buggy. She snatched the bag from the counter, got the shop door open and muscled her way out into the street. She marched along for several minutes, furious with the shop-girl and with Ritchie.

'Why did you behave like that?' she snapped at him. He'd never not done what she told him to before.

Ritchie sat in subdued silence, red-cheeked and upset. Emma marched on, not caring how many pensioners or tiny dogs she hit with the buggy. Oh, that smug cow in the shop, with her silky clothes and her long, prissy hair.

She walked all along the King's Road, past the town hall, and Heal's, and the cinema. Then, when she'd calmed down, she turned around again and went all the way back to the shop.

'No wrapping, please,' she said curtly as the shop-girl was getting another armload of frothy paper ready to cover the truck with.

Outside again, Emma tied a piece of string to the handle of the red plastic truck. She pulled it behind her all the way to the bus stop. The sun had ceased to be a pleasure by this time; it was just a hot nuisance in the sky. The bus blew black fumes into her face. She was tired now, looking forward to lying down.

Ritchie had forgotten all about the truck by

the time they got back to the flat. When he saw it again beside him in the lift, his face lit up.

'Ah-ha-ha-ha,' he chortled, reaching for it. 'Ah-ha-ha-ha.'

In the sitting-room he pushed the truck around, wobbling after it. Emma showed him how to sit on it. It gave him such pleasure, she loathed herself for ever having tried to deny it to him. She went to find her camera.

'Smile for Mummy,' she said.

Ritchie did. They were friends again now. He sat on the truck and beamed up at her; his wide, shy, Oliver smile. Emma clicked the button on the camera.

⋆   ⋆   ⋆

Days later, she woke before dawn, as she often did, and gazed drearily up at the long crack on the ceiling. Were she and Ritchie going to live in this flat for ever? She'd only meant to stay for a while until she got sorted, but a year later, here they still were. Was she going to bring Ritchie up here? Were his childhood memories going to be of these graffitied walls, this grim, treeless view?

She hated this. It was rubbish, being on benefits, having to live where you were told. Having no choice or say or power. She couldn't fault the social workers; they'd been very helpful, but she knew what they must be thinking: yet another single mother, fleecing the system. Her own mother would be ashamed. She'd never taken one penny from the state, and neither had her grandmother before she went on her pension.

But if she did get a job, how would she afford childcare? And what if she did earn enough to move to somewhere nicer, but then got sick and couldn't work? How would she keep up with the rent? At least here was cheap. But she hated the idea of living here for ever. The catch-22 went around and around in her head.

The room grew bright. Ritchie would be awake soon. All the things she had to do that day crowded in on her. She had to dress and feed Ritchie. Do the washing, which meant a trip to the communal laundry in the basement with all the clothes, and the washing powder, and Ritchie as well. Load the washing machine. Come back in an hour to re-load everything into the dryer. Collect the clothes and bring them back to the flat. Give Ritchie his lunch. Go to the shops for nappies and milk and Weetabix and bananas. Do the washing-up. Clean the kitchen.

She lay there, her head throbbing.

At seven, Ritchie woke up and chuckled, hanging over the bars of his cot. Emma sighed and climbed out of bed to pick him up. He'd start crying in a minute if she didn't.

God, she was particularly tired today. Rough. She felt rough. She fed Ritchie, spooning the soggy Weetabix into his mouth with one hand while she leaned her chin on the other and looked at the crumbs on the floor. The flat needed hoovering. Ritchie's clothes were all in the laundry bag, so she dressed him in yesterday's trousers with the splash of baby spinach casserole down one leg. He didn't want to have his jumper put on.

'Grraaghh.' He was in active form, wanting lots of attention.

Emma held him between her knees and forced the jumper over his head.

'Now just shut up,' she told him, 'and give me a chance to get dressed.'

She couldn't be bothered to have a shower. It meant putting Ritchie back in his cot, and he'd stand there and scream the whole time. Who was going to be looking at her anyway? She was only going to Sainsbury's. She pulled a woolly jumper on over her tracksuit and tied her hair back with a scrunchie. Then she stuck her feet into a pair of flip-flops. There. She looked fine.

The lift told a different story. In the mirror at the back, she saw flakes of dandruff in her hair. Her teeth were yellow.

Just as the doors were closing, a high voice called, 'Wait. Wait.'

The doors slid back again and Rosina Alcarez, their neighbour, hurried in, fresh and neat in her blue nurse's uniform.

'Thank you, thank you,' she said, out of breath. 'I am so sorry.'

She smiled at Ritchie.

'How are you?' she asked. 'You never came to see me.'

Emma had meant to visit. But Rosina had a busy job. She hadn't wanted to call at the wrong time and make Rosina feel obliged to invite her in. As time went by, anyway, it just seemed too much trouble, to sit and try to make

273

conversation with a woman she didn't even know.

Rosina was looking at Emma in a funny way. Conscious of her unwashed hair, Emma turned her head away. Rosina went on staring. Emma wished she'd butt out and mind her own business.

'Are you OK?' Rosina asked in a little voice.

'I'm fine,' Emma said shortly.

The lift bounced as it reached the ground floor. As soon as the doors opened, Emma shoved the buggy over the bump between them and walked off as quickly as she could.

The lump in her throat was gone by the time she reached the street.

★　★　★

She kept her eyes down in Sainsbury's, avoiding conversation with the chatty Indian cashier. On the way home, she stopped at a cash machine to check her balance.

Her wallet wasn't in her bag.

Emma scrabbled around again, making sure. She tried in her pockets, then in the buggy and all the plastic shopping bags.

'Great,' she sighed, standing back up again. She must have left the wallet at Sainsbury's. She turned the pushchair around and headed back.

'Did I just leave my wallet here?' she asked the cashier.

He was busy serving another customer; a woman in a pink poncho who swivelled to glare at Emma.

'Your wallet, madam?' the cashier asked.

'Yes.' Emma was too worried to be polite. 'My wallet. I used it to pay for the things I just bought. Less than fifteen minutes ago.'

'Let me check.' The cashier searched all around the desk. Then he bent to check the floor behind.

'No wallet,' he said, re-emerging. 'I am sorry.'

Shit. She'd had forty pounds in cash in that wallet. A week's worth of food for her and Ritchie. Maybe she'd dropped it in the street. Emma retraced her steps to the cash machine, checking the ground as she walked. No sign. Once more, she tried all her bags and pockets. Then she took out her phone. She'd have to cancel her missing card.

'WelcometocustomerservicesDenisespeaking canIhaveyouraccountnumberplease,' the voice reeled on the other end of the line.

'It's . . . er . . . ' Emma hesitated. 'Three. No . . . ' Three or eight? Which? She knew that bloody number off by heart. Why was she suddenly having a problem remembering it?

'I can't seem to think of it at the moment,' she began.

'Can't help you then, I'm afraid,' the voice sang.

'But I need to cancel my card,' Emma protested. 'I think it's been stolen.'

'I need the number.'

'I can give you my name. And the address of my branch in Bath.' Emma recited the details.

A clicking noise from the phone, then: 'I'm sorry. We have no record of that branch.'

'But you must do.' Emma almost laughed at the ridiculousness of it. 'I've had an account there since I was fifteen.'

'What's the sort code?'

'I don't know. Look, can't you just put me through to my branch and I'll deal with it myself directly.'

'We don't do that, madam. Anyway, we have no record of that branch.'

Emma stabbed the end-call button. Stupid cow. She'd go to a high street branch and deal with an actual human.

In the bank, she went to the customer services desk, where an exotically heavy-eyed girl in a suit sat plucking something off her sleeve.

'Nah help you?' The girl examined a speck between her finger and thumb.

'Yes,' Emma said. 'I need to report a stolen bank card.'

'View tried the helpline?'

'Yes, I have. They were no help at all. That's why I came in here.'

The girl gave a long sigh. She reached for her flat-screen.

'Account number?'

'I can't remember it at the moment,' Emma said. 'But I have my branch address, and my own address and date of birth, and all my security passwords, and I can give you a sample of my signature — '

'We need the account number.'

'Look,' Emma struggled to keep her temper, 'if I'd *known* my card was going to go missing today, I'd have brought the number with me, wouldn't I? But since I didn't, and since I don't want someone else using my card, I'm doing everything I can to cancel it. Only none of you seems the slightest bit interested in doing anything to help. I don't. Know. The number. You sort it out. It's your job.'

She had raised her voice by this time. Two beefy-looking men in blue shirts materialized from nowhere and planted themselves one on either side of the bank girl.

'Everything all right?' one of the men asked.

Heads were turning from the cash queue. Ritchie began to sniffle.

Shaking, Emma turned the buggy around and wheeled it out of the bank.

She knew she should go back to the flat and get her number, but she was too angry to talk to anyone else just yet. She steered the buggy towards the river, needing to get away and calm down.

Under Hammersmith Bridge, a group of teenage boys in school shirts and ties were shoving each other into the wall and laughing loudly. Beyond them, on the river path, a man was walking in Emma's direction. Even from this distance she could see that there was something wrong with his face. One eye was lower than the other, the skin on that side reddened, as if scarred.

As he approached them, the boys nudged each other and went quiet. It was fairly obvious what was going to happen. The man reached the bridge and one of the group, a boy with an unflatteringly low hairline, muttered something to his mates that Emma didn't catch. They all started sniggering.

The man stopped.

'Excuse me,' he said, in a pleasant enough way. 'There's no need for that sort of talk.'

'What did you say?' The low-hairline boy straightened at once. He stepped closer to the man, sticking his face forward into his. 'You mutant. How dare you speak to me like that?'

Quickly, the man walked on.

'Fucking retard,' the boy shouted after him. 'People like you shouldn't be out on the streets.'

The man gave no sign that he had heard. With dignity, he kept walking and turned the corner. But Emma felt a sudden surge of rage and hatred so violent it made her jaw clench. She had an almost uncontrollable urge to run over and smack the boy in the face. Really punch him; break all the bones in his nose. Push him over the wall into the river and hope he landed on a rusty spike.

She forced herself to turn around, pushing Ritchie's buggy back up the ramp to the road. Then she turned left on to the bridge, walking quickly to get away. Stop this, Emma! What on earth was happening to her? But the anger grew worse, swelling inside her until she was sick with it. Was this the sort of world Ritchie was going to grow up in? Were these the kinds of people he would have to deal with? Or even turn into one of them one day?

In the middle of the bridge, she tried to steady herself, putting a hand on the railing. The river spun around her. Ornate green and gold lanterns

278

and towers wheeled in the sky.

'You don't matter,' a deep voice said. 'You're nothing.'

Emma jumped, glancing from side to side along the walkway. Who had said that? The bridge was empty. She looked over the railing. Rain spattered the Thames. A million tiny circles slid below her, carried on a surface as black and slow as oil.

Emma went on looking at the water, and a strange feeling came over her. A strong feeling. A certainty.

We're all going to die.

Not just her, but everyone. Everyone in London. Even Ritchie, the most precious thing the city contained. The knowledge of it was as true as the fact that she was standing there. This beautiful, bloated, greedy city would crumble, like the Roman Empire had crumbled. There would be snarling, screams and slaughter, then nothing but silence and water for miles.

An evil presence, very strong, crept towards her over the bridge. It circled her, thickening like smoke. Terrified, Emma shoved Ritchie's buggy away from her, trying to push him away from the evil.

The deep voice again: 'You're useless. You're going to fail him.'

'Who's saying that?' Emma screamed. 'Where are you?'

'Get off the bridge,' the voice spat.

Emma grabbed the buggy and ran. Her feet pounded on the hollow slabs.

Away from the river, the sense of evil faded,

but the fear of it remained. She was trembling so hard the buggy rattled as she walked.

★　★　★

That evening, Ritchie wouldn't eat his mashed pasta and tomato. Emma didn't try to make him. Listlessly, she sat on the couch, a plate of beans on her knee. Ritchie seemed in a great mood. He kept trying to get Emma to play with his plastic tool set. He wanted her to show him how to push the ball through the hole with the hammer. When the ball went through, the machine made a noise: *ding ding ding*. He loved it.

'Be quiet,' Emma snapped.

Her heart was still beating so fast, it felt like there were a million fingers in her chest, trying to poke their way out. She couldn't stop thinking about the river. The boys who had jeered at the man with the burned face. That weird voice on the bridge. The sense of evil. You were always reading in the papers about things like terrorist attacks, global warming, flu pandemic. If something like that happened, the people who would survive would be people like those boys. Not people like her or Ritchie, but people who were strong and hard and ruthless enough to stamp all over others.

Ritchie came to stand beside her. Smiling, he pushed his tool set on to her knee. Her plate tipped over. The beans slid off in a wet lump on to the carpet. Emma jumped to her feet.

'Get off,' she shouted.

She shoved him, a really good, hard shove. For

a second, she felt savage rage. She was thinking about *him*, for Christ's sake. What would become of him if anything happened to her. Wasn't he the slightest bit grateful?

Ritchie flew backwards and landed on his bottom. Plenty of padding; he wouldn't have hurt himself. She glanced to make sure. He sat there, mouth and eyes open, a look of shock and surprise on his face. Emma turned away. She got down on her knees and began to scrape the beans back on to the plate with her fork. After a few seconds, when Ritchie still had made no sound, no screech of outrage, she glanced at him again. His lower lip was out. He was crying. Not loudly, as he usually did, but in silence. Tears slid down his cheeks.

'Oh, Ritchie.' Emma's heart smote her. 'Come here.'

She held her hand out to him but he turned away. The tears slid faster. This wasn't like him at all. Alarmed now, Emma left the beans and went to pick him up. He was stiff in her arms, gouging at his eyes with his fists, twisting his head to keep his face away from hers.

'Ritchie.' She was distraught. 'I'm sorry. What's wrong with us? What have I done? What have I done?'

⋆ ⋆ ⋆

Later, when he was asleep, she went to check on him. The yellow light from the hallway shone into his cot. She rested her arms on the bars and watched him. He lay on his back, one pudgy arm

281

flung above his head, his chest moving up and down in a hiccupy way. His cheeks were wet. He looked unhappy.

Emma's chest ached.

What was the matter with her? Who was this hard harpy she'd turned into? She'd never used to be like this. She'd had friends. She'd been normal. Now look at her. No one to care if she lived or died. A worthless failure. Horrible to her little son.

She undressed and got into bed, but she couldn't lie still. No matter which way she lay, she couldn't get comfortable. She turned and writhed; there was a feeling all over her, like flies crawling around. She ran her hands up and down her body, trying to push it off, the responsibility.

'Help,' she screamed. 'Help me.'

The sound dinged off the walls, ringing away into the silence. Shocked, Emma clapped her hand to her mouth.

In his cot, Ritchie stirred, and was quiet.

Emma lay, still with her hands to her mouth, utterly afraid.

Tuesday, 26 September
Day Ten

The flat was chilly and smelled of old food. Emma dumped her passport and keys on the table. She stood there, still in her outdoor fleece, her hands hanging down at her sides.

'Will you be all right?' Rafe asked.

He had pulled a chair out from under the table. He held it towards her until she sat down.

'He's better off without me,' Emma said dully. 'I didn't deserve to be his mother.'

'Of course you did,' Rafe said. 'Don't be so hard on yourself, Emma. Things haven't been easy for you.'

'I didn't deserve him,' Emma said. 'I didn't want the responsibility of him. Anyway, it's over now.'

She didn't have to worry about him any more. From now on, Ritchie would be looked after. He would be OK.

Rafe hunched beside her.

'Don't give up. There's still plenty you can do. You can follow up the other leads.'

'What other leads?'

'Well, didn't you say the police mentioned a sighting in Manchester? Someone up there saw a child who looked like Ritchie? They're still looking into that, aren't they?'

It took her a couple of seconds to get it. The sensation that hits you when you think you've reached the bottom of a stairs but there's a final step you haven't noticed, and when you take it, the sickening jar goes right through your body.

She sat up.

'You don't think he's mine,' she said.

Rafe wouldn't meet her eyes.

'You don't believe me.' Emma was shocked. Truly shocked. On the journey home, Rafe had been very quiet. She'd guessed it was his reaction to her telling him the real story about what she'd said to Dr Stanford. Even so, she'd still been so sure he was on her side. But it was clear now that even Rafe, so accepting and unjudgemental, had a line that couldn't be crossed, and she, by what she'd told him, had done that at last.

Rafe looked very uncomfortable.

'It's not that I don't believe you, Emma. I know you think it's him. I know you're convinced about that. It's just . . . ' He sighed. 'The DNA, you know. It's hard to argue with it. Maybe we should just face the facts.'

Emma was incredulous. She'd thought he was brighter than that. Surely he must realize what had happened?

'She faked the test,' she said. 'She did something to mix them up.'

Rafe shook his head.

'I've seen these tests done,' he said. 'It's a very strict procedure. Once the swabs are taken, they're put straight into a sealed bag and sent to the lab. It's done that way on purpose, so no one can tamper with them.'

Emma was shaking her head too.

'Is there any way,' Rafe persisted, 'that that little boy could have just looked like Ritchie? That you could just have thought it was him, because you want so much for that to be the case?'

'No,' Emma said. 'No way at all.'

Rafe sighed again.

He said, 'My flight to La Paz leaves in a few days.'

'You should take it,' Emma told him. 'Honestly. Don't miss it on my account.'

'I didn't mean that,' he said.

Then he said something odd.

He said, 'Why don't you come with me?'

'Sorry?' Emma stared at him.

'Well,' Rafe sounded apologetic, 'if, as you say, that *is* Ritchie in France, and you know where he is, then you know that he's safe. You said you didn't think you deserved him because the responsibility was too much for you. Now's your chance to take a break from everything. Come with me for a while. Try again when you get back.'

'Try . . . ' Emma couldn't believe what she was hearing. What was Rafe saying? Go on *holiday* with him? Had he lost his mind? She looked at him again, and saw with a stone heart what she should have seen all along: a young, free stranger in a blue outdoor jacket, all ready for his backpacker tour of the world. What an adventure this must seem to him. A drama in his life, like going to a see a thriller in the cinema. A break in his routine of — how had he put it? Drifting. A vast space opened between them; he was a dot on the other side, and oh, it was a loss, she was amazed she could still feel it, on top of everything, but she could; and it gnawed at her, another frozen gap of pain.

'I'm sorry,' she said coldly, 'but I can't just go on holiday while my son has been kidnapped. I can't just *take a break* from him. I won't start a new life, a life he was never in . . . I won't do that . . . I'll never . . . '

She couldn't continue. The coldness had gone from her voice. Even to keep that there was too much for her now. All that was left was how she felt: profound unhappiness, that everything, everything had gone so wrong.

Rafe was nodding. He had a strange expression on his face.

'OK,' he said. 'OK.'

He didn't say anything more to persuade her. He closed the door quietly as he left.

15

Wednesday, 27 September
Day Eleven

'There's been a change of plan,' Rafe said. 'I'm leaving tomorrow.'

Emma's eyes were puffy and sore. She squinted at the clock. Just gone six. Voices and traffic noises from the street below. Six in the evening then, presumably, rather than the morning.

'I'm sorry,' she said. What was it they'd been talking about? Her voice sounded thick and swollen, as if she had a cold. 'What did you say?'

'I'm leaving tomorrow morning,' Rafe repeated. 'My flight's at seven. Sooner than I expected, but a chance came up of some work abroad and I couldn't say no.'

Emma didn't answer.

'So,' Rafe said, 'it looks like I mightn't see you again before I go.'

'No.'

'Will you be all right?' he asked.

'Yes. Thank you.'

'I'll be in touch,' Rafe promised.

'Uh-huh.'

She crawled back to bed. He wouldn't be in touch. She didn't blame him. Ritchie wasn't his child. Time for him to move on.

★　★　★

Lindsay spoke to Emma about her trip to France.

'How did you get the Hunts' address?' she asked.

Emma didn't reply.

'You know you can't do that again,' Lindsay warned her. 'You could have got yourself into a lot of trouble.'

Emma ignored her. She rested her head on the back of the couch and looked up at the ceiling. They could do what they liked to her now. She didn't care any more.

Over the next few days, people trooped in and out of her flat. There was a social worker called Ziba — something like that — all dressed in black, like she was going to a funeral. A doctor called Hughes, in a striped navy suit. Dr Hughes kept asking her how she was feeling. She said she was very tired but couldn't sleep. Dr Hughes said he'd see about giving her something very mild that would help.

'What would be your thoughts on going into hospital?' he asked. 'Just for a little while? For a rest?'

'Whatever you think.'

Dr Hughes wrote something on a card. More writing. Between the doctors and the police, there must be a whole library on her somewhere by now.

Dr Hughes said, 'We'll talk about this again.'

⋏　⋏　⋏

At one point, someone knocked on the door of the flat, and when she opened it there was a nurse in blue standing in the hall. Emma had been asleep until the knocking woke her up, and for a second she was confused. Was she in the hospital after all, then? But the nurse was Rosina Alcarez, holding a Tupperware box that smelled of spices.

'I'm sorry.' Rosina looked anxious. 'I hope you don't mind me calling. I'm on my way to work, for my night shift, but I've brought you something to eat.'

She held up the Tupperware container.

'Fish,' she said, 'with rice and ginger. Very mild. Plenty of nutrition.'

'Thank you,' Emma said. 'But I'm not really hungry.'

'It is Philippines food.' Rosina said. 'Not everybody likes it. If you would prefer, I can get you something British?'

'No. Really. I'm fine.'

'OK.' Rosina nodded. 'I am sorry to bother you.'

She turned to leave.

Emma wanted nothing more than to close the door and go back to bed. But Rosina's unassuming nod at the rejection, her quiet willingness to take back the unwanted meal, so thoughtfully prepared, gave her a curious pang of guilt.

With an effort, she said to Rosina's back, 'How is your daughter?'

Rosina turned at once, her round face brightening. She came back to the door.

'She is good,' she said eagerly. 'She has grown so big. I have some photographs they sent the other day — '

She stopped, looking down.

'It's all right,' Emma said. 'I was the one who asked. I don't mind if you talk about her.'

But Rosina settled the strap of her bag on her shoulder, and stared at the Tupperware container.

Emma said, 'Do you have any of the pictures with you?'

'I have one.' Rosina glanced up at her. 'But it's OK if you — '

'Please.' Emma widened the door. 'Please. I'd like to see it.'

On the couch, Rosina felt about in her bag and passed Emma a photo. It was a close-up, the face of a smiling baby about eighteen months old. The baby had dark eyes and plump red cheeks. She was wearing something white — whether a top or a dress, it was hard to say. All you could see was the bright whiteness at her throat. She looked like a robin in the snow.

'She's beautiful.' Tears ran down Emma's face. 'Really beautiful.'

Rosina was upset. 'I shouldn't have showed you.'

'No, no.' Emma wiped her cheeks with her hand. 'I'm glad you did.'

But Rosina's distress increased. She turned to Emma, sitting on the edge of the couch.

'I told them,' she said, agitated. 'I told them you should be in a hospital. You should not be here alone. The police say, 'Oh, it is up to such and such' — always up to some other person, to organize everything. That Dr Hughes who came here, I know him from the hospital. I find him in the corridor and I say to him, 'Please, come back and see her again. She is so unhappy.' And he say, 'Oh, so now you are a doctor and can tell me what to do.''

Emma listened, astonished at how much Rosina had been thinking of her all this time. All the things her shy, quiet neighbour had tried to do for her, all without Emma knowing, never expecting any thanks or recognition.

'You're very good,' she said. She wiped her face again with her hands. 'To help me like that. But I'll be all right. Honestly I will.'

'Are you sure?'

'Yes.'

Emma felt very tired. She touched the face of the little girl in the photo.

She said, 'I never asked you her name.'

'Her name is Estela.'

'Estela. It's beautiful.'

'It means 'star'.' Rosina hesitated. 'If you want, I can leave this photo with you.' Her eyes were anxious again, worried she might have somehow said or done the wrong thing. 'But only if you want.'

Emma said, 'If you can spare it, I would love to have it.'

She placed Estela's photo on the low TV table, beside the picture of Ritchie with his tycoon comb-over hairstyle. The two toddlers smiled at each other.

'One day they will meet. I know it.' Tears in Rosina's eyes now too. She moved closer to the photos. As she did so, her arm brushed against Emma's, and Emma did not move away.

The sky over the balcony was dark. Stars, to the east, over the tower. Side by side the two mothers sat, elbows touching, gazing in silence at their children.

⋆   ⋆   ⋆

And then, at one point, Emma woke up and the flat was quiet. No people in suits. No voices. No one there at all.

She lay and floated in the silence, arms and legs spread to all corners of the bed. She was drifting in nothing, in a big white vacuum bowl. Her mind had no anchor. Her head ached from lying down so much. But she didn't want to get up. Or sleep. Or stay where she was. Or be alone, or have anybody with her.

She stretched out her arm and her fingers touched something on the locker by her bed. She frowned. The object rattled when she moved it. She took it and lay back in the bed, holding her arm up in the air so she could see what it was. A small, brownish plastic jar with a lid. The jar Dr Hughes had given her with the pills in, to help her sleep.

Emma pushed herself up on to her elbow. She peered through the side of the jar. Capsules, wobbling about on the bottom, each about the size of a large grain of rice. One half of each capsule was red, the other green. Emma opened the jar and took out one of the capsules. She held it between her finger and thumb, turning it this way and that to examine it. There was writing on the side, some kind of number. She popped the pill into her mouth. Tasteless. Plastic, if anything. She swallowed it. It took a few attempts, as her mouth was dry, but she managed to get it down.

She took out another pill. This time, instead of eating it, she pulled the two coloured halves apart. The whitish powder inside sprinkled all over the sheets. Then she took a third pill and bit into it. The taste was so vile she spat it out again straight away.

She went to take another one, but that was all there was. Emma turned the bottle upside down. Empty. Three was all they'd left her. The first pill was still stuck halfway down her throat. She swallowed again but it stayed where it was. She could feel it sitting there, burning a hole in her neck.

Some time after that, she got out of bed. She went to the fridge to get a drink of something to get rid of the capsule in her throat. But the fridge was empty. Someone had cleaned it out and propped the door open with a sweeping brush.

Emma thought for a while. Then she put on her trainers on, took her bag and headed off out to Sainsbury's.

Closed.

Must be earlier than she'd thought.

What now? She stood there in the street, very low. She could go home again. But she didn't have to. There was no one expecting her. No one waiting to be fed, or changed, or entertained. She could go anywhere. Might as well make the most of it. It was what she'd wanted, after all.

She walked to Hammersmith station and

boarded the first train that stopped at the platform. Eastbound District Line. She sat in the corner, beside the connecting door. Most of the other seats were empty. There were three people in her carriage, all wearing suits and reading the *Metro*. Off to work in the City, probably. Where was *she* going to go? Emma looked at the map above the window. One of the big stations, maybe? She could take a trip out of London. Victoria was coming up in a few stops. The Victoria trains all went south, as far as she knew. To the coast.

Suddenly she wanted to be near the sea again.

A little boy with wispy hair, rolling down a dune.

★   ★   ★

Brighton looked very pale when she came out of the station. Everything painted cream or eggshell or pastel. The whiteness of the sky told her which direction the sea was in. Straight down the hill, through the town. There were people everywhere. Shops and amusements and piers and restaurants. Not what she'd expected, for some reason. Not the sort of sea she was looking for.

'You want the bus east, lovie,' a nice woman washing the floor in a pub told her. 'The coast is quieter there. Might be more what you're after.'

The woman was right. Sitting on the bus, watching the large, cream-coloured buildings give way to smaller towns, and then to villages, Emma felt a huge sense of relief. Finally the bus came to its last stop outside a lone pub in the middle of nowhere. Two cars in the car park. No people. The wrong time of year for tourists. Raindrops dotted her cheeks when she got out.

She could smell the sea. The smell blew from behind a line of grassy hills, like the dune in France. A path — a groove in the sand really — led over the dune. She took it, leaning into the wind.

She didn't notice herself climbing and was surprised, on reaching the top, to see how far she was above the sea. No gentle slope down to the shore, this, but a sheer drop over high cliffs.

She walked right to the edge and looked over. The walls of the cliffs were dazzling white. The sea was blue — not just normal sky-blue, but a surreal, vivid turquoise. Hypnotized, Emma stared down. The colours seemed much too bright to be real. They were like crayon colours, colours you'd find in a child's nursery.

A memory of herself: very small, playing in a white room somewhere, with a doll in a bright blue dress. Where, she didn't know; a neighbour's house maybe, or some child's birthday party. She had hummed to herself as she played.

She'd been happy there.

If she wanted, right now, she could go there again.

Ritchie would be fine without her. He would forget. She could leave him, leave his baby softness and the arms that clung to hers. They wouldn't cling to her for ever anyway. The arms pulled; there was a catch at her chest, and he was gone. When she saw him next, he was running on a beach, chasing something, a kite or a dog. He was older — ten, maybe — strong and healthy and happy. His hair was darker but he still had Oliver's smile. He was tall, and spoke confidently, in a language she didn't understand. The sky grew dark, he ran past but didn't recognize her, and he ran home to a place she didn't know.

The sky darkened further. The wind came up. She couldn't see the waves any more, but she could hear them, crashing and pounding against the rocks. Emma felt like an animal before a storm. As if electrons were running through her body, snapping her alive. Her mind was sharp and clear, like cleaned glass.

'There's a wall between your mother and happiness,' her grandmother had once said. 'It's been there so long now, I think it would take something huge to break it down.'

Emma fingered the scar on her chin.

The eager child, running to her mum. The shock of it as her mother pushed her away. The fright, more than anything else, as she tumbled against the fire-place.

Her mother, white-faced, springing out of her chair.

'Emma. Emma, are you all right?'

Her voice so odd and high. She flew to Emma and scooped her up. She stood with her in her arms, squeezing her tight, rocking her to right and left.

'I'm sorry, I'm so sorry,' she kept saying, over and over again. Her voice was muffled. She had her face in Emma's hair. 'I never should have done that. I love you, sweetheart. I love you,

you'll never know how much.'

Emma didn't remember the exact words but she knew that was the gist. She remembered very clearly how tightly her mother had held her. At the time, she'd been frightened, not used to seeing her mother so emotional; but also she was exhilarated, because it was like in the ad for washing powder where the mother lifted the child out of bed and spun her in the air. Emma had loved that ad.

Her mother was with her now, beside her, her hair, the same colour as Emma's, whipping in the wind.

I needed help, but I was too proud. I'm sorry, my darling child. I should have fought harder for you.

'It's all right, Mum. I know. I always knew.'

The wind was beginning to fall. The waves rolled, rather than smashed, into the cliffs.

She would fight for Ritchie. He would know her when he grew up. She didn't know how she'd get him back, but she would. She had a head start, didn't she? She knew he was alive, who he was with. That was much more than the parents of some missing children ever knew. She'd tried hardly anything yet. There was a way, and whatever it took, she would find it. She wouldn't give up until she did.

★　★　★

Quarter to midnight. No point waiting for a bus at this hour. Emma stepped off the soaking dune and walked along the road until she came to a village. One of the houses had a sign in the window saying 'Vacancy'.

The woman who answered the door took her time, looking Emma up and down in the porch-light before grudgingly admitting that yes, she did have a room. Emma supposed it was her wetness that was the problem. Or her lack of luggage, or the lateness of the hour. The woman led her through to a spotless kitchen with pine cupboards and a long table down the middle, set with a white cloth and cups and bowls for breakfast. She wrote Emma's details into a notebook with a marble-design cover. Then she took some keys and showed her to a bedroom off a hall behind the kitchen.

Emma sat for a while by the radiator in her room, letting the warmth loosen her limbs. She hadn't realized how cold the wind on the cliffs had been.

Funny, the way her mum had come to her so strongly up there. When she had died, Emma had just . . . kept going. She'd never done any of the things you were supposed to do when your closest family member died. Weep, smell her mum's perfume, visit her grave. The sort of things other people said they did. She didn't know why, really. The death had sat inside her like a stone. For a while, Oliver had taken the pressure off, but when he had let go, the stone had come back, heavier than before. Only this time, she'd hardly noticed it, because she'd had Ritchie to carry as well.

'Why does she keep calling?' she'd said to Joanne, when she'd found her mother's messages on the answering machine.

But she knew why now. It was because her mum had never given up either.

The wind rattled the glass, gentler with each gust. Her mum's presence was less strong here than it had been on the cliff. But from up there, you could see down to this house. And all the way to France too, if you looked over the sea.

Emma said, 'If you can see him, tell him I'm coming. Tell him to hold on.'

Then she took off all her clothes and spread everything out on an armchair to dry. She fell into the single bed. She slept as soon as the duvet settled over her. She didn't dream at all.

When she woke, the room was very bright. She'd left the red gingham curtains open. A vase filled with dried flowers stood on the window sill. She could see the branch of a tree, and part of a washing-line with a man's blue shirt and some towels. Somewhere, someone was hammering something. A large-sounding dog barked deeply. Children's voices floated:

'You're a . . . '

'No, *you're* a . . . '

Once Emma realized the voices weren't about to come right up to the window, she relaxed, letting her legs straighten out in the bed. Strange, how her body ached. Her muscles felt used and stretched, as if she'd been running a marathon or lifting heavy weights. She was hungry as well. A toast-and-butter smell wafted from the hall. What time was it? She lifted her head. She couldn't see a clock anywhere. What had she done with her bag? Her phone would have the time on it.

The bag was a couple of feet away under a chair. Still wrapped in her duvet, Emma leaned out of bed to tug it towards her. She felt around inside it, thrusting aside keys and pens with her fingers, until finally she located her mobile right at the bottom. She lay back in the bed, holding the phone up to see the screen.

Then she looked again and blinked.

Twenty-eight missed calls.

Emma frowned and sat up.

Even as she did so, the phone rang again.

'Hello?'

'Emma!'

It was Rafe.

'Emma.' He talked right over her as she tried to answer. 'Where have you been? I've been trying all night. You just disappeared. I rang the police, I rang everyone. No one knew where you were.'

Emma was astonished. He'd been phoning her all night? From Peru or Bolivia or wherever it was?

'I'm here,' she said. 'I'm here, it's all right. I didn't do anything — '

Again, he cut across her.

'I have a message for you,' he said.

'From who?' She was bewildered.

Rafe said, 'From your son.'

16

Monday, 2 October
Day Sixteen

The train from Brighton pulled into Victoria two and a half minutes early. Roused from her trance by the announcement from the driver, Emma glanced up for the first time in an hour. South London had slid past without her noticing any of it. Outside the window, a pigeon with a crisp in his beak fluttered in a panicky way, flapping his wings in circles before getting back on top of things and floating upwards to the grimy glass ceiling.

Rafe, wearing his bright blue jacket, was waiting for her on the concourse. She met him in a daze.

'I can't believe it,' she said. 'Tell me I didn't imagine what you told me.'

'You didn't imagine it.'

He hustled her to the nearest café and sat her at a table by the window. Before he left for the counter, he took something wrapped in a plastic bag from his pocket and passed it into her hand.

Emma sat there, staring at the contents of the bag, turning it over and over between her fingers.

'I'm starving,' Rafe said, reappearing at the table with a trayload of food. 'My flight home was too early for breakfast.'

He sat across from Emma, slid a takeaway coffee cup towards her and began to rip the cellophane off a giant salad roll.

'Just give me a minute to get this down,' he said. 'Then we'll decide our next move.'

Emma tried to let him eat in peace but it was impossible. A thousand questions battled to escape. So many gaps needing to be filled. What came next? What should she do now? But before she could work it out, there were way too many things she needed to know.

'How did you get their phone number?' she asked, starting with the first thing to come into her head.

'It was . . . ' Rafe stopped, waving his hand. He chewed on a mouthful of food, swallowed, and continued, 'It was with the address that my friend Mike sent me.'

'So that was where you were all along.' Emma marvelled at it. 'Not in Bolivia at all.'

'I never actually said where I was going,' Rafe pointed out. 'All I said was that a job came up abroad that I couldn't refuse.'

'A garden that needed work,' Emma said slowly, 'in a house that was suddenly for sale.'

'Precisely,' Rafe said. 'Could have been made for me, eh?'

He took a mouthful of coffee.

'I didn't tell you where I was going,' he said, 'because I didn't want to get your hopes up. I didn't really have any idea what I was going to do. For all I knew, it could have ended up being a total waste of time.'

'How did you get them to take you on?' Emma asked.

'I told David Hunt I was an ex-pat gardener

who offered landscaping services for gardens where the English-speaking owners were trying to sell.'

'What if he'd asked where you'd got his number?'

'I was going to take a chance and say I knew the estate agent. Fortunately, he didn't ask.'

In fact, as he went on to explain, David Hunt hadn't seemed to be that interested in the state of his garden at all.

'It *could* do with some work,' he had agreed in a cautious way, when Rafe had enquired whether his garden was up to saleable scratch.

'Couple of days' worth,' Rafe said firmly. 'Mowing, weeding, hedge-cutting, that kind of thing. You'll find your viewings will shoot up. Garden's the first thing they see.'

'You have a point,' David Hunt said. 'As it happens, though, we have our own gardener.'

'Oh.' *Arse.*

'Yes. I'm not sure why he doesn't seem to have been here for a while. He's normally very good. We've been away, so things seem to have been allowed to slide, but I think you're right. I think we do need to give him a call.'

'Right.' Rafe tried to think of some other way he could get himself invited to the house. Nothing sprang to mind. 'Right. Well, can I leave you my contact details anyway? Just in case.'

'Of course,' David Hunt said. Rafe recited the number and David Hunt repeated it back to him, but there was no way of telling whether he'd written it down.

'I appreciate your calling,' he said.

'No problem.'

Click. The line went dead.

⋆ ⋆ ⋆

But an hour later, David Hunt called back.

'You won't believe it,' he said. 'Our usual chap is having an operation of some sort. He won't be able to work for six weeks. Now you've put the idea in my head, we probably could use you.'

⋆ ⋆ ⋆

'The gods were on our side,' Rafe said. He took another bite of salad roll.

'Didn't you have any kind of plan?' Emma asked. 'Any idea at all what you were going to do?'

'Christ, no. One thing I knew, even if they did let me anywhere near the house, they sure as hell weren't going to let Ritchie out of their sight for one second. I didn't even know if he'd still be there at all.'

Emma looked again at the little bag in her hand. She smoothed the see-through plastic. No diamond could have been more precious.

'I thought you didn't believe me,' she said, 'That he was mine.'

'I *wanted* to believe you.' Earnestly, Rafe leaned forward. 'I knew *you* believed it. I just couldn't see how it fitted with the DNA. I thought, maybe you could have been making yourself think it was him. You know, because of how much you were grieving. I know things have been a bit . . . ' He trailed off.

'It's all right.' Emma rescued him.

'I'm sorry,' he said. 'I didn't mean to — '

'It's all right,' she repeated.

Another glance at the bag on her knee. Time for all that later.

★ ★ ★

And so it wasn't until a long time afterwards that she heard from Rafe the thoughts that had see-sawed through his head as he waited at the airport, his rucksack at his feet. The police had warned him off: 'You hardly know this woman. Don't break the law on her behalf.' In his pocket, plane tickets for two countries.

Keep trying. Or just keep going. It wasn't too late to decide.

Why was he doing this? Getting himself so involved with this woman? In the beginning, he'd felt guilty, and sorry for Emma, who'd struck him as being frankly wretched and pitiful, but now he seemed to have ended up a lot deeper in the whole thing than he'd intended. How *could* that kid in France be Ritchie? Everything pointed against it. The DNA. Everything. You only needed half a brain to see how unlikely it was to be him.

And what the hell had he been thinking, asking Emma to come with him to South America like that? He'd expected her to tell him where to stick it, and she had. In his defence, he'd only been trying, in his big-mouthed, cack-handed way, to make her see that she was a good mother, whatever she said about herself.

Because the way she spoke about Ritchie! She knew every little detail about him. This was no feckless, negligent, abusive parent. And she wasn't stupid. Far from it. Surely her opinion should count for something?

That story she'd told him, about going to the GP and saying she was planning to kill Ritchie. Strong words, you could not deny it. But words were not deeds. Talking about killing him and actually doing it were not the same thing. And then the GP, peeling off like that and running to the police, saying she thought Emma hadn't been coping. Stupid woman. If that was what she'd thought, why hadn't she done her job at the time and tried to help? And didn't doctors have a Hippocratic Oath forbidding them from revealing secrets told to them by patients in their surgeries? Or was that priests he was thinking of?

The police, anyway, were no doubt pleased enough to have what they saw as the answer all nicely laid out in front of them. You couldn't blame them. It was human nature. Take the easy path.

'DI Hill's a tosser,' Mike, his friend, had told him. 'Puts the hours in but that's it. I couldn't see him going the extra mile. Your friend's been unlucky. She doesn't seem to have many people on her side, does she?'

'No,' Rafe said, 'she doesn't.'

'What's your interest in this anyway?' Mike sounded curious.

Rafe paused.

'I think maybe the chickens,' he said.

306

It wasn't a lie. He'd always felt guilty about those chickens. He'd jacked in his probation because of the unquestioning way the police had accepted the paperwork saying the chickens were being properly treated — European directive, number of square metres per bird, blah blah blah — and they'd hauled off the animal rights protestors and refused to investigate any further. And so the farm had stayed open, and it was another year before someone finally got in there with a camera and filmed the workers during their lunch hour, playing football with the chickens, hurling the frantically flapping creatures against the walls, kicking them mercilessly back and forth across the concrete floor.

He'd walked out to make a point. When the point was, if he'd stayed, maybe he could have done something to help.

Sod it. Maybe it wasn't Ritchie at all. But he wouldn't have peace of mind until he knew. It wasn't as if there was much else going on in his life at the moment. His main problem these days was finding ways to stay out of that flea-pit flat over the kebab shop that he shared with Neil, the poet. Poet and cannabis addict. He was finding the days very long. Things were only quiet because he was about to travel, he knew that. But what did you do while you were waiting? Go for a cycle. Do the Sudoku. Meet a mate for a pint. Somehow, when he was a kid, he'd thought he'd have been doing *more* with his life by now.

So. He was going to France. He would see this child again with his own eyes. And if it turned out not to be Ritchie, he'd have done what he

307

could to help and he could move on.

South America. Tents under a canopy. The desert on horseback. The Iguazu waterfall. Polyfilla for the gaps in himself. He would walk in the mountains and rainforests, contemplating life; and when he got bored of that he'd go to the cities and sink into his choice of depravity. Marinade his mind. The trip of a lifetime.

★   ★   ★

He arrived at St-Bourdain in the afternoon. He drove through the tall iron gates, and up the hill around the trees, and when he saw the Hunts' house he whistled. He'd been here before, but at the time he hadn't paid too much attention to the place. This time . . . well, there was no denying it, this was one serious heap of bricks. Three storeys, the same bleached stone as the gate pillars. Windows everywhere, framed with pale blue shutters, the glass black in the light. The rust-red roof pinkened in the sun.

He parked the car in front of the house and turned off the engine. Silence descended like a thick, green blanket; the sort of silence that only money could buy; voice-free, machine-free, broken only by the *zzeeoo* of some passing insect. Rafe hoped it wasn't a sign he'd got here too late. He got out of the car. The three stone steps to the wooden front door were dotted with orange trees in square wooden pots. Beside the door, under some creeper, was a push-button doorbell. He pressed it, and heard a fairly ordinary *ding-dong* die away inside the house.

308

The green silence again. He stood on the step, looking around. The only car he could see was his own. At the front of the house, a willow tree shaded a flagstoned courtyard and a white, wrought-iron table and chairs. The only items missing were a jug of lemonade and a chick holding a frilly umbrella.

Still no answer to the doorbell. Where had the Hunts gone? Shopping? A day out? Taken the kid and moved to Australia? Then footsteps echoed inside the house, and the wooden door was opened by a tall, slim woman, dressed for the heat in white trousers and a pale green shirt. She held the door and stared.

'Hello.' Rafe put on his most jovial, gardener-type smile. 'I'm Rafe Townsend. I spoke to Mr Hunt the other day, about doing some work in the garden.'

'My husband did mention it,' the woman said. 'I'm Mrs Hunt.'

Mrs Hunt — or Philippa, as he knew her name was — looked good for her age, which was probably early forties. Very preserved. Plucked eyebrows, the lot. She also looked much more suspicious than her husband had sounded.

'I'm very sorry,' she said, 'but I must tell you that we would normally require references before employing someone like this. We've been very busy recently, and unfortunately my husband completely forgot until this morning to inform me about this arrangement.'

OK. If he was in a circus, this was the part right now where he'd be out on the tightrope. Right out in the middle. Rafe kept his smile.

'I understand,' he said. 'You can't be too careful these days.' He let his gaze fall to a clump of nettles growing through the stones on the bottom step. 'Of course, if you need a reference, I'd be only too happy to provide one.'

Mrs Hunt's gaze dropped, with his, to the nettles. Then towards the gate, where the wooden estate agent's sign faced the road. Her expression went blank for a moment.

She looked back at Rafe.

'Where are you living?' she asked.

'I'm based in Domme,' Rafe lied, having picked the name at random from the map. It was a village far enough away that she'd be unlikely to know anyone there, or want to know what street he lived on. He hoped.

'Domme,' Mrs Hunt mused. 'Isn't that where they have that marvellous market on the hill?'

'That's the one,' Rafe agreed. 'Great vegetables. I stock up there every Saturday.'

'Really?' Mrs Hunt looked surprised. 'I thought that market only opened on a Thursday.'

'No, it . . . changed.'

'Oh. How very interesting.'

Mrs Hunt looked closely at Rafe's clothes. He was wearing his heavy brown boots. They were still clumped and stained with mud from his last gardening job.

'If I were to employ you,' she said, 'I would need that reference.'

He'd done it. Done it! She was coming in.

'No problem,' he said.

Philippa Hunt paused again, then opened the front door wider. Rafe was looking everywhere as

310

soon as he entered, taking in as much as he could. The hall was double height, with cream and pale blue tiles on the floor. An iron chandelier with candles hung from the ceiling on a long chain, almost low enough to touch. A marble table with ornate, gilded legs stood under a massive, gilt-framed mirror. The rest of the furniture was dark wood: a hat-stand and a chest of drawers, and what looked like a church pew along one wall.

'If I could have a contact number for your referee?' Philippa was standing before him with a pen. Rafe gave her the number of the landscaping agency he'd been with in England. He hoped she'd be happy with that and not insist on a reference from France as well.

As he'd guessed she would, the first thing Philippa did was to call directory enquiries to confirm that the number he'd given her belonged to the address he said it did. Then she went off to a room somewhere to ring the agency. Rafe used the opportunity to continue his recce of the hall. Five doors leading off, including the one Philippa had just gone through. A polished stone staircase with an iron banister. Halfway up, the staircase curved to the right, so he couldn't see all the way to the top. No child visible or audible anywhere. No photos. And then, just as Philippa's footsteps came tapping back into the hall, he glanced under the marble table and spotted a pair of tiny red wellies, scuffed with mud.

Philippa appeared, closing her phone.

'Your reference is satisfactory,' she said. 'When

would you be able to start?'

Rafe said calmly, 'Today, if you like?'

'Excellent.' Philippa opened a drawer and took out a set of keys. 'I'll show you where the gardening things are kept.'

She led him out again through the big front door.

'I see you have children,' Rafe said, indicating the boots under the table as they passed.

'Yes, we do.'

Philippa closed the door behind them. Rafe followed her down the steps, unable for the moment to think of a follow-up child-related question that wouldn't sound too nosy.

They went around the side of the house, past a grassy, fenced-off area, like a dog-run, with a tree on a small hill in the middle. Then they crossed a paved area to a low white building.

'This is where Frank' — Philippa pronounced it Frrronk — 'keeps the gardening equipment.'

She turned keys in two separate locks. Inside, the building consisted of a long, white-painted room with shelves all down one side. Fronk seemed to have been very organized. Sets of shears hung on hooks in order of size, all of them gleaming and clean. Hoes and rakes lined up against the wall. Boxes of weedkiller and fertilizer on the shelves. The hoses were stored beneath. Dimly, Rafe glimpsed their dark green coils.

'Through there you'll find a kitchen and lavatory,' Philippa said, indicating a door. 'The kitchen is quite basic, but there is a microwave in case you need to heat up anything.'

In other words, no reason for him to go back into the house.

'What would you like me to do?' Rafe asked.

'Frank tends to keep to a list.' Philippa showed him a printed page on the wall. 'He carries out the jobs in rotation, but as it's been a while, you might find that just about everything needs doing.'

The list was in French. Rafe nodded, arms folded, sucking his lower lip. He couldn't read a word of it.

'As you can see,' Philippa said, 'it's mostly mowing and weeding the areas around the house, and tending to the vegetable garden at the back. Through those trees over there is the goose farm, and Frank doesn't garden there, obviously.' She looked at him. 'My husband said you thought a couple of days should be enough?'

'That's right,' Rafe said. 'Say if I aim to finish by Monday?'

'That's fine.'

Philippa turned to leave.

'When are you planning to move?' Rafe asked, hoping to keep her talking.

She paused.

'In a couple of weeks.'

'Going anywhere nice?'

Mrs Hunt glanced towards the shelves.

'The lawnmowers are in a separate shed at the back,' she said. 'The sit-on was giving us trouble, but I think Frank has fixed it. Any problems, do let me know.'

She tapped across the paving stones, back to the house.

313

Right, missus. I hear you.

Rafe took another look around the room. What he was looking for, he wasn't sure. Children's stuff, maybe: old cots or prams in storage. Boxes with useful photos. But all he could see was weedkiller and watering cans.

There was another door, besides the one to the toilet and kitchen. He went to check it out. Behind the door was another large room, with shelves and a counter along one wall. The shelves were stacked with empty jars and plastic containers, all with dust on the top. A plastic sheet covered something on the counter. He lifted a corner to have a look. A cash register. Obviously the place was used, sometimes anyway, as a shop. Some of the containers had labels on the sides: *'Ferme des Chasseurs: Huile de Noix', 'Ferme des Chasseurs: Foie Gras'.*

Foie gras. Well, that explained the geese. Poor things. But a small country farm like this wouldn't make the Hunts the money they seemed to have. Possibly David was something or other in the City, and this was Philippa's thing on the side.

Anyway. Time was passing. He'd better look as if he was doing something. He took the lawn-mower out, deciding to concentrate for today on the area at the back of the house. Beyond the lawn were orchards of walnut and apple trees, and beyond them again, fields of dark maize. No child's toys anywhere that Rafe could see. No slides, swings, trucks, balls, cars. Nothing. It was as if no kid had ever lived here. Or maybe they had everything all packed up already.

314

After cutting the grass, Rafe took the hoe to the walled-in vegetable garden. More evidence of Fronk's impressive organizational skills. Carrots in rows like a passing-out parade. The tomatoes, however, were falling off the vine and lay, over-ripe and rotting, in the soil. The pumpkins were in better shape but needed re-staking and harvesting. Rafe didn't plan to bother too much about harvesting. His brief for now was just to make things look good. He dug weeds and cleared rotten fruit, and took the lot to the compost heap near the garden-room. Each time he wheeled the barrow past the house, he took a different route so he could look in as many windows as possible. At first he just glanced in, turning his head in a casual way as he passed. But then, as all the rooms seemed empty, he stepped closer, staring frankly in. Where were they all? The house was deserted. Philippa, at least, must be somewhere, surely. She was either upstairs or in some inner room with no windows; or perhaps she'd gone out altogether without him noticing.

As late in the evening as he reasonably could, he put away the hoe and barrow and rang the doorbell to let the Hunts know he was leaving. No answer. Well, whether they were out or hiding, with the gardening things put away he couldn't risk hanging around here much longer. Anyway, he was starving. He'd had nothing to eat all day.

★　★　★

He left the house and drove to a village a prudent twenty miles away. He booked himself into a guest-house, under the walls of yet another ancient castle. In a pizzeria under a stone arch, he more or less inhaled two portions of garlic bread and a twelve-inch pizza with extra toppings. Then he took a bottle of lager to a table on the outside terrace, looking down over some fields. The sun sank behind distant trees, turning the castle walls orange.

All right. What the hell was he doing here?

Even if he saw this kid, how was he going to know whether he belonged to the Hunts or to Emma? He didn't have a photo of Ritchie, though he'd seen a couple. Now it seemed moronic not to have brought one. Emma had mentioned he looked like her ex, who naturally Rafe had never met. And, despite what he'd naively thought, it didn't look as if he was about to witness any incriminating conversations between Philippa and her husband — but then, what had he been expecting? To burst in on them throwing their heads back and shouting: 'Mwa-ha-ha, we got away with it at last'? This was one couple who kept themselves very much to themselves. Which of course you would do, if you'd just kidnapped someone; but it could also be the reserve of the English upper middle classes, walking around all day with a pinched expression on their faces, as if someone had put a clothes peg up their arse.

Rafe took a mouthful of beer, swishing it thoughtfully through his teeth.

Emma. Emma Turner. What was it about this

woman? Why was he so convinced that she knew better than all of these people here? Better than the Hunts, in their stone, silent house; better than their family, the neighbours, the police. The DNA lab, for Christ's sake! Emma, who was so defensive and so suspicious of everyone, so hostile and prickly and angry. It was only now occurring to him that his bringing her here might have done her no favours at all. It might have been premature to have been so encouraging about the word 'Bergerac'. She might have heard it wrong. That woman in the café might have said something else entirely. She might have been a different woman entirely.

The Kronenbourg seeped down his throat. Rafe tipped his head back. His shoulders were killing him from today. He found himself looking straight up into the sky. Blue ink and orange. No moon tonight.

That day on the sand dune. The evening he'd driven her back to Bergerac, and they'd stood in the hall outside her room with the moonlight coming in. Those few seconds when all of her hostility had been suspended and just for that short time he'd seen . . . something so valiant and slender and vulnerable and sweet that . . .

Rafe lifted his head. He took another mouthful of beer.

All right. If he was going to continue with this, he should try to get into the house. Poke around a bit. See if he could find out where the Hunts were moving to. He could say he'd accidentally cut through a pipe and wanted to check that their water still worked. Or that he'd electrocuted himself on the mower and thought he might be having a heart attack.

Or he could just chuck in the whole thing and catch his flight to La Paz.

Another sip of the lager. He looked at the bottle. Where did they make this stuff? He'd drunk it in London, but it had never tasted this good. The light on the castle walls deepened to red.

No. He wasn't ready to leave here yet. He'd stay until he finished what he'd come to do.

⋆ ⋆ ⋆

The next morning, he was at the house by seven. He tackled the sloping lawn at the front with the sit-on mower, keeping a close eye on the house as he worked. Still no sign of anyone. In bed, in the house, gone out already for the day, who knew?

One day left. The frustration was getting to him. It was looking more and more as though Ritchie — if it *was* Ritchie — wasn't here. At this rate, he mightn't even get to see Philippa or David again either. OK, he'd have to meet one of them to get paid, but that would likely be a quick hand-over of an envelope and goodbye. There had to be some way to start up a conversation. Get some decent information without coming across as seriously inappropriate or obvious.

No point hanging around the house if no one was in. He took the hedge-trimmer down to the gate and began to cut away the heavier branches

318

that hung over the walls, keeping a sharp eye through his goggles for any cars coming in or out. His mind worked as he chopped. Which of the two of them might be easier to crack? Philippa or David? He had an idea from the phone that David might be the type to cave in and reveal more. But so far, Philippa was the only person he'd actually met.

He could always just break into the house. But what would that gain him? Apart from getting felt up under a tree by a couple of gendarmes.

It was after eleven. The sun was beating down. Rafe's throat prickled with dust and bits of hedge. He turned the trimmer off and trudged up the drive to the garden-room to get some water.

He was pulling a splinter out of his thumb, concentrating on his hand as he reached the house. Just as he rounded the corner, he glanced up. Then he threw his arms out, leaping back with a yelp, as if he'd just spotted Damien from the *Omen*.

There, in the grassy, fenced-off enclosure, sitting under the tree, a yellow plastic soother jammed in his mouth, was Ritchie.

★ ★ ★

'It nearly finished me,' Rafe admitted to Emma. 'I'd been thinking about toddlers all morning, and obviously sensitized myself so much that when I saw one I got a serious shock.'

'How did he look?' Emma whispered.

Rafe had painted the picture so perfectly. She

was there, not in an egg-and-bacon-smelling café near Victoria station, surrounded by the chatter of tourists and the shriek of milk being steamed, but right there, right there in the garden in France.

Rafe said, 'He looked great.'

He said, 'He looked exactly like you.'

★ ★ ★

Emma had said he resembled her ex, but he looked like *her*. A mini, male, blond her. The same eyes: dark blue, kind of tipped down at the sides. The same mouth, the lower lip fuller than the upper.

The last time, the time he'd been here with Emma, Philippa Hunt's arms had been in the way and Rafe hadn't been able to see the child. This time he had a ringside view. He watched the child playing with something in the grass, and all vestiges of doubt left his mind.

This was him. This was Emma's baby.

Rafe coughed to clear the dust from his throat. The sting made his eyes water. It was strange, seeing the kid here like this. Knowing the enormous injustice that had been done to Emma, and how much she would have given to be here and see him too. He cleared his throat again. Still dusty.

Now what?

The enclosure had a gate with thin wooden bars. Rafe watched Ritchie through the bars. He was still poking at the grass, rather aimlessly, just sitting there. His legs stuck out in front of him.

His head was down, his chins on his chest. He looked grave and thoughtful. Not like you'd expect a kid that age to look, all happy and crawling around.

Should he snatch him? Sweat trickled down Rafe's back. But then what? How would he get him to London?

He edged forward. No sign of anyone, but the back door to the house, only a few feet away, was ajar. Rafe opened the gate and stepped into the enclosure. The child was still intent on whatever he had in front of him in the grass. Keeping one eye on the back door, Rafe waved to attract his attention.

'Ritchie,' he whispered. 'Ritchie.'

Ritchie looked up at once, his face creased in puzzlement. Man, it was Emma again. Definitely. The way one of her eyebrows went lower than the other when she was trying to think of something.

'Over here, mate. This way.'

Ritchie's face cleared. He smiled, his cheeks puffing up like a chipmunk's around the soother. He lifted his finger and pointed, gazing past Rafe, as if he could see something behind him. Rafe glanced quickly over his shoulder. Nothing there but the wooden gate.

'Hey.' He turned back. 'Who are you looking at?'

He bent his knees to lower his face, trying to get Ritchie to focus on him.

'This way, mate. There's nobody here but me.'

Ritchie was still pointing at the gate and smiling. Then he seemed to change his mind. He switched his gaze to Rafe and held out his other hand. Something was in it, clutched in his grubby fist. Rafe couldn't see what it was. He inched forward, an ingratiating grin fixed to his face, hoping the little blighter wouldn't take a sudden dislike to him and start crying. Then the door to the house creaked open, and Philippa Hunt came out.

Hastily, Rafe transformed his step forward into a crouch. He patted the ground — checking the worm-count? — and nodded at Philippa in an amiable way. She gave him a swift look and strode into the enclosure. She went straight to Ritchie and picked him up, hoisting him on to her hip.

'Come along,' she said.

Rafe watched the tail of her shirt flutter as she marched away.

Two more seconds. Two more seconds and . . . what? He could have . . . he could have got some kind of repeat sample for DNA. A hair or something. Shit, why hadn't he thought of it in time? No way was he going to get another chance like this.

Philippa had stopped by the gate.

'What's this?' Rafe heard her ask Ritchie. 'What have you got there?'

She took something from his hand; the object he'd been holding out to Rafe. She tutted.

'Nasty,' she said to Ritchie, wrinkling up her nose. 'Nasty.'

She dropped whatever it was into the grass. Then she took Ritchie through the gate and back to the house. The door slammed shut behind her. Rafe heard the scrape and clang of a bolt.

He kicked at the grass. What a fucking loser! What was he, a fucking rabbit in headlights? He should have taken him while he had the chance. He kicked again. Now what? Carry on gardening? He looked around the enclosure. He'd been planning to take a strimmer to that part around the walnut tree. The tree stood on a short rise, almost a hill. Green fruit, still not quite ripe, hung from the branches like dark pears.

Rafe stared at the fruit.

He loves sour things.

He crouched down again, hunting in the long grass where Philippa had dropped the object Ritchie had been holding. He found what he was looking for and picked it out of the grass.

A dark green walnut, with toothmarks in it.

Rafe looked up. The back door was still shut.

He got to his feet, with the green fruit in his hand.

Saliva glistening all over it.

17

Emma's eyes were full. She still had so many questions. What else had Antonia said to Ritchie? Had she seemed angry with him? How had he looked when he smiled?

But she looked at the walnut in its plastic sandwich bag, with the surprisingly large bite mark in the side, and all she said was, 'We have to tell the police.'

★   ★   ★

Lindsay answered on the second ring.

'Emma,' she exclaimed, 'where have you been? We've all been so worried. You weren't in your flat, and your phone — '

'I'm fine,' Emma interrupted, cutting her off. 'I've got something I need to tell you.'

'Really?'

Emma announced, 'We've got proof.'

'Proof?'

'That that's Ritchie they've got there in France. That's my baby that woman has in her house.'

There was a silence. Then Lindsay said, 'Emma . . . what have you been doing?'

'Listen,' Emma said. 'Listen, and I'll tell you.' She did her best to give as clear an outline of the story as possible, but the coffee grinder at the counter had upped its setting to Road Drill, and the women at the table beside her were laughing in great, cackling shrieks. The noise pressurized her. She got mixed up, speaking faster instead of louder until all her words came tumbling out on top of each other. Lindsay had to interrupt to ask her to slow down.

'Emma . . . Emma, take it easy,' she said. 'I'm not getting everything you're saying. What was that last bit again? Did you say you had a sample from France, of that boy's DNA?'

'Yes.' Emma took a breath. 'I told you, didn't I? I told you it was him. I knew that woman messed with the DNA test. I *knew* she did.'

'But how — '

'You need to check this new sample against *my* DNA. Then you'll see he's mine. You'll see he really is Ritchie.'

Lindsay said, 'And this DNA is on a fruit?'

'On a walnut, yes.'

There was a pause. Then Lindsay said, 'Emma . . . '

'What harm can it do?' Emma asked. 'You keep saying you want to help me. If you do, then this is the way.'

'I do want to help you,' Lindsay said.

'Then where's the problem?'

'Come in,' Lindsay said. 'Come and meet me at the station today, and we'll talk about it.'

'But you'll do the test?' Emma persisted.

Lindsay hesitated.

'I'll have to talk to the DI first,' she said, 'before I can authorize anything like that.'

She suggested a time for them to meet at the Fulham Palace police station. Emma ended the call in frustration. She was no closer to knowing whether things were going to go anywhere than before she'd picked up the phone.

She said to Rafe, 'I don't think Detective Hill is going to like this.'

'I thought this might happen.' Rafe was hunched forward, stirring the remains of his coffee with a spoon. 'I don't know much about DNA, but I do know that we've got no proof of where I got that walnut from, or who was eating it. Plus, it's contaminated. I touched it, and so did that woman Philippa. Though to be honest, I don't think either of us touched the sticky part of it that Ritchie chewed. But still. It might be hard to convince the police.'

'Well, then,' Emma cried, 'we won't wait for them to make up their minds. We'll just go ahead and organize our own test.'

'Maybe,' Rafe said. He sat back, flipping the spoon between his fingers. 'I think we're going to need some extra muscle here. Maybe I should phone Mike again.'

'Mike? Your friend who gave us the address?'

'Yeah. Mike's a bit of a golden boy. Detective Sergeant since January, in the Drug Squad. But he's a decent bloke. He'll vouch for us at least. Make a couple of calls on our behalf.'

'Ring him, then,' Emma urged.

Rafe dug his phone out of the back pocket of his jeans. It was lunchtime, and the queue for the cashier stretched back as far as the door. The customers had to bellow their orders to be heard. Rafe took his phone outside to talk in peace. While she waited, Emma stroked the bag on her lap, smoothing the gnawed, misshapen fruit inside.

Come on, little walnut. It's all up to you now. Don't let us down.

★　★　★

Emma had thought it was just going to be Lindsay meeting them at the police station but, to her surprise, when she and Rafe were shown into the room where she'd watched the tape of Ritchie at the airport, Detective Inspector Hill was there as well. So were a couple of other people she didn't recognize. One of them, a large, untidy-looking man with very fair hair and eyebrows, nodded at Rafe in a friendly way.

'Mike!' Rafe sounded pleased and surprised.

Detective Hill, on the other hand, didn't look any friendlier than usual. He was leaning against a table, his arms folded, his bulgy blue eyes colder than ever.

'I've told DI Hill what's happened,' Lindsay explained to Emma.

Five pairs of eyes bored into her. Emma didn't waste any time.

'This,' she said, holding up the plastic bag with the walnut inside, 'has got Ritchie's saliva on it. We got it from him in France. If you compare the DNA with a sample from me, it'll prove once and for all that I'm his mother.'

Her hand shook. The bag crackled. She took a firmer grip on it, holding it straight out in front of Detective Inspector Hill. He kept his arms folded and stroked at his moustache.

'All right,' he said. 'All right. Without for the moment even going into how you managed to *obtain*,' a glance at Rafe, 'this item, my main question for now is: are we to just keep on repeating DNA tests on this French child until you get the result you want?'

Lindsay looked compassionately at Emma.

'I only want it repeated once,' Emma said. 'That other test was wrong. How can it hurt to just do this? You'll see it shows he's mine.'

'It may well do,' Detective Hill said, 'but we've already had a test done that shows he's someone else's. There'll need to be some quite solid grounds to order a repeat. And, with respect, how do we know that this . . . what, walnut? . . . came from that child in France? That it's not something Ritchie was eating here in London before he disappeared?'

Rafe said, 'Walnuts don't grow in the UK.'

There was a silence.

The other detective, a thin man with a biggish nose, spoke up: 'Actually, they do. My aunt has an orchard in — '

'I doubt if Ritchie was in your aunt's orchard recently,' Rafe snapped.

Emma burst out: 'Anyway, so walnuts grow in the UK. So what? There could be walnut trees all over London for all I care. But how many of them grow outside my flat? And even if Ritchie found a walnut somewhere before he was kidnapped and chewed it, why on earth would I have kept a half-eaten piece of fruit lying around the flat and not thrown it away?'

She thrust the plastic bag out again, so they all

had a clear view of what was inside.

'Look,' she said, 'you can see it's just starting to go ripe. Ritchie's been gone for over two weeks. If this walnut had been lying around the flat for that long, don't you think it would have gone rotten by now?'

She waited for Mr Orchard to say that walnuts never rotted, or something like that. But he didn't. Nobody spoke for a minute.

Then Detective Hill said to Mike and Rafe, 'Could I have a word?'

'Of course.'

Detective Hill got up off the table. His coat made a swishing noise as he left the room. Rafe caught Emma's eye and made a face, a quick, comical downtwist of his mouth at the sides. Then he followed Detective Hill and Mike out to the hall. After glancing at each other, so did Lindsay and the man whose aunt grew walnuts.

Emma was left on her own. The room had a tight, cloying smell: crisps, and the harsh, chemical tang of marker. Beside the table, a whiteboard was propped on a frame, with writing on it, as if someone had been giving a lecture. 'Public Perceptions of the Community Support Officer' was circled on the board. Arrows pointed out from the circle. At the end of one of them, a cartoon stick-man flexed his biceps and brandished a gun. Underneath him, someone had scribbled the word 'Rambo'.

They'd been gone a long time. What were they all talking about? Surely it was a case of a simple yes or no? Then it struck Emma that what Rafe had done, pretending to be a gardener like that,

329

might well be against the law. Oh, this was great. Just wonderful. Were they going to arrest him now, thanks to her, on top of everything else?

The door opened, and Lindsay came back into the room. She closed the door behind her.

'We've decided,' she said.

Emma waited.

Lindsay glanced down, delicately spreading the fingertips of both hands on the table as if she was playing the piano. Then she looked up again.

'First,' she said, 'I need to say something. There are still several other leads we're following up on. That child in Manchester I told you about, for one. We've got a car number, we're — '

'If you follow that lead,' Emma said in a hard voice, 'you'll be wasting your time.'

Lindsay sighed.

'Emma,' she said, 'we're going to do the test.'

Thank God.

'DI Hill isn't happy,' Lindsay said. 'You really shouldn't have gone back to that house at all. Or Mr Townsend shouldn't. Another thing you should know is that the DI has discussed this with one of our colleagues, an expert in DNA, and he says there's a high chance that the walnut will show up nothing at all. The acid from the fruit will almost certainly have destroyed any DNA that was on it. And since it's been lying around for quite a while, and handled by several different people, testing it is going to be very difficult. It could take days. Weeks, even.'

'But I — '

Lindsay held up a hand. 'But Detective

Sergeant Evans,' she said, 'assures us that your friend Rafe wouldn't have done what he did unless he honestly thought there was a very good reason. So that's our decision. We're going to go ahead with it.'

Emma breathed again. 'Thank you,' she said. 'Thank you very much.'

'One other thing I must tell you,' Lindsay said, 'If Ritchie's DNA does shows up on the walnut, all it means is that we would have grounds to have the official test repeated. On its own, the walnut won't be enough for us to just go out there and take him back. Do you understand that?'

'Yes.'

'All right then.'

Lindsay nodded.

Then she said, 'We've always looked for him, you know. I know you think we haven't, but we have.'

She sounded quite emotional, for her.

She said, 'I would love if the test showed it was Ritchie.'

'So would I,' Emma answered simply.

She didn't want to spend any more time talking. She wanted to get things moving. Take the next step.

'What happens now?' she asked. She was prepared to go anywhere for the DNA test. To a lab, or a clinic, or the hospital. Whatever she had to do.

Lindsay said, 'We're going to check the walnut against a sample of Ritchie's DNA from your flat. We'll take a sample from you as well. Also one from Mr Townsend, so the lab will be able to tell which DNA on the walnut is his. We can do that for you today. A specialist is on his way right now.'

The specialist, when he arrived, took details from Emma: her name, her date of birth, her address. He filled out them all out on a form. Then he held up a stick with a white cotton-wool ball on one end, like a giant ear-bud.

'Open your mouth, please,' he said.

It was like being at the dentist. Emma sat on the grey plastic chair and opened her mouth wide. She felt a ticklish pressure swooping around the inside of her cheek. This was what it had been like for Ritchie. She was almost certain he'd have tried to bite the stick.

The ear-bud was whisked away. Emma's lips and the inside of her cheek were dry. She licked around them with her tongue. The specialist rubbed the cotton-wool ball over a square of card. Then he folded a flap over the card, sealing it shut. He put the card into a plastic bag, along with the form he'd filled out with Emma's details.

'That's it,' he said. 'You can go.'

She left the room, elated. Finally. After all that, Ritchie's walnut was on its way. Where had Rafe got to? They'd never have agreed to this if it wasn't for him. She'd never have *got* the DNA if it wasn't for him. Imagine if this was it. The final proof. She couldn't wait to talk it over with him.

Outside the police station, Rafe's friend Mike was standing with his hands in his pockets, swaying a little on his heels as he looked out over the street. He was a big man, as tall and bulky as Detective Hill, but kinder-looking, with small, crinkled eyes. When he heard the door opening, he turned at once.

'Emma,' he said, and came to shake her hand. 'Mike Evans. Good to meet you.'

'Thank you for being here,' Emma said, suddenly shy in front of Rafe's friend. She didn't mention his having given them the address in France, in case she wasn't supposed to know where that had come from.

'No problem,' Mike said. 'I owe your friend Rafe. We trained together in Brixton; he got me out of a couple of situations. He's got a good head in a crisis.'

'Where is he now?' Emma asked.

'Having a little chat with the Governor. Probably getting a slap on the wrist for what he's been up to.'

'A slap on the wrist.' Emma was dismayed.

'Don't worry. Our Townsie'll be all right. As long as he doesn't get up to anything else before he heads off to South America, or Juliet won't be too happy with him.'

'Juliet?'

'His girlfriend.'

Emma was startled. Rafe had a girlfriend called Juliet?

'I'm sorry.' Mike put his hand to his forehead in a comedy-slap kind of way. 'I forgot you and Rafe don't know each other that well. Come to think of it, I haven't seen Juliet for a while myself, but they've been going out for . . . what? Two years? Last I heard, she was making plans to take a gap year and join Townsie on his travels.'

'Oh, I see.' Emma was still recovering from the surprise. Rafe had never mentioned anything about a girlfriend. But then, why would he have?

The door to the police station clattered open. Rafe arrived out on the steps.

'Brrr,' he said, rubbing his hands together in a dramatic way. 'I have to tell you, I'm very happy I don't need to deal with that kind of shit any more.'

Mike said, 'You know, mate, you never should have left the job.'

'Yes, I should. Best decision I ever made.'

'I don't think so.' Mike looked at him. 'You were a loss to us.'

Rafe didn't respond to this. He said to Emma, 'We were thinking of going for something to eat. Will you join us? There are a couple of decent old places on the river.'

Emma shook her head. 'Would you mind if I went for a walk by myself?' she asked. 'I'm grateful, really I am. But right now, I just need to clear my head and be on my own for a while.'

As soon as they'd left her, she went straight to her flat. From the cardboard box at the top of her wardrobe, she took her emergency credit card and driver's licence. She wiped a film of dust off the licence with her sleeve. The last time she'd driven a car was when she'd managed to pass her test, first go, in Bristol when she was eighteen. Her passport was still in her backpack, along with the map of France she'd bought with Rafe. She stuffed a few more items into the pack and left the flat again without looking back.

At Liverpool Street station, she took cash out of the ATM, as much as the machine would allow her in one go. The next train to Stansted was leaving in two minutes. She hurried to catch it.

When she was settled in a seat by the window, she sent Rafe a text.

'Tired. Going to have early night. Don't call.'

Then she put her phone back in her bag.

It felt wrong, lying to Rafe after all he'd done. But she didn't want to waste her energy arguing. Or get him into any more trouble.

She sat back, pushing her hair out of her eyes.

In a way, she supposed, she'd come to see Rafe as a sort of extension of her and Ritchie. He had come into her life almost at the very moment of Ritchie's disappearance. Ritchie was all they'd ever discussed in any great depth; he was the only thing that filled her mind, and, she'd assumed, Rafe's too. He'd even postponed his trip to South America to help her.

But Rafe had his own life, of course he had. Stupid of her not to have seen it before. With Mike on the scene, and now this Juliet person as well, Rafe was turning out to have a whole other world, filled with people and interests she knew nothing about.

Juliet. The name gave her a funny little thud. It was a lovely name. Classy and romantic. She was probably very beautiful. Rafe wouldn't settle for anything less. Well, he deserved it. Funny, just, that he'd never mentioned her at all. But then, why would he have? The topic had never come up. And it wasn't as if he'd ever acted in any way

335

inappropriately. He'd been nothing but a good friend to her and Ritchie when they needed it most.

She looked out the window. London was behind them now. Scrubby fields spread beyond the tracks. Behind them, trees pointed at the sky; black, spiky pencil drawings on a pink background. Stansted airport was less than fifteen minutes away. Last stop before France.

Emma felt a rush of determination.

She'd been there before, and come away without him.

It would not happen again.

⋆   ⋆   ⋆

Her excitement had risen by the time she got to the airport.

'Next flight to Bergerac, please,' she said breathlessly, holding her passport out to the girl at the reservations desk. She waited, tapping her foot, as the girl keyed a couple of sentences into her computer.

'Sorry.' The girl made a regretful little moue. 'You've just missed one.'

Emma nodded. 'All right, then. I'll go on the next one.'

'No more flights to Bergerac this evening,' the girl said.

Emma couldn't believe it. Of course, Bergerac wasn't a major city but she'd never thought of there being no more flights for the day. Now what was she going to do? How was she going to wait another whole night to get back to Ritchie?

The girl pressed another couple of keys on her computer.

'There's a flight first thing in the morning,' she said. 'Seven fifteen. Is that too early for you?'

'No. No, it's not. I'll take it. Thank you.'

It was better than nothing. Emma handed over her credit card and took the precious plane ticket. She folded it into her passport and zipped everything carefully into the side of her pack. Then she stood there, looking around the concourse. Now what? She could hardly hang around here for the night. But she didn't fancy going all the way back to the flat again either.

She bought a sandwich from one of the coffee outlets and sat at the end of an empty row of seats to eat it. It was quiet there, and warm. She must be under a heating vent or something. By the time she'd finished the sandwich and screwed the wrapper up, not one person had come to sit near her, or even walked past. Emma got up to poke the wrapper through the hole in a nearby bin. A lone passenger wandered in the distance, his footsteps echoing behind him on the tiles. The airport seemed to have quietened down for the night.

Someone had left an *Evening Standard* folded in half on top of the bin. Emma took it back to her seat. She opened it out, spreading it across the cushions to protect them from her shoes. Then she lay down sideways across three of the seats, using her backpack as a pillow. She got herself into a comfortable position, bunching the backpack up, moving it around so that a soft part of it ended up under her cheek.

She lay for a while, waiting for someone to come and tell her she couldn't sleep there. But no one did. The only sounds she heard were the muted *ding-dongs* heralding the passenger announcements, followed by various unintelligible speeches in the soothing tones the announcers always seemed to use. It was comforting. Peaceful. It felt right to be here. Closer, in a way, to France than to London.

Emma closed her eyes.

★ ★ ★

She was the first passenger to board the next morning. The plane filled up behind her with couples and families, children dressed in shorts and sandals, with jumpers on top as they were still in England. The windows were squares of white, watery light. The air from the doors was crisp and cool.

The plane took off five minutes early. Emma felt a surge of control. She was in an aisle seat this time. The stewardess bumped her shoulder, rather painfully, with her metal trolley a couple of times as she passed. A woman leaned across the aisle to ask if she could borrow Emma's in-flight magazine. The man beside her knocked his laptop against a pile of papers, sending them slithering off his fold-down table on to the floor. Emma bent to help him to pick them up. When you were in the aisle seat, rather than the window, you had no choice but to be part of what was going on around you, instead of a little mote, floating by yourself in the clouds.

All of these people, united on the plane, suspended for a time from carrying out their real purpose.

And her, one of them, with her purpose too.

Very calm.

I know what I'm doing now.

★   ★   ★

At the car-hire desk in Bergerac, she had her driver's licence out and the correct money ready before the man could even ask her.

The car was similar to the one she and Rafe had had the last time. Out of habit, Emma went to the passenger door. She was actually sitting in the seat, wondering where the steering wheel was, before she remembered that she should be on the other side. She got out again and swapped over, and spent a few minutes in the driver's seat, adjusting the mirrors, checking to make sure she knew where everything was. She folded open the map to the right page and located the green twisty line representing the road to St-Bourdain. Then she pulled the seatbelt around her, and started up the engine.

'Keep the bitch in the ditch,' she said nervously to herself a few times as she drove out of the car park, reminding herself to keep on the correct side of the road. The town of Bergerac was busier than it had been the last time. More people in the shops and on the pavements, more cars and bustle about the squares. Maybe because today was Tuesday instead of Sunday. Emma made her way cautiously through the traffic, only stalling once at a left turn, and was soon on her way to St-Bourdain.

The weather was more changeable this time, the fields overhung by low, grey clouds. Now she was here, and so close, the house couldn't come quick enough. She refused to let herself think that the Hunts might no longer be there. Antonia had told Rafe they weren't moving for another week or so, but there was a high chance she was lying. Even with the DNA on their side, time was running out for the Hunt family. They must know that Emma wasn't going to give up. They must know she'd be back. Come on, house, come on. The green and yellow fields flew past. The tyres hummed and swished on the road. In Emma's pack on the seat beside her, her phone began to ring.

Keeping her eyes on the road, Emma felt about in the pack with one hand. The ring tone grew louder, then softer, as the phone kept pushing into things. She got it out before the ringing stopped, and switched it to her left hand, so she could keep the steering wheel in her right.

'Hello?'

'Emma!' It was Rafe.

'What's happening?' Emma was suddenly tense. 'Is the DNA back?'

'If it is, I haven't heard,' Rafe said calmly. 'The police would have called you.'

'Oh.'

'Not that they'd have been able to reach you,' Rafe added. 'I was trying you earlier. Your phone kept saying 'Out of range.''

'Er . . . did it?'

There was a pause.

'You're there, aren't you?' Rafe said. 'You're in France.'

'How did you guess?' Emma found she was smiling at the phone.

Rafe said something, swore or something, she couldn't make it out. She thought he might have been smiling too. But when he spoke again, it was in a serious voice.

'Emma, what are you doing?'

Emma concentrated on a tight bend in the road.

'All I know,' she said when the car had straightened out again, 'is that I need to be near him. Not hundreds of miles away in another country.'

'Don't antagonize them, Emma. You need to wait for the DNA result. Your case will be a lot stronger then. You'll have the police on your side. Don't give the Hunts an excuse to disappear.'

'What if they already have?'

That threw him, she could tell.

He said, 'They didn't seem in any rush when I was there.'

'Yeah, well, I doubt if they'd have filled you in on their plans.'

She was here. There was the sign for St-Bourdain, tilted sideways into a hedge. Beyond it, the trees rose on the hill. The red roof of the house was just visible at the top. Emma slowed, a short distance from the gates. She brought the car to rest in a lay-by behind the hedge. Were the Hunts still there? You couldn't tell, just from looking at the roof. It wasn't as if they'd have covered the house in a dust sheet if they'd left.

'Where are you now?' Rafe asked.

'At the house.'

'Man.' He swore again.

Emma pulled up the handbrake. The engine idled, grumbling into the road. She turned the key and the engine shuddered into silence.

'I need to see him,' she said. 'Anything else isn't an option. I need to be where he is.'

'I'm not going to talk you out of this, am I?'

Emma said simply, 'What else can I do?'

There was a pause.

'Nothing,' Rafe said at last. 'Nothing at all.'

'So, then.'

'Yeah.' A long, heavy sigh. 'So, then. I see your point. All right, good luck with your watch. But Emma, please try to stay out of sight. Don't confront them on your own.'

'I know.'

When she'd hung up, she sat and waited. Gaps opened in the clouds. The light slanted through them in bright, straight lines, like ramps down to the fields.

If the Hunts were there, they'd have to show themselves some time. She was going to wait here until they did. One more glimpse of him. And then, when she'd seen him, she'd . . . well. What would she do? Start up her car again, and go. Drive away from here. Sit in a room somewhere, and twiddle her fingers, and wait until the police got around to giving her a call.

Rafe had said to follow the rules. He'd said that she had to, because she had no choice. So she'd done as he suggested, and she'd played their game, and in the end it had got her nowhere. Rafe had been wrong.

The sun was out properly now. The car grew warm. Sweat trickled from under her arms. Emma rolled down the window and pushed her seat back from the steering wheel to give herself more space.

If the Hunts were out somewhere, they'd have to come back. If they were in, they'd have to go out. If they drove past her in a car, it might be hard to get a proper look at Ritchie. But perhaps they'd take him out for a walk. Even just on to the driveway, like last time. Every time an engine sounded on the road, she twisted to see if it was them, but it was always some man in a tractor, or a tourist people-carrier, packed with children and tents.

She waited.

After what seemed a long time, movement flickered at the top of the drive. Emma sat up. A man, passing between a gap in the trees, carrying something in his arms. Antonia's husband? Emma leaned forward, narrowing her eyes. Too far to see his face. But he was carrying a box of some kind. Heavy looking. He had to use both arms. He went to a car and did something to the back of it, turning sideways to jab at it with his elbow. The boot of the car sprang open. The man loaded the box inside.

Emma thought hard. If that was Antonia's husband, what was he doing loading things into a car? She watched the man as he passed back behind the trees. She kept her gaze fixed on the exact branch where he'd disappeared, waiting to see if anyone else came out. Nothing.

The car was very warm now. The backs of Emma's legs itched and stuck to her jeans. She rolled the window the rest of the way down. The smell of grass floated through the window. A dove or wood-pigeon cooed in the fields.

Here came the man again. Emma stiffened. Heading for the car on the drive. With a suitcase this time.

And then a woman. Carrying a child.

Emma took a sharp breath in. It was a child! Ritchie! It had to be! Oh, thank God. Thank God he was still here. What were they doing now? Christ, she really needed a pair of binoculars. She leaned forward again. The man hoisted the suitcase into the boot, and the woman went to the side of the car. She opened the door and leaned in, still with the child in her arms. She fiddled about for a minute or two, then stood back. Her arms were empty.

Ritchie was in that car now. Definitely.

The car with all those boxes loaded into it.

Oh, she had a bad feeling about this. Stones crunched on the road behind her. A car was slowing down. Emma twisted to see. A black jeep drove around her, flashing its indicator, then sped up again, whizzing over the hill. Oh, bloody hell. Even if the DNA came through right now, the police would still take for ever to get here. There'd have to be phone calls between England and France, everyone talking to each other in broken language. It could take hours. And would the police take it seriously enough to send a proper number of people and cars to the house? Or would it be the local junior constable, ambling along to ask a couple of questions when he'd finished his morning croissant?

Another car. Not the police.

Ritchie was there. He was there right now. And if she didn't do something soon, he wasn't going to be there any more.

Emma opened the door of the car. She climbed out, into the grass-smelling morning. Refreshing, after the rubbery heat. The air cleared her mind. She closed the door, but didn't latch it. Then she stole across the road to the gate. She began to walk up the drive, quietly at first, avoiding obvious patches of crackly stones. And then, all of a sudden, she didn't care any more. So what if they heard her? Time to put an end to this.

In her pocket, her phone began to ring. She pressed the stop button, and walked on.

At the top of the drive, Antonia was leaning into the car again, rearranging something on the seat. Her back was to Emma, her fawn-clad bottom moving from side to side. More boxes were stacked around the car. Her husband was nowhere to be seen. A bird chattered somewhere, *ack-ack-ack*, and the sun filtered through the trees. Branch-shadows rippled and dappled the golden walls of the house. Ritchie was in the car, up high in a seat. He was facing away from her. Emma could see the top of his head.

'Hello,' Emma said.

Antonia tried to spin and jump backwards at the same time. Her head knocked off the top of the car. When she saw who it was who had spoken, her mouth opened. She staggered back, the colour flying from her face.

'I'd like my child back now,' Emma said.

Antonia was chalk-white.

'David,' she called in a high-pitched voice. 'David.'

She said to Emma, 'What are you doing here again? This has gone far enough. We'll get the police back here.'

'You do that,' Emma said. She was staring beyond Antonia, trying to see Ritchie in the car. Footsteps crunched on the stones. Emma spun around. A tall man in long shorts, coming around the side of the house. She recognized him at once. The man who had said sorry to her, and closed the door in her face.

'Pip?' the tall man said. 'Pip, are you all — '

Then he saw Emma and slowed.

'Oh,' he said. 'Oh.'

His face gave nothing away. He came to a stop a few feet from the car.

Emma turned back to Antonia.

'I'm going to take him now,' she said.

She stepped forward. Antonia moved quickly. She slammed the door of the car and placed herself directly in front of it.

'Hold on,' she said. 'Hold on just a minute. You leave my son alone.'

'He's not your son,' Emma said. She kept her eyes on the car. The child in the back sat facing away from them. The windows were tinted. All she could see was his hair. She longed to call him, longed for him to twist around and beam his wide melon grin when he saw her. But she didn't want to frighten him before she could reach him.

She was going to have to get past Antonia first.

She made herself focus properly on Antonia for the first time. You had to hand it to the bitch, her grooming was as immaculate as ever. The hair freshly washed and smooth, all strands moving together as one. The shirt and trousers, ironed and matching. Cream, of course. The lipstick, frosted pink, perfectly applied.

'I can understand.' Emma forced herself to speak as calmly as possible. 'I can understand why you want him. I'm not trying to take him away from you. You can still see him. We can work something out.'

'You're insane,' Antonia sputtered. 'You need help. Why have you attached yourself to our family like this? I know your son has disappeared, but why don't you just go and look for him? Why do you have to fixate on *our* child?'

'How can you lie like that?' Emma was amazed. 'You know perfectly well that this isn't your child. You took him from me at the tube station.'

'I haven't been in a tube station for years,' Antonia sounded exasperated. 'The only thing David or I did wrong was to take a simple flight home through London after a holiday. And now we find ourselves caught up in all of this. For God's sake.' Her voice shook. 'We've had every sympathy for you. We even had that DNA test done, at great inconvenience, I might add, but we did it to help you. To help *you*! But enough, now, please. Enough. Just go away, and leave us alone.'

Emma was astonished. What was going on here? Antonia was behaving as if there was a microphone nearby recording everything she said. What was the point of this ridiculous denial? Surely she must see that Emma knew what she'd done. Lying to Emma like this was like lying to herself.

She looked again. She wasn't imagining things. This *was* Antonia. Wasn't it? This was the woman who'd been in Mr Bap's that evening and disappeared with Ritchie. Her hair had been blonder then, but everything else was the same. If you were really pushing it, perhaps, there was a difference under her eyes. If you looked closely, the skin below them seemed older than she remembered. Baggy and shadowed. The areas around her nose and mouth were yellowish in colour.

Rafe's voice: *I've seen these DNA tests done. No one can tamper with them.*

This was crazy. This was crazy. That was Ritchie, right there in the car. All right, so she couldn't see him so well right this minute, but she'd seen him on the tape from the airport, she'd seen him here the last time, right here on the driveway. The car windows were dark, and he was facing away. That was his hair, though. Browner, as well, but Antonia had *dyed* it. Those were his ears. She *knew* him. All she had to do was push past Antonia and go to him and she'd —

Footsteps again behind her. Emma swung to face David Hunt. But it wasn't her he was looking at.

'Pippa,' he said. 'Pip.'

'Call the police,' Antonia snapped at him.

'Pip,' David said again. He was holding out his hand. 'Let it go, Pip,' he said.

'What are you talking about?' Antonia snarled.

'It was never going to work. My mother's been asking a hundred questions since we brought him here, and she's not the only — '

'Shut up,' Antonia screamed at him. 'Shut up, you fool. Do you want them to take Xavier?'

David's eyebrows lowered. His face shrank on itself, a paper bag, crumpling in a fist.

'Xavier's dead,' he said.

'What are you saying?' Antonia's voice broke in a squeak.

'He's dead,' David shouted. All of a sudden, his teeth were clenched. The muscles in his neck stood out. 'Do you hear me? He's dead, and he's not coming back.'

'Shut up. Shut up.' Antonia backed away, her hands to her face. Emma's phone was ringing but she hardly heard it. From the car floated a child's fretful wail.

'Our son . . . ' David looked at Emma. He could hardly say it. 'Our son died. In India, four months ago.'

'No, he didn't,' Antonia yelled at him. 'No, he didn't.'

'Yes, he *did*.'

Ritchie's hot, despondent wail tugged at Emma like a wire, pulling her towards him. She took another step, but Antonia was still between her and the car.

'She wouldn't let me tell anyone,' David

349

whispered, twisting the ring on his wedding finger. 'She said if we didn't say it, then it hadn't happened. I went along with it. She was so . . . I couldn't get her to come home. She wouldn't leave him in India on his own. Then when I finally persuaded her to come to London, she met you and said you couldn't look after your child properly and begged me to take him away with us and I . . . God help me, I . . . '

Antonia hissed at Emma, 'You weren't fit to look after him. For God's sake, you let him get trapped on a train. When I met you at that tube station you were a mess. Filthy clothes, hardly able to speak. You looked like you should be in a hospital. I had to get him away from you.'

'That's not your decision to make,' Emma shouted. She'd forgotten to keep quiet so as not to upset Ritchie. The crying from the car stopped, as abruptly as if a switch had been pressed. Then Ritchie gave a shrill scream.

'Muh,' he shrieked. 'Muh.'

Emma couldn't hold herself back any more.

'Ritchie. Oh, Ritchie, sweetheart, I'm here.'

She rushed towards the car. Ritchie was twisting and wriggling, struggling to free himself from his seat.

'Get back,' Antonia cried.

Emma didn't quite catch what happened next. Antonia was reaching somewhere — into the car, a box, wherever — but the next thing she was up again, holding her arm out, and something long and pointed gleamed in her hand.

'Get. Back,' she said.

Emma's reflexes had jerked her back against

her will, even before she knew what the gleam was. Then she realized, and felt an eerie horror. Antonia had a knife, and she was pointing it straight at her.

'Pippa.' David sounded alarmed. 'Pip, what are you doing?'

'Don't touch me,' Antonia roared. David had been about to do just that, but he took a hasty step back. 'I'll stab you too,' she warned him. 'Don't think I won't. I wanted to leave here days ago, but oh no, *you* kept saying to wait. What was *wrong* with you? If it wasn't for me, we wouldn't be going at all. Anyone would think you *wanted* them to take Xavier . . . I *said: Get! Back!*'

This last was for Emma, who had tried again to move to the car. Antonia swung the knife back to her. Her hair, which she'd run her hand through a couple of times, didn't look so tidy now. In fact, it looked as if a hundred bats had been nesting in it. Her eyes were bloodshot. Emma stayed where she was. No knife was going to keep her back now. Not a knife, nor a gun, nor a herd of wild elephants.

'Philippa,' she said. She almost called her Antonia. 'Philippa, please. Can't we talk about this?'

'I'm not discussing anything with you,' Antonia said. Emma had a clear view of the knife now. It was a long, wide kitchen blade, for chopping meat or vegetables. 'Stay away from my son. I'm warning you.'

'Muh,' Ritchie squealed, still furiously kicking.

'You helped me, that time.' It took all of Emma's strength to stay calm. 'On the train, remember?

You saved Ritchie from getting lost. If it wasn't for you, where might he have ended up? Please don't think I'm not grateful to you for that.'

Antonia, still holding the knife out, was backing around the car towards the driver's side. That was OK, though. The further she went that way, the clearer the path to Ritchie would be. Antonia moved again, and Emma took her chance. She lunged for the car. As she passed Antonia, she felt something knock against her arm. The blow caught her above the elbow, spinning her to the side. Strangely, Antonia seemed to be holding on to Emma's arm, following it as it moved, as if her hand was stuck there. With her other hand, Emma gripped the roof of the car and used it to wrench herself away. A weird feeling shot along her arm and down into her fingers, a sizzling, pins-and-needles sensation, as if she'd touched the exposed wires of a plug. Then it was gone.

In the distance, David was calling, 'Philippa. Philippa. Stop.' Emma could only see Ritchie's door. She was about to go for it again when something made her stop.

Antonia. Still holding the knife. Leaning from the front of the car into the back. Pointing the knife straight at Ritchie.

She said, 'Do I have to hurt him as well?'

Emma recoiled. The tip of the knife, so close to Ritchie's round, defenceless little face, made her want to vomit, actually vomit.

She said frantically, 'Don't — '

'Then I won't tell you again. Stand back from the car.'

'I will. I will.' Emma backed away. 'Please. Just take the knife away from him. Take it away from him.'

Antonia eyeballed her.

'You're not taking Xavier,' she said. 'You're not taking my child. No matter what happens. That's one thing I promise you.'

She lifted the knife. Then she whirled around and swung herself into the driver's seat. The second her back was to Ritchie, Emma flew to his door to get him out. She scrabbled at the handle, but for some reason she couldn't get her fingers to work. There was the door handle, there was her hand, but the fingers were all curled over and wouldn't open, what the fuck was going on? Her hand was useless, she couldn't straighten her hand.

'Ritchie,' she screamed.

Around the driver's side of the car, David was shouting as well. Emma had time to glimpse a blur, the frightened round blob of Ritchie's face at the window, then the engine roared to life. The car jumped, then burst away, spraying dust and hot stones. Still revving, it shot off down the drive towards the road. David raced after it. Car and man disappeared around the trees.

Shit, shit, shit. Emma fumbled for her phone. It was in her jeans pocket, on the right-hand side. She tried several times to get it out. The pocket seemed to be stitched shut in some way. Then she remembered it was because her hand wasn't working. Her fingers were all red now. Blood dropped from the tips, gathering the dust on the ground into dark pellets. The sound of the car was fading on the road.

'FUCK,' Emma shouted. She reached around with her left hand, twisting her shoulder and elbow to pull the phone out of her jeans.

David returned from the trees, gasping and sweating. Then he saw Emma's arm and stopped. His lips whitened. He said, 'Oh, Christ. She did it. She actually stabbed you.'

'Help me,' Emma said. 'Help me get my phone.'

'My wife is not responsible,' David whispered. 'She's ill.'

'Yeah, well, she's got my son in the car with her.'

The phone was out at last. One-handed, Emma flipped it open.

'What's the number for the police in France?' she demanded.

'I . . . it's . . . '

The phone rang just then, making them both jump. It was Rafe's name on the screen. Emma pressed the button and jammed the phone to her ear.

'She's taken him,' she said.

'What?'

'She's got a knife. She's got Ritchie in the car with her, and she's got a knife.'

'Shit.' Rafe's voice dropped. She heard him in the background, talking to someone else. Then he was back. 'Hold on, Emma. Just hold on. The police are on their way.'

'Hurry. Please.'

When she hung up, David was staring at her in misery. She'd almost forgotten he was there.

354

Deep lines ran from his eyes, down the sides of his mouth. The last few weeks hadn't been easy for him either.

'We should have got help,' he said. 'If we had, this would never have happened.'

'Why did you take him from me?' Emma cried. 'Did you look after him? Were you cruel to him?'

'I swear to you.' David put his hands to his chest. 'We loved him like our own child. We looked after him as best we could, we did everything for him.'

'How could you do it? How could your family lie like that? How could they not see he wasn't yours?'

'They hadn't seen him for months.' David's face was grey. 'We told them, if he looked different it was because he was better. The child he should have been.'

Emma had been waiting for so long to confront these people. She'd been over this moment a thousand times in her mind, had a million questions prepared. The questions were still there, all ready and bursting in her head. But now she was here, and David Hunt was standing right in front of her, she found she didn't want to ask them any more. She went to turn away, but David hadn't finished yet.

'He'd have wanted for nothing,' he said after her. 'Nothing! He would have been so happy.'

Emma turned to look at him again.

'She would have stabbed him,' she said. 'You know that, don't you?'

'No, she wouldn't have.'

'Yes. She would.' Emma showed him her arm.

'You didn't know her.' David was shaking his head. 'The old Philippa would never have . . . my old Pippa . . . she . . . '

Then he was collapsing, one hand to his face, the other groping to the wall for support. 'My son,' he said, 'my son,' and Emma had no way of telling which child he meant: Ritchie, or his own lost boy, far away in the ground in India.

She turned away again. Down the hill, beyond the curve of the driveway, the road divided in the fields, separating again and again into smaller and smaller lines. Which road was hers? Surely she could still see a haze of dust on one of them, marking their path as they fled? She tried to follow it, so she could point it out to the police when they came, but the haze shimmered and spread. The clouds billowed down to hide it, and her blood dropped in the dust at her feet, glistening like grapes.

18

'Lieutenant Eric Perrine,' the man in the brown corduroy jacket said, 'of the French police.'

He had his hand out to shake Emma's before realizing that she couldn't take it. She was lying on a trolley, surrounded by people, and a man in a white tunic was cutting off her sleeve with a pair of scissors.

'Have you seen them?' Emma tried to lift her head off the pillow. 'Have you found them?'

'No, *madame*. But we will.'

'You know she's got a knife? Are you chasing them? Have you put up roadblocks?'

'We are doing everything we can,' Lieutenant Perrine said. He had short dark hair, grey at the sides. His voice was soft and courteous. 'Trust me, *madame*. We have the description of the car, we have many people looking for them. They will be found.'

A man in a blue paper hat appeared, and began to prod at Emma's arm.

'You can feel this?' he asked. 'Or this?'

She couldn't feel anything. The arm was numb. It was still joined to her shoulder, but it wasn't hers, it wasn't a part of her any more. The man in the hat said something to Lieutenant Perrine and he nodded.

'For now,' he said to Emma, 'I need to let the doctors treat you. Your arm has been very badly damaged. This surgeon here says that you must have an operation.'

'An operation?'

'Yes. As soon as possible.'

Emma was shocked. 'I can't. I can't have an operation. Not while Ritchie's still out there.'

Lieutenant Perrine listened to the surgeon again and translated. 'The blood and nerve supply to your arm have been badly damaged,' he said. 'If they don't fix them immediately, your arm could die.'

'I don't care.'

'This is very serious. You must think about your son. Please, Ms Turner.' Lieutenant Perrine's brown eyes reminded her of someone she knew. 'Things are difficult enough at this moment. Do not make them worse.'

The kindness in his voice silenced her.

He said, 'You have done your son a service today, Ms Turner. We have spoken to Mr Hunt. They were leaving for Italy this afternoon. They would have gone if not for you.'

A nurse in white was folding a dressing over her arm.

'I will go now,' Lieutenant Perrine said, 'and see what is happening. As soon as there are developments, I will contact you.'

'Will you do everything?' It came out as a sob. 'Everything you can do?'

'I will.' Lieutenant Perrine looked grave. 'You have my word of honour, *madame*. I will do everything I can.'

He left her, and the man in the hat and the people in white had drifted away too. Emma hardly noticed. The lights were too bright. Trembling, she turned on her side, facing herself to the wall. That woman had had a knife. She'd pointed it at Ritchie. She'd stabbed Emma, just like that; she was a psycho. And now Ritchie was somewhere in a car with her. Emma gripped a corner of the sheet in her fist. She shouldn't be here. She should be out in a police car, searching the roads for him; be there when they found him, be the first person he saw. He'd been calling her: 'Muh. Muh.' Aah! She pressed her fist to her chest. He'd known she was there. He must be wondering why she hadn't come to him, why she'd gone off again and left him.

'I didn't mean to . . . ' She had to tell him. 'I didn't . . . '

She struggled to sit up again. No way was she going to just lie here. She could have the operation some other time. For now, she was going to find Lieutenant Perrine and insist that one of the police cars took her along with them. She tried to sit straighter, but her right arm hung behind her, floppy as the damaged wing of some giant bird or bat. The dressing stuck to her skin, dragging open the wound above her elbow so she could see the pink mass of muscle inside. Red lines streaked towards her wrist. Her arm was like a white and red road map. Faint, she looked away.

The nurse reappeared by her bed.

'Are you all right?' she asked.

'I'm fine.' Emma was looking around her for a towel or sheet. 'I just need something to . . . '

Then she looked at her arm again and

slumped in defeat. She hadn't lost the plot so much that she couldn't see the mess she was in. She couldn't do anything, go anywhere, with her arm like this. The nurse looked at it too and frowned.

'You have decided?' she asked. 'You will have the surgery?'

Emma was thinking fast. 'If I have it, how soon can I leave here? Can I get out straight away?'

'If the surgery is successful, then yes, maybe.' The nurse wrinkled her forehead. 'But you should have it immediately, *madame*. The knife has done a lot of damage. Your hand has no blood supply. That is why you can't feel anything.'

'Will they be quick?' Emma asked. 'You see, I don't have time. I need to be awake . . . I . . . my son . . . '

'I understand,' the nurse said. She came to put her hand on Emma's shoulder. 'Of course I understand. We will try to be as quick as we can.'

★   ★   ★

As soon as the nurse had told everyone she was having the surgery, Emma's cubicle filled with people again. Emma searched the crowd for Lieutenant Perrine. She wanted to hear him promise the police would keep looking for Ritchie while she was in the operating room.

'Excuse me,' she kept saying. She raised her voice. 'Excuse me, I need to see that policeman again. The one who . . . Is anybody listening?'

The man in the blue hat was back, barking

360

orders at the crowd.

'*Tout de suite*,' he snapped. Emma recognized the phrase. It meant 'immediately'. Within seconds a group of people had taken hold of Emma's trolley and were wheeling her along a corridor. White windows flew past. A breeze blew on her face. Then she was in another room, filled with machines. A chemical smell, strangely familiar. Nail varnish? More people in tunics, blue this time. Everyone seemed to be doing something. Opening and closing cupboards. Hanging things on poles. Flicking liquid from the tops of syringes.

A woman asked her questions, ticking them off on a clipboard: 'When did you last eat? Have you had an anaesthetic before?'

The quicker Emma cooperated, the quicker the surgery would be done. She answered all the questions. The woman's pen flew down the clipboard. A man wearing a paper hat and mask tied something around the top of Emma's good arm.

'To make the vein,' he explained. He tapped the back of her wrist. 'Move your hand, please.'

Emma didn't know what he meant. Move her hand? She twisted her wrist forward and back. The woman with the clipboard saw she didn't understand and returned to the trolley to help.

'Open and close your fist.' She demonstrated. 'Like this. Pretend you are trying to grasp something that is just out of your reach.'

Emma got it. She opened and closed her left hand. Then something sharp stung the back of it. Seconds later, the room spun. She tried to grip the side of the trolley, but her left hand was still being held and the other had no life in it at all.

'Please,' she said, not knowing what it was she was asking for. 'Please.'

Voices in the background. Antonia appeared beside her, wearing a blue hat and mask. Emma could only see her eyes. She was holding a knife up and touching her finger to the tip of it.

'Do you know Solomon?' Antonia asked. Her voice was deep and dry and cold. 'Solomon was the king who ordered the baby to be cut in half.'

Emma tried to wrench her hand away from whoever was holding it.

'Let go,' she shouted. 'I've changed my mind.'

But the shouting must have been just in her head, because the French voices with their soft 's's and 'g's murmured on in the background. Terrified, Emma twisted her hand, until she felt someone's fingers and squeezed.

'It's all right,' a different voice said. 'I'm here.'

'Sleep now,' the doctor said.

Her hand was released. It floated by her side, as if in water. Something was on her face, pressing on her eyes, making everything dark. A cool flow in her nose. The nail varnish smell grew stronger.

From a distance, a woman said, 'You do not need to grasp any more.'

Emma realized she was moving her hand again. Open. Close.

Just out of your reach.

I'm here.

Startled, she opened her eyes. Something was blocking her hand from moving. She pushed it away and grasped again, reaching out as far as she could. Then everything went dark. Her hand fell to the sheet. Her fingers curled, coming to rest, and when they closed, they closed only upon themselves.

★ ★ ★

Everything was swirling. Brightness speared her eyelids. Her stomach heaved.

'Good morning,' a voice said.

Emma opened her eyes. The swirling stopped. A girl in white was pushing back curtains at a window.

Emma blinked, getting used to the light. She stared around her. This wasn't the operating theatre. She was in a bed in a normal room, with a white wardrobe and locker, and a TV up near the ceiling in the corner. Her right arm, bulky with bandages, was propped on a pillow.

'Have I had it?' She was bewildered. 'Have I had the operation?'

'Yes.'

She was amazed. The last thing she remembered was the woman with the clipboard showing her how to move her hand.

'The surgery took a long time,' the nurse was saying. 'Seven hours. We do not yet know whether — '

Seven *hours*?

Emma shot up in the bed.

'What time is it?' she asked.

'Almost eight o'clock in the morning.'

'Eight o'clock in the *morning*?' She'd been

asleep the whole night! If she'd known the surgery would take this long, she'd never, never have agreed to it. 'Did they find him? Did they find Ritchie?'

'I'm sorry, *madame*.' The nurse looked away.

Emma was aghast. 'Why?' Sitting up had made her nausea worse. Her stomach seemed to be forcing itself into her throat. 'Why? They said they couldn't have got far. They said — '

The nurse put her hands up.

'There is a lady outside,' she said, 'from the British Embassy. She has demanded that she can speak with you when you are awake?'

'Yes. Yes, please.'

The nurse left the room. Seconds later she returned, accompanied by a blonde, short-haired woman in a knee-length skirt.

'Tamsin Wagstaff.' The woman introduced herself. 'From the Consulate.'

'What's going on?' Emma pleaded. 'Why haven't they found Ritchie?'

Tamsin Wagstaff said, 'Unfortunately it hasn't been as easy as that. St-Bourdain is in a very isolated area. No cameras, very few cars. Even with such a quick response, it was difficult to know which way they might have gone. The police are doing their best.'

'What's going to happen now? What will they do?'

'They've put out a country-wide alert,' Tamsin said. 'Borders as well. Everyone's looking for them now. Philippa Hunt's husband says that as far as he knows, she has very little money with her. So if she needs to buy anything, she'll have to use her cards and that'll show us where she is.'

'What if she doesn't buy anything?'

'She'll have to, sooner or later,' Tamsin said. 'Petrol, for a start.'

Petrol! How much petrol could a tank hold? How long could it last, if it was full? Hours? Days? What if Antonia just decided to steal another car?

'The police are very hopeful,' Tamsin was saying. 'They will find them. I'm sure they will. In the meantime, if there's anything I can do to help, please, just ask.'

Once she had left, the nurse tried to persuade Emma to have some breakfast.

'You need it after the anaesthetic,' she coaxed. 'Your body fluid is low.'

Obediently, Emma picked up a rectangle of butter in gold foil. The butter squished under her fingers. The room was much too warm. The sun steamed through the window. Heat rolled in waves from the radiator. The smell of melting butter made her gag. A wasp rattled gaspily on the window ledge.

All night, and Ritchie still not found. What was happening to him? Where in God's name were they?

That knife to his face.

Emma threw the butter down.

You're not getting him back.

* * *

Rafe phoned from London.

'The DNA from the walnut came back,' he

365

said. 'He's yours all right. He's Ritchie.'

Emma couldn't see anything. The sun spangled through a knot in the glass, straight on to her face.

'I know,' she said.

The sun was still in her eyes. She turned her head.

Rafe said, 'I kept ringing you yesterday, and when you didn't answer your phone, I knew something must have happened. Mike called everyone he knew, they put massive pressure on the lab to rush the result. I'm just sorry we couldn't have got there in time.'

'She was so mad,' Emma wept. 'So completely mad. And she had a knife. She held it to him. She held it to his face.'

'Shh. Shh.'

'What if she's hurt him, what if — '

'I'm coming over there,' Rafe said. 'I'm booking a flight right now.'

Emma sniffled. Then she gave a deep sigh. She pressed the phone to her cheek. It would be so great to have Rafe there. He would know exactly what to do. His warm eyes, his strength. Always with him the sense that she could lean on him, and he would make everything all right.

She said, 'No.'

'It's not a problem. I'm happy to come.'

'You'll miss your trip again,' she said.

'That doesn't matter.'

'Why do you keep doing this?' Emma asked. 'Putting your life on hold like this? It's crazy. Why do you keep on and on wanting to be involved?'

366

It came out so vehemently that he was silenced.

She answered for him, more gently, 'Because you feel guilty, that's why. That you didn't save him. But you don't need to. You did everything you could at the time. And you've done everything since. People are listening now, and it's all thanks to you.'

'Emma, you don't need to do this all on your own. Believe it or not, there are people who care about you.'

'Because they're paid to. It's their job.'

Rafe said, 'It's not *my* job.'

She didn't know what to say to that.

'I want to be there,' he said. 'I want to be with you.'

Emma said in a cold voice, 'Do you think this is helpful to me? Do you think this is an appropriate conversation for us to be having right now?'

'I . . . ' Rafe sounded startled. 'I didn't mean it like that.'

'Goodbye,' she said softly.

She hung up. The phone was warm. She clung to it as if it was his hand.

Rafe didn't deserve that. After all he'd done for them, he certainly didn't deserve that. But he had his own life to lead. He had Juliet. If she thought for one minute that there was anything more he could do for Ritchie, she'd have him over here in a heartbeat. But there wasn't. The police, at last, were doing everything now. And when Ritchie came back, she needed to be strong for him. Not to be depending on someone who wasn't hers to depend on.

When Ritchie came back.

When he came back, things were going to be so different from how they'd been before. This could never happen again; that they were so isolated, that when things went wrong they had nobody to help them. She could see now how it had been. For herself, she could manage on her own; she didn't need anyone. But Ritchie did. Ritchie needed people. For him, she would climb out of her rut of self-pity and stop retreating from the world. There were decent people out there, people who'd look out for Ritchie and be kind to him. People like . . . well, people like Rafe. But others as well. Rosina Alcarez. Mrs Cornes. They existed, they were in the world, if she would only open her eyes and look for them.

And if he didn't come back?

Uneasy, Emma turned from that dark stretch of wasteland at the edge of her mind. She wasn't ready to face that yet. But go there she would, if she had to. If that was all that was left.

★   ★   ★

Tamsin Wagstaff, with her slim skirt and slicked-back bob, looked very French, but turned out to be from Taunton, in Somerset.

'Practically neighbours,' she said with a smile, when she discovered that Emma was from Bath.

Emma was in no mood for small talk, but Tamsin seemed to know that, and didn't try to make any. She made herself useful, acting as translator when any of the nurses or doctors didn't speak English. She even managed to persuade one of the nurses to open the window to ease the overpowering stuffiness in the room. The police had told Emma they would call if there was any news, but Tamsin ignored this and phoned them every hour or so for an update.

Ritchie was famous at last. He was on TV; one of those twenty-four-hour news channels that showed the same stories on a loop. He was the lead item. Every twenty minutes or so he appeared on the screen; the photo of him on his red truck with his surfer T-shirt, smiling at the camera.

'He's beautiful,' Tamsin said, looking up at the TV, her fingers to the hollow of her throat. 'A really beautiful child. He's a credit to you.'

'Thank you.' The sight of him was so painful. She couldn't keep looking at him. She couldn't turn away.

Tamsin said, 'What *I* want to know is how Philippa Hunt fixed that DNA test. It turns out that the doctor who did their test was the family GP. The police have spoken to him. It seems he did Ritchie's swab all right, but while he was doing it, Philippa went to the bathroom saying she felt unwell, and when she came out she had her own swab already done and sealed in a bag. Dr Ridgeway shouldn't have accepted it, but he did. He was so sure he knew them. Of course, it's obvious now she must have done something to her swab while she was in there, but —

Emma said grimly, 'If she went to that much trouble for him, she's not going to want to give him up.'

369

You're not getting him back.

If she never saw Ritchie again, almost his last memory of her would be of her shouting and pushing him away. He had been such a lovely child. Such a loving, cheerful, kind little boy. He'd wanted so little from her, except just to be with her and for her to love him. And how had she repaid that? By bringing him, the very day after shouting at him, on that vile visit to Dr Stanford.

Oh, God. Emma moved in the bed. Those things she'd said about him that day. They were disgusting. Truly disgusting. Had he heard them? Had he understood? He'd been sitting right there beside her.

'People say things they don't mean,' Rafe had told her.

But he hadn't been there, had he? He didn't know. He didn't know.

★   ★   ★

Emma was still drowsy from the anaesthetic. The hospital room came and went. She knew she was in France, but sometimes, when she opened her eyes, she couldn't understand why the room was all white and not the pink and brown of the B&B. People were phoning in from all over the country, claiming to have spotted Ritchie and Antonia. Tamsin continued to relay updates from the police. Emma tried to keep track of all the calls, but she kept forgetting which ones had been made. She kept asking Tamsin questions, only to realize when she heard the answers that

370

she knew them already.

'Someone's spotted Philippa's car,' Tamsin said excitedly after one of the calls. 'Fifteen minutes ago. On the A20, driving north from Limoges.'

But a half an hour later, the police phoned again to say that the car, driven by a middle-aged French man, had a different registration number to Philippa's.

Then, later in the afternoon: 'Someone's seen a woman and toddler,' Tamsin reported. 'At a petrol station near the Italian border. The toddler didn't seem to want to be with the woman. He was crying and trying to get out of the car. They're sending someone straight away.' Tamsin clasped the phone to her chest. 'This could be it, Emma. This really could be it. I have a feeling.'

Shortly afterwards, however, the phone rang again.

'I see,' Tamsin said. 'A Swiss mother and her child. A red-haired girl. Aged five. Thanks anyway.'

She slammed down the receiver.

'I know people are trying to help — at least, I assume they are — but why on earth do they do this? Why does every attention-seeker in the country feel they have to call in with these ludicrously inaccurate sightings? It's such a waste of police time. Not to mention the strain on you.'

In the evening, a team of doctors arrived to check on Emma's arm. They stood in a circle around her bed.

'It was a difficult procedure,' one of them began. 'We will have to wait to see if the arm will survive. The axillary artery, at the exit from the sub-clavian . . . '

Emma's mind wandered. She was staring over the doctor's head at the TV. Ritchie was on again, smiling down at her from his truck. Someone touched the doctor's shoulder and he stopped talking at once. In silence, they all filed from the room.

★ ★ ★

Night-time came, and the air, at last, began to cool. Still no news. And then it began to rain. The nurse drew the curtains and switched on the lights, but the steady pattering continued on the glass outside.

At three a.m., unable to sleep, Emma dragged herself and her bandaged arm out of bed and over to the window. It was cold now, despite the heater. The rain was heavier. Under the lamps in the car park, yellow cones of droplets thrashed and swirled.

The bedroom door opened. Bleary-eyed, Tamsin came in.

'They've found it,' she said. 'They've found the car.'

Emma turned.

'The real thing this time,' Tamsin added. 'Not a false alarm.'

Then Emma was light-headed, stumbling near the glass. Tamsin caught her arm.

'Were . . . ?' she said, dry-lipped. 'Was . . . ?'

Tamsin said, 'I'm sorry, Emma, but Ritchie and Philippa weren't in the car. It had been abandoned. It was almost out of petrol, that's probably why she left it.'

Emma caught the window sill, righting herself. Her bandaged arm plopped back into its sling.

'Where?' she asked.

'Behind an empty house, on a back road in Alsace. Near the Swiss border.'

'How long ago? When did they leave it?'

'They reckon at least twenty-four hours.'

'Twenty . . . ' Emma stared at Tasmin. She'd thought that Tamsin had meant they'd only recently left the car. 'But that's ages ago. They could be anywhere by now.'

'They could,' Tamsin said. 'But the police say it's unlikely. Not if they're on foot. It narrows things down considerably.'

'But someone could have picked them up.'

'Yes. But Ritchie would have been recognized. He's been all over the news.'

'Not everyone might have seen the news.'

'This is a very big story.' Tamsin tried to make Emma see things her way. 'Chances are, most people have at least heard about Ritchie from somewhere. I would say that Philippa is too intelligent a woman to risk it. There's a high chance they're within walking distance of the car. The police have got dogs there now. They're searching all over.'

Tamsin was almost pleading, trying to make Emma see this as *good* news, a *good* thing, that a sick woman and a baby didn't have a car, or any shelter or food, two days on the run, in the middle of a wet night with nowhere to stay.

The Swiss border! Wasn't that where the Alps were? If the weather was bad here, what must it be like up in the mountains?

Outside, the rain beat harder. The hospital was in an old building. The window frames were warped, the panes old-fashioned, single-glazed. Icy air wisped around the edges of the glass.

Two days.

A dull certainty settled over Emma. It was too long now. He was too small. After all that, it was over. They weren't going to find him in time.

She looked at her mobile phone.

'My battery's gone red,' she said. 'I didn't bring a charger.'

'Don't worry,' Tamsin reassured her. 'If your phone runs out, there are plenty of other ways they can reach us.'

But Emma was afraid. She gripped the phone. She just had a feeling. In the car park, under the lamps, the dense, yellow cones swirled faster.

'Please stop,' she said to the rain. 'Please stop, please stop, please stop . . . '

Her voice disappeared. Tamsin came to the window. Tamsin was so full of hope. Emma needed it so badly, her own supply had run out.

She leaned on Tamsin. Clung to her, and felt the hope flow back into her, and cried and cried and cried.

★ ★ ★

At dawn, the rain stopped.

Tamsin said to Emma, 'You need some air.

I'm going to see if we can get you out of here for a while.'

She went to speak to the nurse to try to negotiate Emma some day leave.

'All set,' she reported on her return. 'You're not due a dressing change until tomorrow. There's no reason for you to stay in the room here all day.'

The nurses were getting the other patients up and ready for their breakfast. Six o'clock in the morning, and already they were shaving the man in the room next door. They seemed glad to have one less patient to wash and feed. One of the nurses came to help Emma dress and re-fix her sling. Emma took her phone from her locker. The battery was so low now, the phone had started to beep every couple of minutes.

Ritchie was on TV again, over the nurses' desk in the hall. A cluster of people in white stood around it, watching. When Emma came out of her room, the people turned and murmured, and she saw the sympathy in their faces, the fresh ones coming on for the day, the tired ones from the night.

'Some friends of mine own a vineyard,' Tamsin said as they walked across the hospital grounds to her car. 'They're away at the moment. It'll be a peaceful place to go for a walk. No one will disturb us there.'

Emma said, 'You work long hours.' It had occurred to her that Tamsin had been with her for most of the night, and now here she was again, driving her around.

'I'm not working today,' Tamsin said. 'I just

375

came anyway. I didn't want to leave you.'

They pulled up outside a shuttered bungalow. Around it lay fields filled with rows of dark-leaved plants. A breeze lifted the leaves, uncovering shiny green and purple grapes. Emma and Tamsin walked through the rows of grapes to a long stone wall. Beyond the wall spread the countryside, dotted here and there with clusters of white or yellow houses that blended into the landscape, almost part of the trees and the earth.

The sun was up. The grass brushed damp against Emma's ankles.

Ritchie, lying in a field somewhere. Please, God.

Every couple of minutes, her phone beeped.

She just had this feeling. If they didn't reach her in time, if her battery ran out and there was no word . . .

They walked on together across the grass.

★ ★ ★

And then Emma's phone rang. She looked at the screen.

'It's a French number,' she said, and her heart began a heavy *thump-thump-thump*, like a drumbeat from the depths of doom.

Up till then, it had always been Tamsin's phone that the police called. She had a French mobile, she could translate; it made sense. Emma and Tamsin looked at the phone, then at each other, and even Tamsin's face was pale.

Emma turned. She walked away, the phone

still ringing, until she was behind a little clump of trees and alone. Everything seemed extra clear, the grass and sky in pale yellow, the tree before her in strange close-up, each grain standing out, the damp boughs, the smaller branches, trembling with leaves.

She pressed the button.

'Hello,' she said.

Beep. The battery warning sped up at once.

'Ms Turner?'

'Yes.'

'Eric Perrine here.'

Beep.

'I am phoning to inform you that, fifteen minutes ago, Mrs Philippa Hunt was found — '

Beep. Beep.

' — attempting to cross the border at — '

Emma couldn't wait for any more.

'Ritchie?' she said. A dark bag seemed to have come down. It shrouded her head, obscuring the light, cutting the oxygen off from her face. 'What about Ritchie?'

Beep. Beep. Beep.

Lieutenant Perrine's voice did not change. It stayed soft. Soothing. Very kind. Emma didn't know what it was, his words or his tone, or how she first knew, but she was breathing into the airless bag, and the battery warning became a long, single note, and the bag burst about her head, opening her up to the sky, and the soft voice, though the phone was silent now, went on sounding in her ears: 'He is safe, *madame*. The infant is safe. He is with our gendarmes.'

377

19

**Thursday, 5 October
Day Nineteen**

So she waited in a room at the Consulate, with armchairs around the walls with lace on the backs, and a glass cabinet with plates in it, and a grandfather clock in the corner.

Tamsin Wagstaff came in, tucking her sleek, shiny bob behind her ears.

'Another couple of hours at most,' she said. 'They're at Clermont-Ferrand.'

'How is he?' Emma asked. She'd been asking it every fifteen minutes since the phone call. 'Is he OK?' She saw Ritchie in the police car, speeding across France, his flushed little face bouncing up and down in the back.

'He's absolutely perfect,' Tamsin said. 'He's been fed, he's well wrapped up. Stoical little chap, the police said. They're hoping to recruit him.'

Emma smiled.

Lieutenant Perrine's voice: 'The infant is safe, *madame*. The. Infant. Is. Safe.' She was on her knees again, under the trees in the vineyard, screaming and crying so incoherently that it was several minutes before a terrified Tamsin could manage to understand what she was saying. It was a dream, just like a dream. She wouldn't believe it was real until Ritchie was here, right beside her, where she could see and touch him.

'Philippa Hunt is in a bad way, as you can imagine,' Tamsin said. 'She collapsed when they found her. She'd guessed the police would look for them in Switzerland so she tried to go further north instead, to Germany. Thirty miles, she walked, all along back roads and in fields. She carried Ritchie the whole way.'

Emma pictured them, stumbling along in the wind and cold. Ritchie had had no bottle. Nothing to eat. His nappy wouldn't have been changed for hours. Maybe even days.

'She walked most of the night,' Tamsin said. 'So it'll probably be a while before she can be questioned. *I* still want to know how she fixed that DNA. Someone suggested that maybe if she'd substituted a sample of your DNA for hers while she was in the bathroom — but of course, that's ridiculous. How would she have got a sample from you?'

'She did have a sample,' Emma said. She'd had plenty of time to work it out.

'She did?'

'She had a tissue. With my blood on it.'

'*Had* she?'

That day in the tube station. Antonia — she still kept calling her that — being so helpful and considerate. *Would you like another tiss-yoo. Give that old one back to me.* Had she taken Emma's blood on purpose? Even then, thinking ahead, knowing what she was planning to do? Had there been any moment at all when her motive was simply kindness to a fellow mother, so clearly in distress?

'Good Lord,' Tamsin was saying. 'I can't

believe it. The police will check it, of course. She'll be questioned all right, don't you worry.'

'It's just a possibility.' Emma shrugged. 'She might have done it some other way. It doesn't matter now.'

Tamsin was looking at her curiously.

'You must hate her,' she said.

Antonia in the café, looking away.

Yes, we do. We have a little boy.

All the things that Emma knew, Antonia knew them too. The terrible pain of childbirth. The loss of youth and freedom. The loss of yourself. You were the soil now, not the flower any more. And it was blimmin' dark and lonely down there. You worried, and you would worry for ever. You could never, ever go back. Only forward, pulled by the world; and your reward, the touch of the future, the glory of that face against yours.

Tamsin was still looking at her. Emma shook her head.

'I don't hate her,' she said. 'I understand.'

★ ★ ★

'Personal call for you,' said a girl at the door, looking across at Tamsin, who rose, smoothing her pale grey skirt.

She said to Emma, 'I'll be in the office if you need me.'

She left, and the only sound was the ticking of the grandfather clock in the corner: *Lock. Lock. Lock.*

Suddenly Emma's palms were sweaty. She hoped Tamsin wouldn't be too long. She'd been hoping she'd stay with her until Ritchie came. Be with her when he came, even. What must she look like, all scrawny and pale and wrapped in plaster? With her arm so heavy and strange? Ritchie might be frightened when he saw her.

Lock. Lock. Lock.

She couldn't go on sitting here. Tamsin had left the door open. Emma re-tied the sling on her arm and stood up. She wandered out into the hall. The last time she and Rafe had been here had been at night. Now, the sun came down in a cone from the round, high window in the roof. Dust floated around the edges. Emma felt as if she was walking on her toes. She was suspended like one of the dust-dots, floating in the lightness of her head. Her arms and body and mouth and face tingled, the nerves buzzing as if they'd made contact already, but not yet, not yet, hold on, you've been here before.

You weren't fit to look after him.

What if Ritchie had forgotten her? Or didn't want to be with her any more? What if he wanted to stay with Antonia? Antonia had been good to him. He had liked her at the tube station; she had handled him as if she knew him. She had dressed him in beautiful clothes, and held him so lovingly in her garden, and carried him all night in the rain.

Whereas she . . .

You weren't fit.

When Emma opened the door to Dr Stanford's surgery, the rain came in with her from the street. The floor was wet. The waiting-room was crowded and smelled of pus and bad breath.

'It's an emergency,' Emma said.

The receptionist looked her up and down. Ritchie was in his buggy, squalling for his lunch.

'You don't have an appointment,' the receptionist said. 'You can see the locum tomorrow.'

Emma shook her head.

'I have to talk to someone,' she said. 'It has to be today.'

* * *

Don't think about this now. Why are you thinking about this?

* * *

Dr Stanford gave a tight smile.

'Hello again, Emma. What brings you in today?' She was looking at a card on her desk. 'I see we'd arranged an appointment for the week after next? A final check on Ritchie's ear?'

'Yes.'

'So what was it that couldn't wait until then?'

Emma thought she'd planned this. She thought she'd known what to say. She sat there, looking at Dr Stanford, and not a single word came out of her mouth.

Dr Stanford's smile grew tighter.

'You did say it was an emergency,' she said.

'I'm going away tonight for a week. You can see how full the waiting-room is.'

*   ⋆   ⋆

This should be such a precious day. Don't spoil it. Emma stood in the sun-cone, under the high, round window, and tried everything she could to push Dr Stanford's surgery away, but it kept coming back. Nudging at her. A persistent child offering a toy.

⋆   ⋆   ⋆

'You see,' she said to Dr Stanford, 'I can't leave Ritchie behind.'

'Of course not.'

In the pushchair, Ritchie sobbed, his voice a hoarse, used croak.

'Things can be tricky, can't they?' Dr Stanford said. 'A small child. And the weather's been terrible these past few days. Awful when you can't get out.'

Ritchie cried on.

'Look.' Dr Stanford glanced at the clock on the wall. 'Now doesn't seem the best time for us to talk. Why don't I ask Alison, our health visitor, to call and see you over the next couple of days? You know Alison? She's been away for a while, but she's due back next week. She's very nice, very approachable. You two can have a good, long chat. All right?'

She made a note. Then she looked back up at Emma.

'All right?' she said again, a little impatiently.

The noise Ritchie was making stabbed right through Emma's head. He was crying so hard his voice had almost disappeared and his chin sunk in fatigue, but still he persevered. She'd never seen him like this. She couldn't make any move to soothe him because she was sinking too. She let him cry for her, because she had nothing left.

Dr Stanford said, 'Was there anything else?'

* * *

In the hall in the Consulate was a huge, marble statue that Emma didn't remember seeing the last time. And yet something about it struck her as familiar. A pale, robed woman leaned over a child in her lap. The peaks of her robe glowed in the sunlight. The child reached up with dimpled arms and a half-smile. The woman had her hand in the air, caressing the space above his head, guarding and protecting him, and the expression on her face as she gazed at him was one of awe and tenderness and wonder.

* * *

It had to be something quick. She'd thought about it, over and over. Some way he wouldn't suffer. Because she loved him, more than anything; more than she could have ever have thought possible. In her whole life, she'd never thought that one human being could love another this much. But she had to think of something soon, because she was shrinking,

shrinking in her coat. A cold, shrivelled worm in the dark.

All she knew was that she didn't want to hurt him.

She said to Dr Stanford, 'I'm going to throw Ritchie under a train.'

★   ★   ★

When he came, it was after five.

Emma and Tamsin were in the room with the grandfather clock. Someone had brought a tray with coffee and cups.

'Message for you, Tamsin,' said a girl at the door.

Tamsin stood up. 'Another message,' she said to Emma. 'I seem to be quite popular today. You go ahead; have your coffee before it gets cold.'

The pot was heavy, awkward to manage with just one hand. Concentrating on it, Emma thought she heard something: a high, sweet babble in the distance. Frowning, she steadied the pot and listened. Nothing. She lifted the pot again to pour. Then there were footsteps outside, and all of a sudden she was putting the pot down in a rush before she dropped it because everything was happening at once: the footsteps, the squeak of the door handle, the sharp, clear rectangle of light. Tamsin's voice: 'Emma, Emma, he's here.'

She rose in confusion. Shapes in the hall, the light streaming past. For a second, the light was in her eyes and she couldn't see. Then the blindness went away, and she looked at the doorway, and there he was.

Something burst in her when she saw him. He was wearing a blue jumper, and trainers with real laces, and stripes on the sides. His eyes were big, and too bright; he was clutching a woman's hand and babbling about nothing, the way he always did when he was tired, just before he started to get upset. Then he saw Emma and the babbling died away.

He still held the woman's hand. He was staring at Emma in utter astonishment, as if he couldn't believe what he was seeing. Emma's chest squeezed, she was taking long, drawing breaths, as if she'd just come up from under water.

'Muh,' Ritchie said. He pointed at Emma, looking uncertainly up at the lady beside him.

The woman said, 'Yes, Ritchie. That is your mum.'

Ritchie turned to gape again. The woman prised his fist from her skirt and stepped back. Ritchie went on standing there, still gaping, his fist still in the air.

Oh, how tiny and funny he looked, standing there all by himself. How small and bewildered and overwhelmed. Emma's chest squeezed tighter. She was on her knees without noticing. 'Hello,' she whispered. Ritchie's face was bright red. His lower lip was trembling. His eyes were like the eyes in a cartoon. She was afraid to touch him. She stretched out her hand and her fingers brushed his sleeve. Ah, how quiet it was in here, how strange. All those people, where had they gone? Just the two of them here: her and her baby. The light from the hall came in and pinned them there. She went on stroking his sleeve, and when he didn't pull away she moved her hand, very slowly, to his arm, then to his shoulder, and so at last . . .

. . . and so at last to . . .

Ritchie came closer.

'Muh,' he said. He was puzzled, she could see. He looked into her face and she read the questions in his wet, heavy eyes: Mum. Why don't you talk to me? Why is that white thing on your arm? Why do you look so strange?

Why are you shaking?

Then he put his arms around her. He pressed into her, his warm, fierce, soft little body, his pudgy cheeks, his smell. The curve of his cheek below his ear. 'Muh,' he said again, his breath on her face. She wanted to speak, but it was too big, what she had to say, it swelled inside her, surging outwards until their chests touched. *I'm here*, she said, and the message passed straight from her heart through to his. *We're both here*.

Epilogue

August
Cornwall

Four o'clock. Emma stood in the doorway of the Pie and Lobster in Polbraith, and smelled warm beer and the sea.

'Finished for the day?' Susan, the bar supervisor, asked.

'Yeah.'

'See you tomorrow, then, Emma.'

'See you.'

Emma walked on down the small main street. The Spar shop had its wire racks out, hung with buckets and spades and postcards of Cornwall: horses at sunset, and woolly-hatted fishermen mending nets in the harbour. Beside the Spar was Dr Rudd's surgery with its brass plaque at the entrance. After that came a row of houses in a terrace, then a shop selling wetsuits and surfboards. At the end of the street was a white-washed cottage with a wooden sign by the door: *The Dolphins Nursery: 0-5 Years*. Below the lettering, a painting of a cheerful blue dolphin, leaping out of a wave.

Jess, the friendly girl who ran the nursery, opened the door.

'Hi, Emma,' she smiled. 'Come on through. He's in the garden.'

They walked through the narrow hall. Jess

388

cleared the way, pushing tiny chairs back against the wall. The walls were decorated with stencils of Winnie the Pooh, and a poster of a giant smile saying: 'Be Kind to Your Teeth.'

'Was he good?' Emma asked.

'He's always good,' Jess assured her. 'He spent the afternoon talking about ghosts. I had to put a towel on my head and say, 'Woo-ooo.''

'Oh, poor you.' Emma had to laugh. 'He loves ghosts. He saw one on TV a couple of weeks ago and he's been going on about them ever since.'

They were in the kitchen. The door to the garden was open.

'Well,' Jess said, 'there he is.'

She'd already seen him, crouched beside the sand-pit, his head bright in the sun. His tongue was sticking out of his mouth as he emptied some bricks out of a bucket. Beside him, another small boy was covering a plastic dinosaur with sand. Then Ritchie looked up and saw her. He dropped the bucket and came running. Emma knelt to meet him.

'Kiss?' she said.

Ritchie's wet mouth bumped heavily against her cheek. 'Mmmm-AH!'

'What did you do at school today?'

'No.' Violently, he shook his head.

'Go on. You must have done something.'

'No. No.' He shook his head again, dying to be off. He ran to the door of the hall and hung off the handle.

'School must have got easier since my day,' Emma said to Jess.

They laughed, and said goodbye.

Juliet's just a friend. That's all it's been now for a long time. We did plan to meet up when she came to South America, but so far our paths haven't crossed. At this stage, I don't think they will.

Ritchie was thrilled to be back at their little cottage on the cliff. He rushed to his red truck, parked in the middle of the sitting-room, and attempted to steer it into the kitchen, but Bob the Builder was lying under the front wheel.

Emma watched him trying to drive the truck over Bob.

'Do you remember Rafe?' she asked.

Ritchie had spotted Bob's limp form.

'Uh-oh,' he said.

He climbed off the truck to pull him out.

'Rafe's back from his year in South America,' Emma said. 'He's coming to visit us tomorrow. For the weekend.'

Ritchie glanced up briefly, but Bob was well and truly stuck in the axle. Getting him out was going to be a big job. Breathing heavily, he returned to the task.

Later, when Ritchie was asleep, tucked up with Gribbit in his little box-room beside the kitchen, Emma sat out on the doorstep of the cottage, listening to the tide. She stretched her right arm out, opening and closing her hand, the way the physiotherapist had taught her.

She'd been busy today. She and Susan and some of the others had finished clearing out the back office of the pub. They'd removed every stick of furniture, along with what seemed like hundreds of old boxes, books and piles of papers. They'd scrubbed all the floors, windows, walls, even the ceiling. They'd had a bit of a laugh. There was a satisfaction in seeing the once dingy room transformed into a bright space, all ready for re-painting.

It was Dr Rudd, at the health centre, who'd suggested Emma take the job at the Pie and Lobster.

'Some friends of mine have taken it over,' she explained. 'They're going to expand and redecorate, and set up a new restaurant, all while trying to keep the bar up and running. If you need something to do over the next few weeks, they'll be glad to get some extra staff in to help.'

Dr Rudd had been very good to Emma and Ritchie since they'd moved to Polbraith. They were only here for the summer, but they'd had to register with a GP because of Ritchie, and because Emma was still getting physiotherapy on her arm.

They'd come after the court case, which had happened in May. Emma had only been required in court for one day to give evidence, but she'd had to meet up a few times before that with Lindsay and Detective Inspector Hill, to give her statement saying how the kidnap had affected her and Ritchie. Detective Hill, still wearing his tan coat, had barely been able to meet her eye. In the statement, Emma described how awful she'd

391

felt when Ritchie had disappeared, how unbearable her terror and pain had been. She talked about her injured arm, which was now slowly recovering, but only after three operations and many months of physiotherapy. But she was also honest enough to admit how bad things had been before Ritchie had disappeared. How she was getting treatment now for the way she'd felt then, and how, even though she still didn't know what the future held, thanks to what the Hunts had done, she didn't think she would ever feel quite that way again.

In the end, David Hunt got a three-year prison sentence. Philippa got four years, but she hadn't started serving it yet. She'd gone straight back to hospital from the Old Bailey, and, as far as Emma knew, she was there still.

She'd seen the Hunts, that day at the Old Bailey. They'd been sitting with some other people at the back: David in a grey suit, staring straight ahead; Philippa in black, her head down, not moving at all. A woman beside her had her arm around her. Emma only had time for a quick glance at them before the lawyer began his questions and she'd had to turn to him and concentrate. Later that day, however, on her way out of the building, she'd seen David Hunt again, standing with a group of men in the hall.

The shock of seeing him so close caused her to stop. Lindsay, beside her, suggested in a low voice that they return to the waiting area until David had gone. But then David had turned and seen them too. He seemed older, his hair thinner. He looked very tired. He had lost everything: his job, his beautiful house in France, his wife, to all intents and purposes, even if they did end up staying together. And of course, he had lost his son.

Emma looked at him, and he looked back, each of them acknowledging the other. There was no change of expression from either of them. No smiles, obviously. But no anger or hatred either. Not from him, not from her. If she could have spoken to him, she might have, though it might have taken a while to find the words. Then Lindsay put a hand on her arm, and they moved on together until they were out in the street.

At the entrance to St Paul's tube station, Lindsay gave Emma a warm hug.

'Congratulations, Emma,' she said.

'Congratulations to you too.' Emma smiled. An oval-shaped diamond glittered on Lindsay's engagement finger.

'You're quite sure you won't take that lift?' Lindsay asked. 'The car isn't very far away.'

Emma shook her head. 'I'll be quicker on the tube,' she said. 'My neighbour is minding Ritchie, and I don't want to keep her too long.'

'All right, then.'

They looked at each other for a moment. They both went to speak at the same time. Then they laughed. They hugged again, and wished each other well. Then Lindsay walked away. Her dark coat and neat, glossy bun vanished quickly into the crowds. Emma stood on the long escalator and watched herself being carried down to the platform. She felt several different emotions at once. The main one was a great sense of peace and relief. That was it. She would not see any of those people again.

Mrs Cornes had a friend who owned a couple of summer-rental cottages in Cornwall.

'You need a break after that court case,' Mrs Cornes said. 'Your mother used to holiday in Polbraith as a child. She often said how much she loved it. The cottage is only a tiny two-bedroomed terrace but my friend, Mrs Castle, will let you have it for a very low price for as long as you need.'

Emma said, 'We'd love to take it. But only if you'll promise to come and visit us while we're there.'

People had been so kind. Rosina, glowing with happiness, had called to say she was going home to the Philippines for three whole months. She asked if Emma and Ritchie would like to go with her for a while, to stay with her family by the sea. Emma thought that the journey might be too long for Ritchie, but Rosina had told her not to worry because the invitation would still be there for when he was older. Even strangers like Dr Rudd had gone out of their way to help; and Mary and Tom, the owners of the Pie and Lobster, who had given her the job. Emma and Ritchie had been in all the newspapers for weeks, their photos in every shop and news-stand, everywhere you looked. It seemed, at one point, as if everybody knew them and wanted to do something to show their support. But these days, fewer and fewer people were recognizing them. The photos in the papers were out of date now; she and Ritchie were not the same people they'd been then. Ritchie wasn't the tiny child on the red truck any more. He was huge. People thought he was three, not two. He was learning how to swim. He was a little boy now, not a baby. And when the newspapers published the report on the court case, Emma was surprised to see the picture of herself that they used. It was one that had been taken a few months before the kidnap. A health visitor had taken a photo of her holding Ritchie when he was about five months old. She was thin, with black circles under her eyes. Angry and hostile-looking. Her eyes were slitted, her head lowered, her hair scraped back off her face. Had she really ever looked like that?

Life was not perfect now. Emma still didn't know what she and Ritchie would do once the summer was over. Would they go back to their flat in Hammersmith? Maybe ask for a bigger one, now that Ritchie needed a room of his own?

She'd seen Joanne a couple of times in London. Joanne and Barry had split up soon after Christmas. Joanne had come home from work early one day and caught Barry in bed with one of his female colleagues.

'I'm well shot of him,' Joanne told Emma over coffee in Emma's flat. 'He was so controlling. It was only *his* friends he wanted us to meet up with, never mine.' She put a tentative hand on Emma's arm. 'I'm so sorry we lost touch, Ems. We should meet up more often now. Never let it happen again.'

But was that what Emma wanted? To go on living in social housing, even in a larger flat where Ritchie had his own room? To go on meeting Joanne for coffees and pretending that their friendship could ever go back to what it had been?

And money was still an issue. She was very much enjoying the camaraderie of the work at the Pie and Lobster, but the job was for the summer only. Once it was over she'd have to go back to dipping into her savings.

At night, sometimes, she worried about all of these things.

But the other day, walking home with Ritchie from the beach, where both of them had paddled in the sea and she'd laughed at Ritchie's face when he'd seen a crab, the afternoon had been so lovely she'd caught herself humming a song she'd heard on the radio earlier.

The tide *whooshed* again. Emma stretched her arm out, opening and closing her fist.

Tomorrow evening, Rafe would be here. How would things go between them? Would they get on well together? Run out of things to say? It was almost a year since she'd seen him. He'd been all around South America since then. He had emailed photos: the bar where he'd worked in Rio de Janeiro, a campsite by a glacier in Chile, a canoe he'd floated in, down through a gorge: 'I felt like Indiana Jones.' Her and Ritchie's life would probably seem very dull to him. Well, she hoped he'd enjoy the weekend. She'd like to show him Rich paddling, and the cliffs, and the places where the surfers went. It would be good if they could be friends.

If you're serious about re-applying for the

police, she'd written, *you can put Ritchie and me on your CV.*

Three months. And here she was, still in Polbraith. She'd never intended to stay this long. She could see why her mum had loved it so much. People here looked out for each other. It would be a lovely place to bring up a child.

★ ★ ★

A couple of evenings back, Ritchie had come flying into the kitchen to find her.

'Muh.' He hauled on her sleeve, pointing towards the sitting-room. 'Muh.'

'What is it? What's going on?'

'Oh. Oh.' He panted, desperately trying to tell her.

He pulled her into Mrs Castle's chintzy sitting-room, and scrambled up on to the window seat. Outside, it was getting dark. The flowers on the bush below the window glowed luminous pink. The line where the sea met the horizon was pink as well, the sky navy.

'Woo,' Ritchie kept saying. 'Woo-ooo.'

'A ghost?' Emma peered. 'Where?'

Ritchie pointed vigorously into the garden, but it was clear he wasn't too sure where. His eyes searched. Then he was on his knees, pointing again and gasping dramatically.

Emma said, 'Oh, now I see.'

She did. A pair of white barn owls, swooping in the dusk over the bush. Ritchie's eyes, following them ecstatically, were filled with the pink light from the sea.

'They're beautiful ghosts,' Emma told him.

She looked down at him, at his heart-shaped face, his broad, intelligent forehead, and thought again, for the thousandth time, how incredibly privileged she was to have him.

The owls swooped again. Their reflections flitted past the glass in a photo on the window sill. The photo was the one of Emma with her mum and gran, taken on the day of her gran's birthday. Her mum and her gran sat on the couch together, smiling at the camera. Across their faces, the two pale owls floated and soared.

Ritchie pointed at the ghostly shapes in the glass.

'Woo,' he said. 'Woo-ooo.'

* * *

At work on Friday, Susan said to Emma, 'What's this? You're all dressed up.'

'I am not.'

'Yes, you are.' Susan came around the bar and put her hands on her hips. 'Definitely.' She looked Emma up and down. 'New top?'

'Haven't I worn this before?'

'No.'

'Oh, well.' Emma wiped a smudge of peanut dust off the bar top. Over the past few weeks, she and Susan had become good mates. Susan had a little girl a year older than Ritchie who was in the Dolphins as well. Emma didn't know why she felt suddenly shy with her.

'A friend of mine is coming to visit today,' Emma said. 'After work.'

'A friend, eh?' Susan gave a knowing smile. 'Well, you look great.'

After work, Emma collected Ritchie from the Dolphins. He came in from the garden at a funeral pace, his tongue sticking out, concentrating on a squashed yellow flower in his fist. He went to Emma and presented the flower to her. She took it from him, with difficulty, as the petals were stuck to his fingers.

'Ah.' Jess tilted her head. 'Isn't that sweet?'

'It's beautiful. Thank you.' Emma tried to kiss him, but he was busy wiping his hands on the front of his T-shirt.

'Mess,' he said.

Emma put the mashed flower into her bag. She said to Ritchie, 'We'll go home along the cliff path.'

★　★　★

My last week in South America. My flight leaves from Lima on Tuesday. Right now, I'm in the Andes, and we've been trekking since dawn. We just got into this village an hour ago. The views are spectacular, but I can't appreciate them at the moment because I'm hot, and my feet are killing me, and the altitude is melting my brain.

And now here, in this tiny market square, miles from anywhere, I find this message from you.

It's great to hear from you, Emma. I'm really looking forward to seeing you both.

★　★　★

The way home from the Dolphins took them up the hill. At the top of the hill, all that was left was the sea, sparkly in the distance, deep blue near the shore. *Shhwooo* it said as it came in, and there was a crackle as it slid back out again. They were on a cliff path with a wooden fence. Beyond the fence, twisty stone steps led down to the long, sandy beach. Further along the cliff, an old copper-mine tower, overgrown with creeper, stuck straight into the sky.

Ritchie ran ahead, holding a long, spiral shell. Then he stopped, pointing down the cliff path.

'Man,' he said.

There *was* a man, halfway down the path. Leaning on the part of the fence that ran outside their house. A black rucksack lay at his feet, and his bright blue T-shirt matched the sea. The man had seen them too. He straightened, shading his eyes with his hand. Then he lifted his arm, fingers spread, a high, full-on salute. Emma waved back. She felt the smile in her eyes, then her mouth, then all over, every part of her involved. She waved again, standing on tiptoe to make sure he saw. The man came out to the middle of the path to wait. Emma's heart was beating faster. But of course, that would be the steepness of the path from the village. It was a very warm evening.

'Come on, Rich,' she said.

Ritchie had to sort his shell out first. He hunched down, carefully, to place it in the grass. The shell tipped a little; he steadied it in the grey curve of a rock. Then he stood up again and took Emma's hand. Together, they walked on down the path.

400

Other titles published by
The House of Ulverscroft:

TRUST ME

Jeff Abbott

Luke Dantry tragically lost his parents when he was a teenager — his father was murdered by a crazed operative, his mother died in a terrible accident. Brought up by his step-father, Luke now works with him on his research, monitoring extremist groups on the internet. Yet within the seemingly harmless world of the internet lie untold dangers. And Luke suddenly feels the full force of them when he is kidnapped at gunpoint in an airport car park. He's an ordinary guy who's led a blameless life, so why has he been targeted. He just knows that he must escape — somehow.

THE LIAR'S DIARY

Patry Francis

School secretary Jeanne Cross is an ordinary wife and mother with a seemingly perfect life when Ali Mather, the new music teacher, arrives on the scene. Ali is everything Jeanne isn't: flamboyant, reckless and sexy, with a habit of breaking rules and hearts wherever she goes. Despite their differences, the women are drawn to each other and an unlikely friendship develops. But beneath the surface, both of them are troubled. For Ali, it is the suspicion that someone has been breaking into her house — not to steal, but to terrify her. For Jeanne, there are secrets too dark and too brutal to face alone; secrets that will be dragged into the light with devastating results for her family and her friend.

DARK ECHO

F.G. Cottam

She is a seductive ship: a magnificent sailing yacht built for an American playboy. Yet her history is full of fatal accidents and three of *Dark Echo*'s owners met tragic, violent deaths. Now she has been rebuilt, crossing the Atlantic with new owners, and only the truth about Harry Spalding, the man who built her, can save them from the same fate. . . . And this is the story of an evil man, an incredibly brave woman and a secret more powerful than any of them . . .

TWILIGHT HOUR

Carol Smith

Alone on Dartmoor, campaigning journalist Erin O'Leary is in hiding from Russian assassins. In a gated community, built on the ruins of an ancient manor house, she shares her exile with a disparate group of new neighbours. They are Gerald and Sylvia, early retired with social pretensions above their means; Ned and Lisa, newlyweds who know each other through work, though not very well; and beautiful embittered Auriol, left with the dog her husband no longer wants. None is exactly what they seem. And when the killing begins, they all have motives. Winter approaches; the nights draw in. The mists roll down and eclipse the moor, and shadowy figures among the trees appear to be watching the houses. Out there, a terrible evil exists.

THE ANATOMY OF DECEPTION

Lawrence Goldstone

Philadelphia, 1889. In the morgue of the city hospital, physicians uncover the corpse of a beautiful young woman. What they see takes their breath away. Within days, one of the doctors, Ephraim Carroll, strongly suspects that he knows the woman's identity. His investigation takes him from the bloody and brutal medical world in which he practises and into the drawing rooms of Philadelphia's high society, where he soon learns that nothing — and no one — is what it seems. Plunged into a maze of deception and deadly secrets, Carroll is forced to choose between exposing a killer, undoing a terrible wrong and, quite possibly, protecting the future of medicine itself.